Witchlight

Jessi
Zabarsky

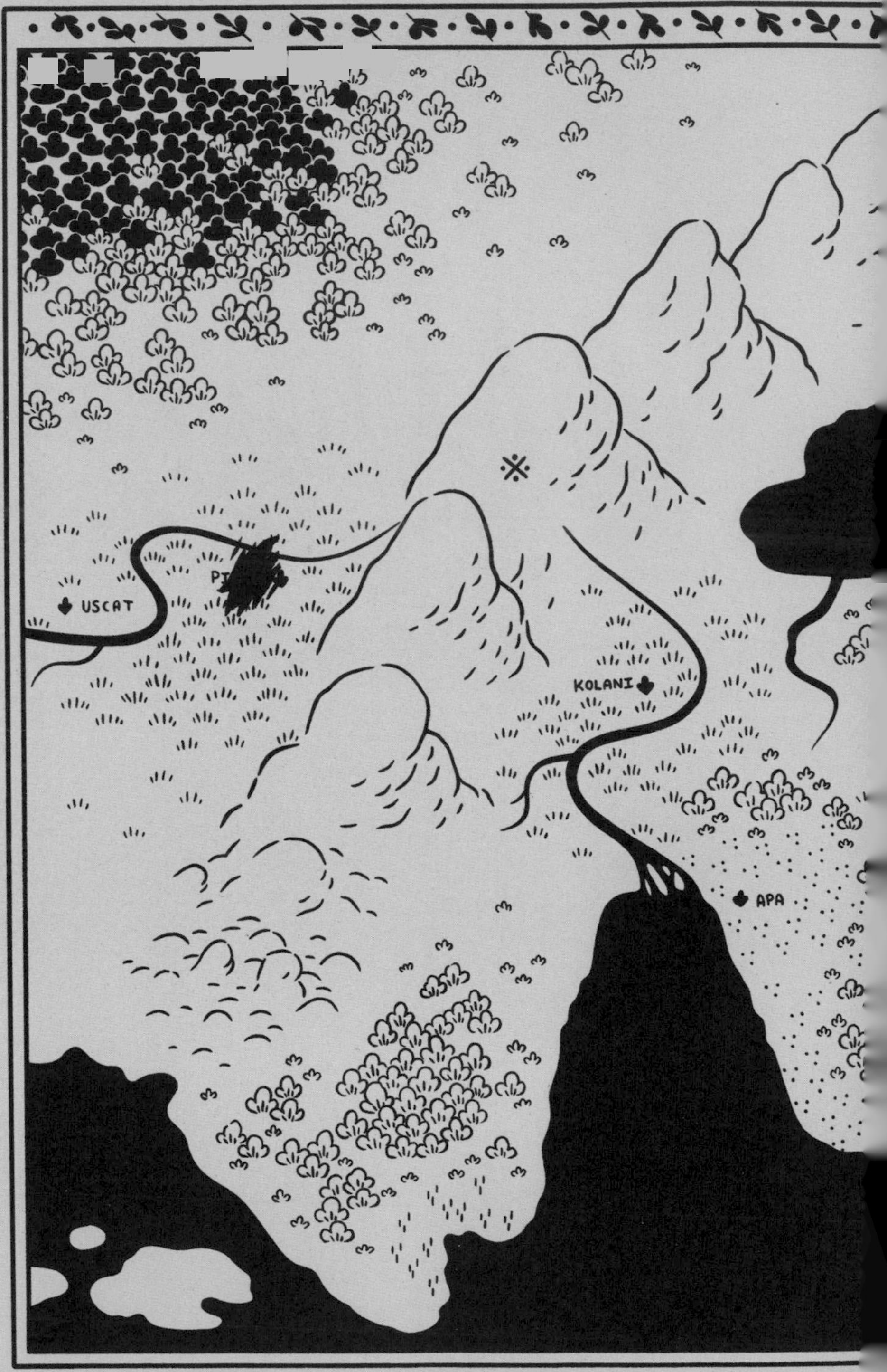
USCAT
PI[redacted]
KOLANI
APA

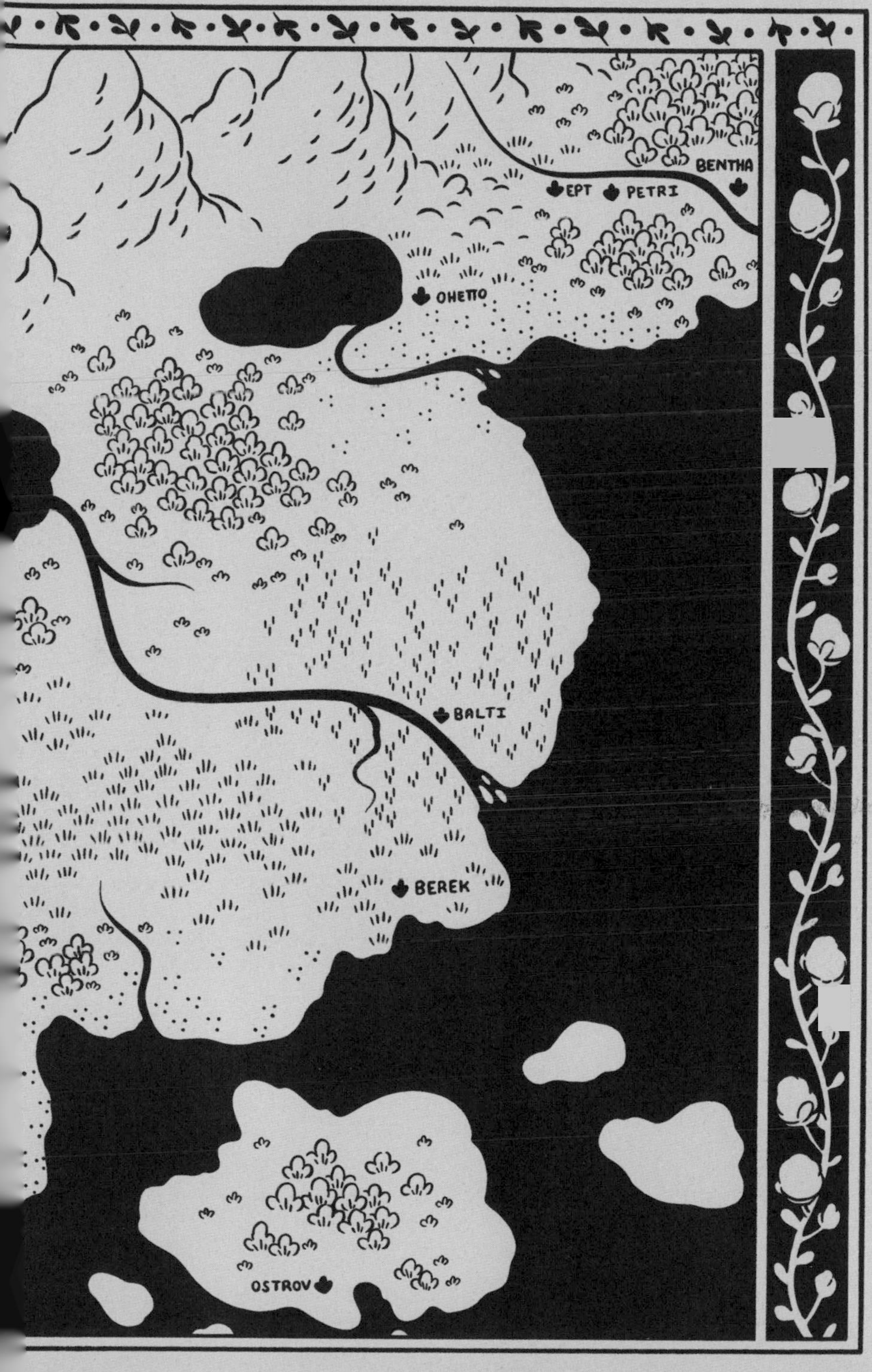
BENTHA
EPT
PETRI
OHETTO
BALTI
BEREK
OSTROV

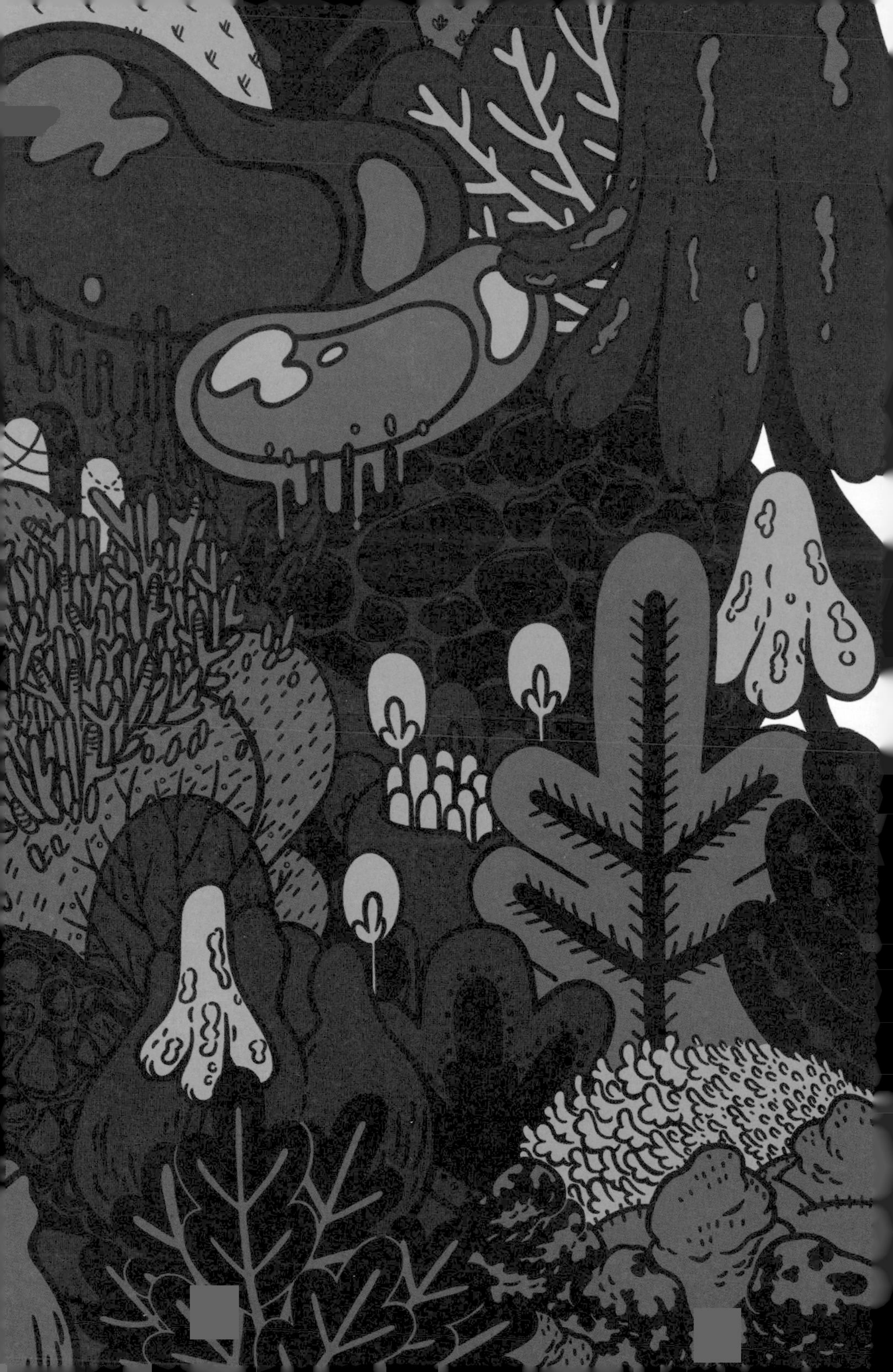

Witchlight

Jessi Zabarsky

with coloring by Geov Chouteau

RH GRAPHIC

Witchlight was drawn with ink on paper, then lettered and colored digitally.

Text and art copyright © 2016, 2020 by Jessi Zabarsky
Cover art copyright © 2020 by Jessi Zabarsky

All rights reserved. Published in the United States by RH Graphic, an imprint of Random House Children's Books, a division of Penguin Random House LLC, New York. Originally published in the United States in different form by Czap Books in Providence, Rhode Island, in 2016.

RH Graphic with the book design is a trademark of Penguin Random House LLC.

Visit us on the Web! RHKidsGraphic.com • @RHKidsGraphic

Educators and librarians, for a variety of teaching tools, visit us at RHTeachersLibrarians.com

Library of Congress Cataloging-in-Publication Data
Names: Zabarsky, Jessi, author, artist.
Title: Witchlight / Jessi Zabarsky.
Description: First RH Graphic edition. | New York : RH Graphic, [2020] | Audience: Ages 14–18 | Audience: Grades 10–12 | Summary: "Sanja gets taken by Lelek, a witch, and they find themselves on an adventure to discover the truth about Lelek's powers and each other"—Provided by publisher.
Identifiers: LCCN 2019025813 | ISBN 978-0-593-11999-0 (paperback) | ISBN 978-0-593-12418-5 (hardcover) | ISBN 978-0-593-12001-9 (ebook) | ISBN 978-0-593-12000-2 (library binding)
Subjects: LCSH: Graphic novels. | CYAC: Graphic novels. | Witches—Fiction. | Ability—Fiction.
Classification: LCC PZ7.7.Z33 W58 2020 | DDC 741.5/973—dc23

Designed by Patrick Crotty
Colored by Geov Chouteau

MANUFACTURED IN CHINA
10 9 8 7 6 5 4 3 2 1
First RH Graphic Edition

A comic on every bookshelf.

To the best park in
the Cuyahoga River Valley

Part 1

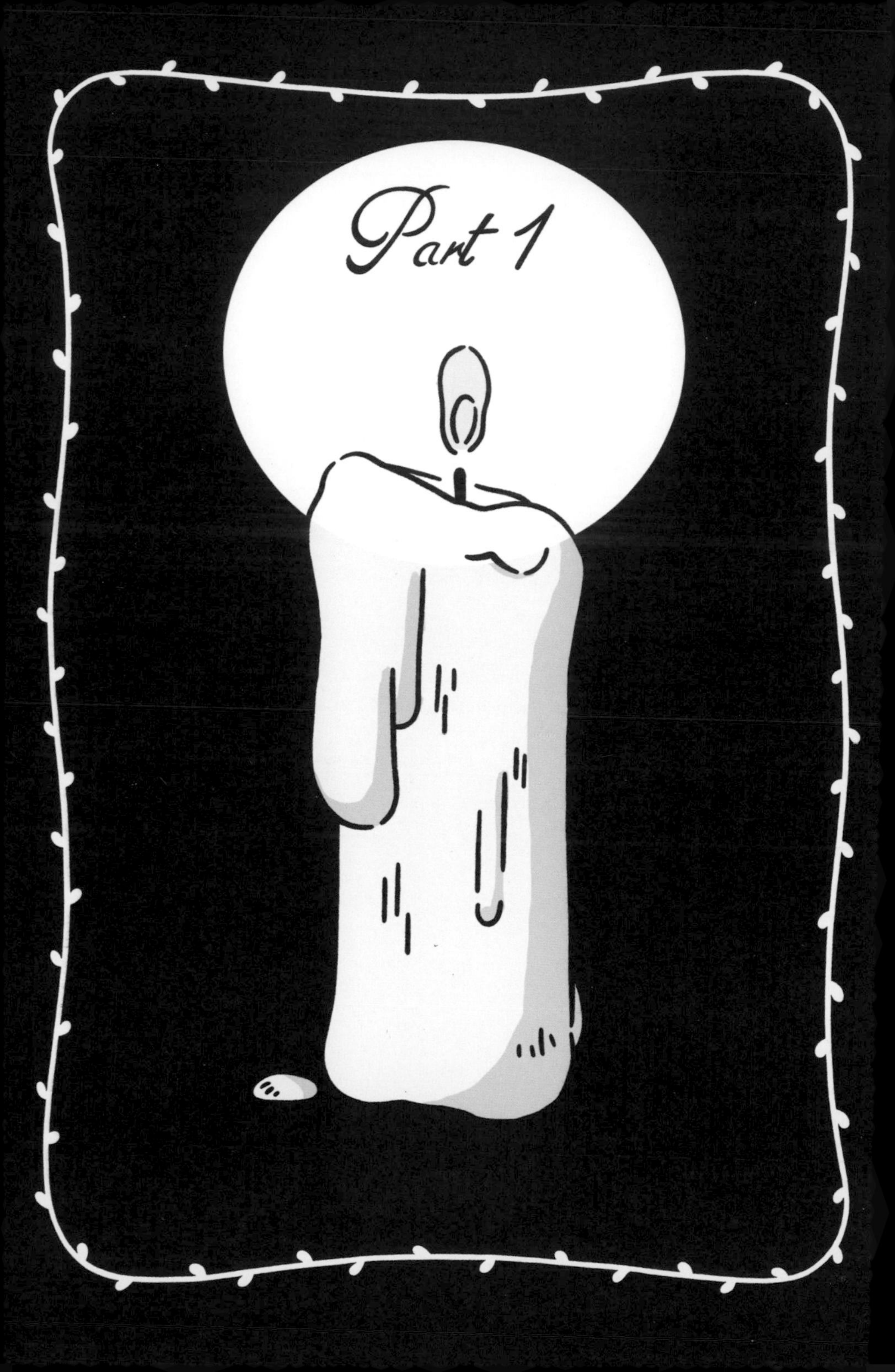

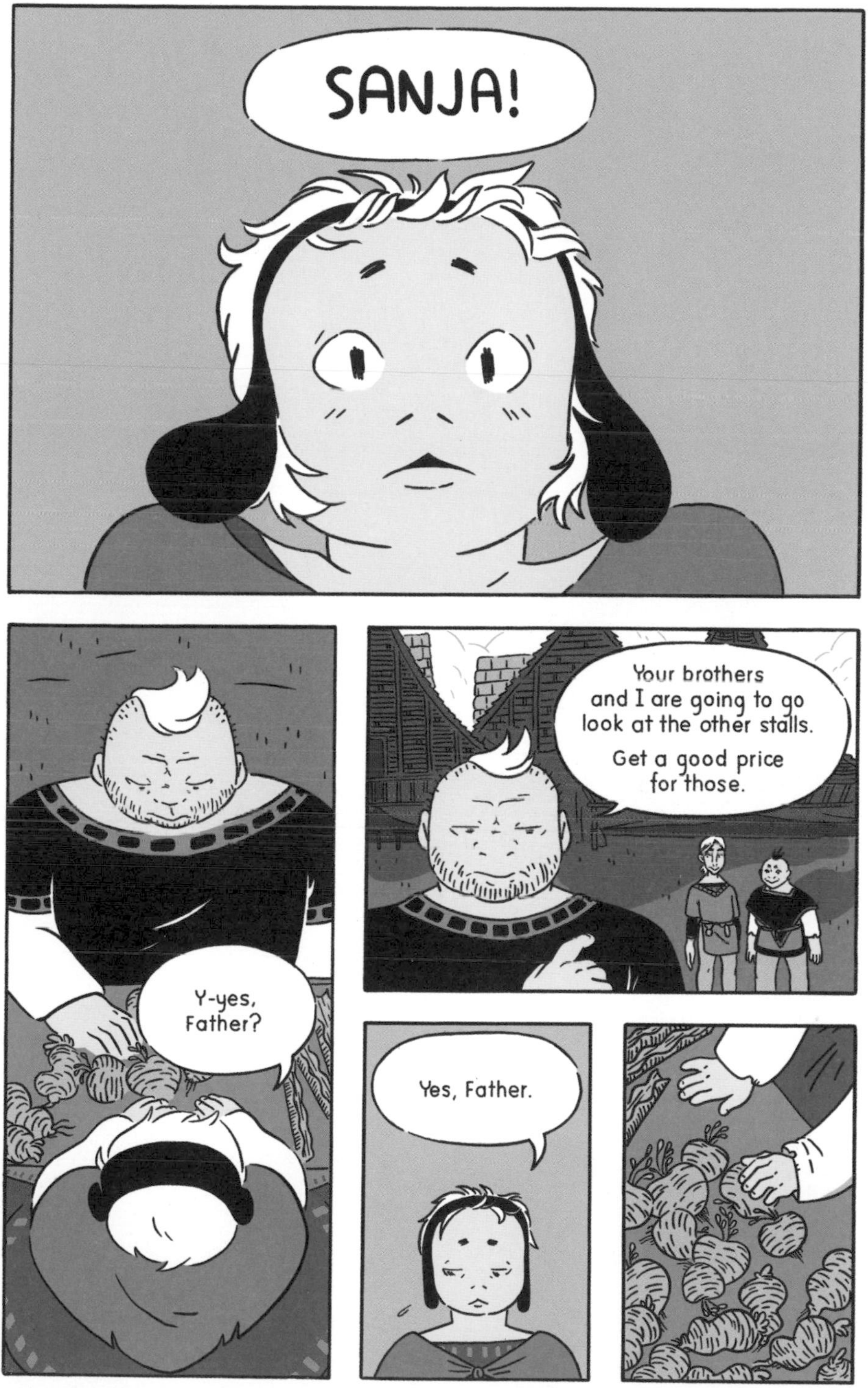
SANJA!
Y-yes, Father?
Your brothers and I are going to go look at the other stalls.
Get a good price for those.
Yes, Father.

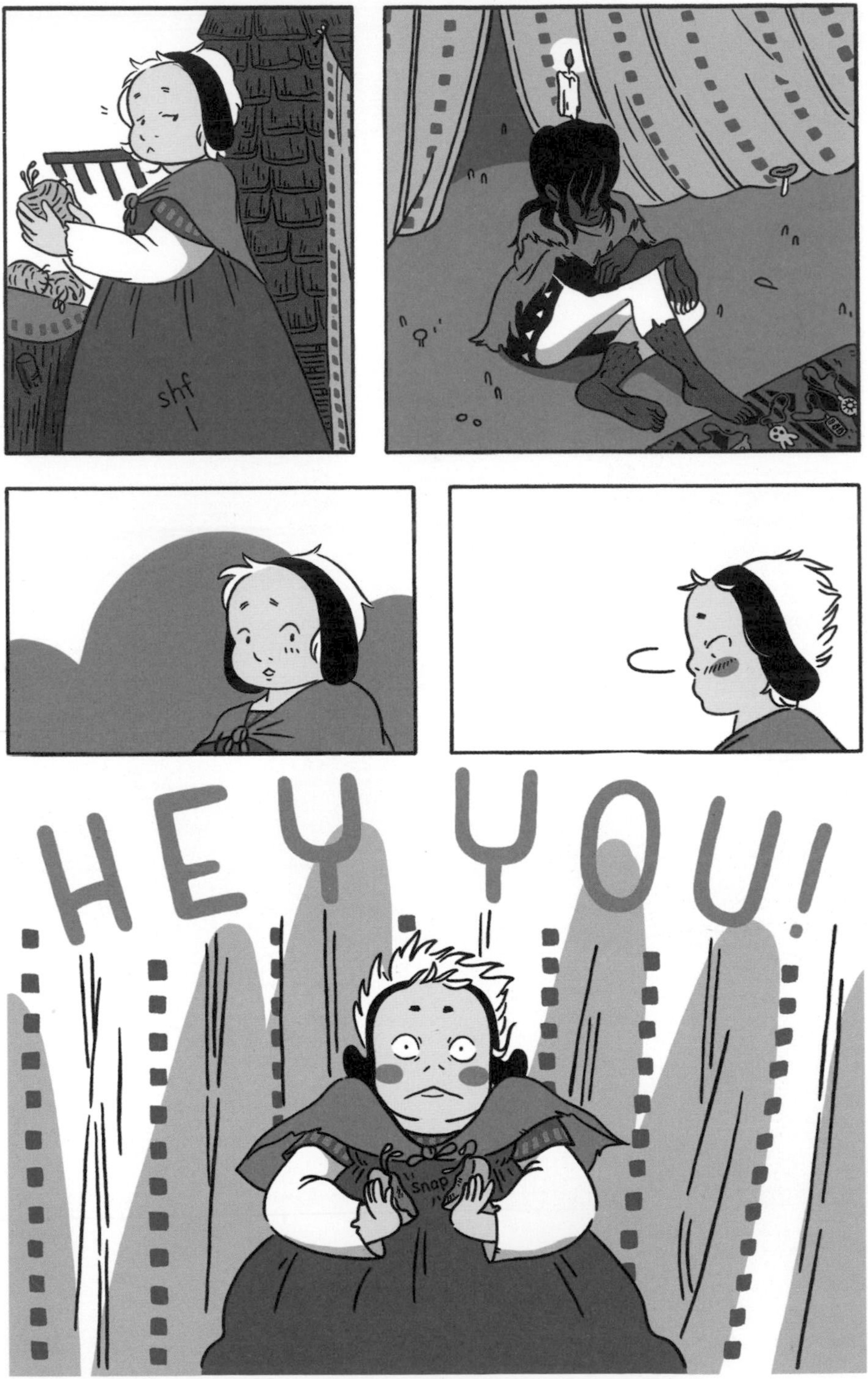
shf
HEY YOU!
snap

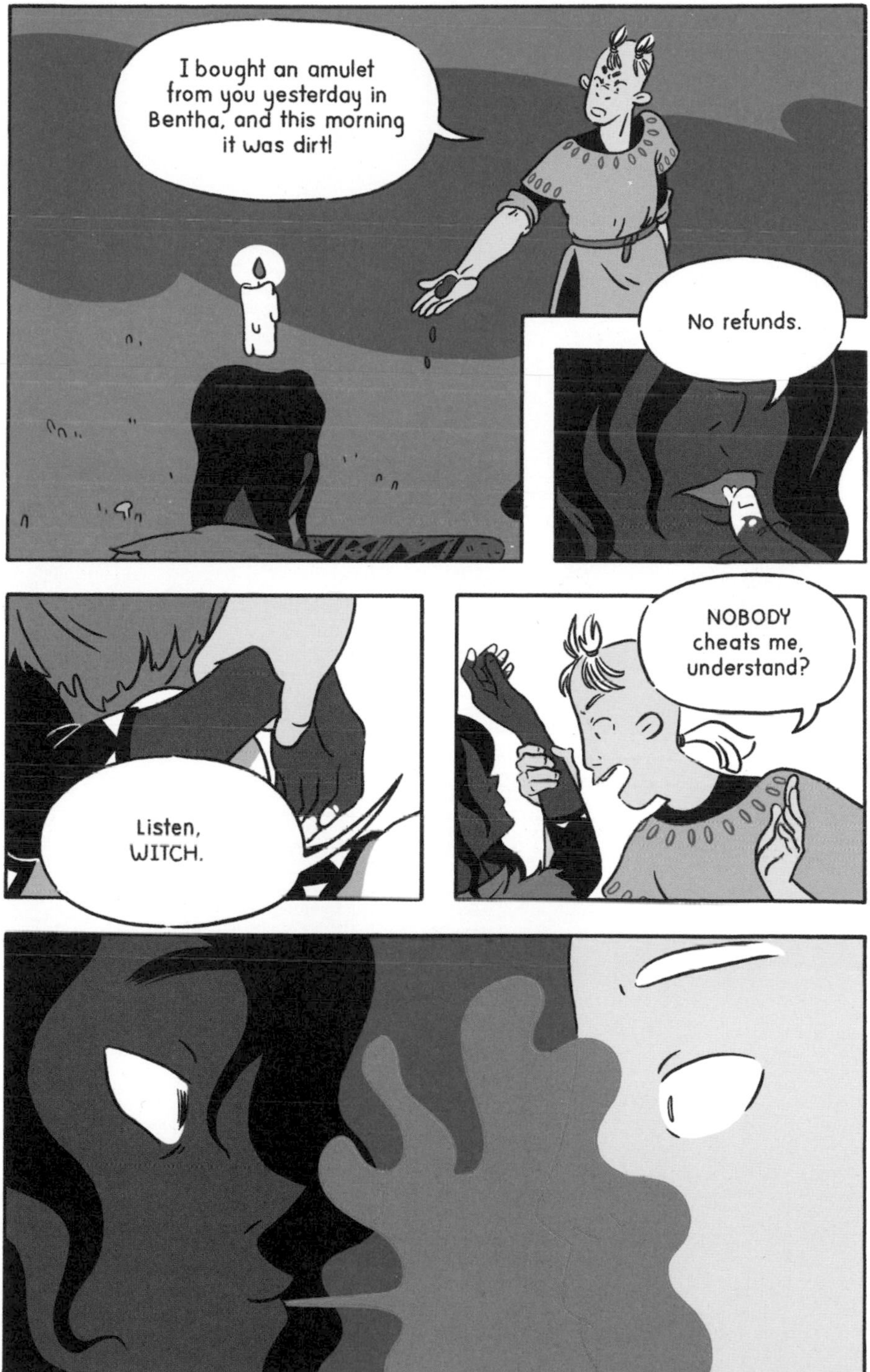
I bought an amulet from you yesterday in Bentha, and this morning it was dirt!
No refunds.
Listen, WITCH.
NOBODY cheats me, understand?

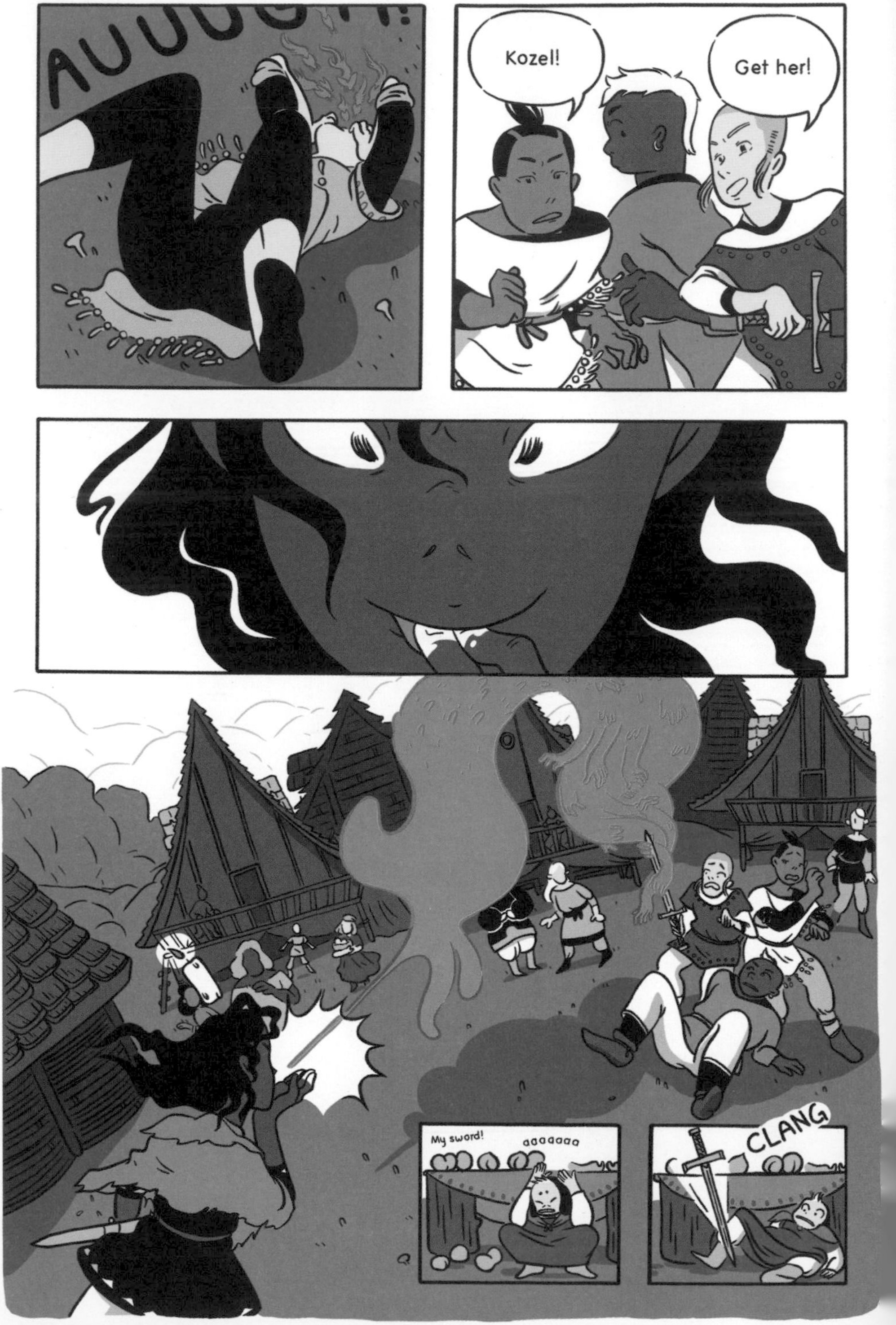
AUUUG
Kozel!
Get her!
My sword!
aaaaaaa
CLANG

tmp
tmp
tmp
Blast!
ugh
Koff
Koff

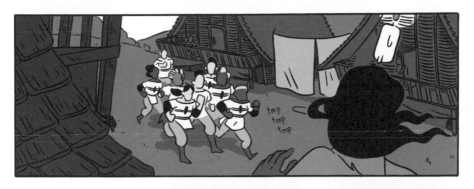

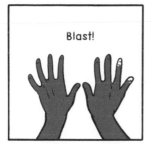

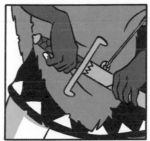

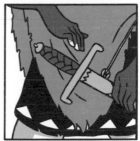

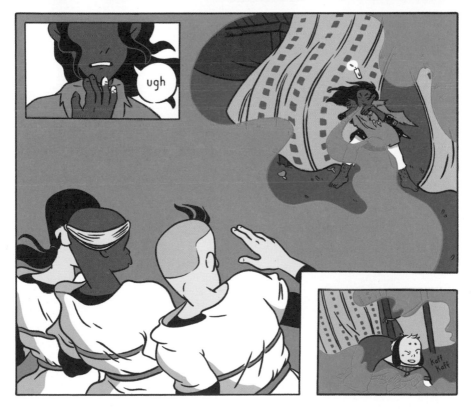

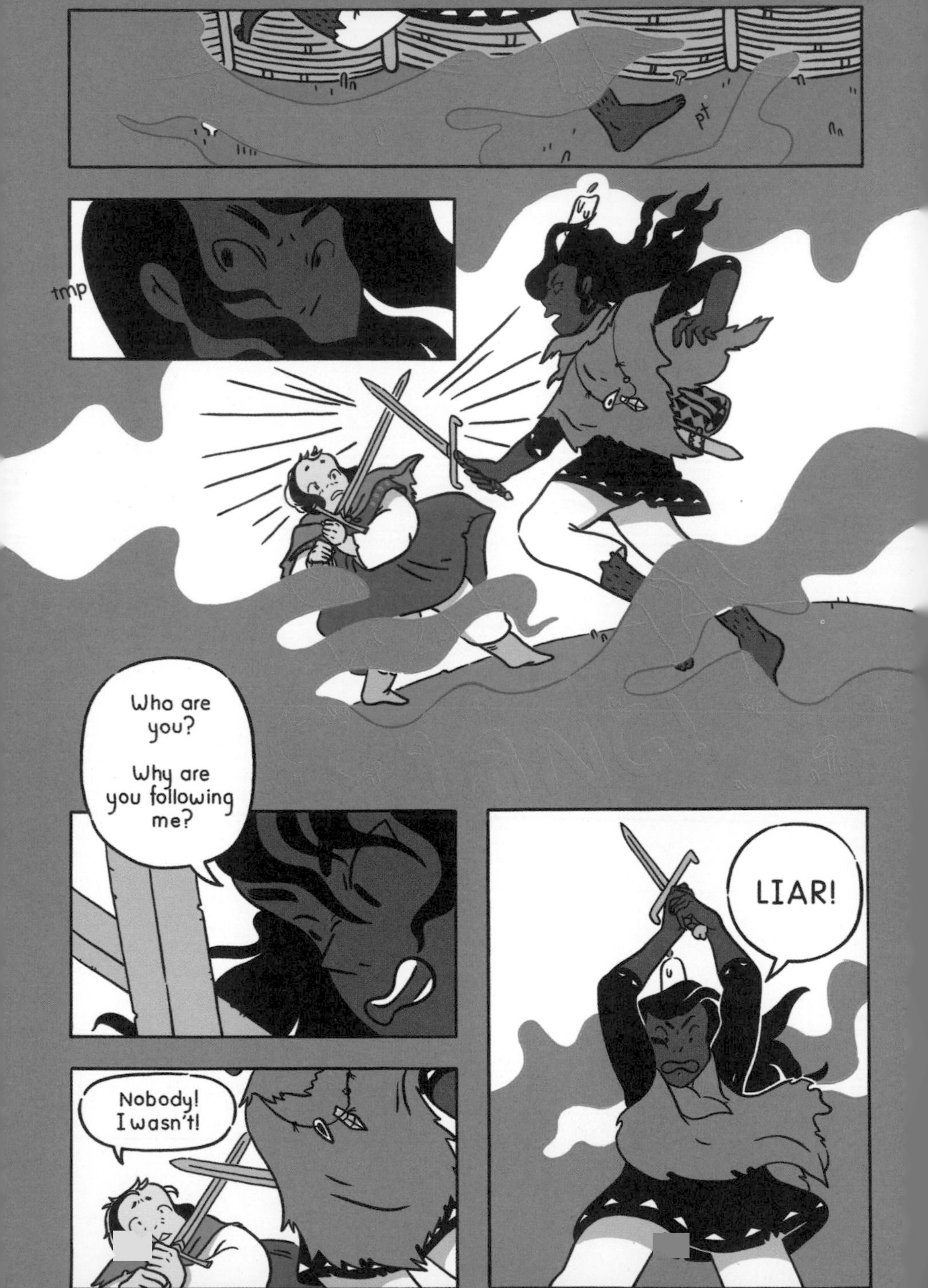
pt
tmp
Who are you?
Why are you following me?
Nobody! I wasn't!
LIAR!

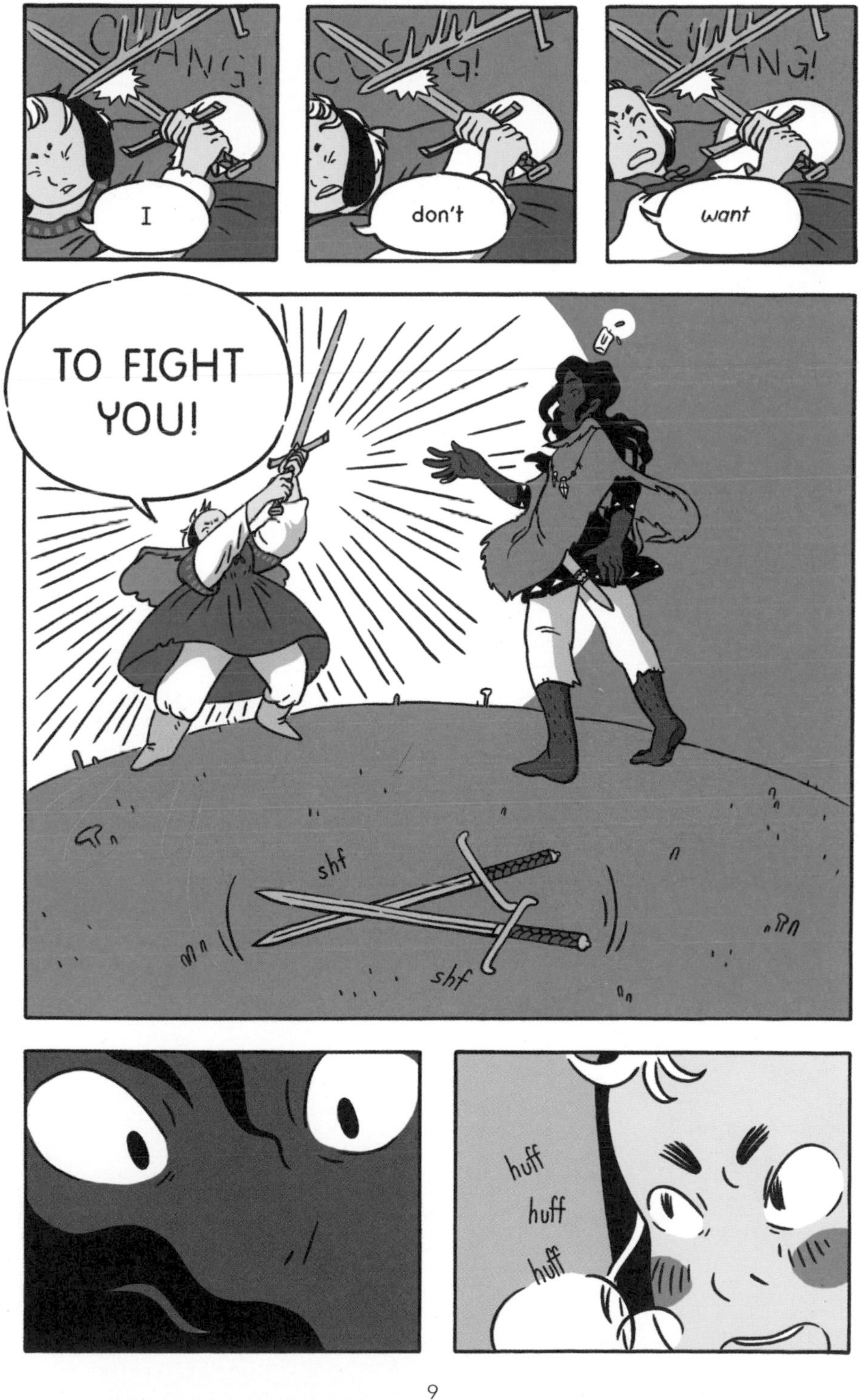
I
don't
want
TO FIGHT YOU!
shf
shf
huff
huff
huff

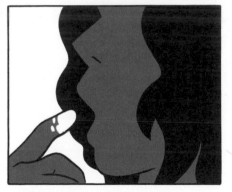

PFOO!

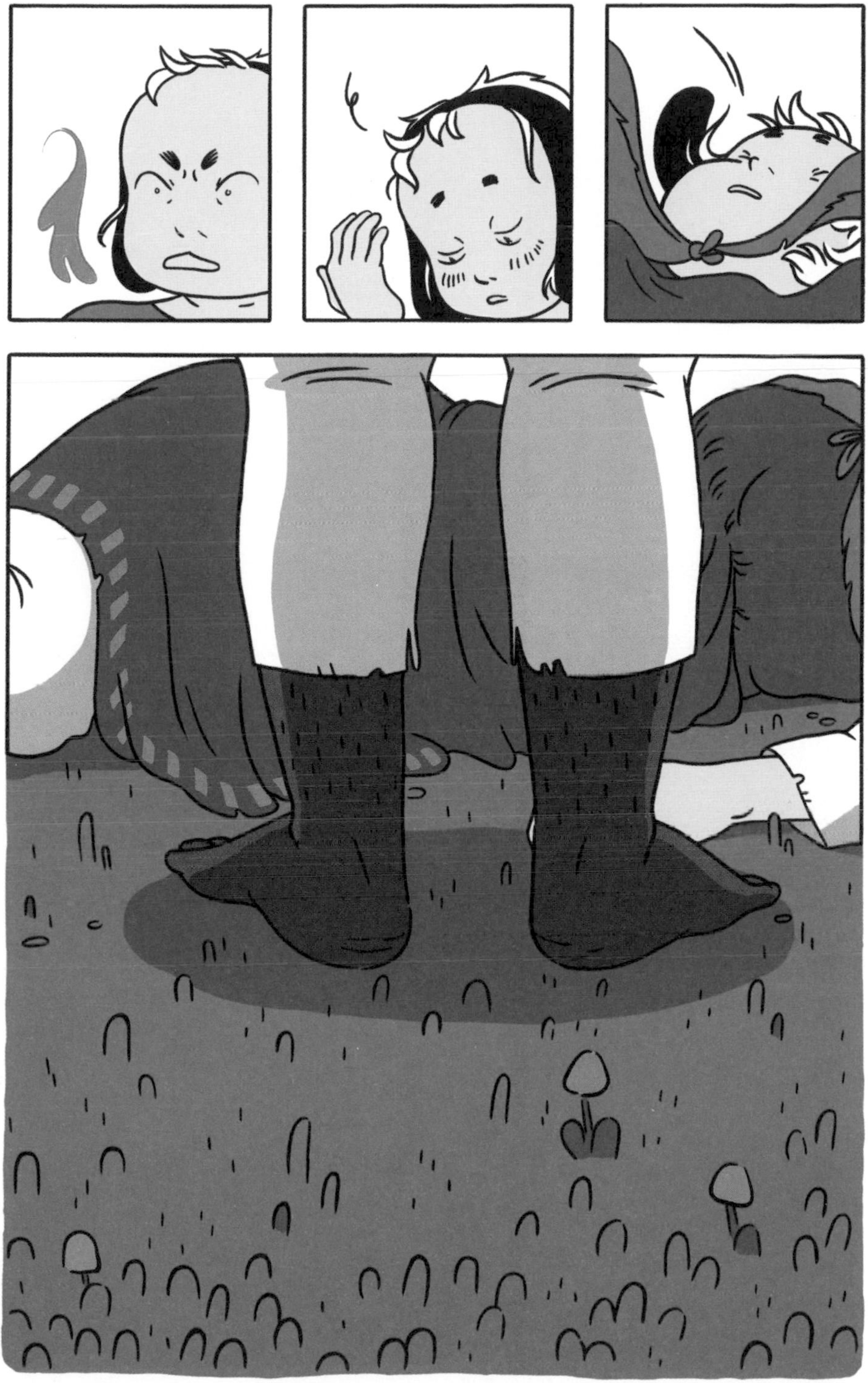

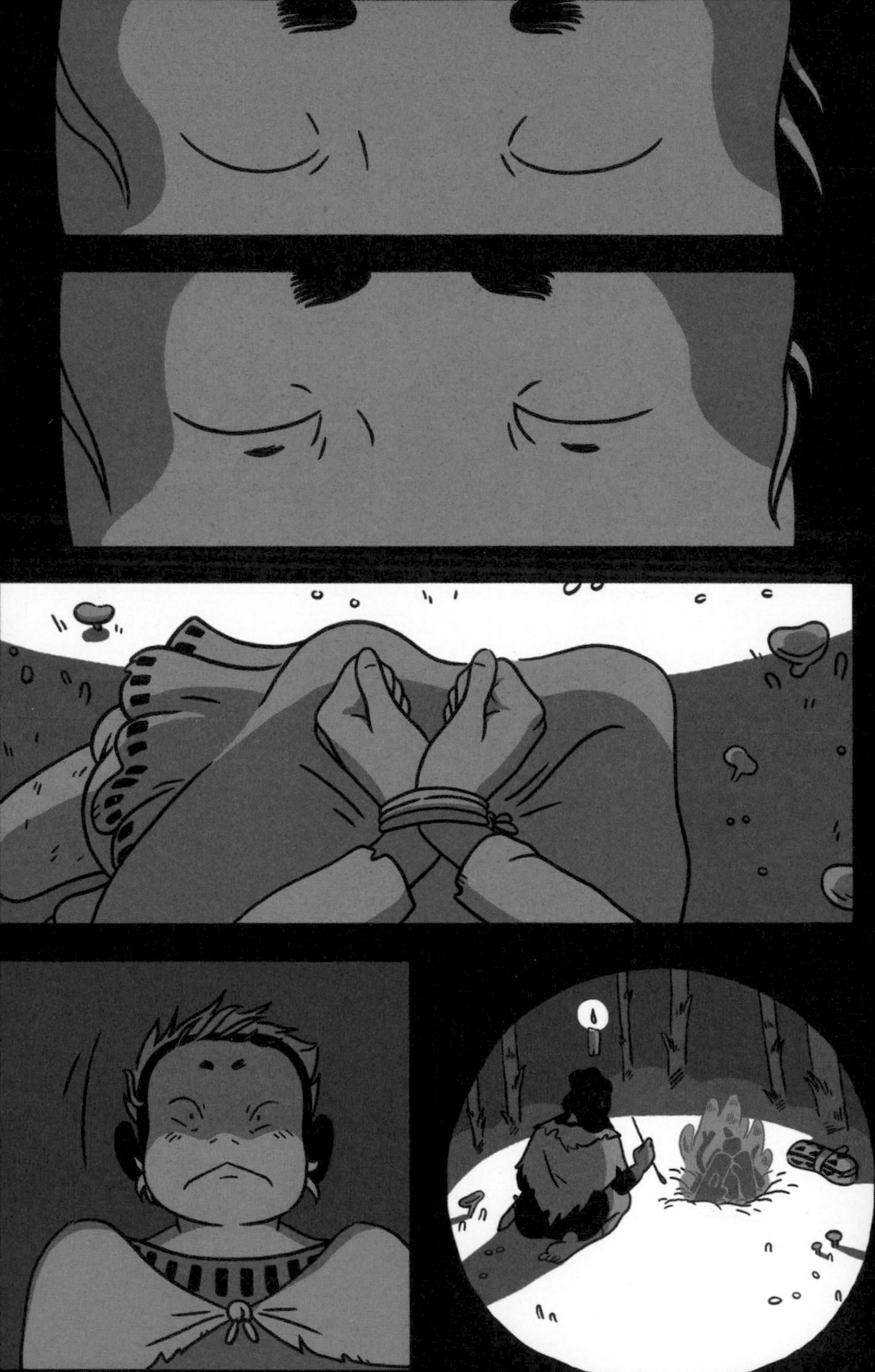

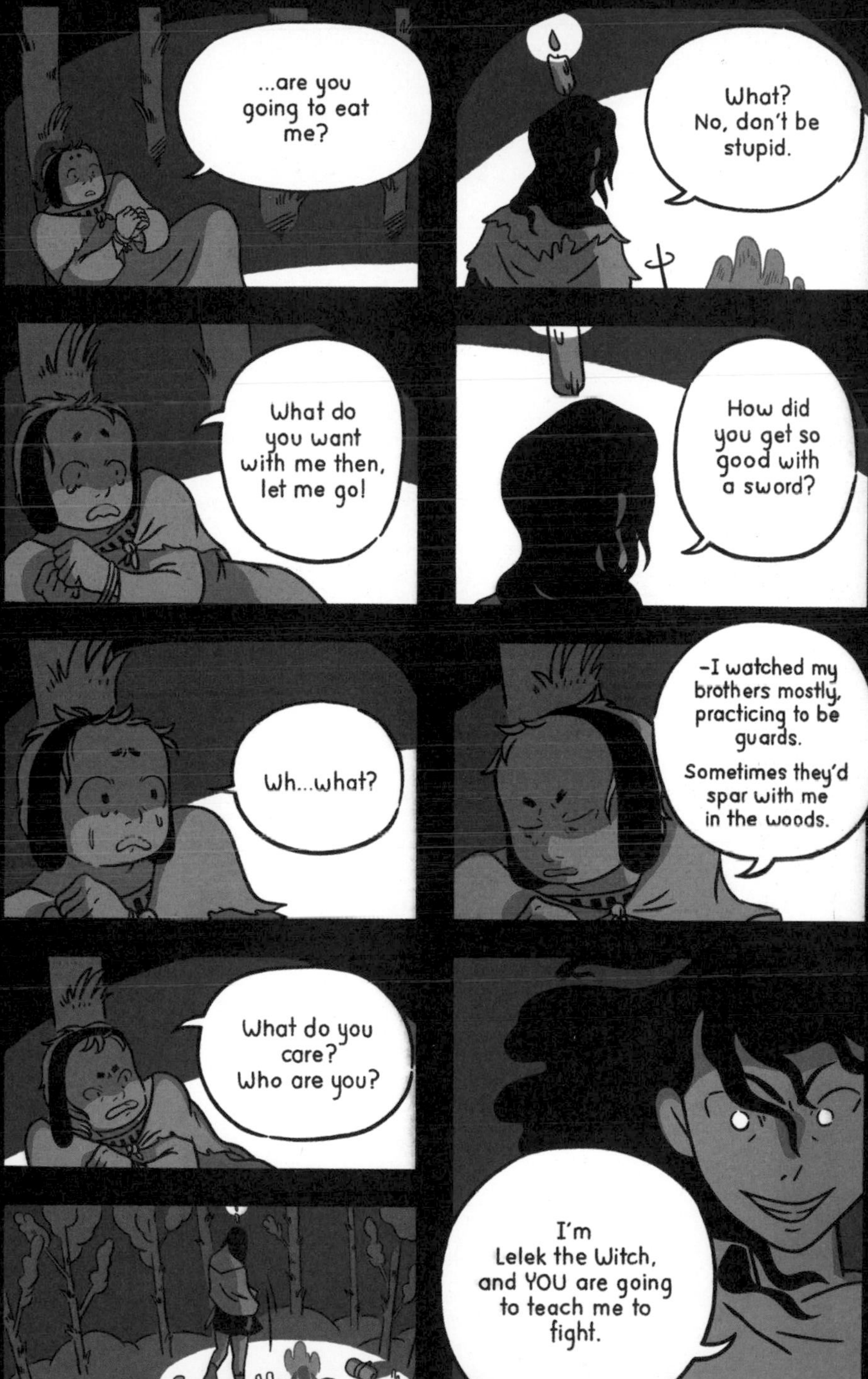
...are you going to eat me?
What? No, don't be stupid.
What do you want with me then, let me go!
How did you get so good with a sword?
Wh...what?
-I watched my brothers mostly, practicing to be guards.
Sometimes they'd spar with me in the woods.
What do you care? Who are you?
I'm Lelek the Witch, and YOU are going to teach me to fight.

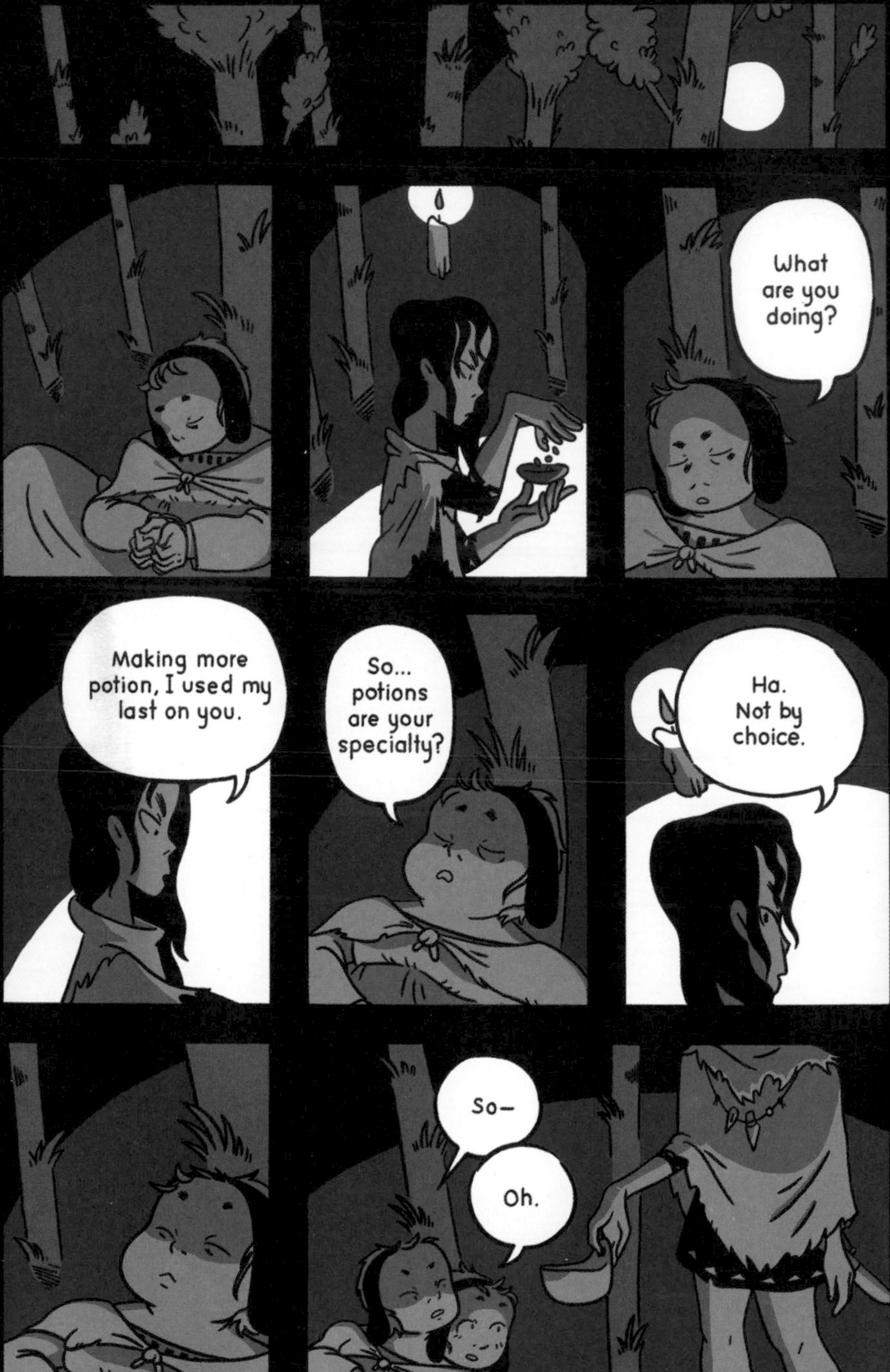
What are you doing?
Making more potion, I used my last on you.
So... potions are your specialty?
Ha. Not by choice.
So—
Oh.

Here, eat.

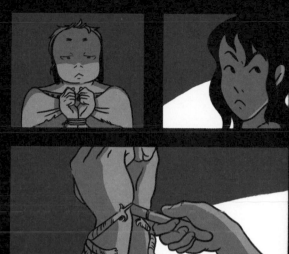

bmBMP
bmBMP

Eat!

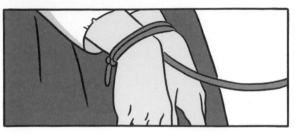

Where are we going?

I'M going to the next town.

YOU'RE staying, hmmm...

...right here.

HEY!

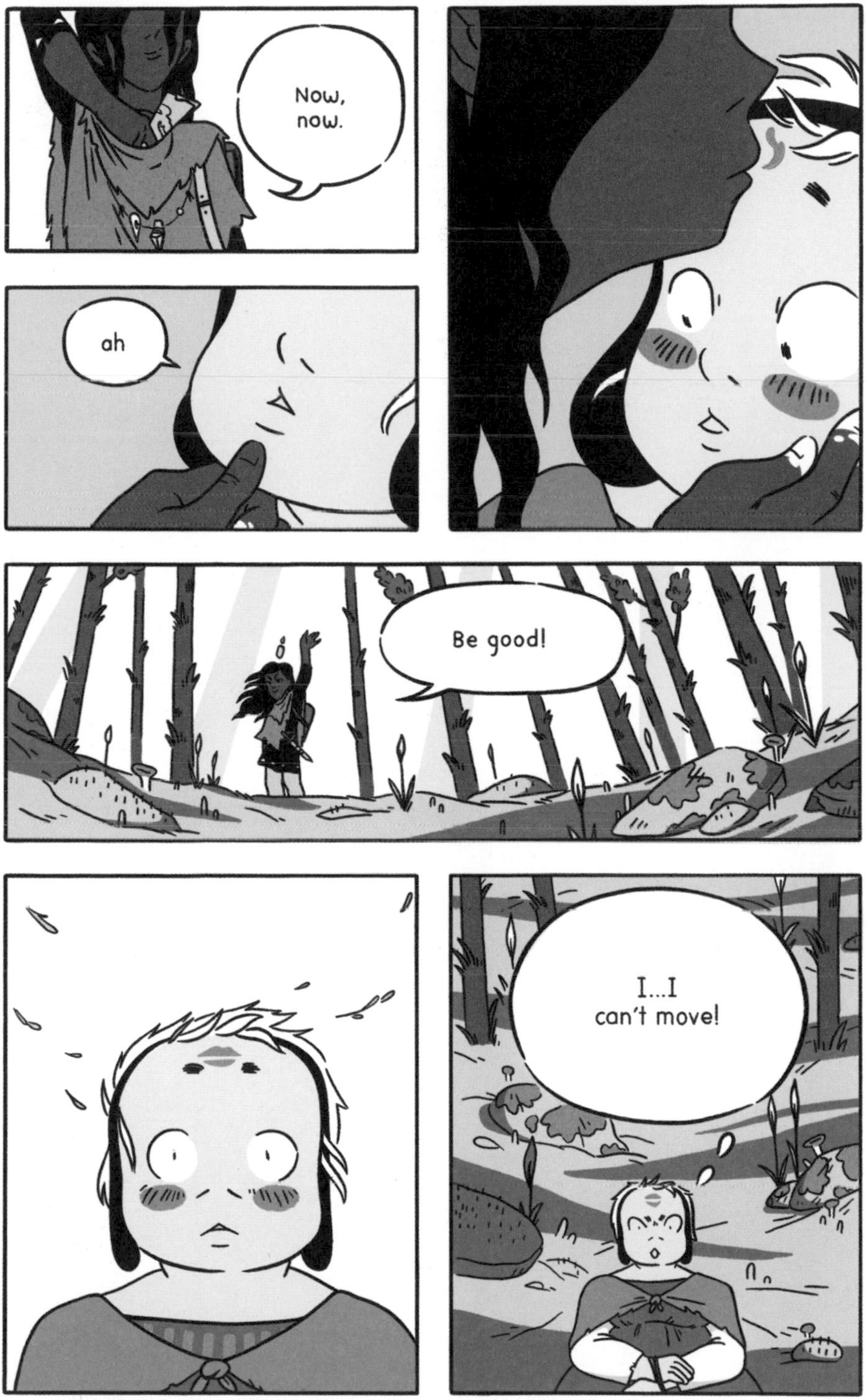
Now, now.
ah
Be good!
I...I can't move!

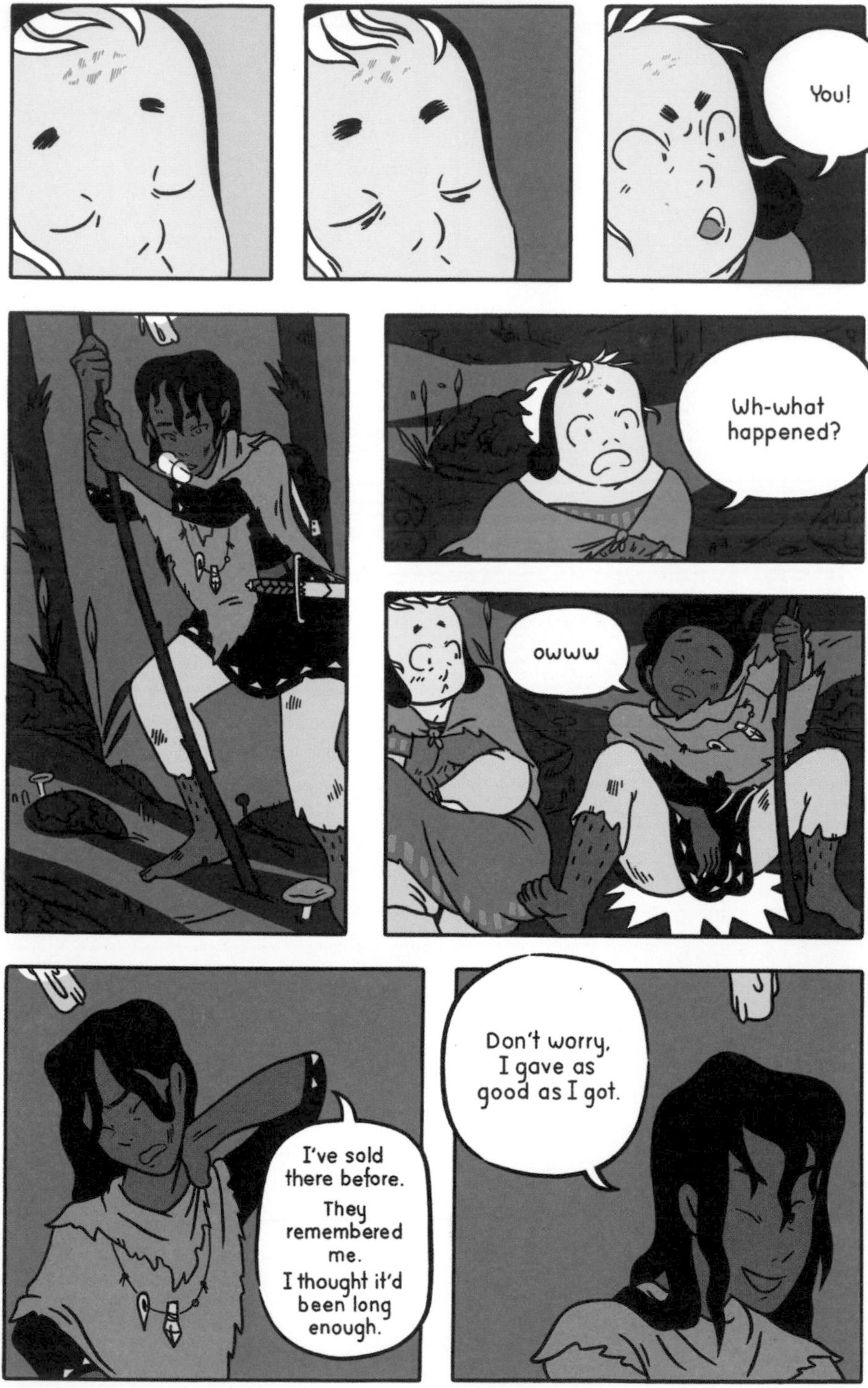
You!
Wh-what happened?
owww
I've sold there before.
They remembered me.
I thought it'd been long enough.
Don't worry, I gave as good as I got.

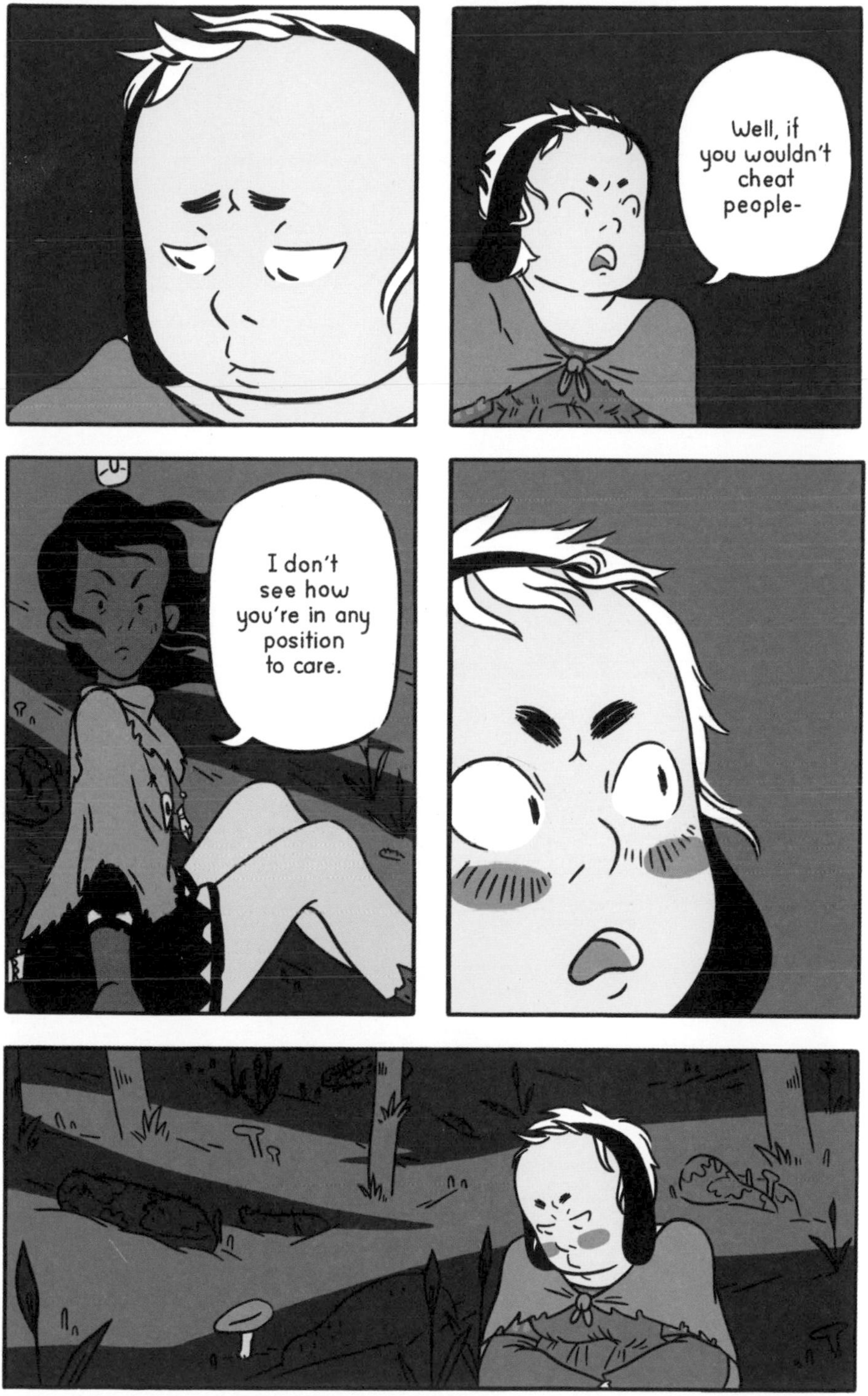
Well, if you wouldn't cheat people-
I don't see how you're in any position to care.

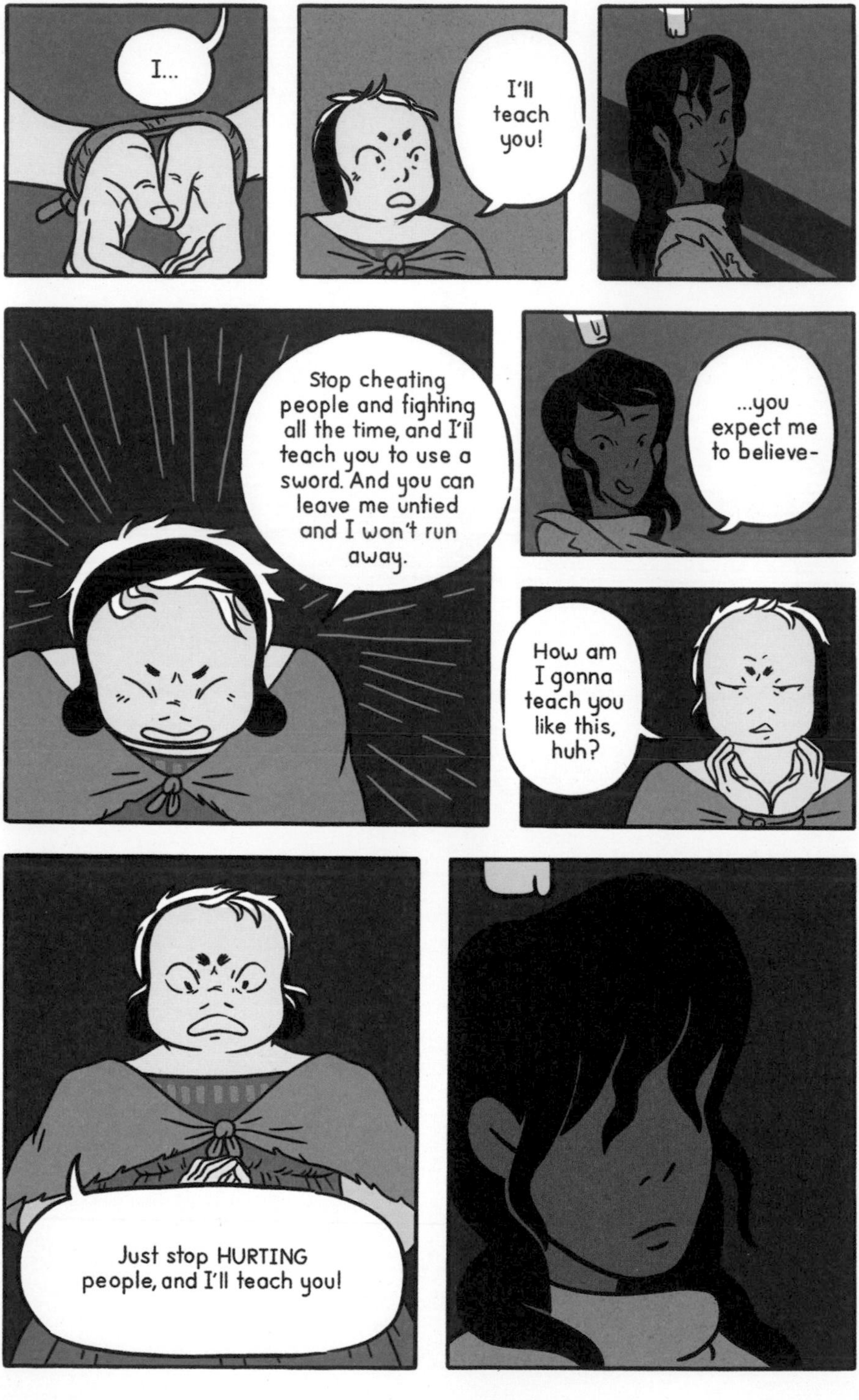
I...
I'll teach you!
Stop cheating people and fighting all the time, and I'll teach you to use a sword. And you can leave me untied and I won't run away.
...you expect me to believe-
How am I gonna teach you like this, huh?
Just stop HURTING people, and I'll teach you!

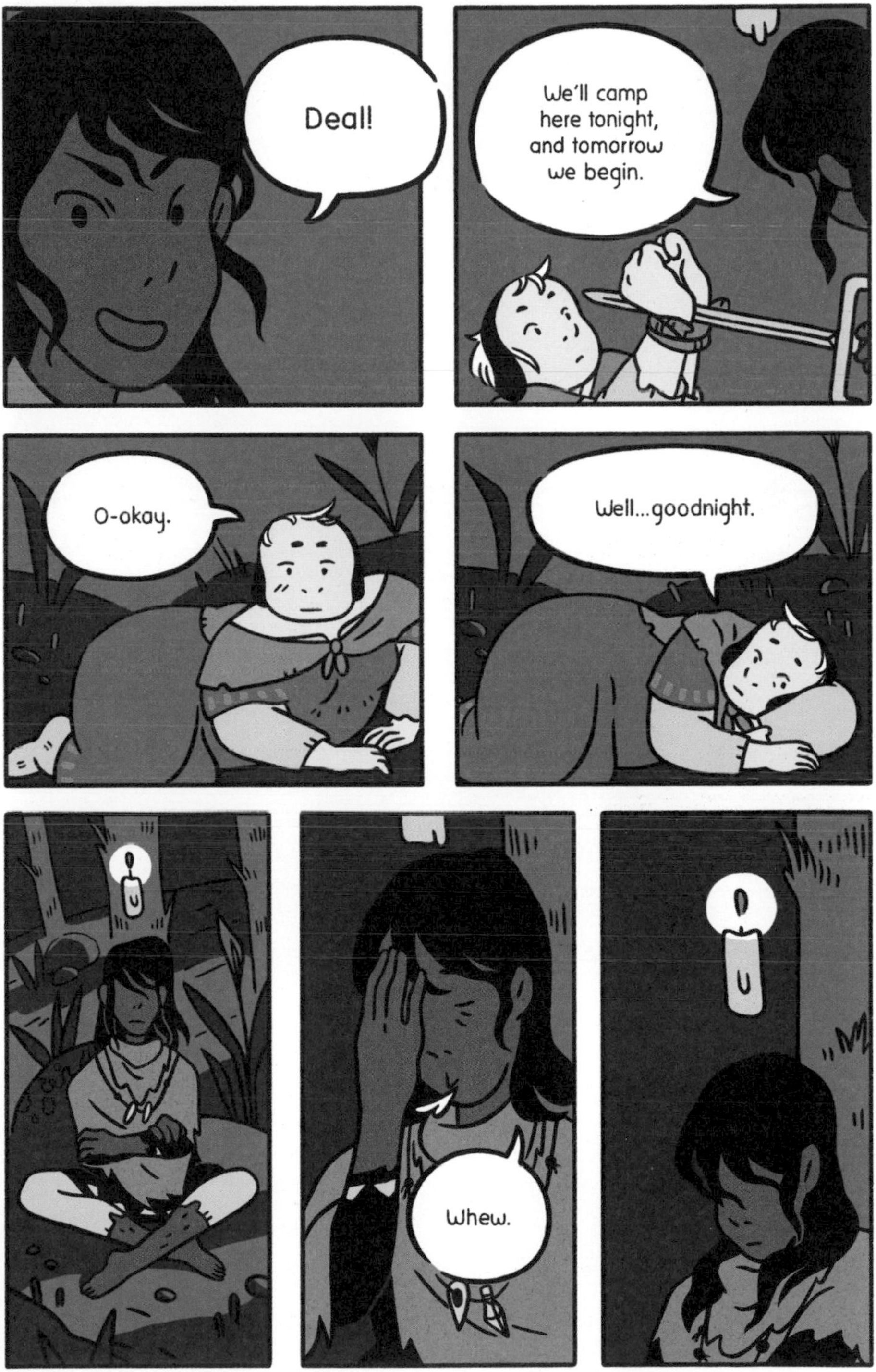
Deal!
We'll camp here tonight, and tomorrow we begin.
O-okay.
Well...goodnight.
Whew.

Part 2

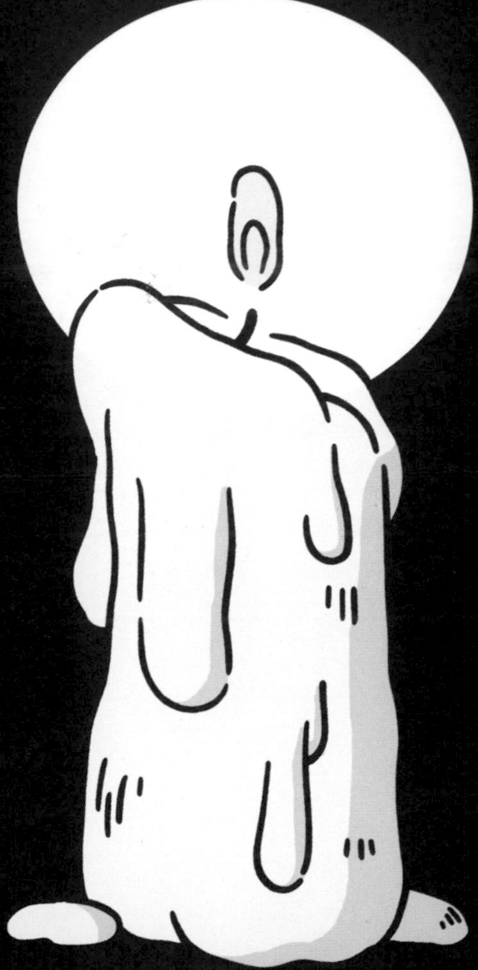

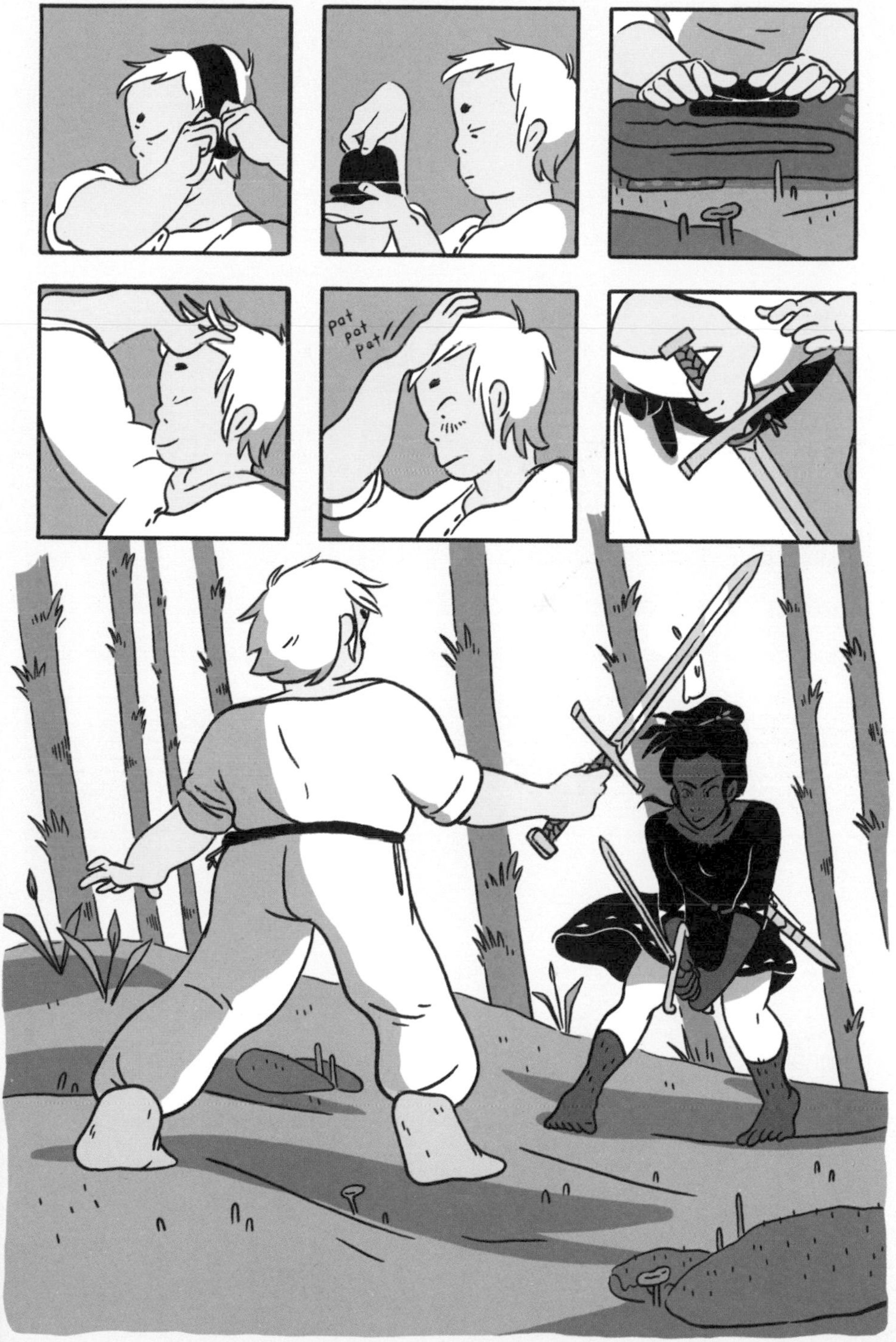
pat
pat
pat

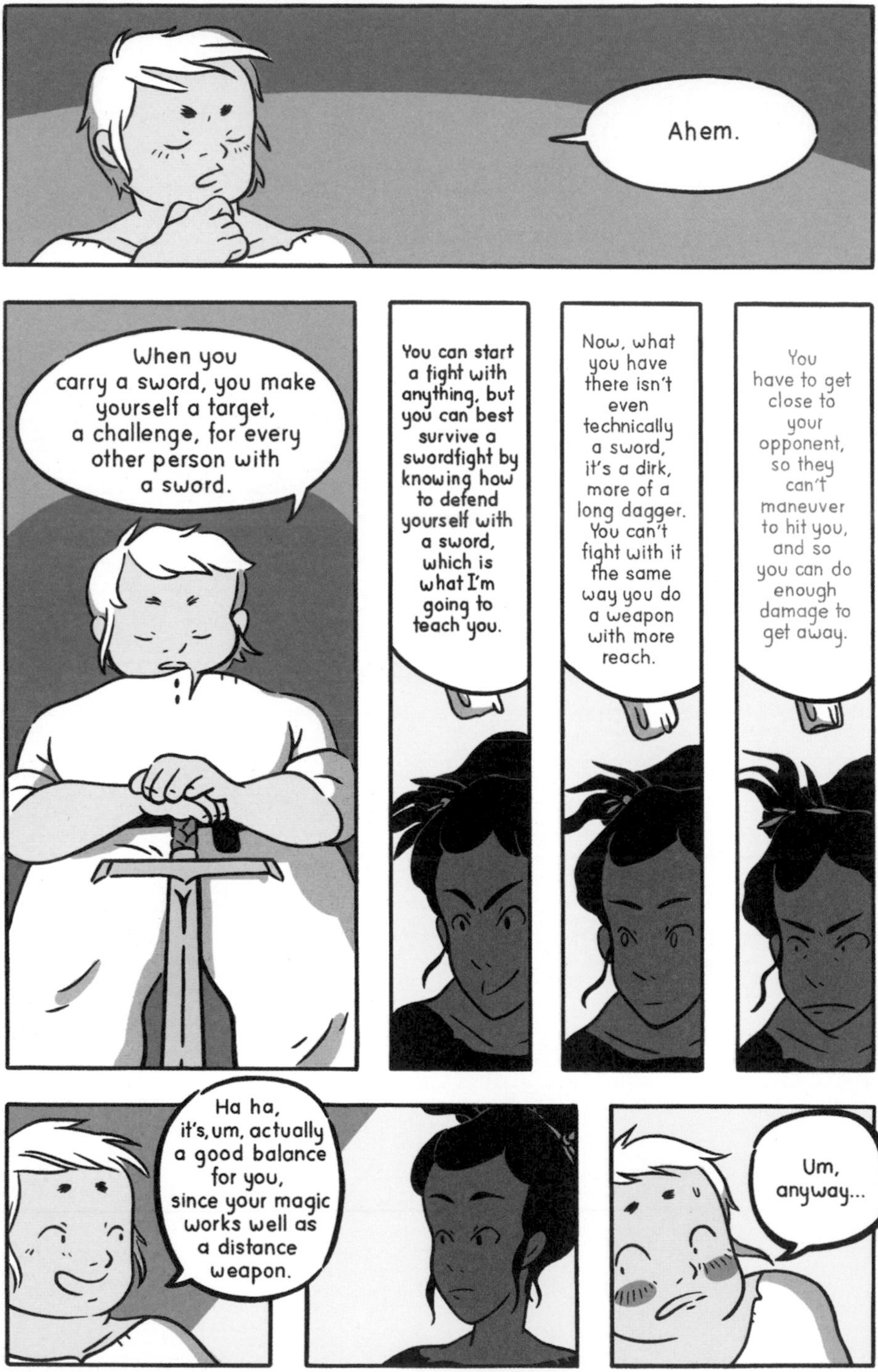
Ahem.
When you carry a sword, you make yourself a target, a challenge, for every other person with a sword.
You can start a fight with anything, but you can best survive a swordfight by knowing how to defend yourself with a sword, which is what I'm going to teach you.
Now, what you have there isn't even technically a sword, it's a dirk, more of a long dagger. You can't fight with it the same way you do a weapon with more reach.
You have to get close to your opponent, so they can't maneuver to hit you, and so you can do enough damage to get away.
Ha ha, it's, um, actually a good balance for you, since your magic works well as a distance weapon.
Um, anyway...

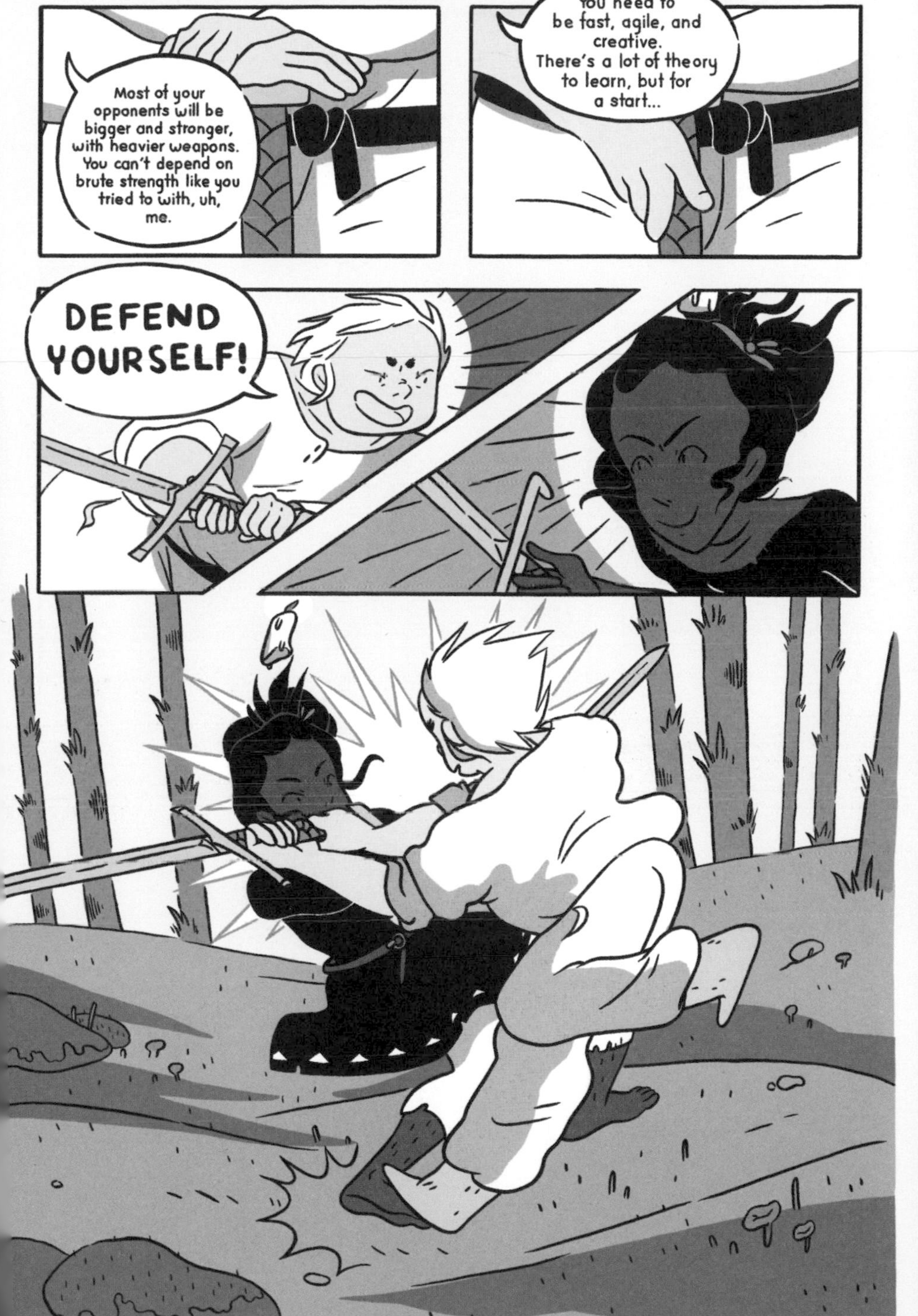
Most of your opponents will be bigger and stronger, with heavier weapons. You can't depend on brute strength like you tried to with, uh, me.
You need to be fast, agile, and creative. There's a lot of theory to learn, but for a start...
DEFEND YOURSELF!

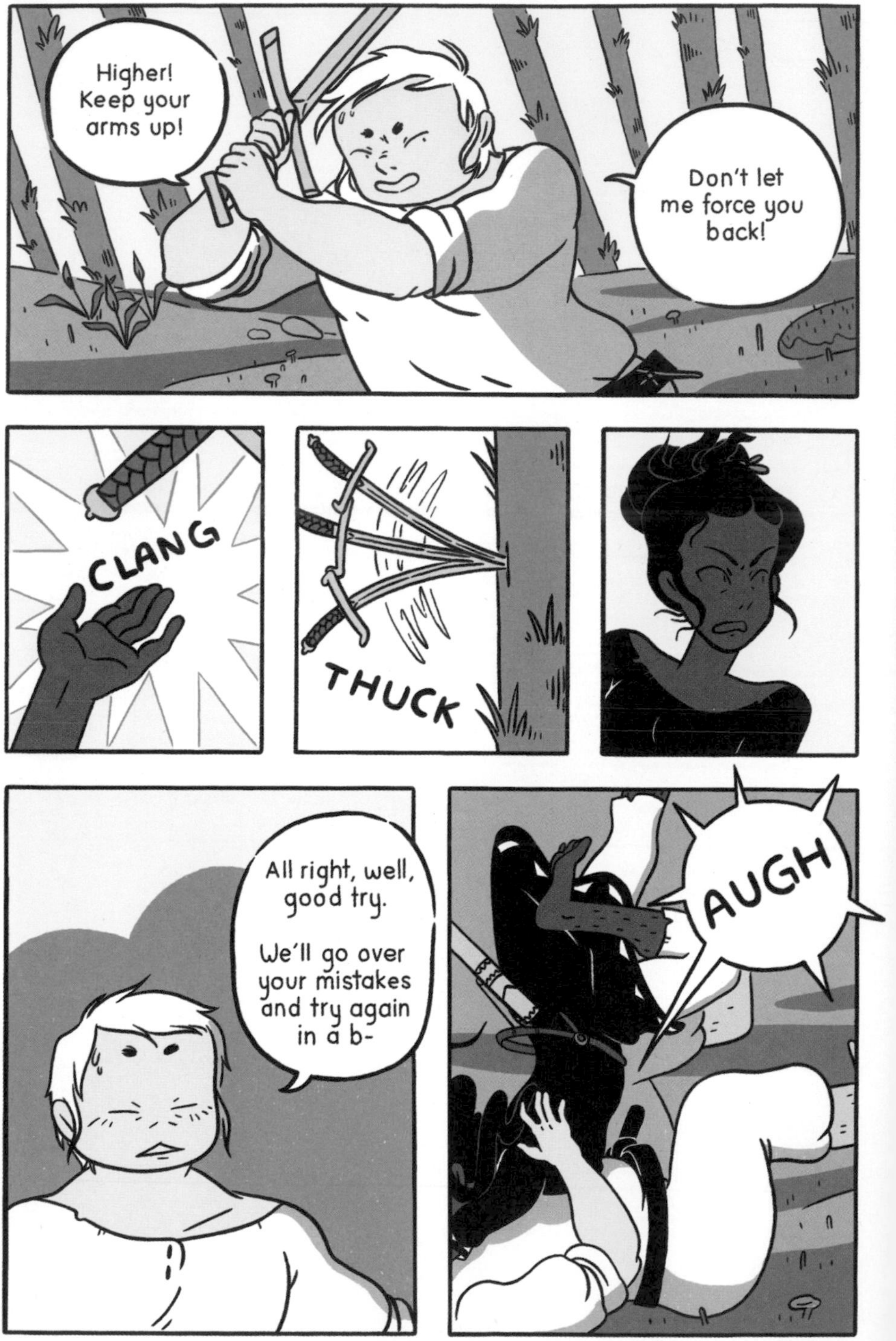
Higher! Keep your arms up!
Don't let me force you back!
CLANG
THUCK
All right, well, good try.
We'll go over your mistakes and try again in a b-
AUGH

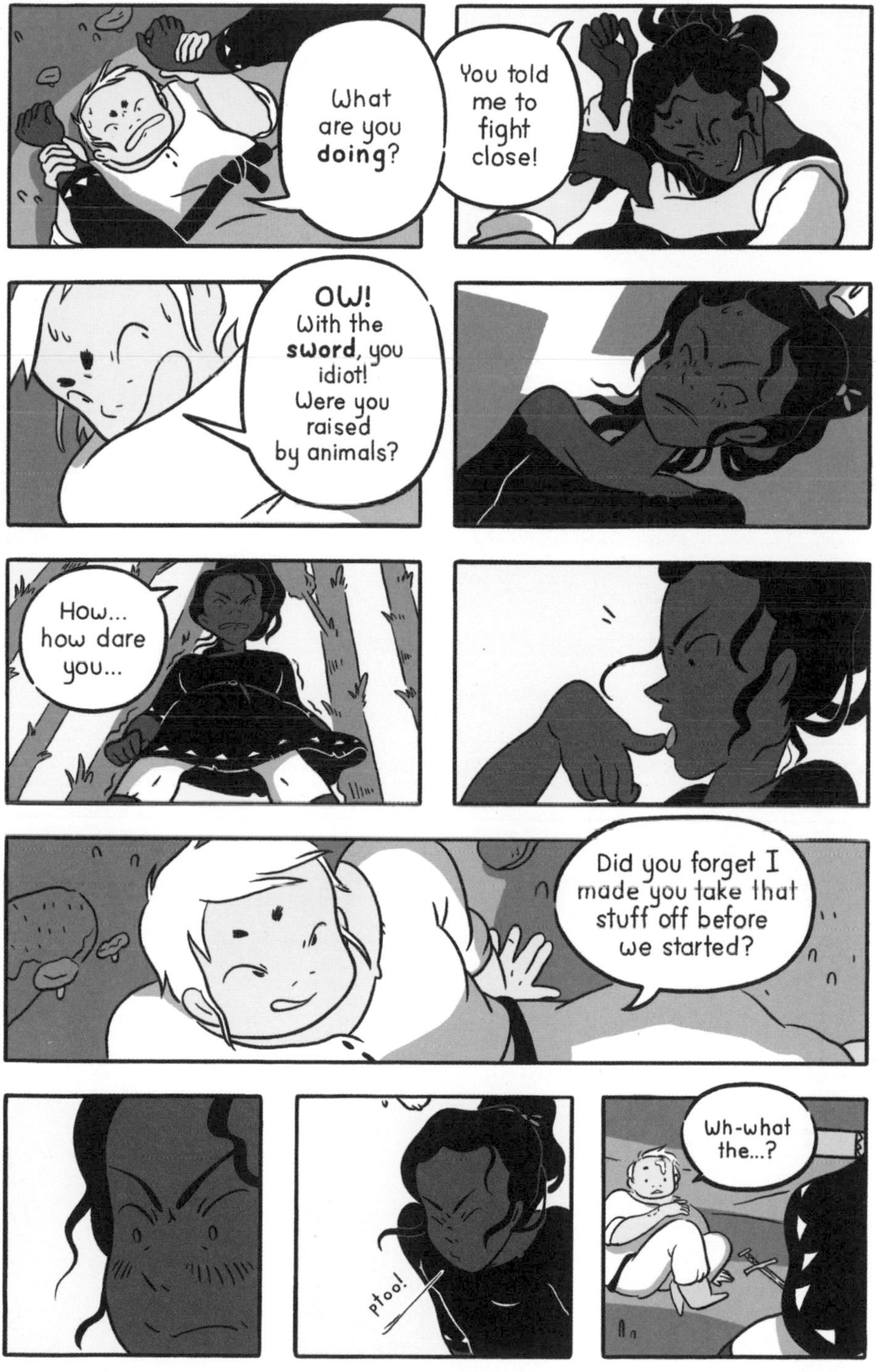
What are you **doing**?
You told me to fight close!
OW! With the **sword**, you idiot! Were you raised by animals?
How... how dare you...
Did you forget I made you take that stuff off before we started?
ptoo!
Wh-what the...?

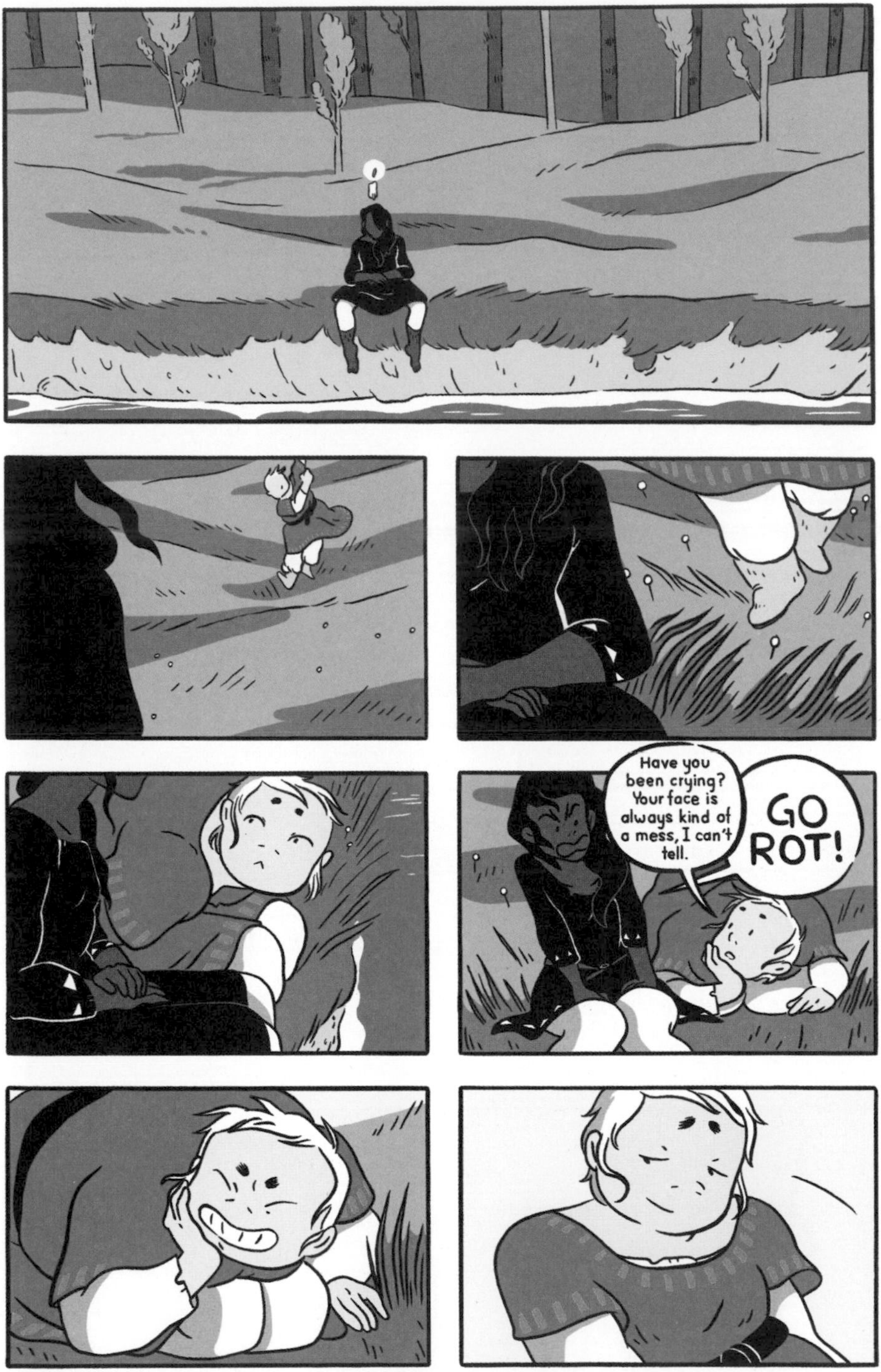
Have you been crying? Your face is always kind of a mess, I can't tell.
GO ROT!

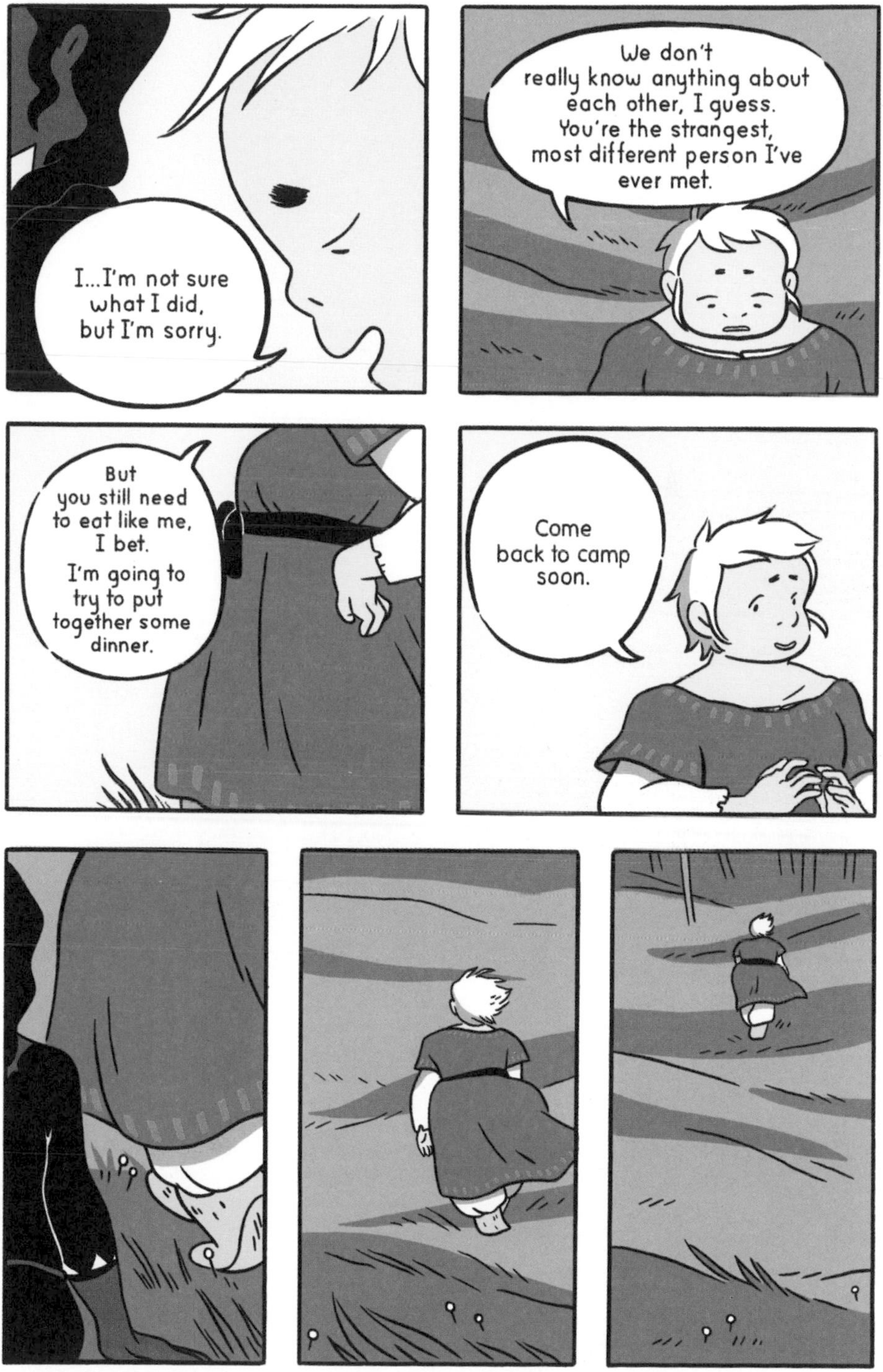
I...I'm not sure what I did, but I'm sorry.
We don't really know anything about each other, I guess. You're the strangest, most different person I've ever met.
But you still need to eat like me, I bet. I'm going to try to put together some dinner.
Come back to camp soon.

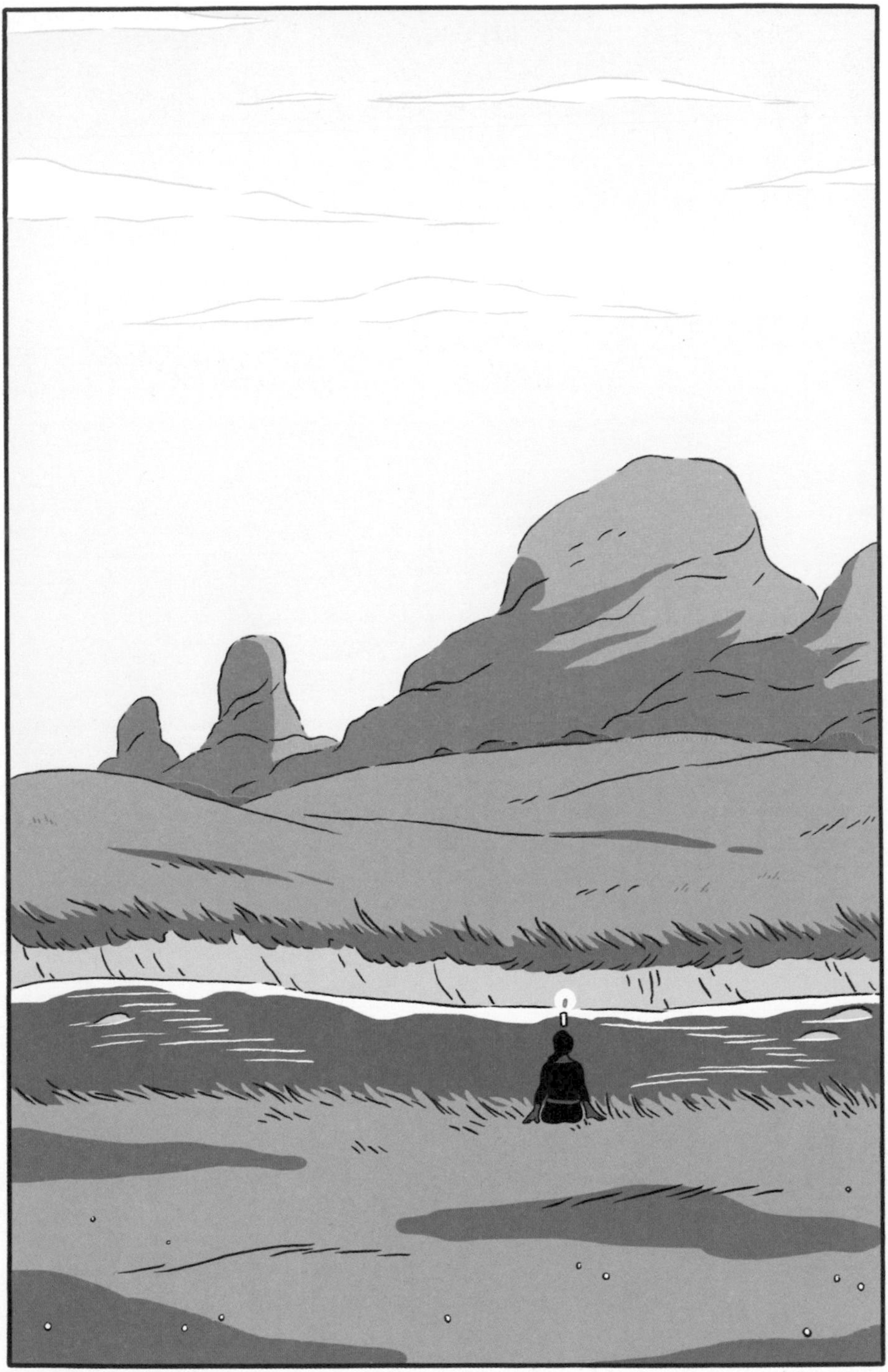

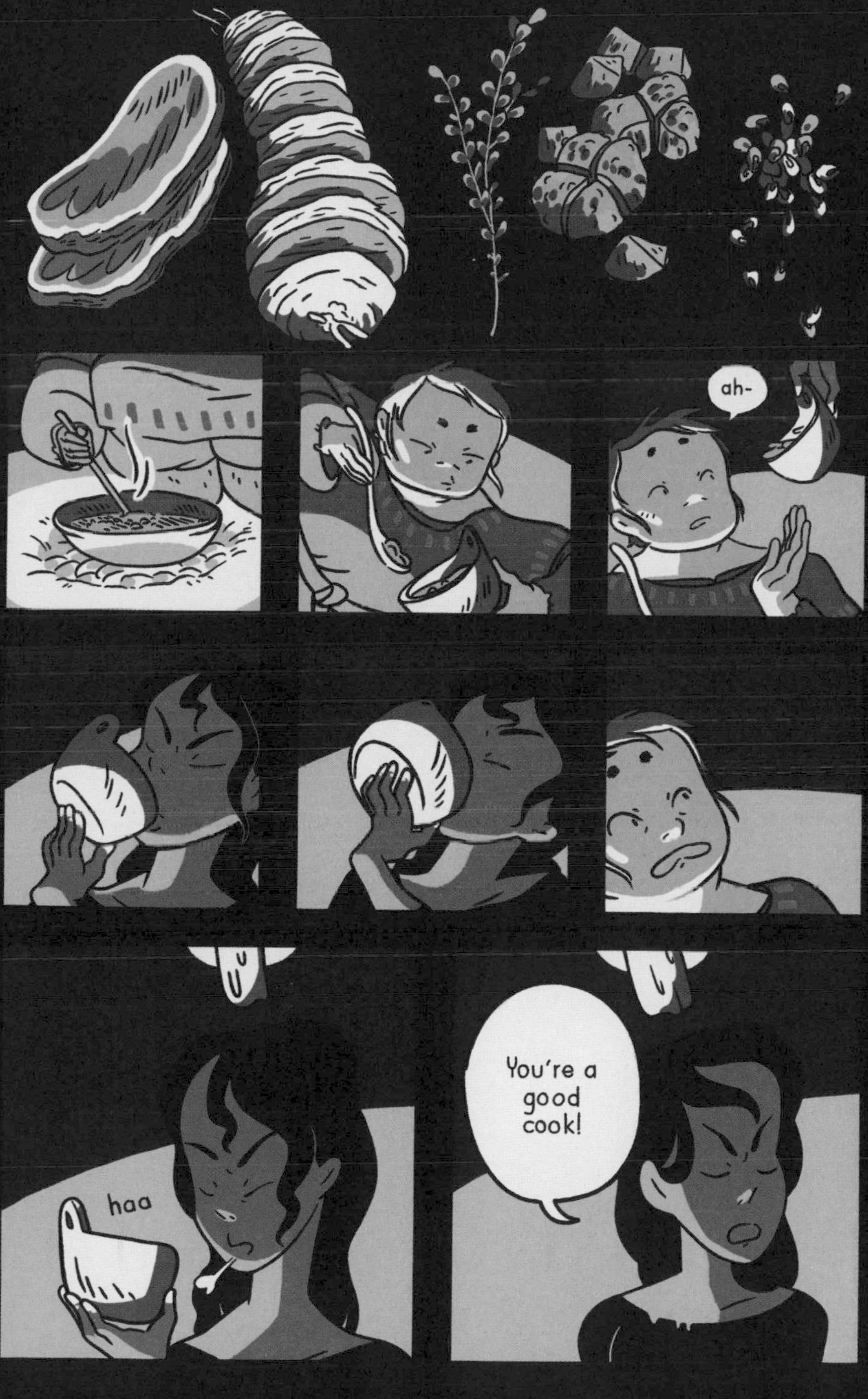
ah-
haa
You're a good cook!

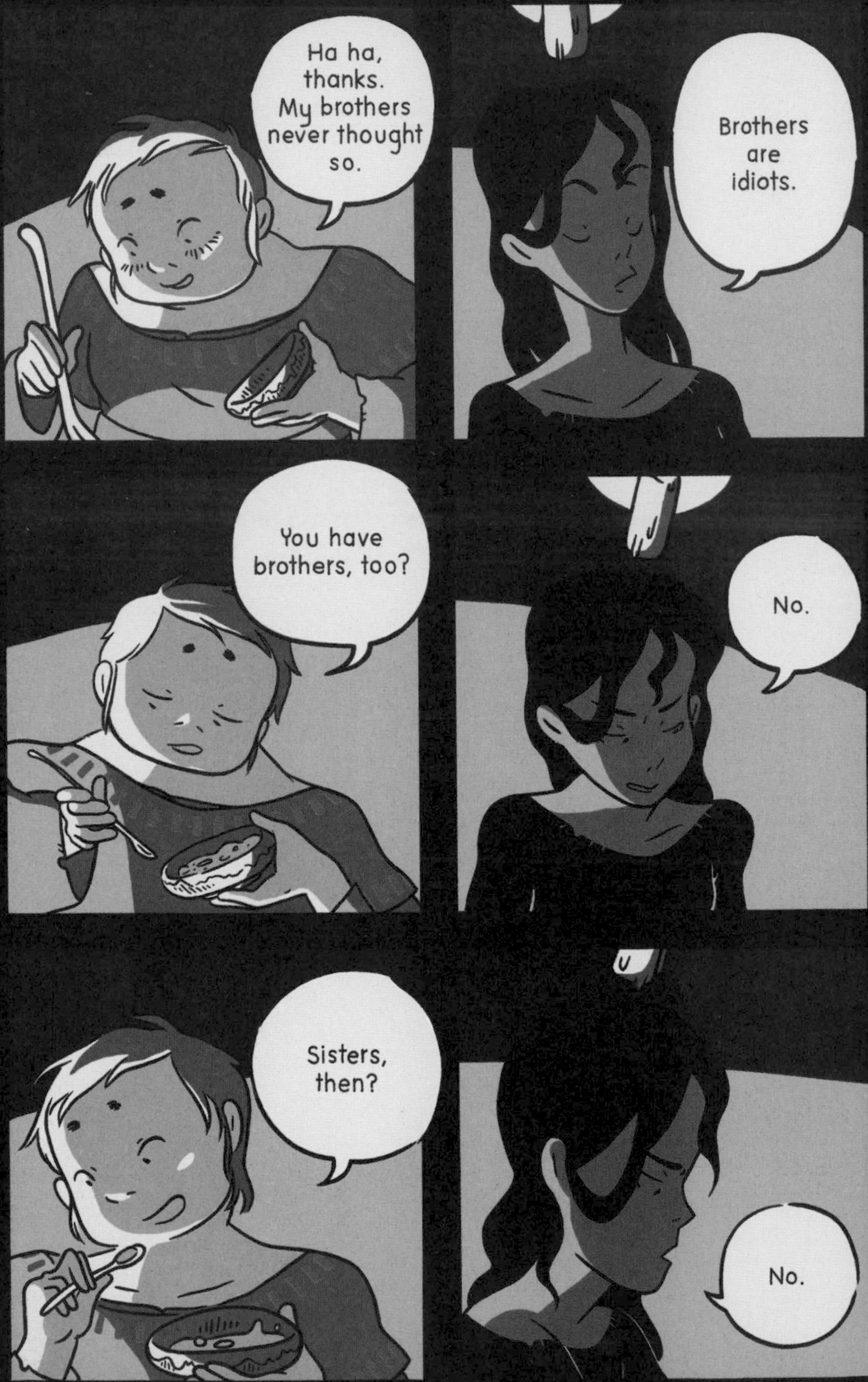
Ha ha, thanks. My brothers never thought so.
Brothers are idiots.
You have brothers, too?
No.
Sisters, then?
No.

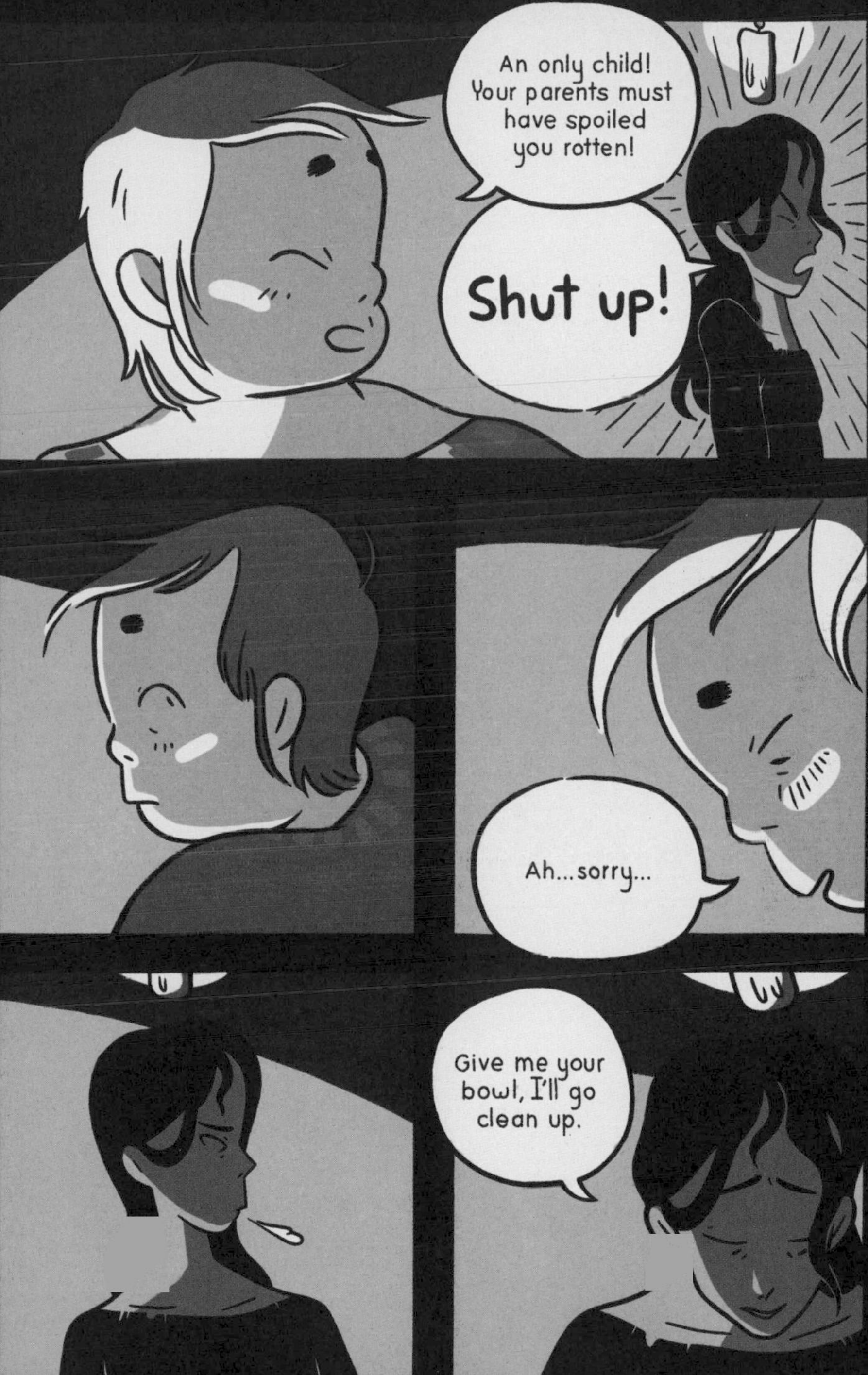
An only child! Your parents must have spoiled you rotten!
Shut up!
Ah...sorry...
Give me your bowl, I'll go clean up.

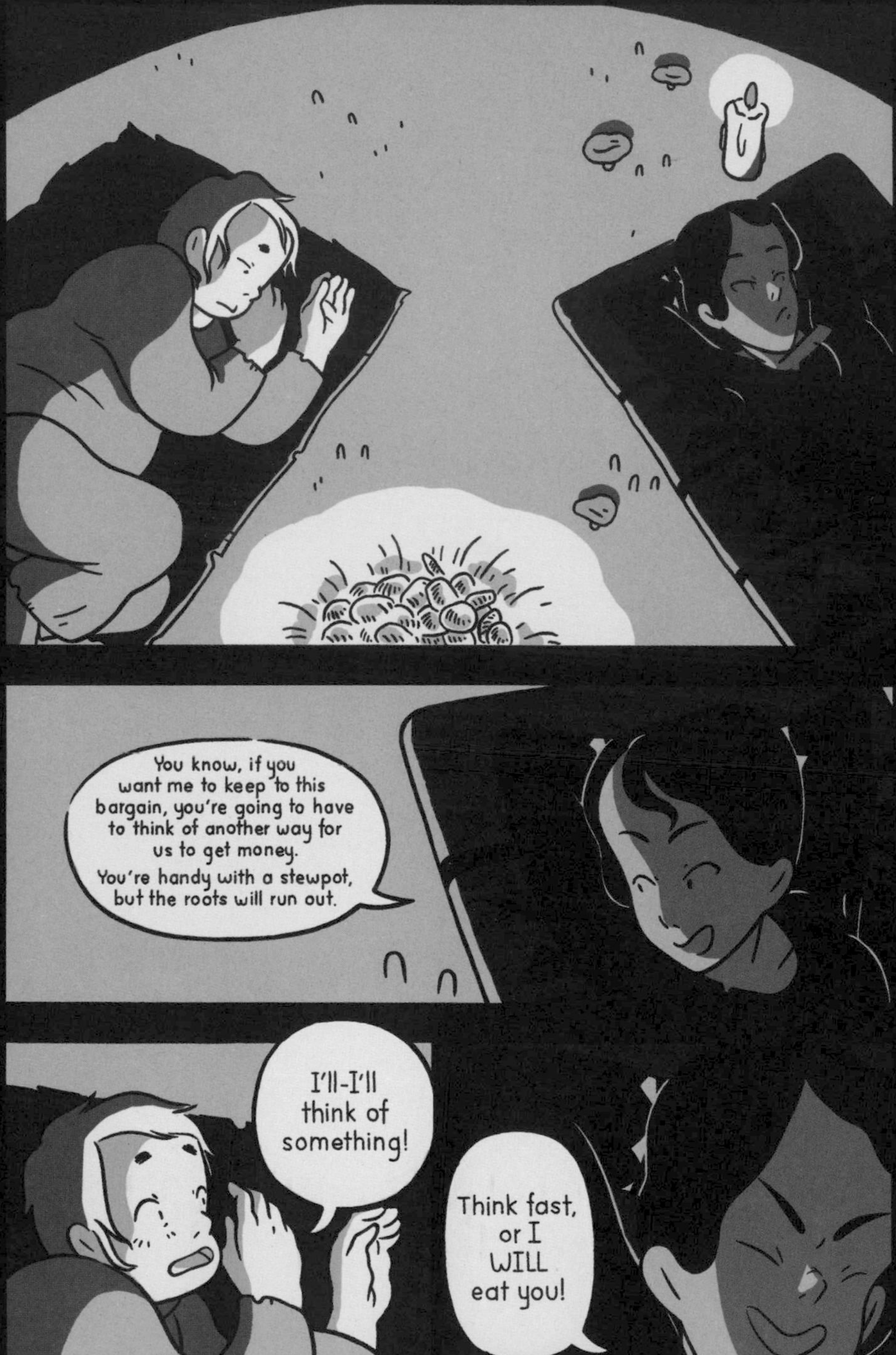
You know, if you want me to keep to this bargain, you're going to have to think of another way for us to get money.
You're handy with a stewpot, but the roots will run out.
I'll-I'll think of something!
Think fast, or I WILL eat you!

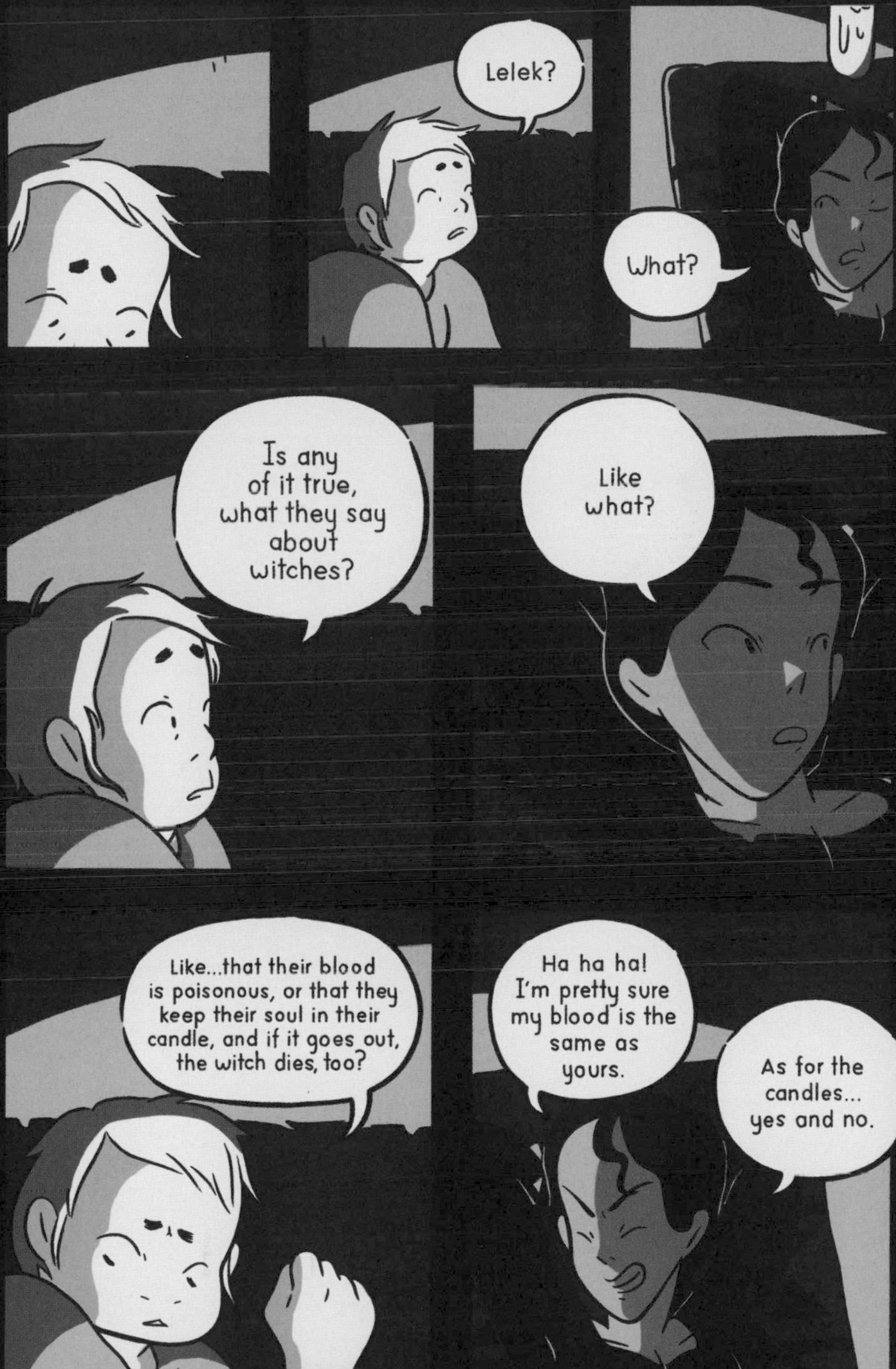
Lelek?
What?
Is any of it true, what they say about witches?
Like what?
Like...that their blood is poisonous, or that they keep their soul in their candle, and if it goes out, the witch dies, too?
Ha ha ha! I'm pretty sure my blood is the same as yours.
As for the candles... yes and no.

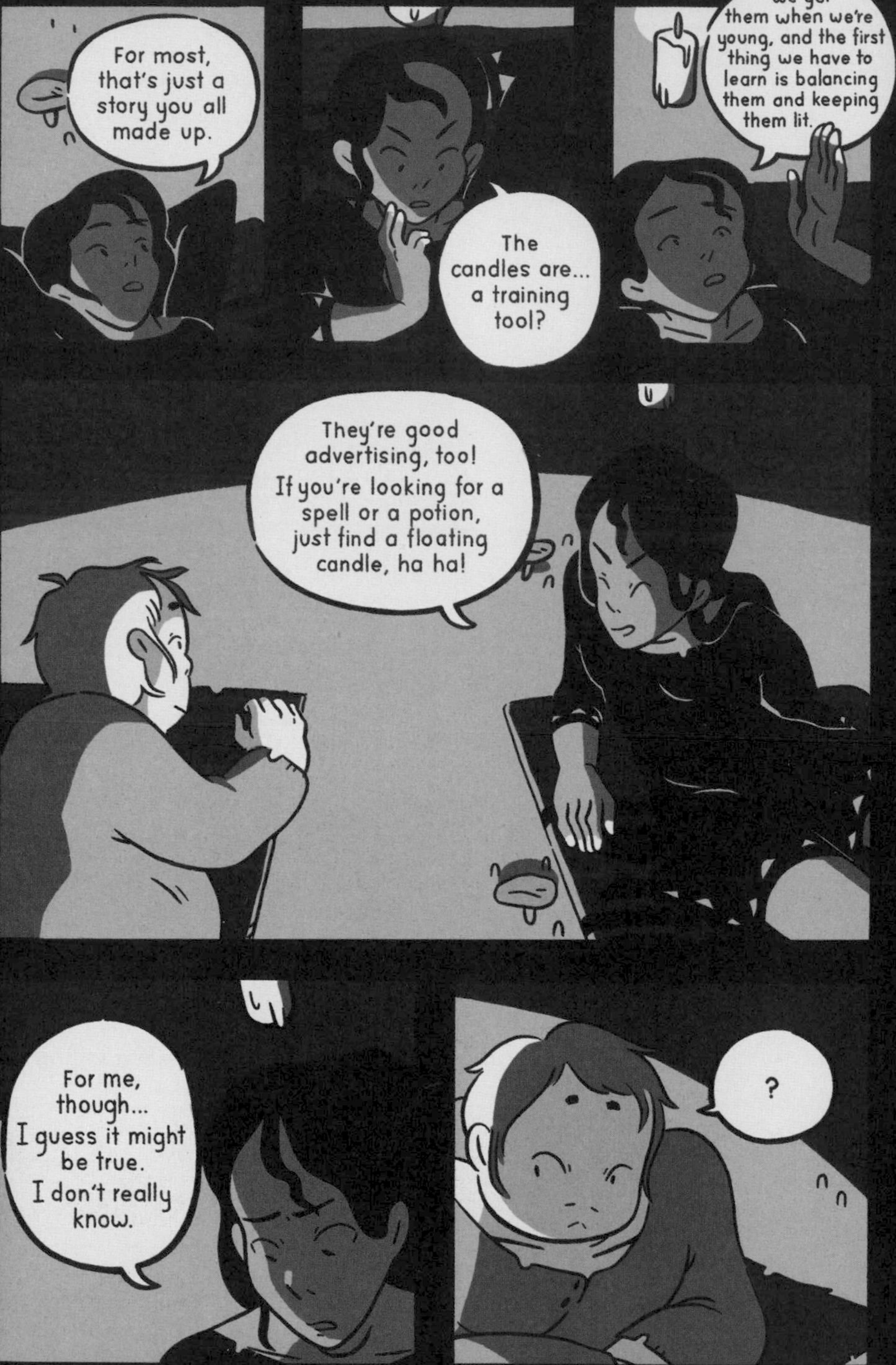
For most, that's just a story you all made up.
The candles are... a training tool?
We get them when we're young, and the first thing we have to learn is balancing them and keeping them lit.
They're good advertising, too! If you're looking for a spell or a potion, just find a floating candle, ha ha!
For me, though... I guess it might be true. I don't really know.
?

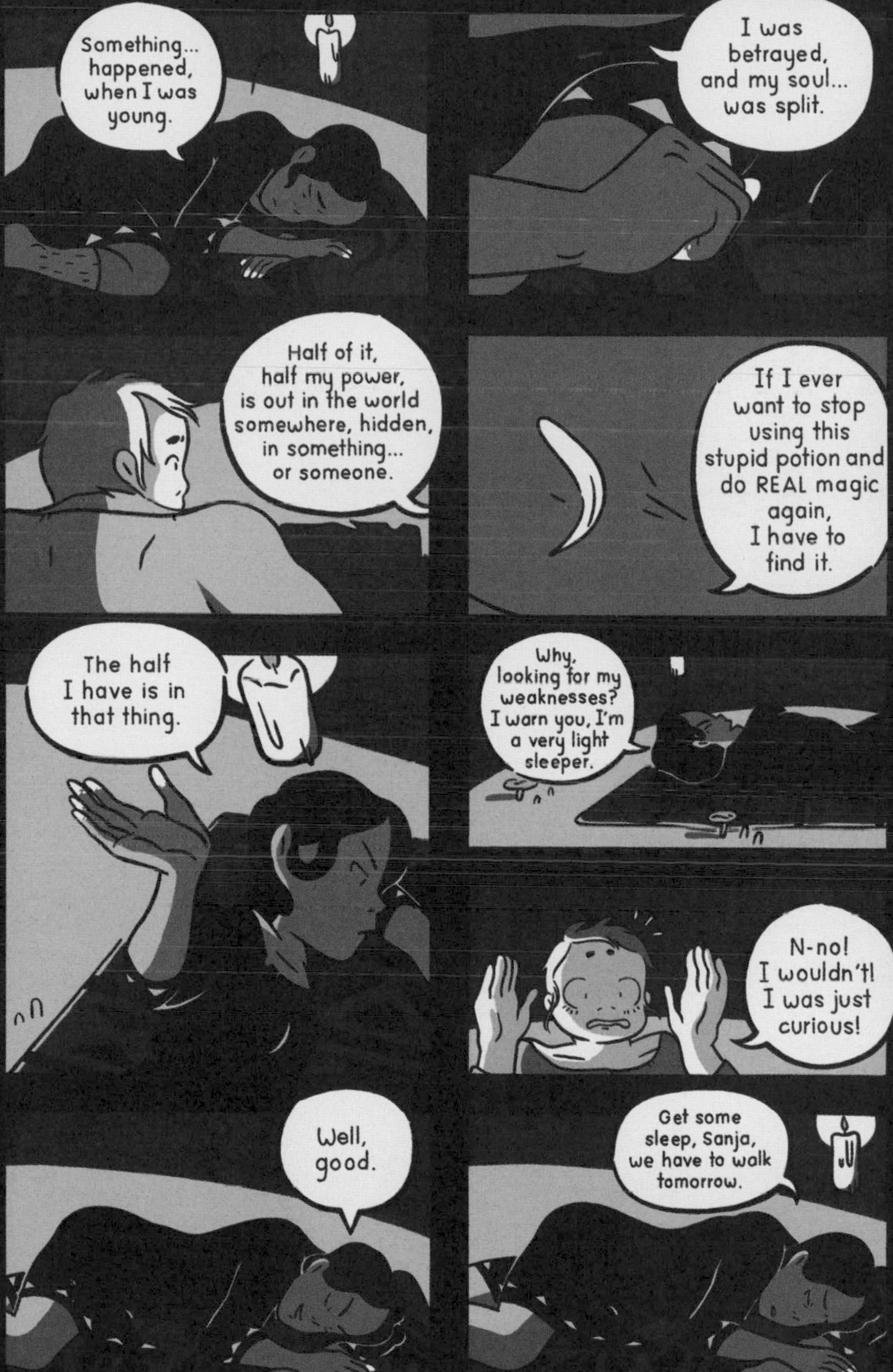
Something... happened, when I was young.
I was betrayed, and my soul... was split.
Half of it, half my power, is out in the world somewhere, hidden, in something... or someone.
If I ever want to stop using this stupid potion and do REAL magic again, I have to find it.
The half I have is in that thing.
Why, looking for my weaknesses? I warn you, I'm a very light sleeper.
N-no! I wouldn't! I was just curious!
Well, good.
Get some sleep, Sanja, we have to walk tomorrow.

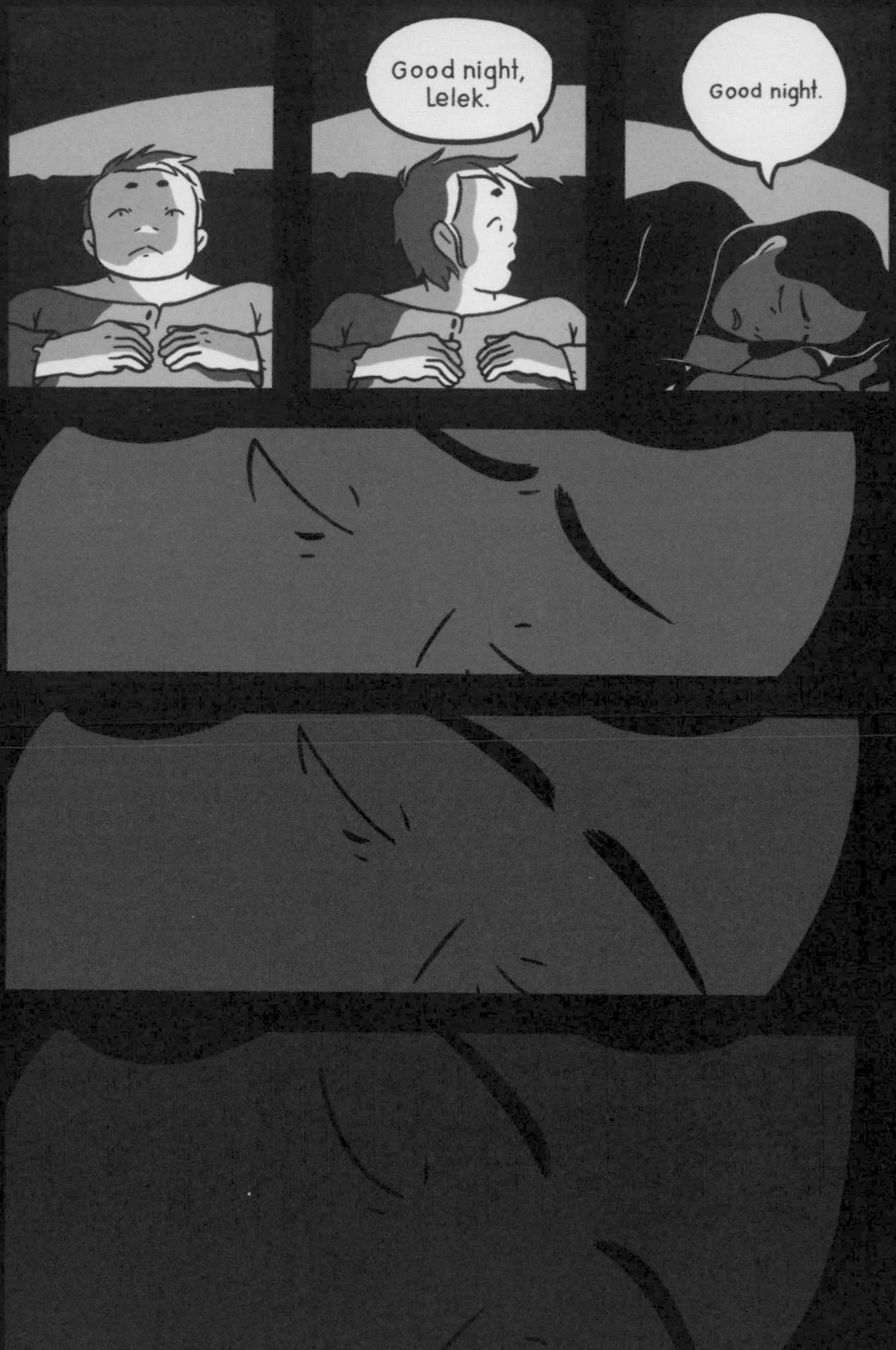
Good night, Lelek.
Good night.

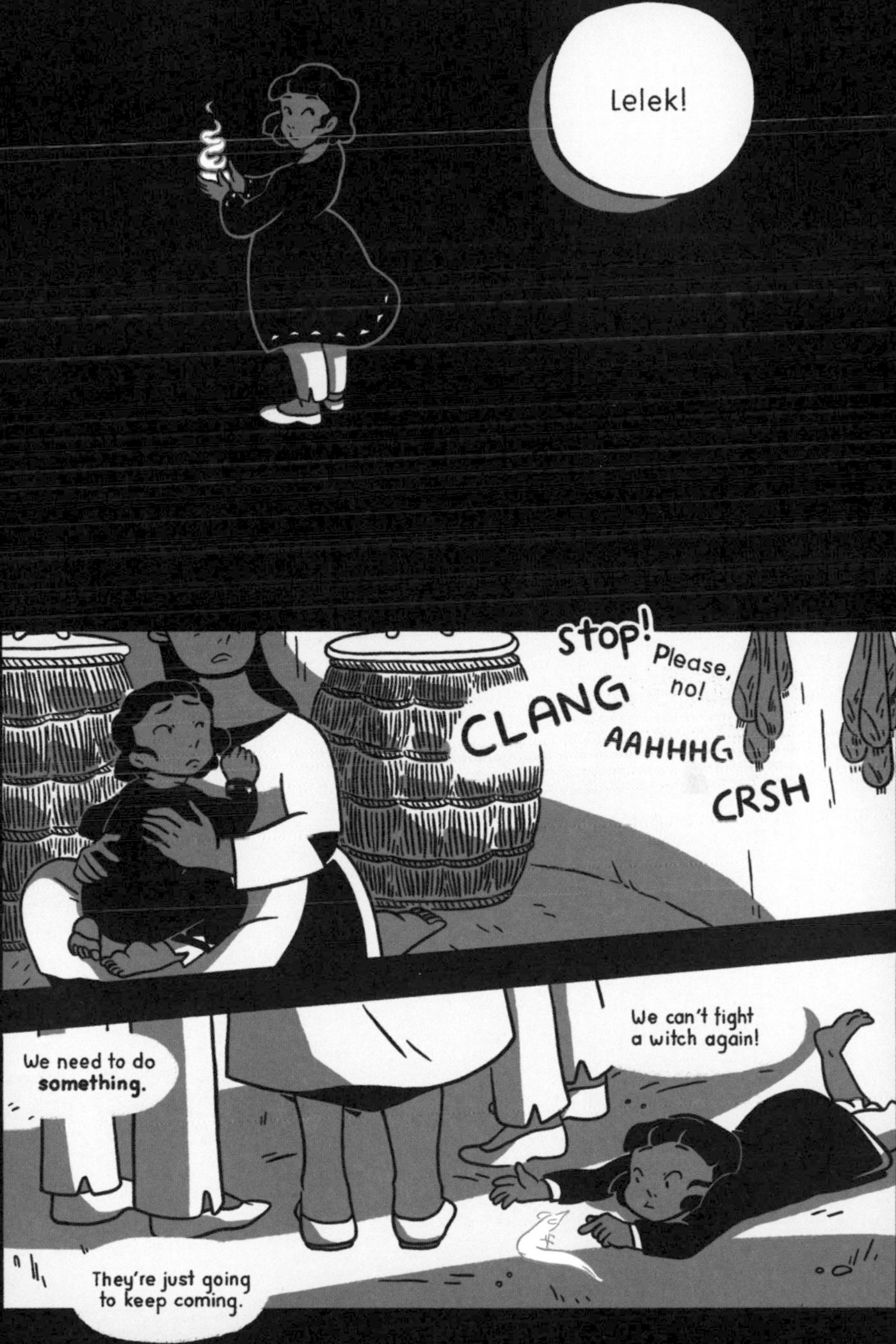
Lelek!
Stop!
Please, no!
CLANG
AAHHHG
CRSH
We need to do **something**.
We can't fight a witch again!
They're just going to keep coming.

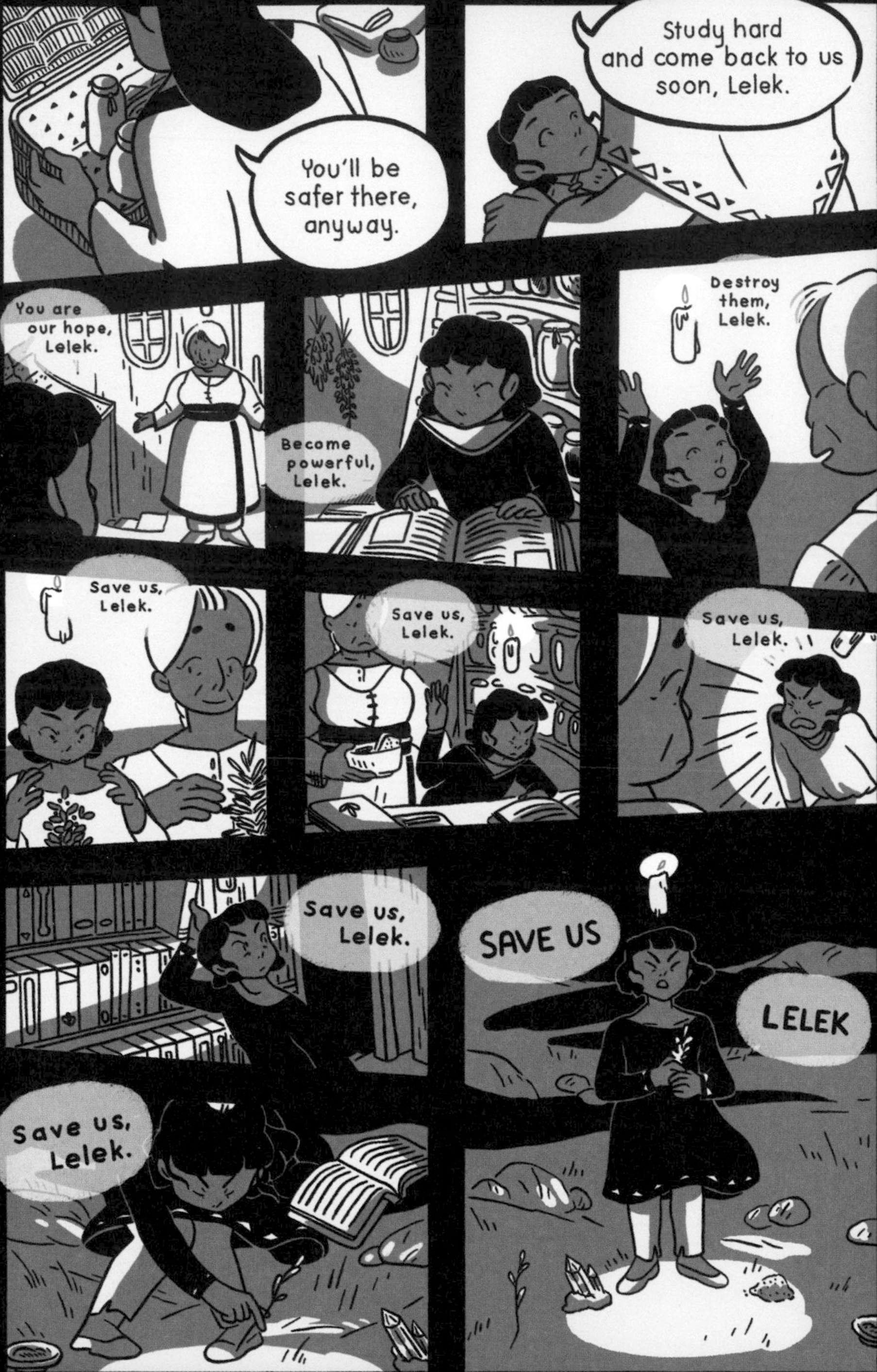
You'll be safer there, anyway.
Study hard and come back to us soon, Lelek.
You are our hope, Lelek.
Become powerful, Lelek.
Destroy them, Lelek.
Save us, Lelek.
Save us, Lelek.
Save us, Lelek.
Save us, Lelek.
Save us, Lelek.
SAVE US
LELEK

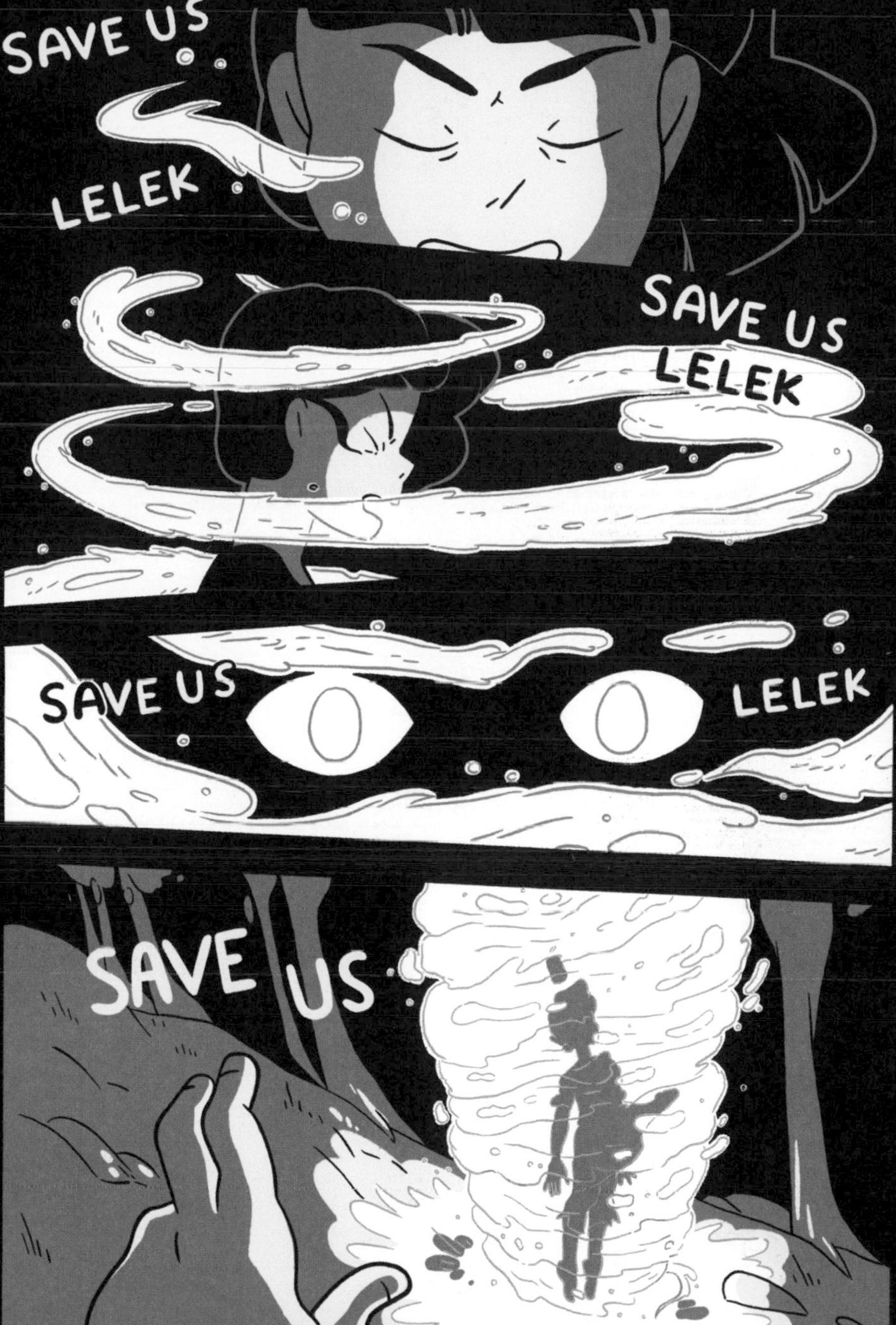
SAVE US
LELEK
SAVE US
LELEK
SAVE US
LELEK
SAVE US

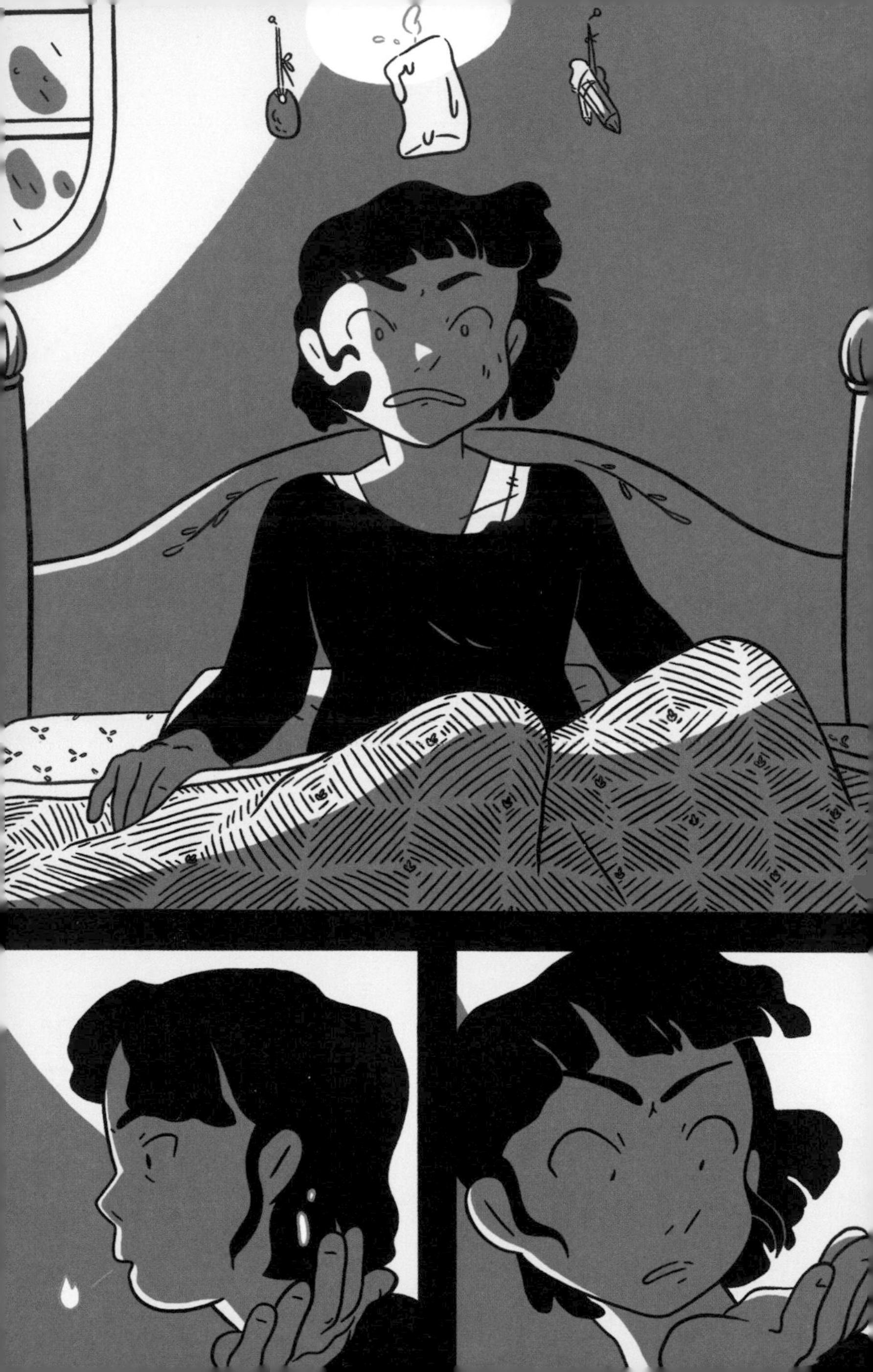

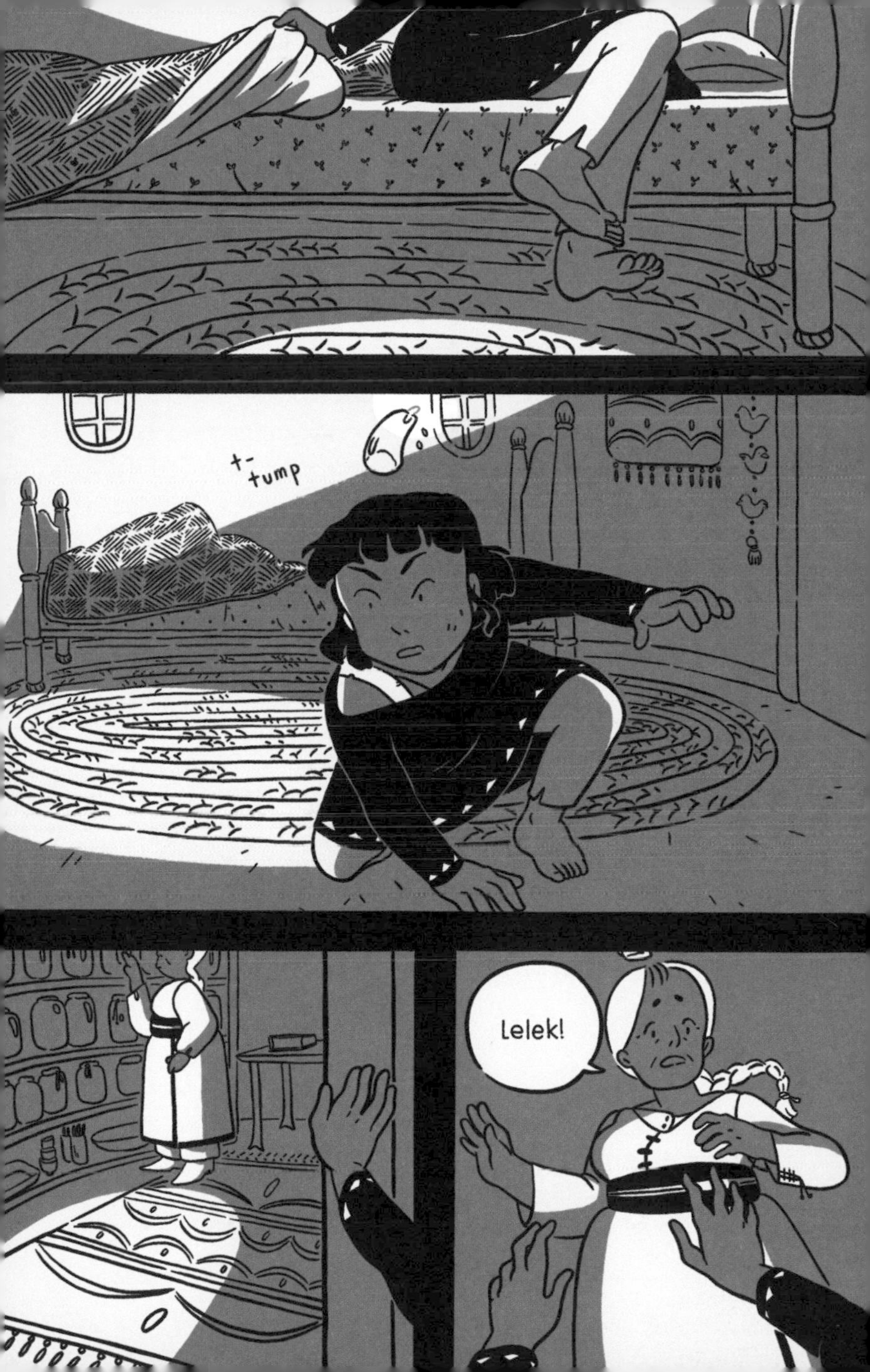
t-
tump
Lelek!

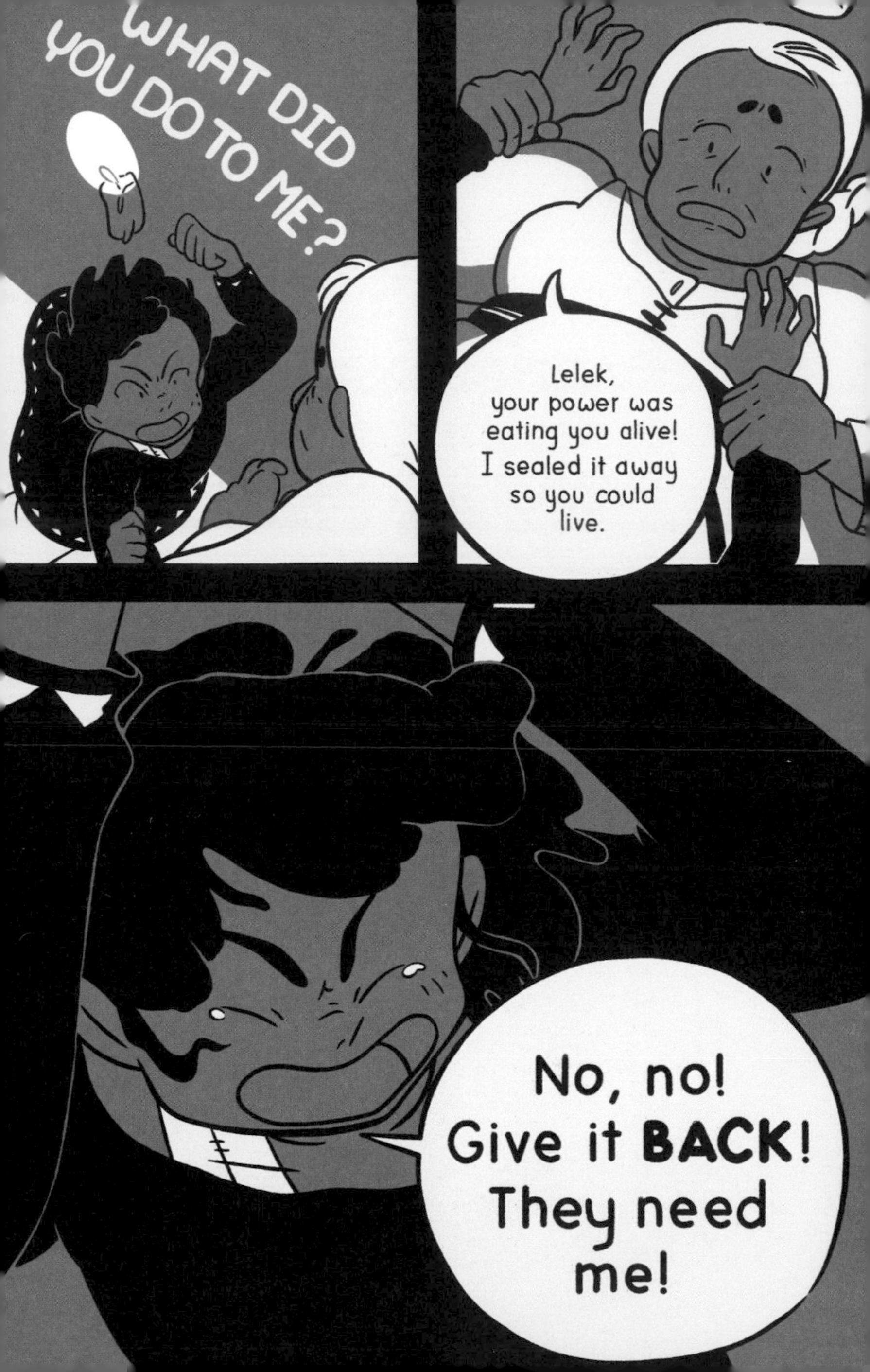
WHAT DID YOU DO TO ME?
Lelek, your power was eating you alive! I sealed it away so you could live.
No, no! Give it **BACK**! They need me!

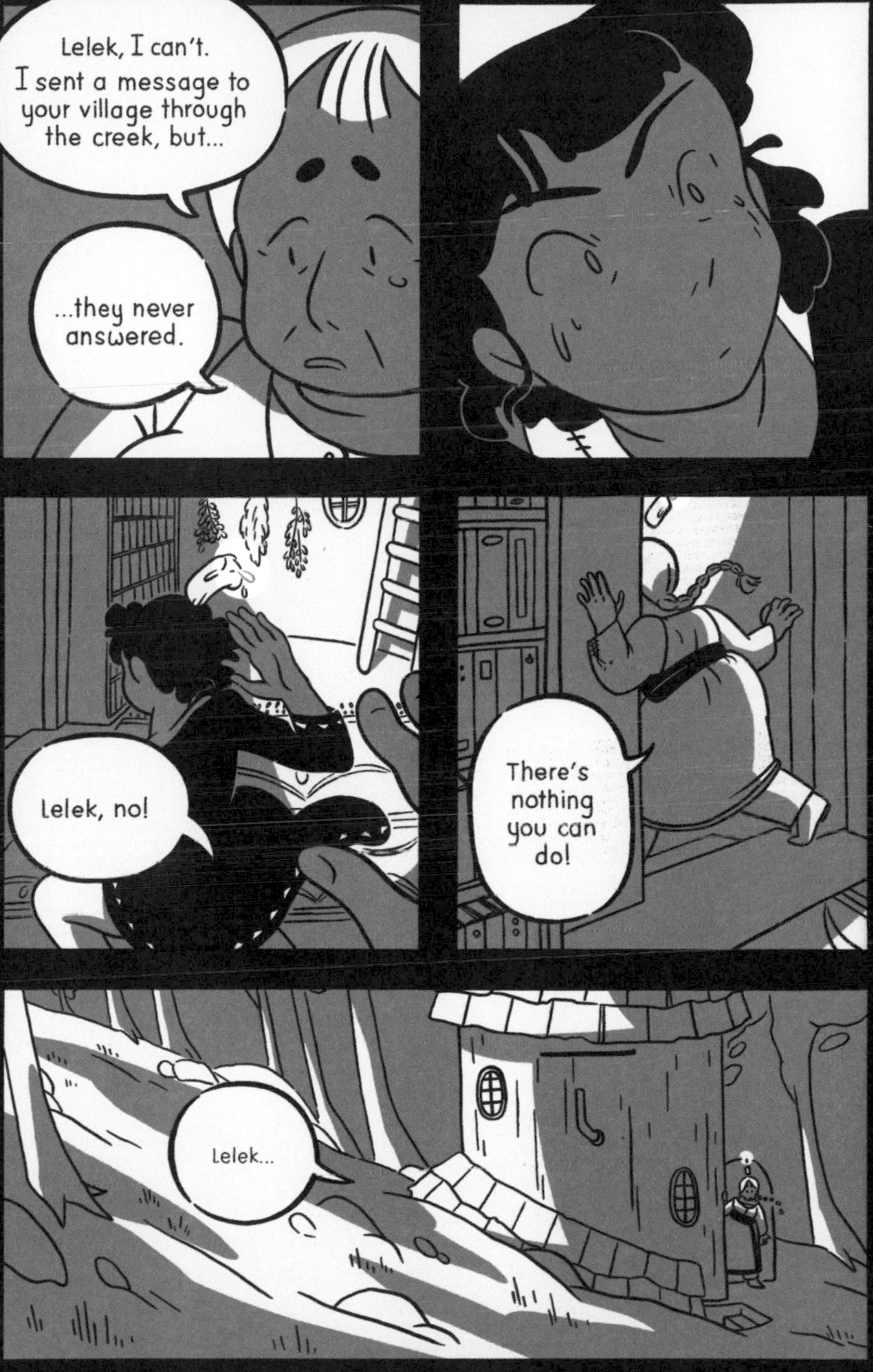
Lelek, I can't. I sent a message to your village through the creek, but...
...they never answered.
Lelek, no!
There's nothing you can do!
Lelek...

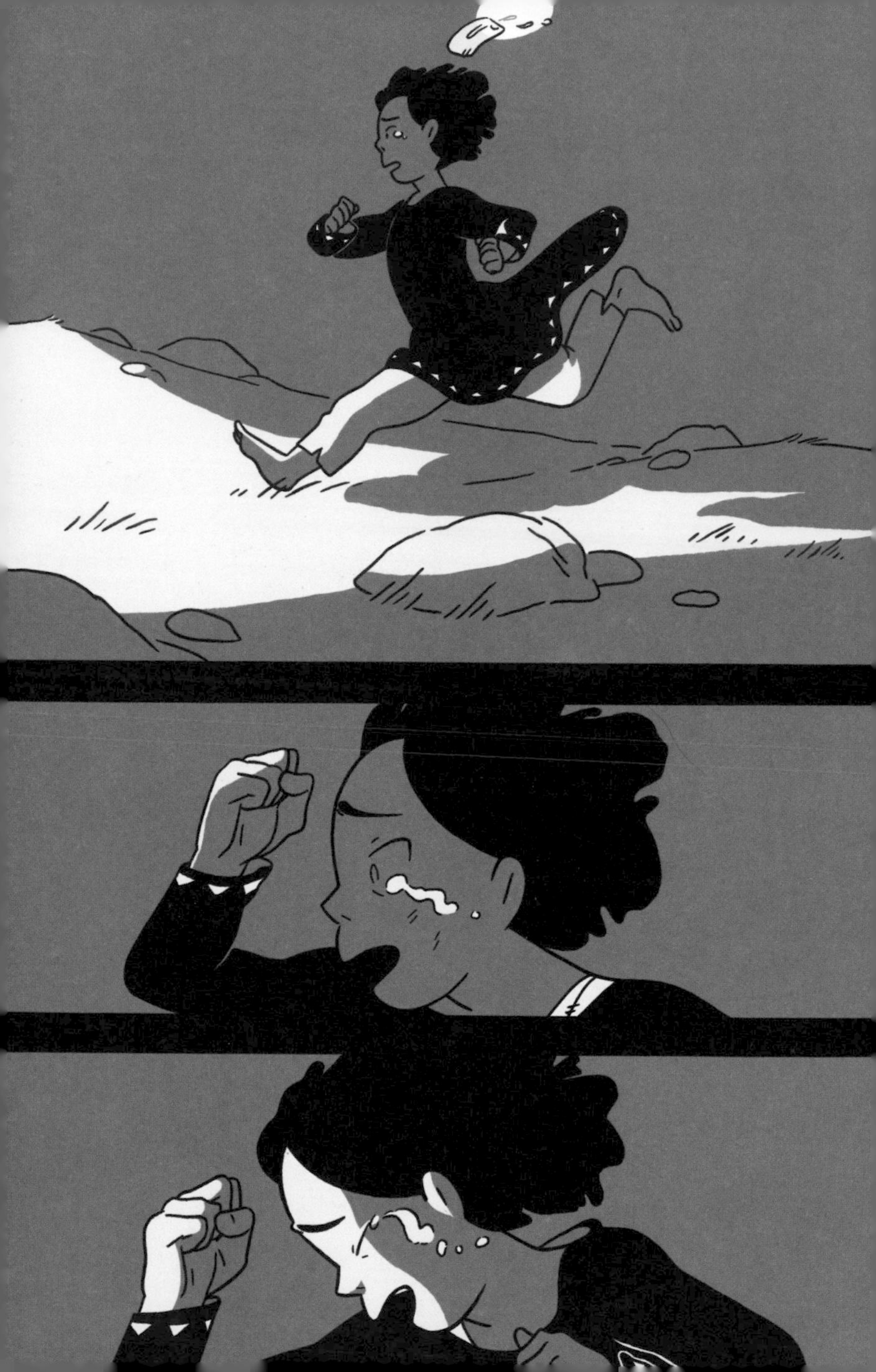

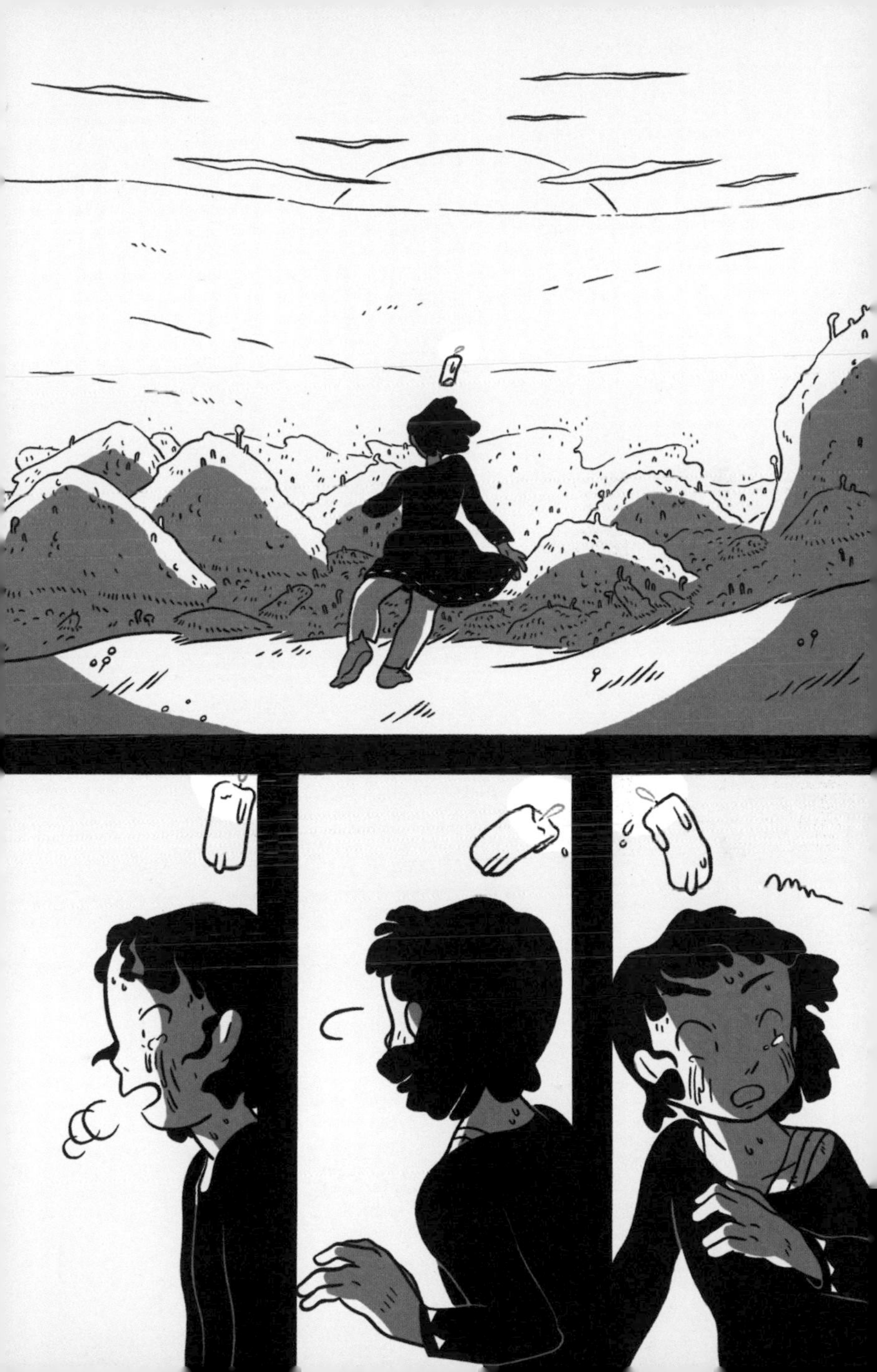

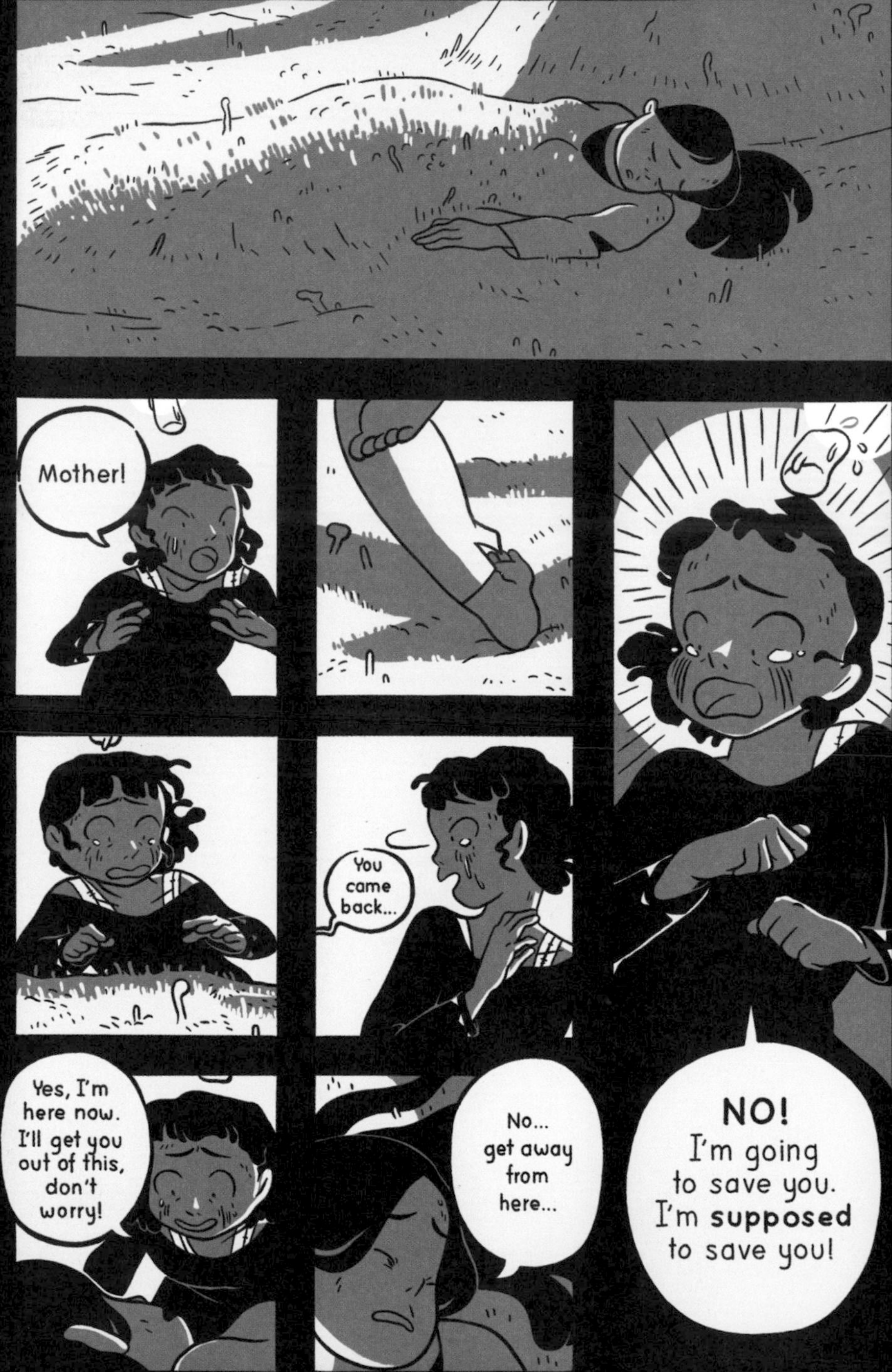
Mother!
You came back...
Yes, I'm here now. I'll get you out of this, don't worry!
No... get away from here...
NO! I'm going to save you. I'm **supposed** to save you!

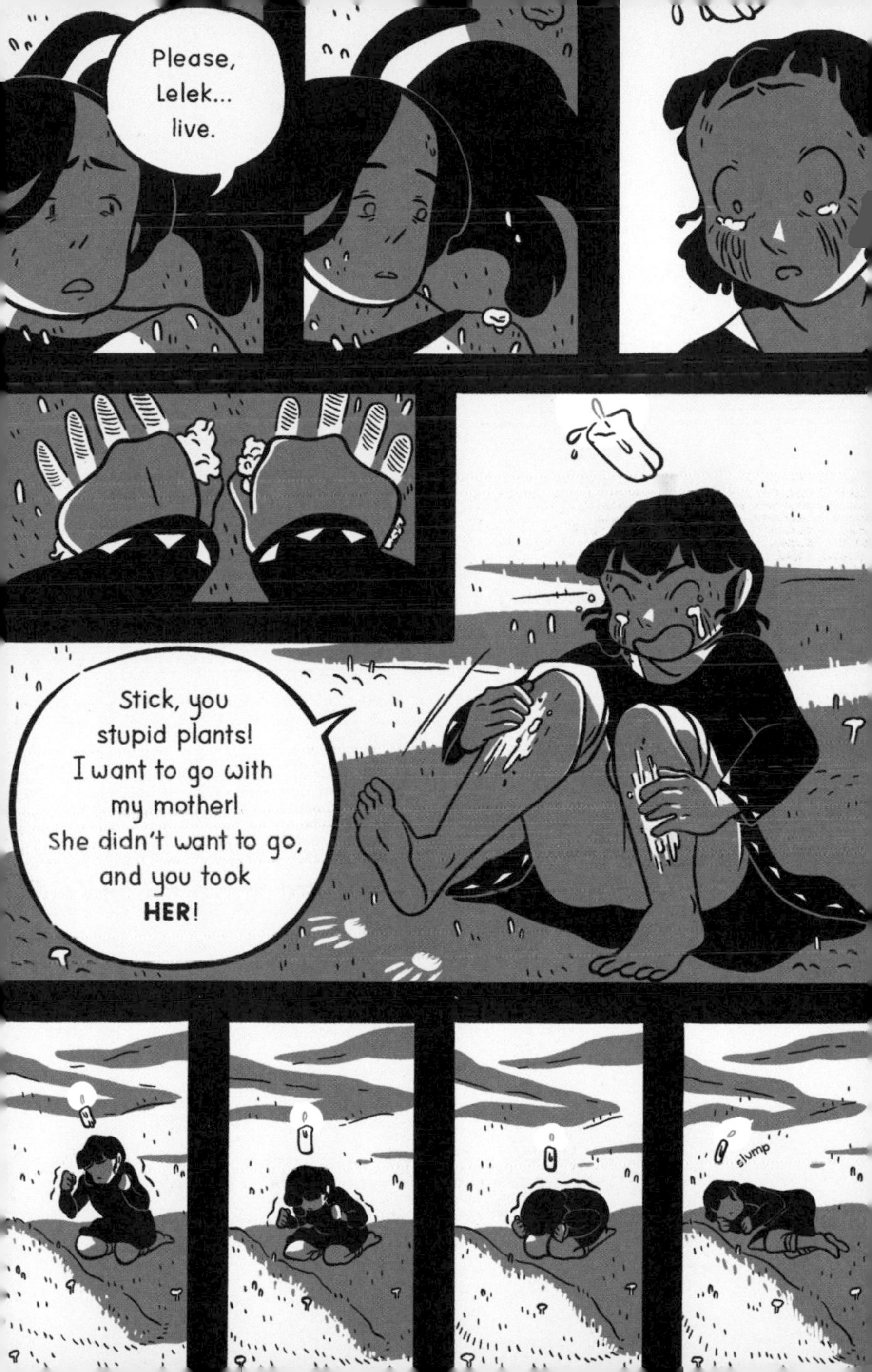

Please, Lelek... live.
Stick, you stupid plants! I want to go with my mother! She didn't want to go, and you took **HER**!
slump

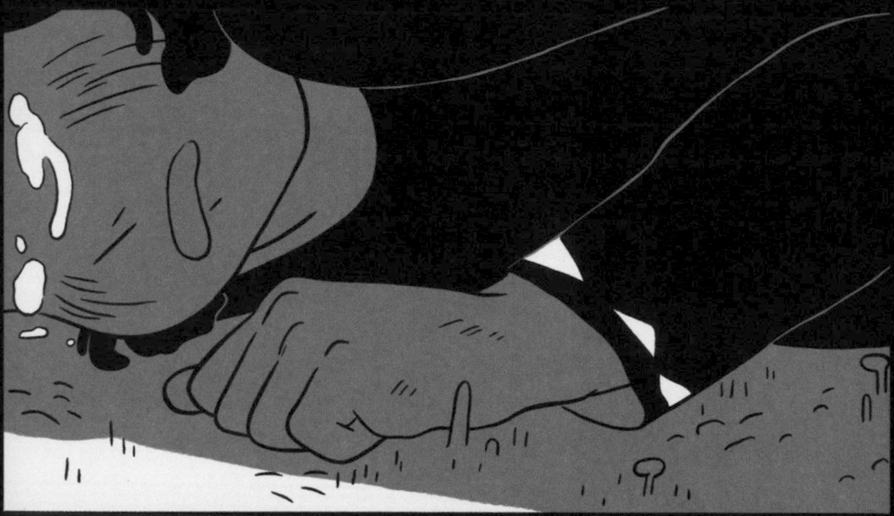
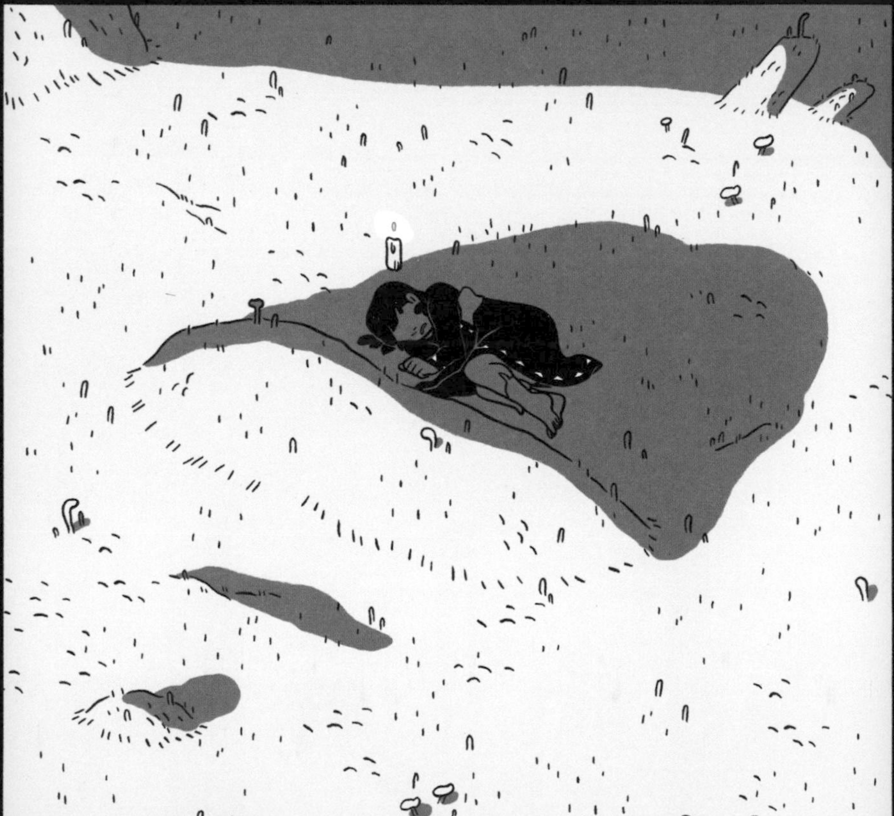

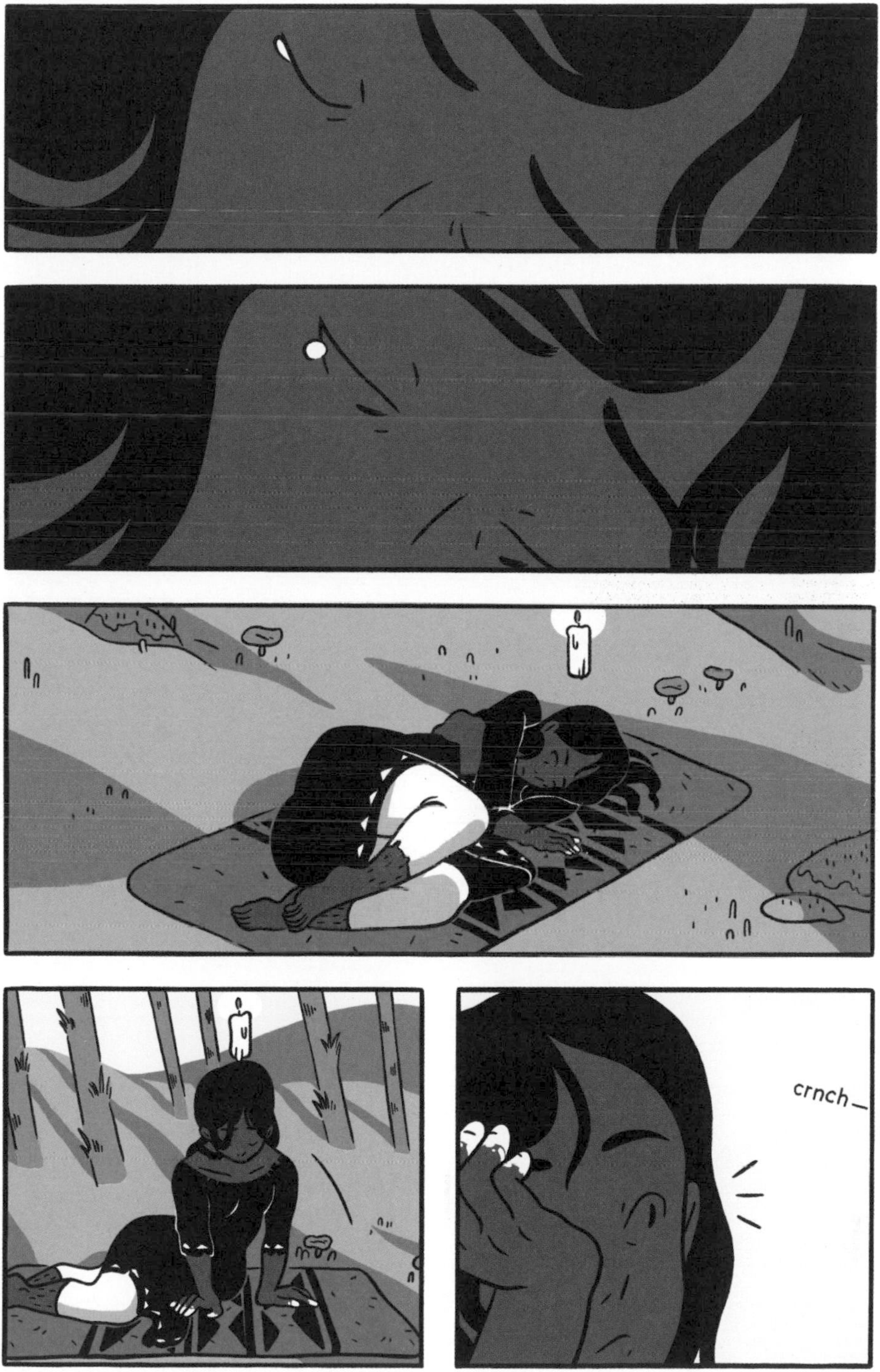
crnch—

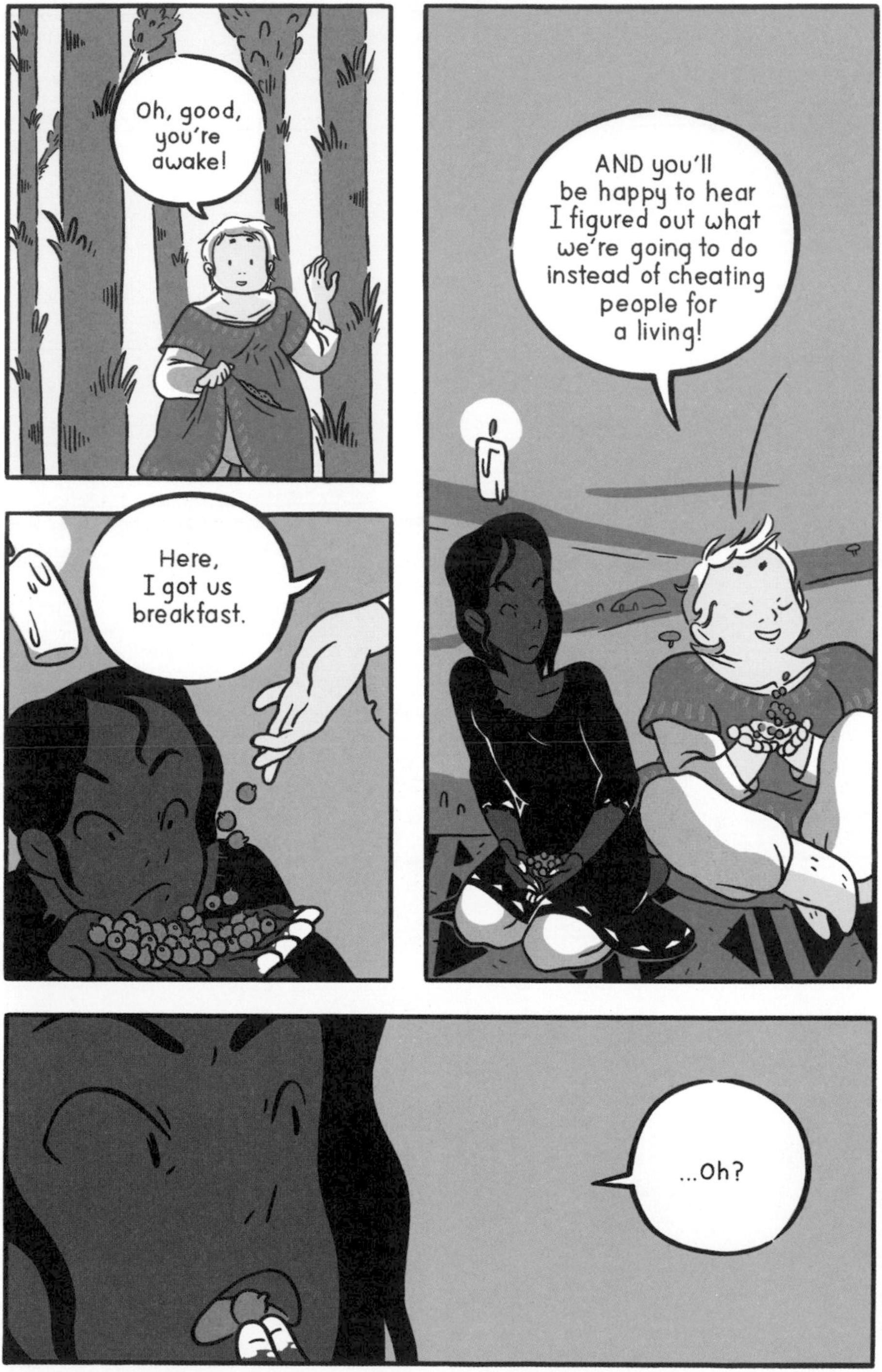
Oh, good, you're awake!
Here, I got us breakfast.
AND you'll be happy to hear I figured out what we're going to do instead of cheating people for a living!
...Oh?

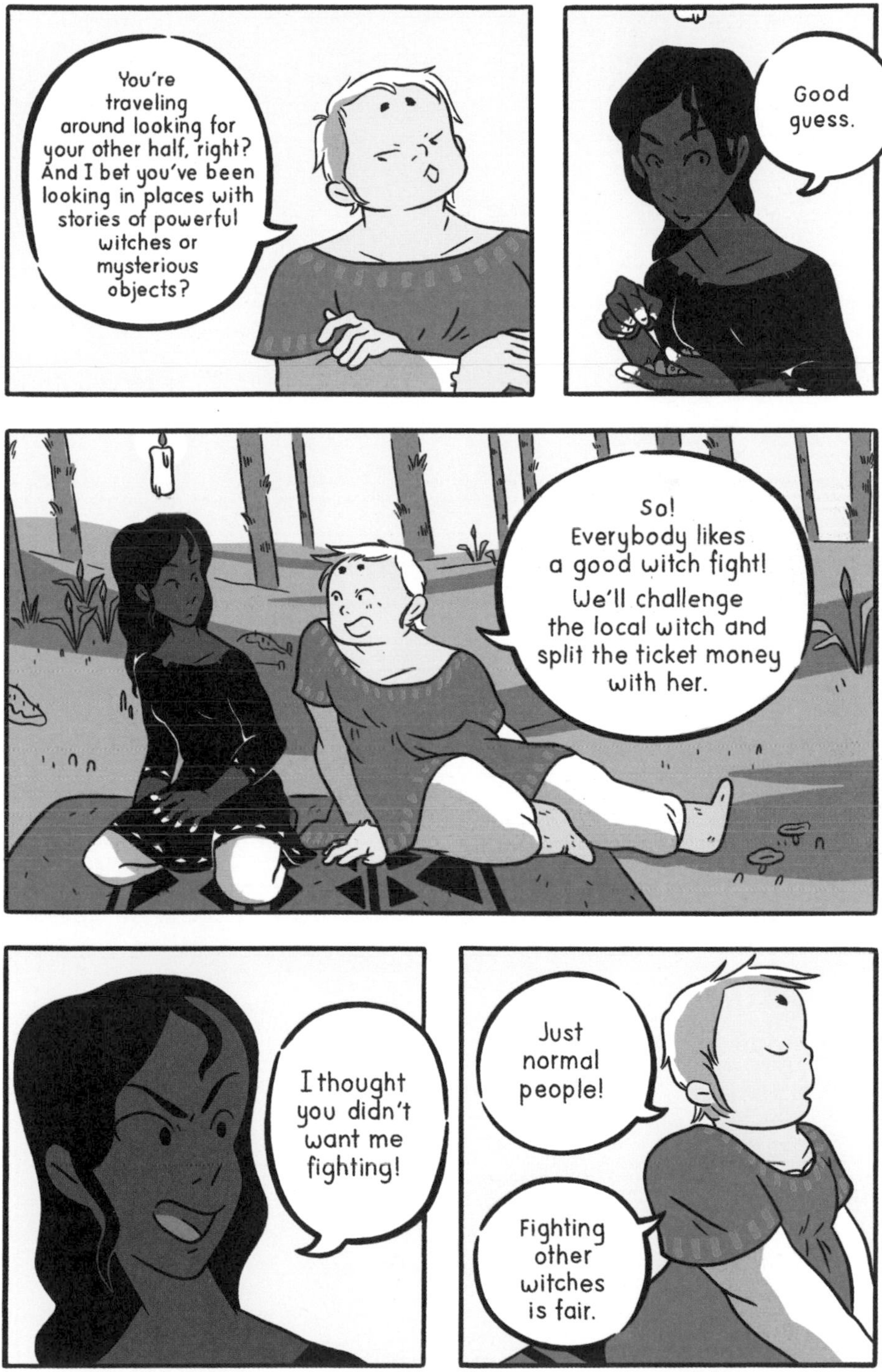
You're traveling around looking for your other half, right? And I bet you've been looking in places with stories of powerful witches or mysterious objects?
Good guess.
So! Everybody likes a good witch fight! We'll challenge the local witch and split the ticket money with her.
I thought you didn't want me fighting!
Just normal people!
Fighting other witches is fair.

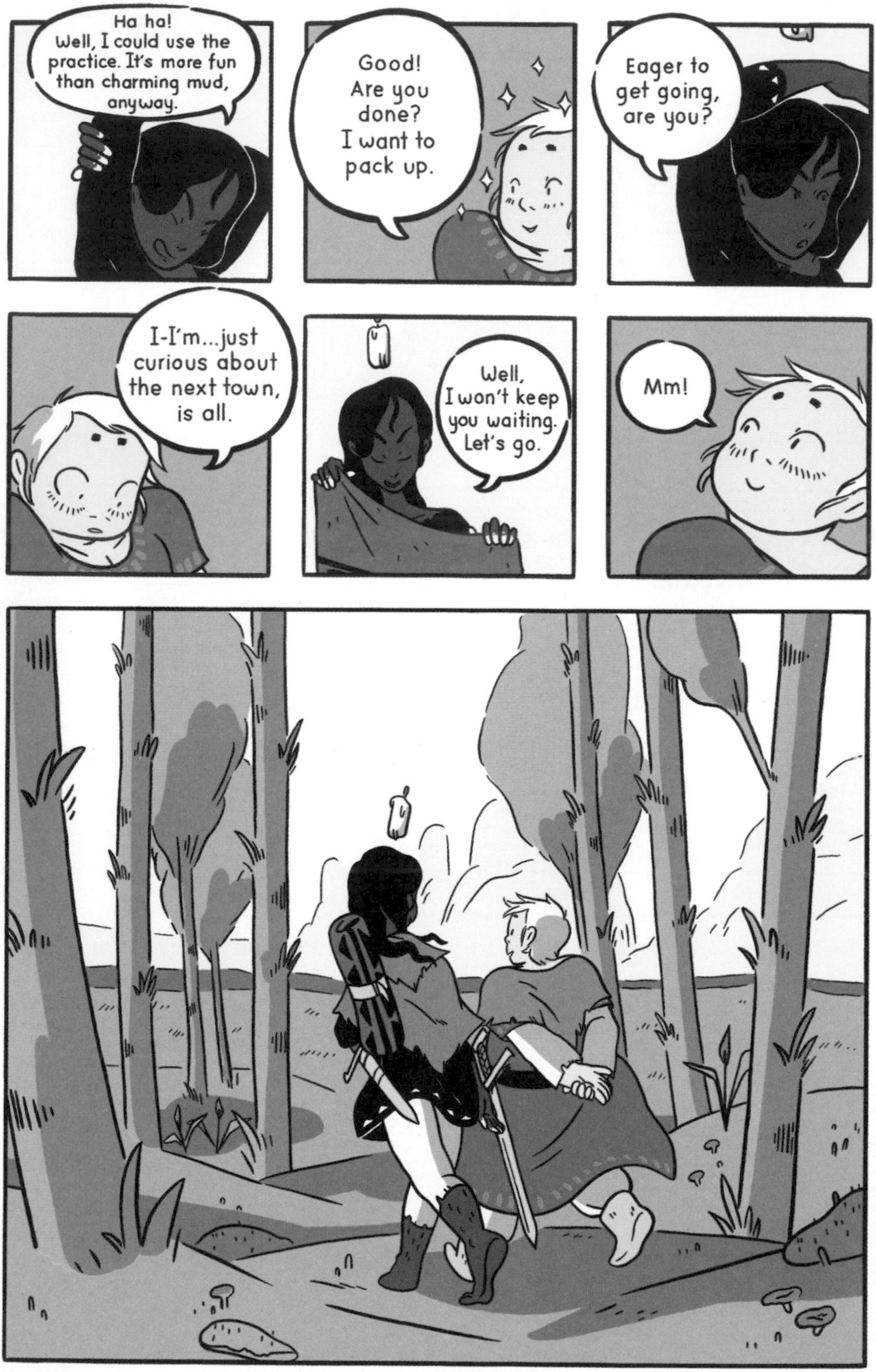
Ha ha! Well, I could use the practice. It's more fun than charming mud, anyway.
Good! Are you done? I want to pack up.
Eager to get going, are you?
I-I'm...just curious about the next town, is all.
Well, I won't keep you waiting. Let's go.
Mm!

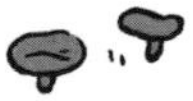

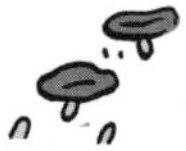

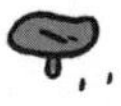

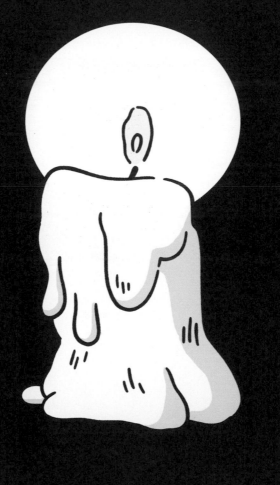

Part 3

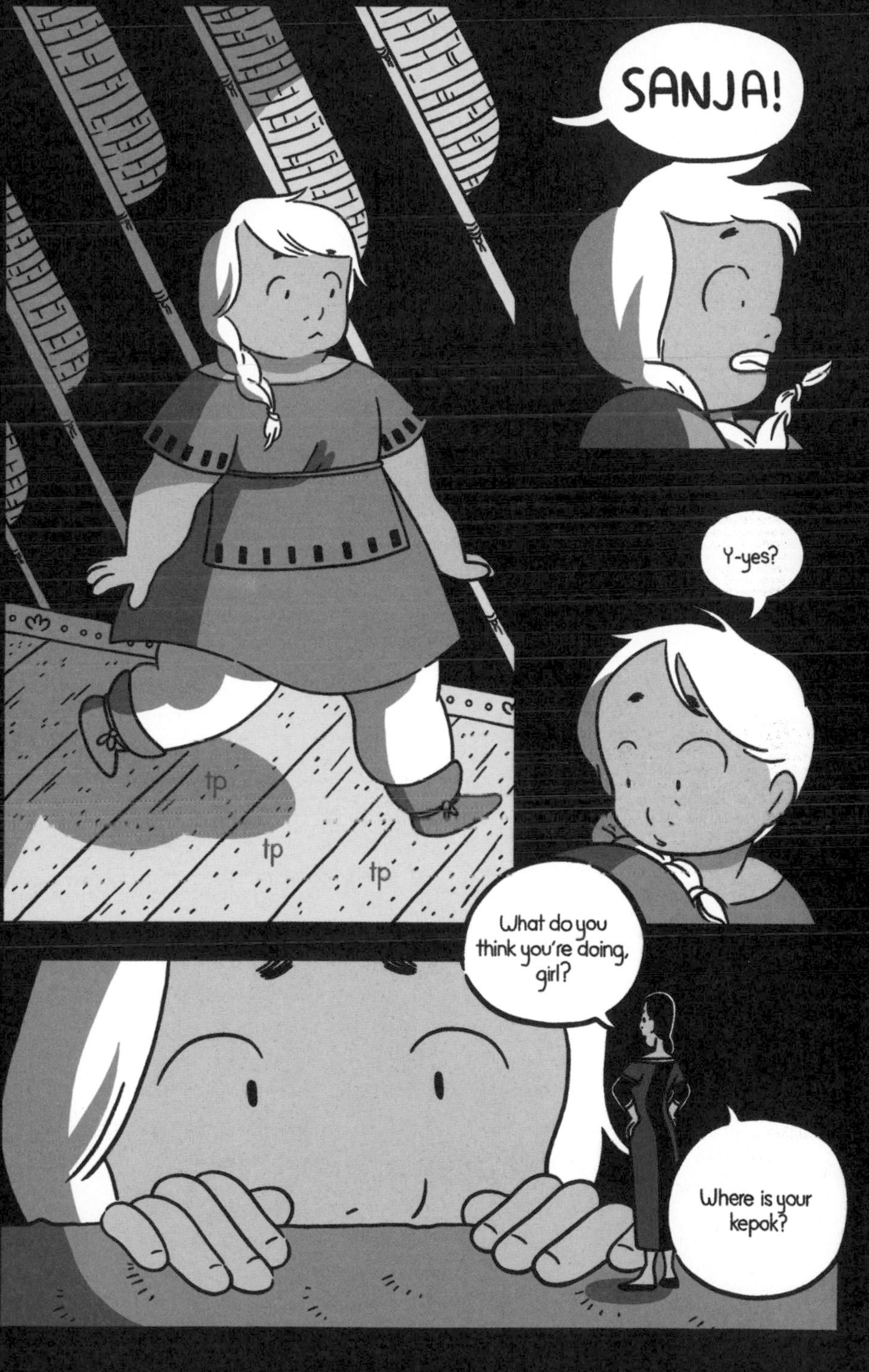
SANJA!
tp
tp
tp
Y-yes?
What do you think you're doing, girl?
Where is your kepok?

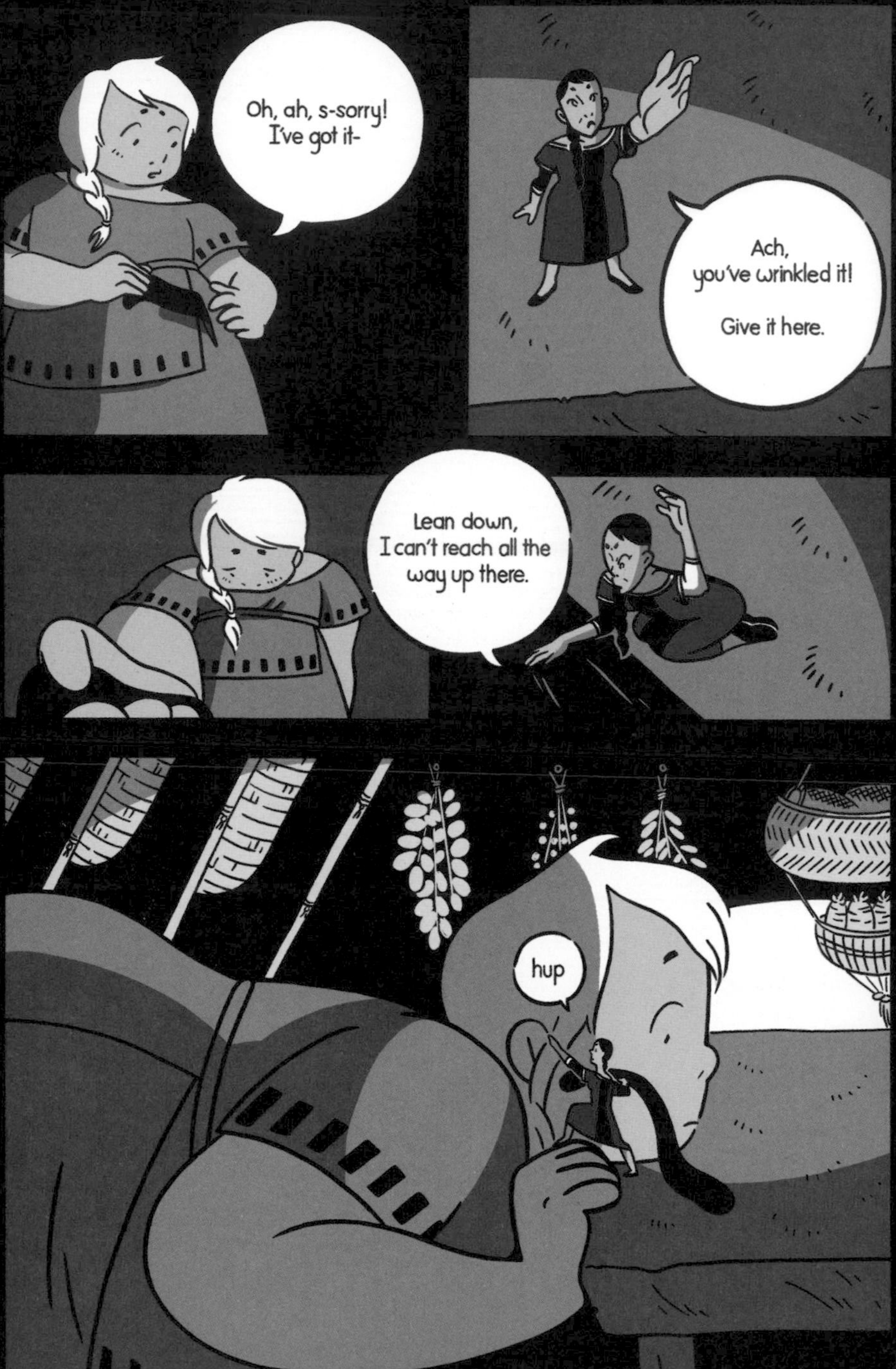
Oh, ah, s-sorry! I've got it-
Ach, you've wrinkled it!
Give it here.
Lean down, I can't reach all the way up there.
hup

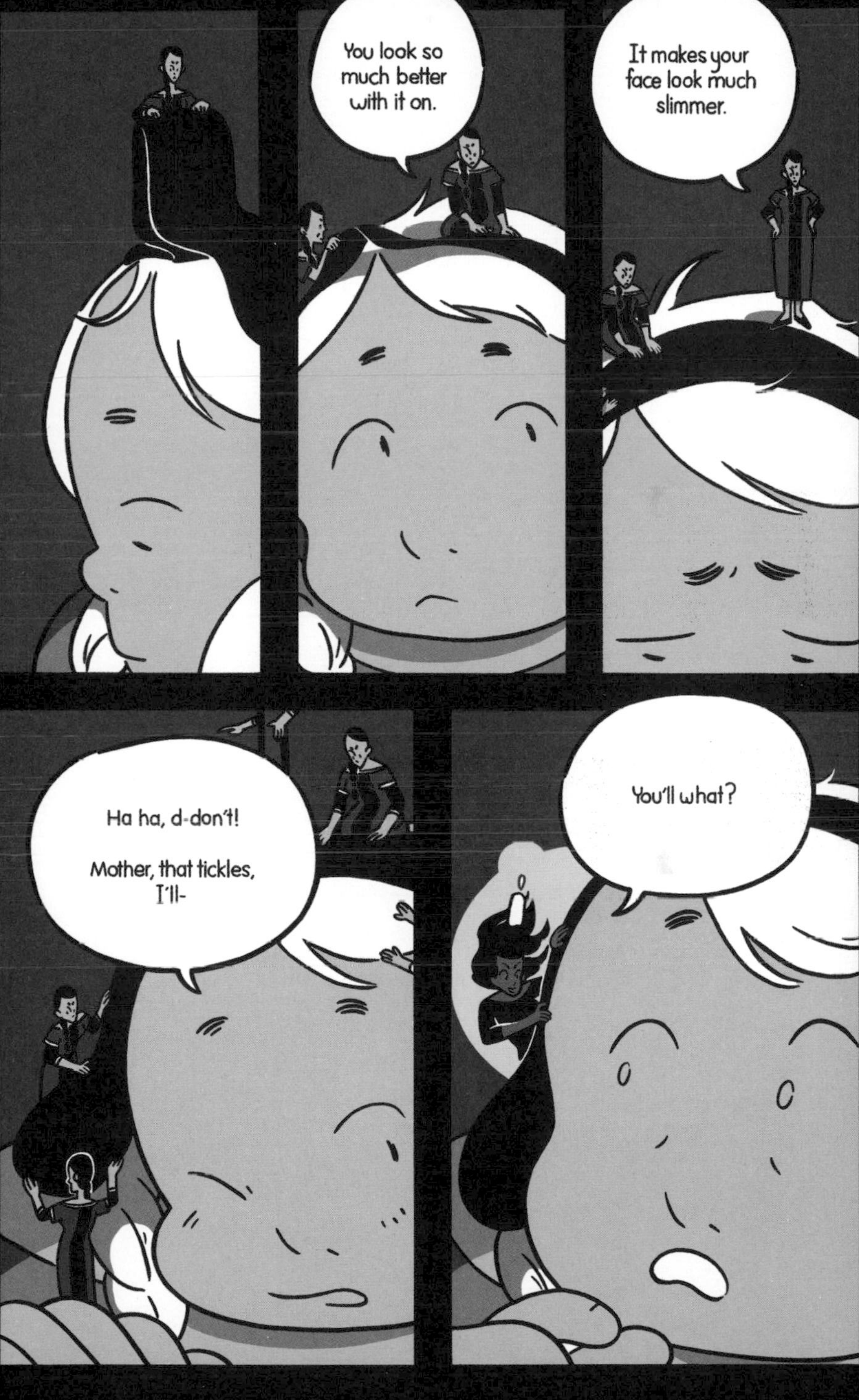
You look so much better with it on.
It makes your face look much slimmer.
Ha ha, d-don't!
Mother, that tickles, I'll-
You'll what?

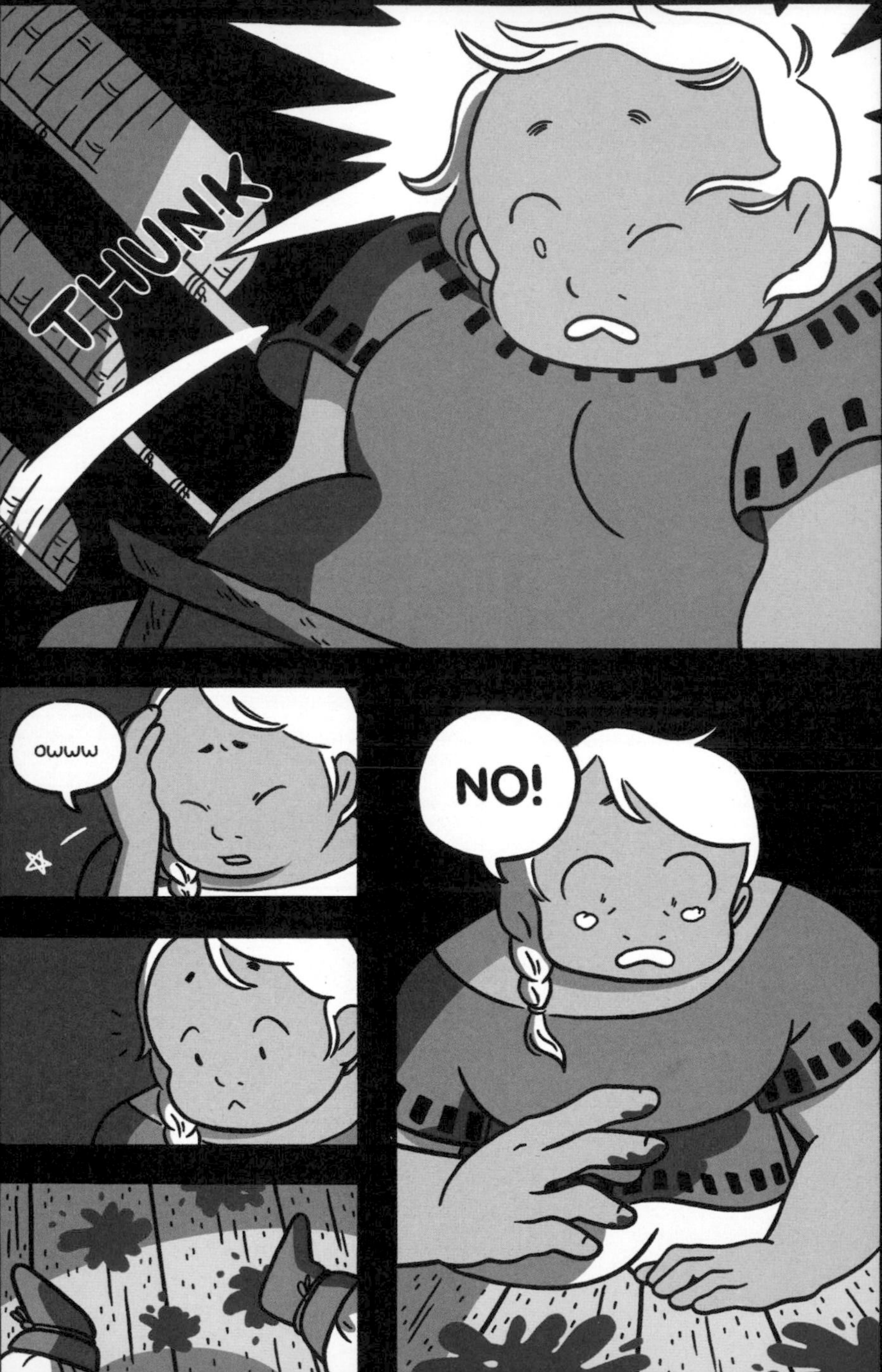
THUNK
OWWW
NO!

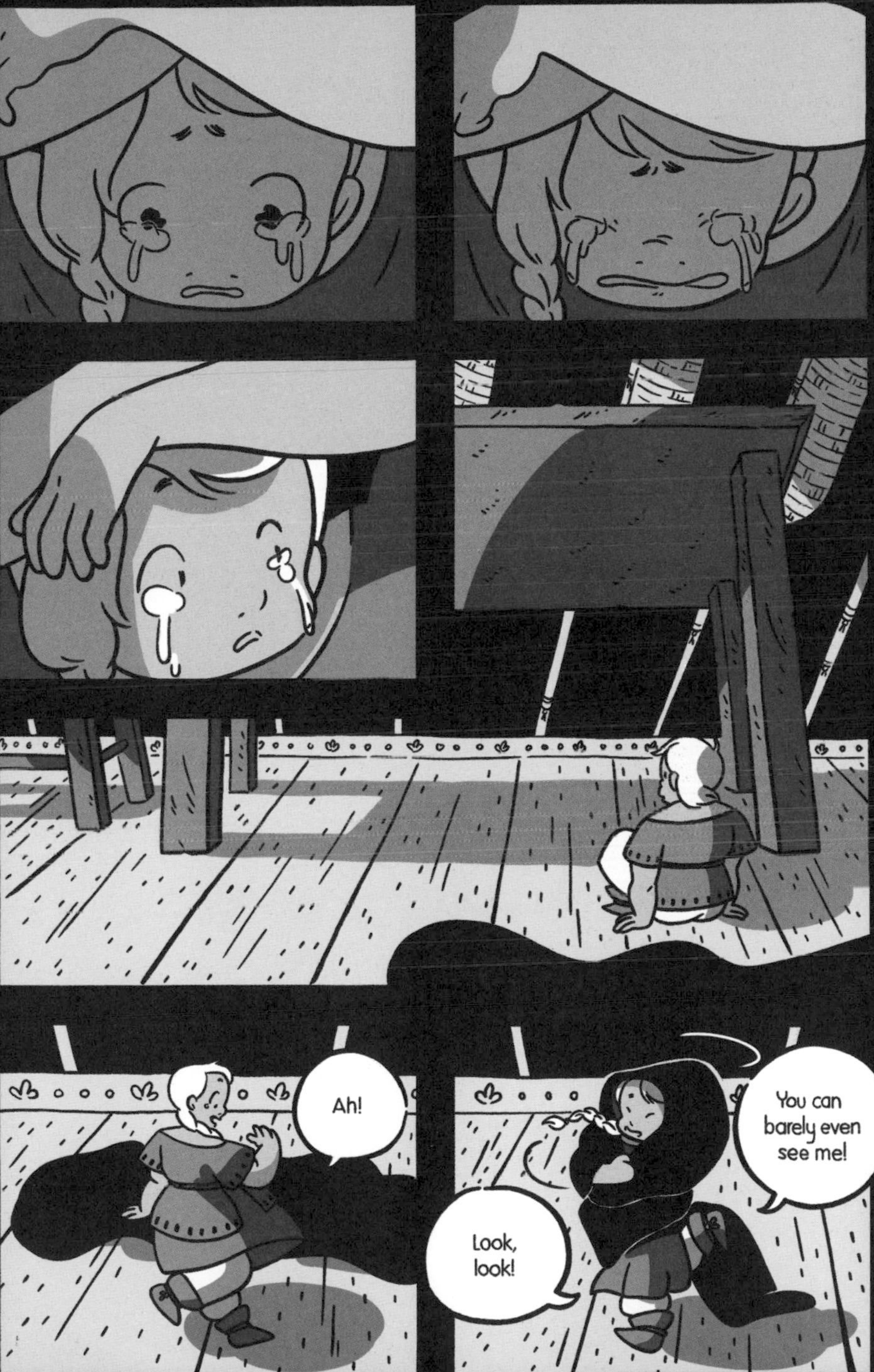
Ah!
You can barely even see me!
Look, look!

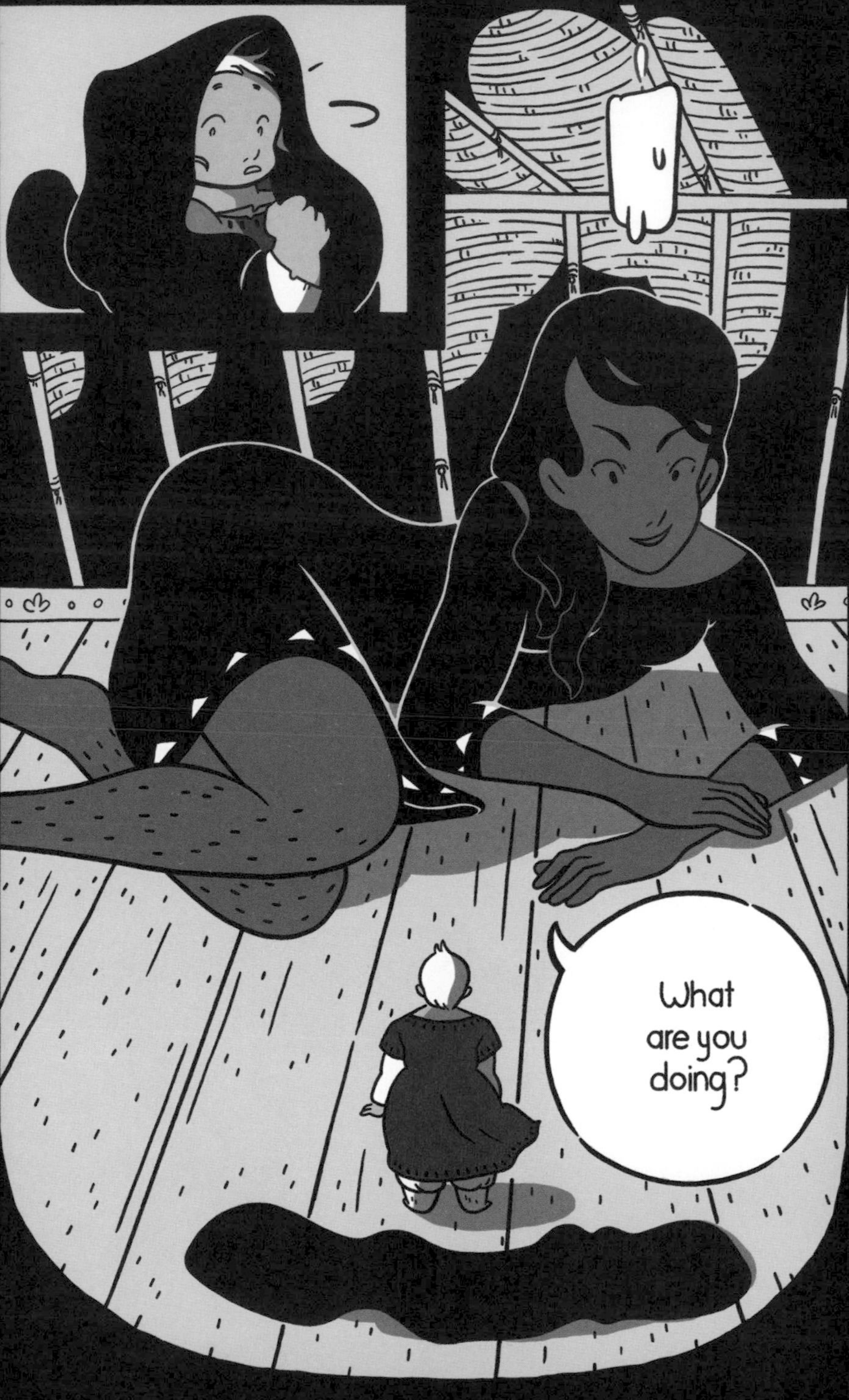
What are you doing?

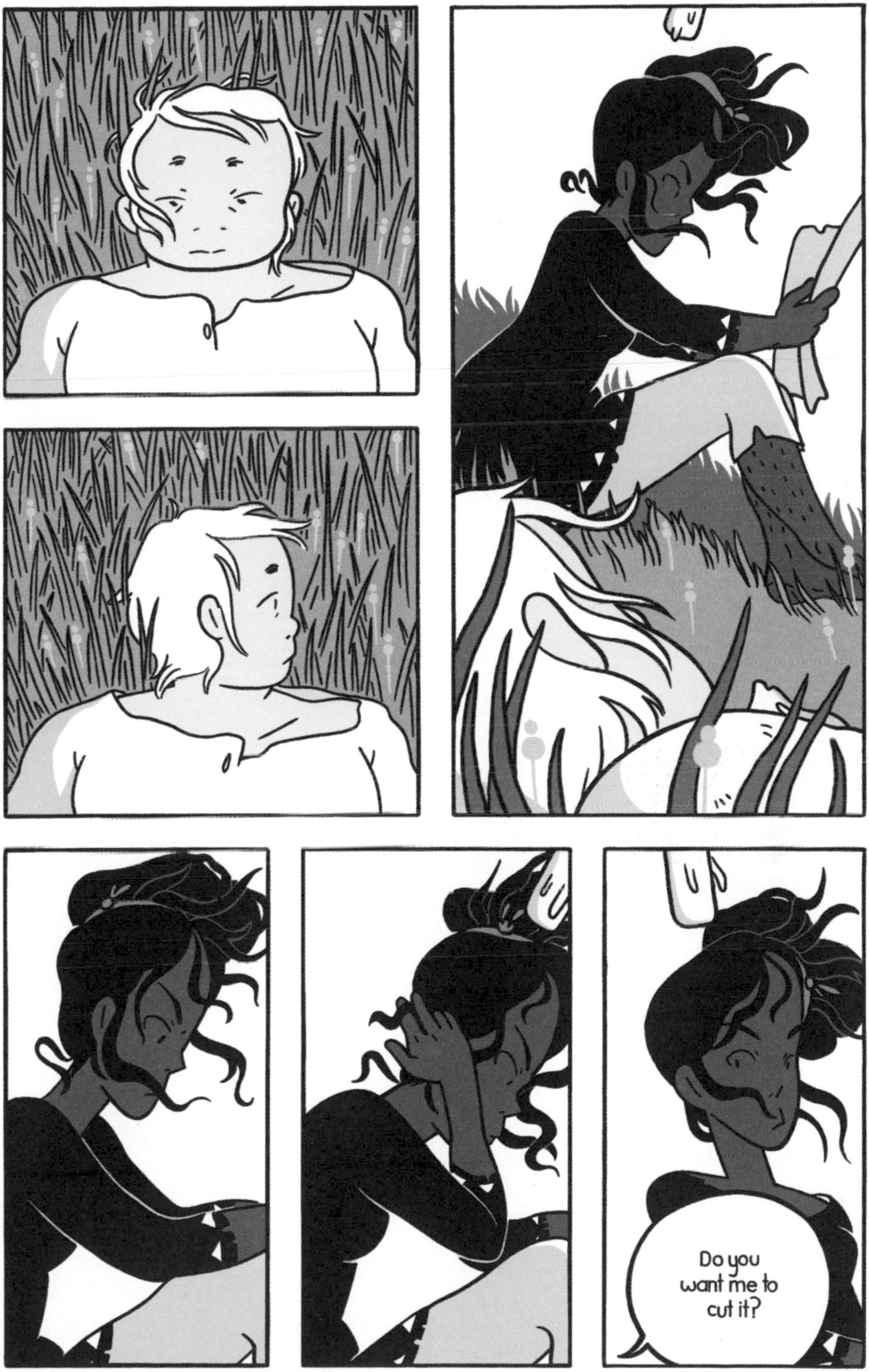
Do you want me to cut it?

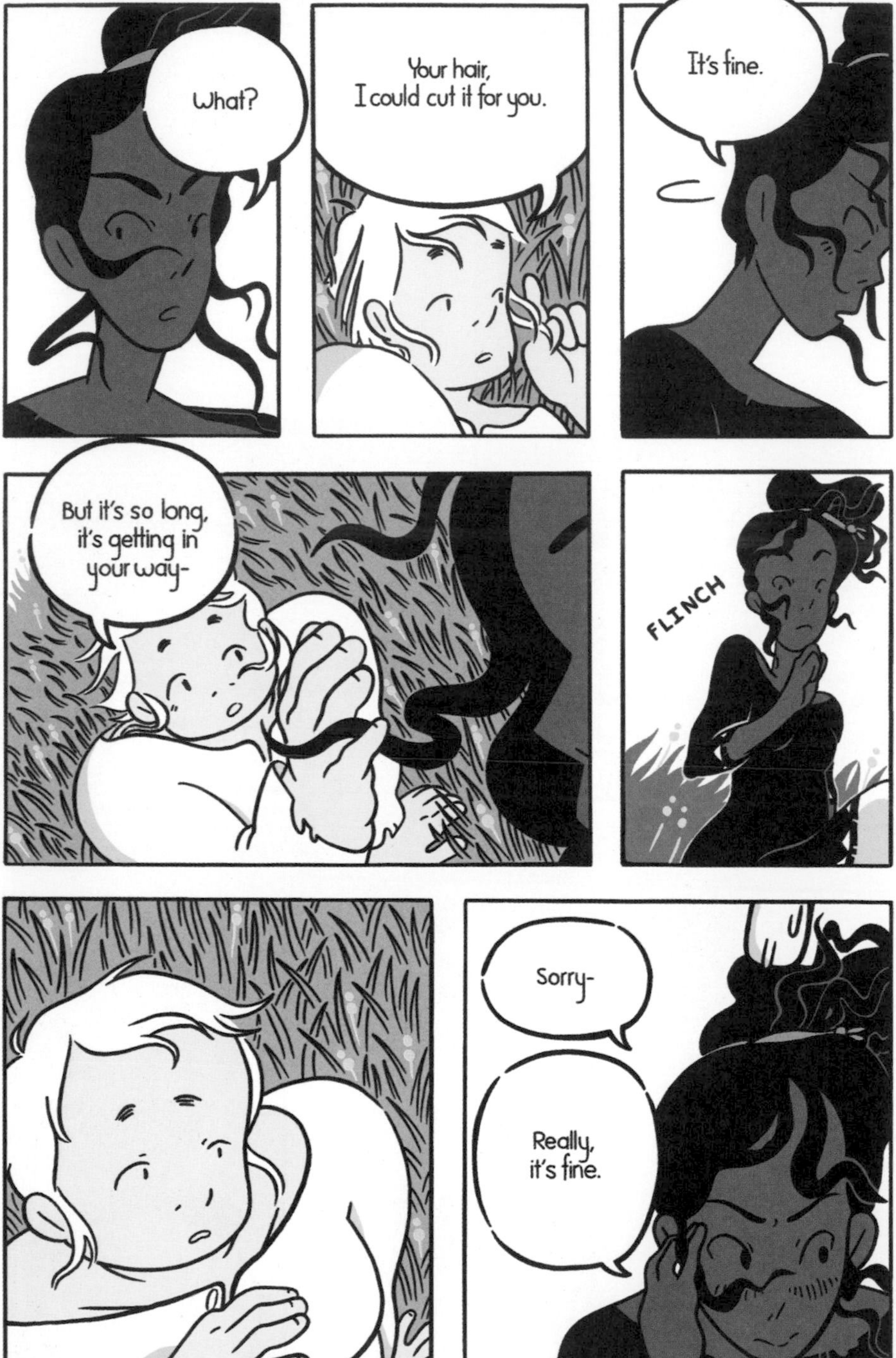
What?
Your hair, I could cut it for you.
It's fine.
But it's so long, it's getting in your way-
FLINCH
Sorry-
Really, it's fine.

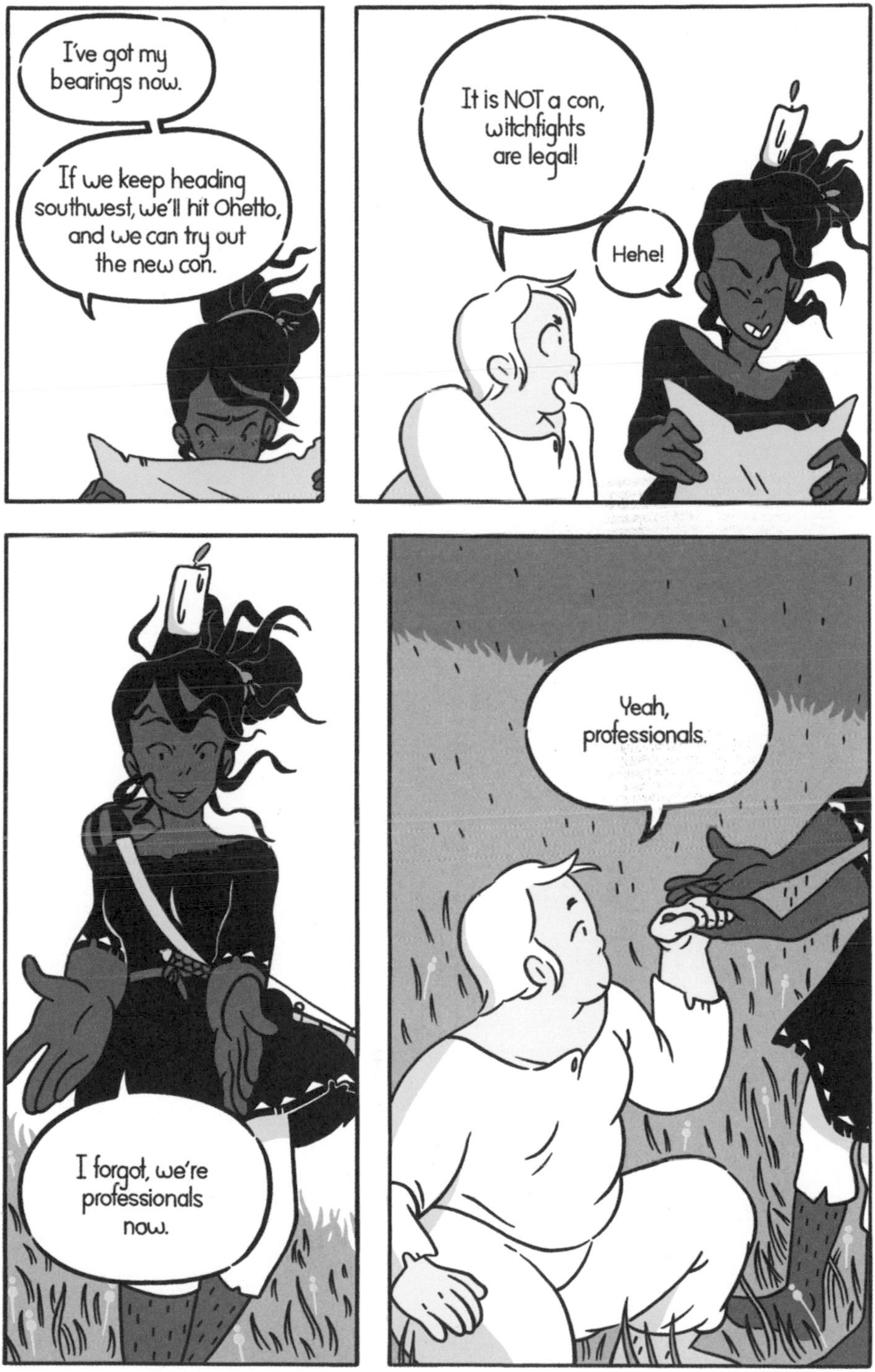
I've got my bearings now.
If we keep heading southwest, we'll hit Ohetto, and we can try out the new con.
It is NOT a con, witchfights are legal!
Hehe!
I forgot, we're professionals now.
Yeah, professionals.

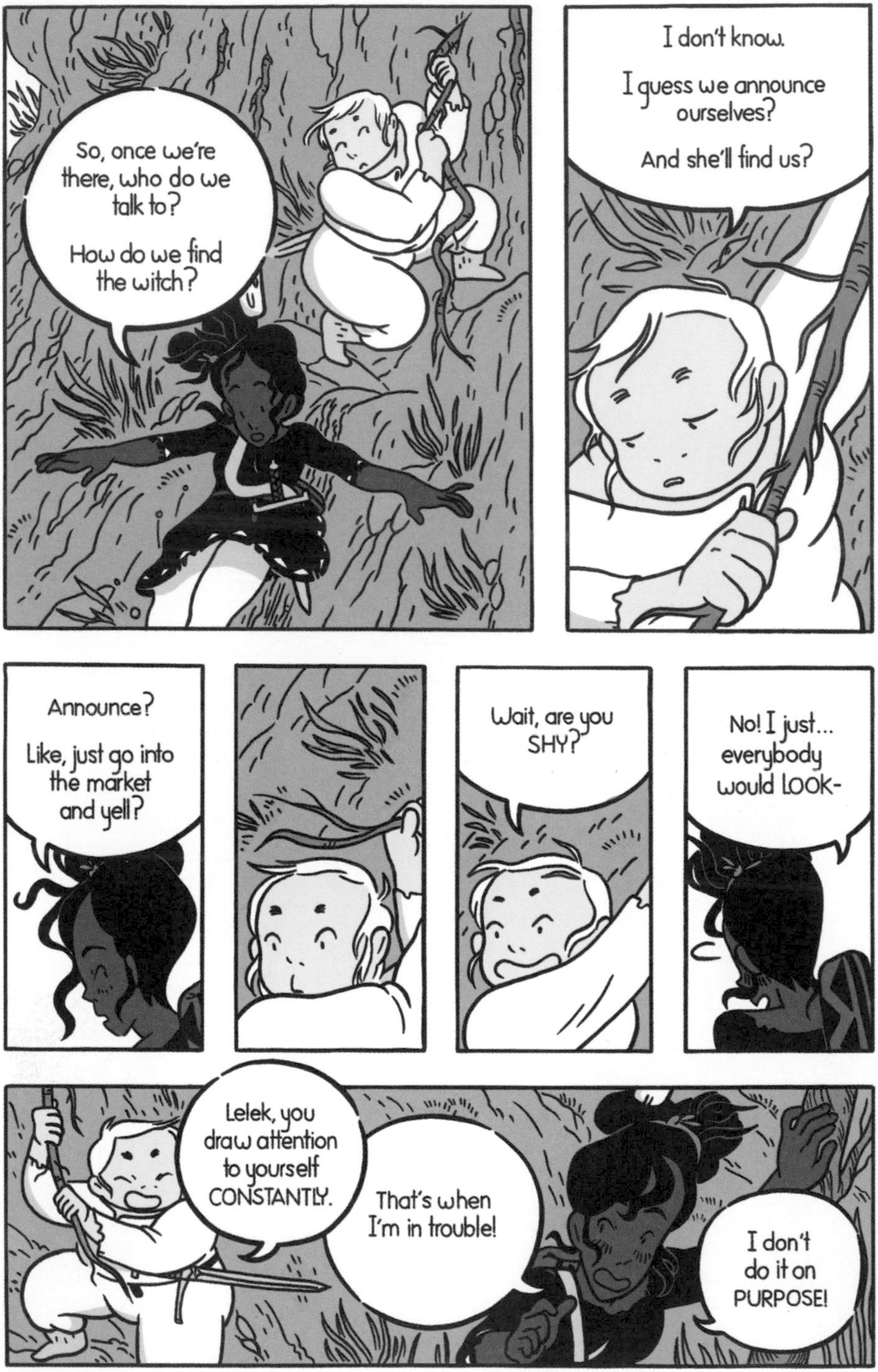
So, once we're there, who do we talk to? How do we find the witch?
I don't know. I guess we announce ourselves? And she'll find us?
Announce? Like, just go into the market and yell?
Wait, are you SHY?
No! I just... everybody would LOOK-
Lelek, you draw attention to yourself CONSTANTLY.
That's when I'm in trouble!
I don't do it on PURPOSE!

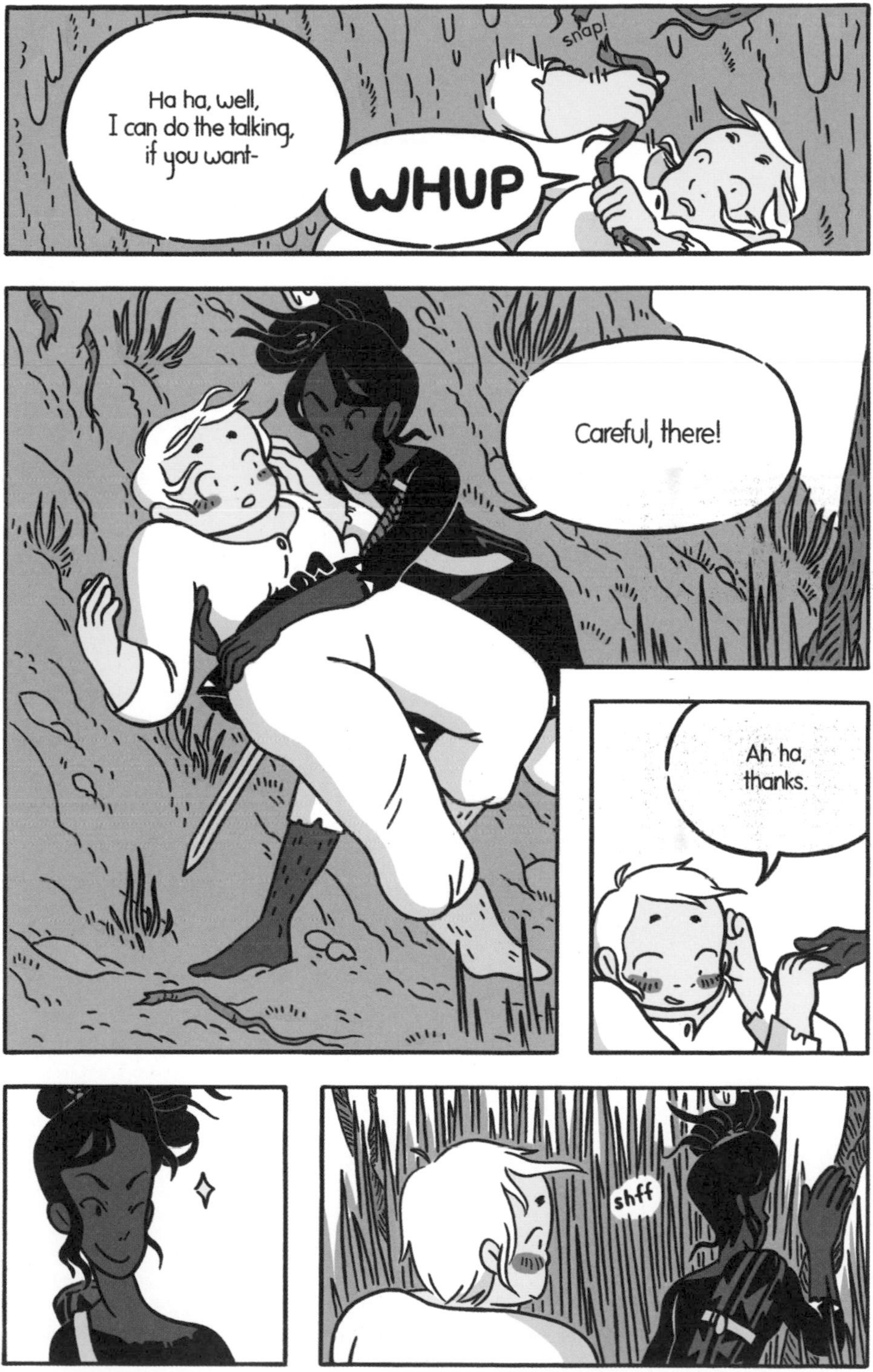
snap!
Ha ha, well,
I can do the talking,
if you want-
WHUP
Careful, there!
Ah ha,
thanks.
shff

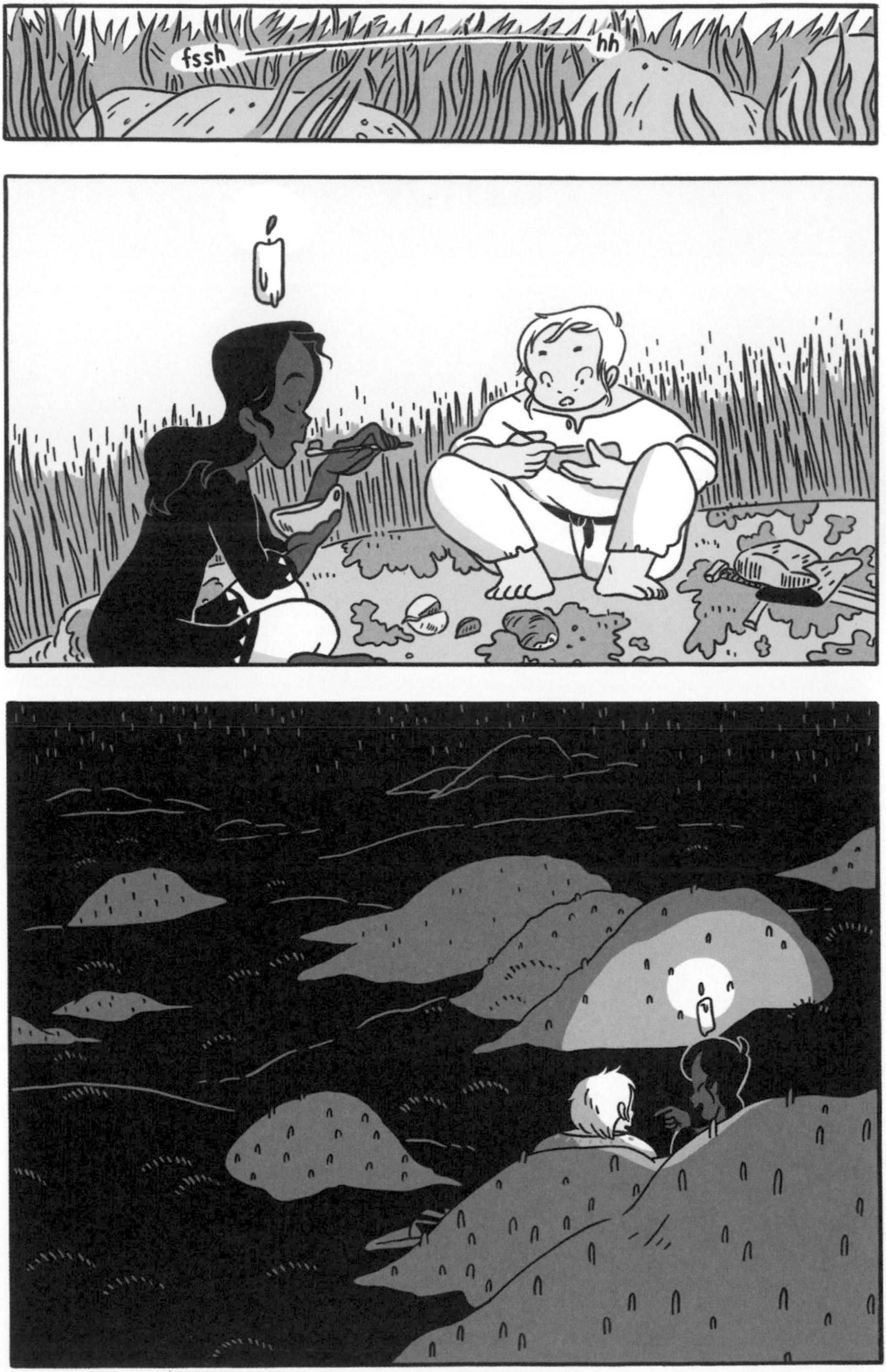
fssh
hh

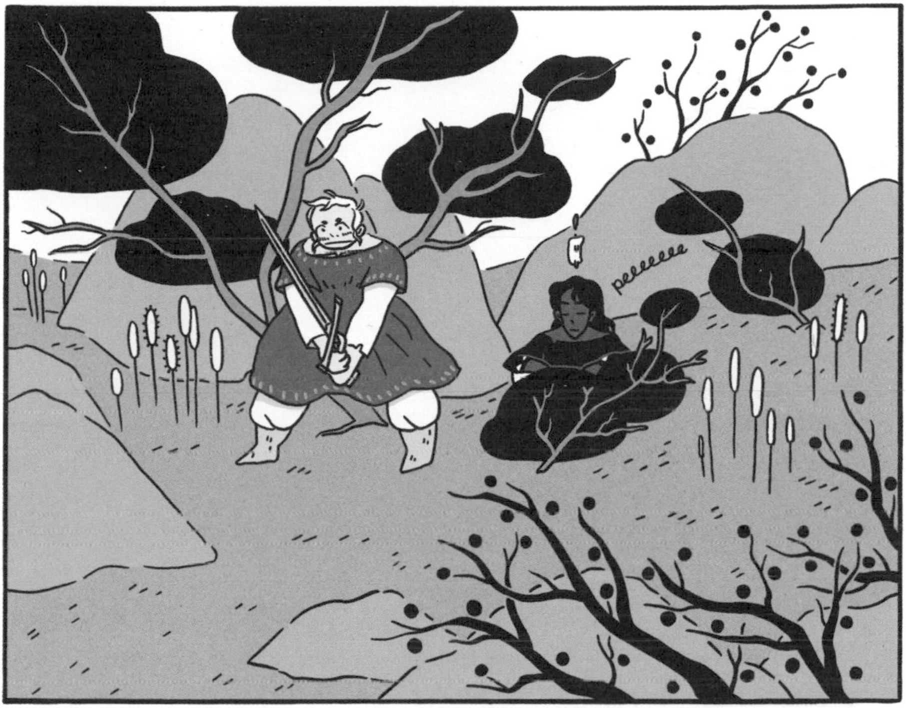
peeeeeee

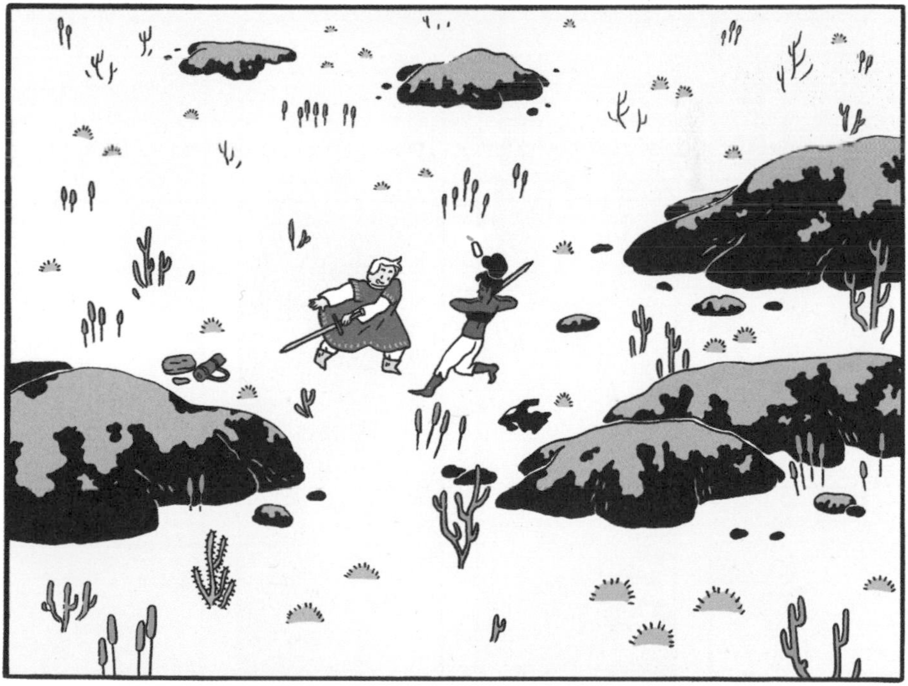

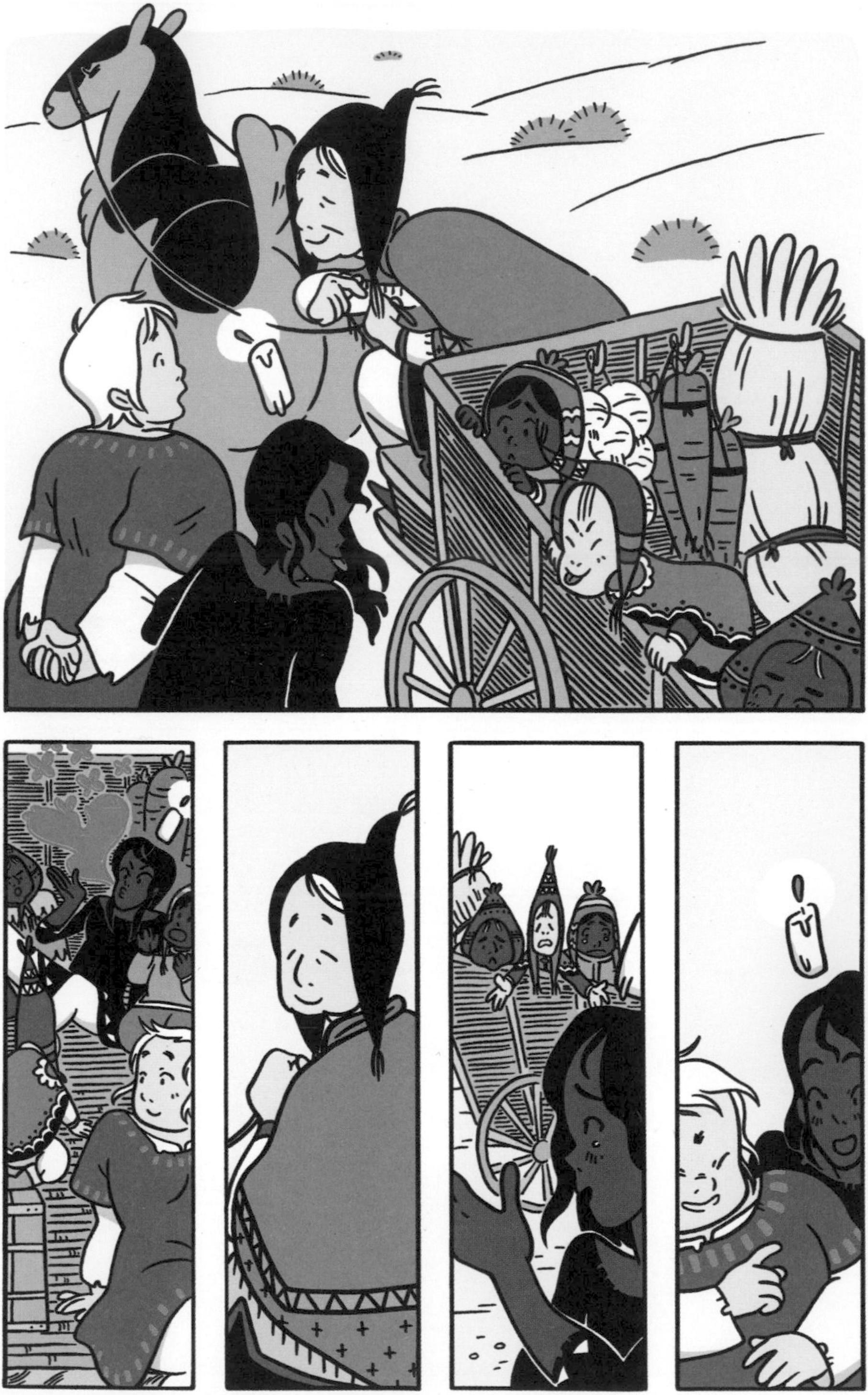

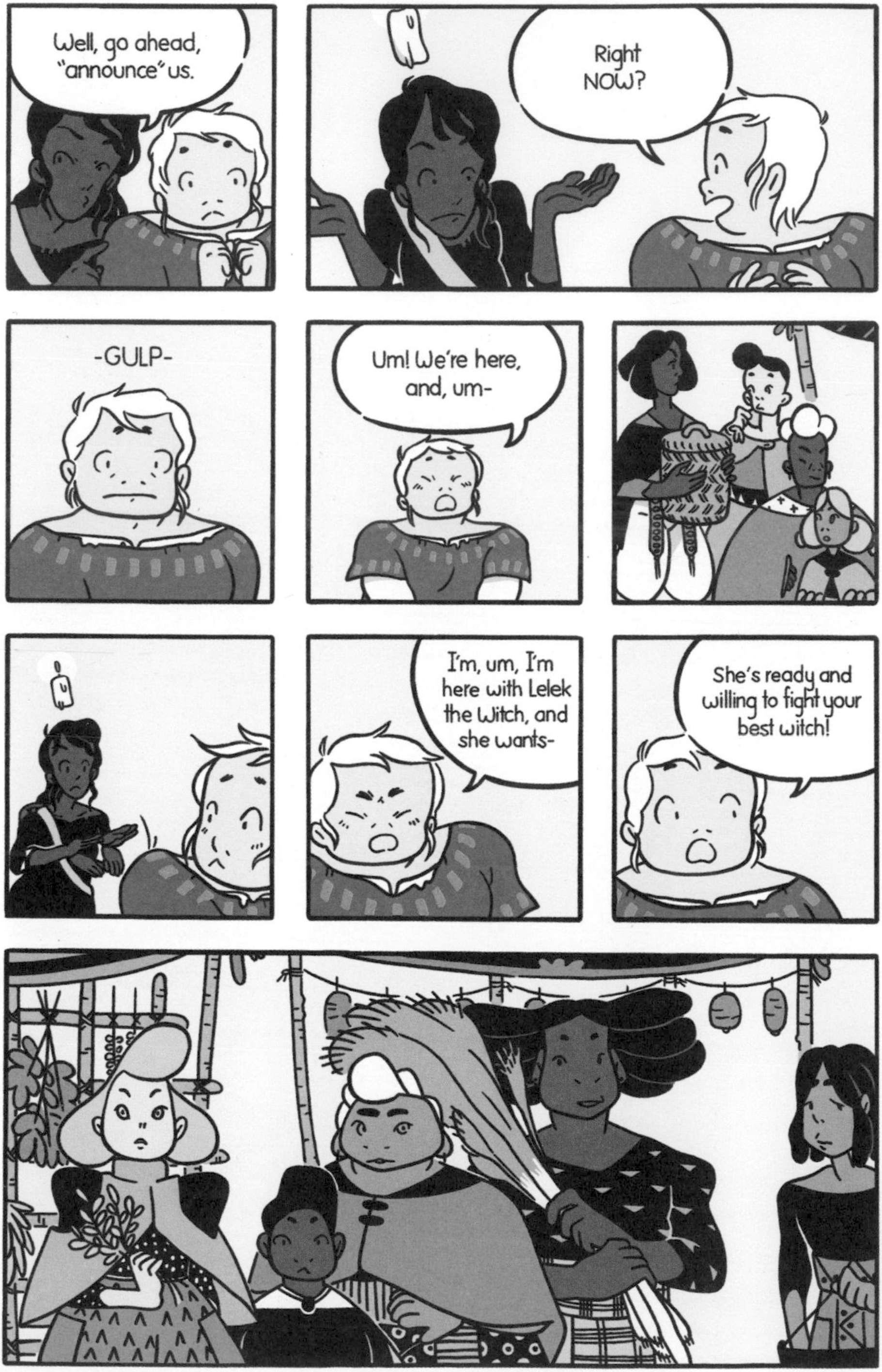
Well, go ahead, "announce" us.
Right NOW?
-GULP-
Um! We're here, and, um-
I'm, um, I'm here with Lelek the Witch, and she wants-
She's ready and willing to fight your best witch!

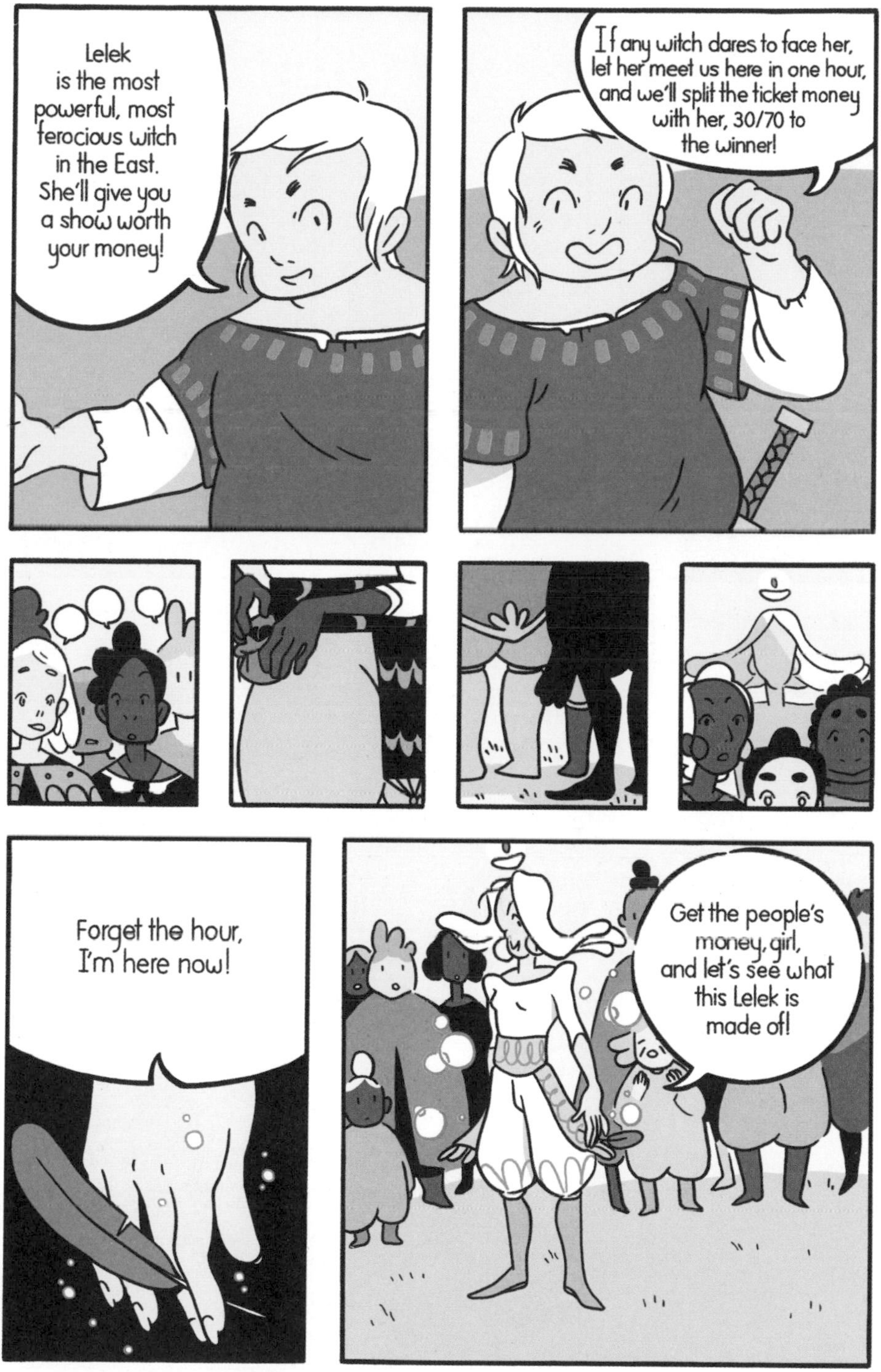
Lelek is the most powerful, most ferocious witch in the East. She'll give you a show worth your money!
If any witch dares to face her, let her meet us here in one hour, and we'll split the ticket money with her, 30/70 to the winner!
Forget the hour, I'm here now!
Get the people's money, girl, and let's see what this Lelek is made of!

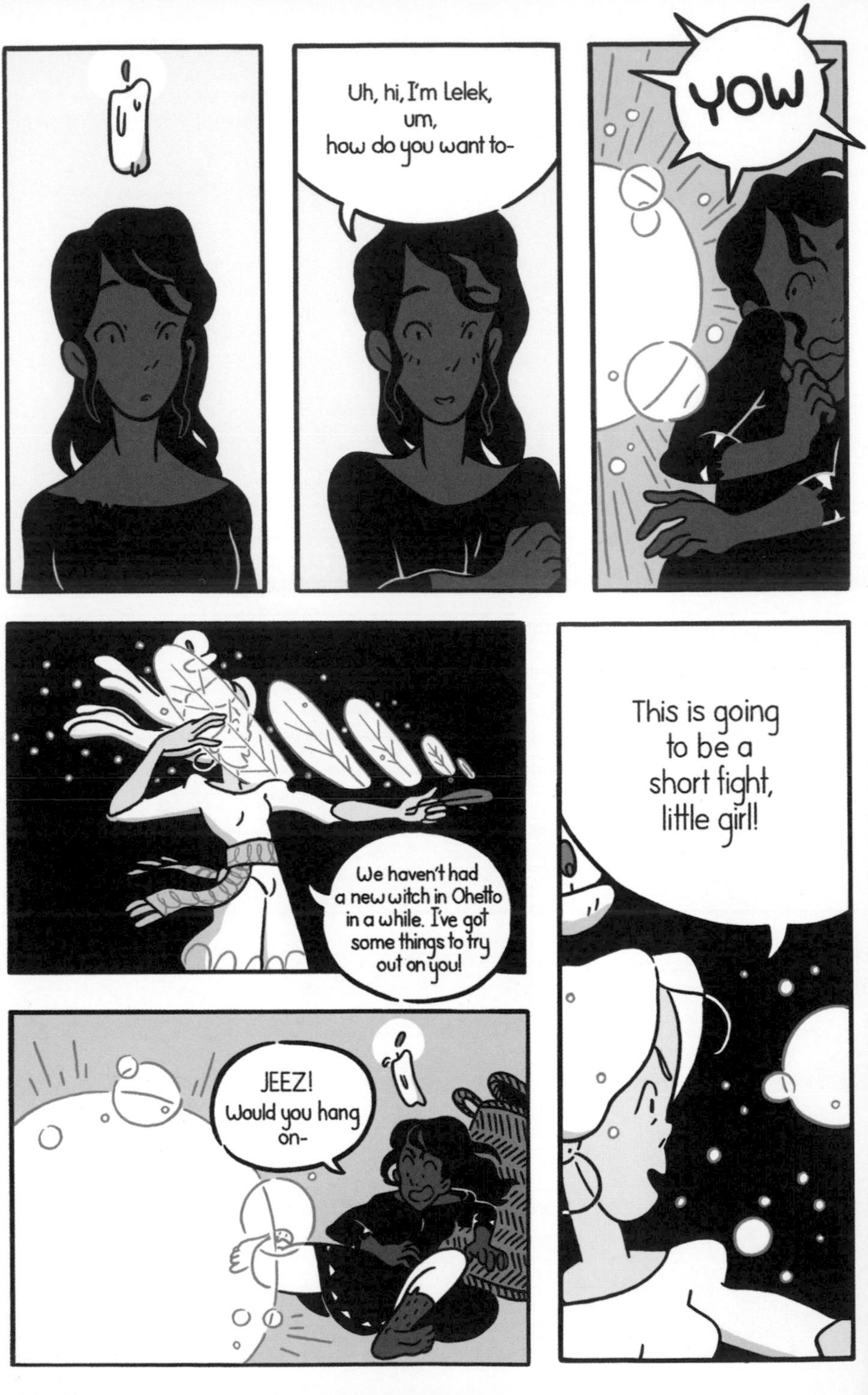
Uh, hi, I'm Lelek, um, how do you want to-
YOW
We haven't had a new witch in Ohetto in a while. I've got some things to try out on you!
This is going to be a short fight, little girl!
JEEZ! Would you hang on-

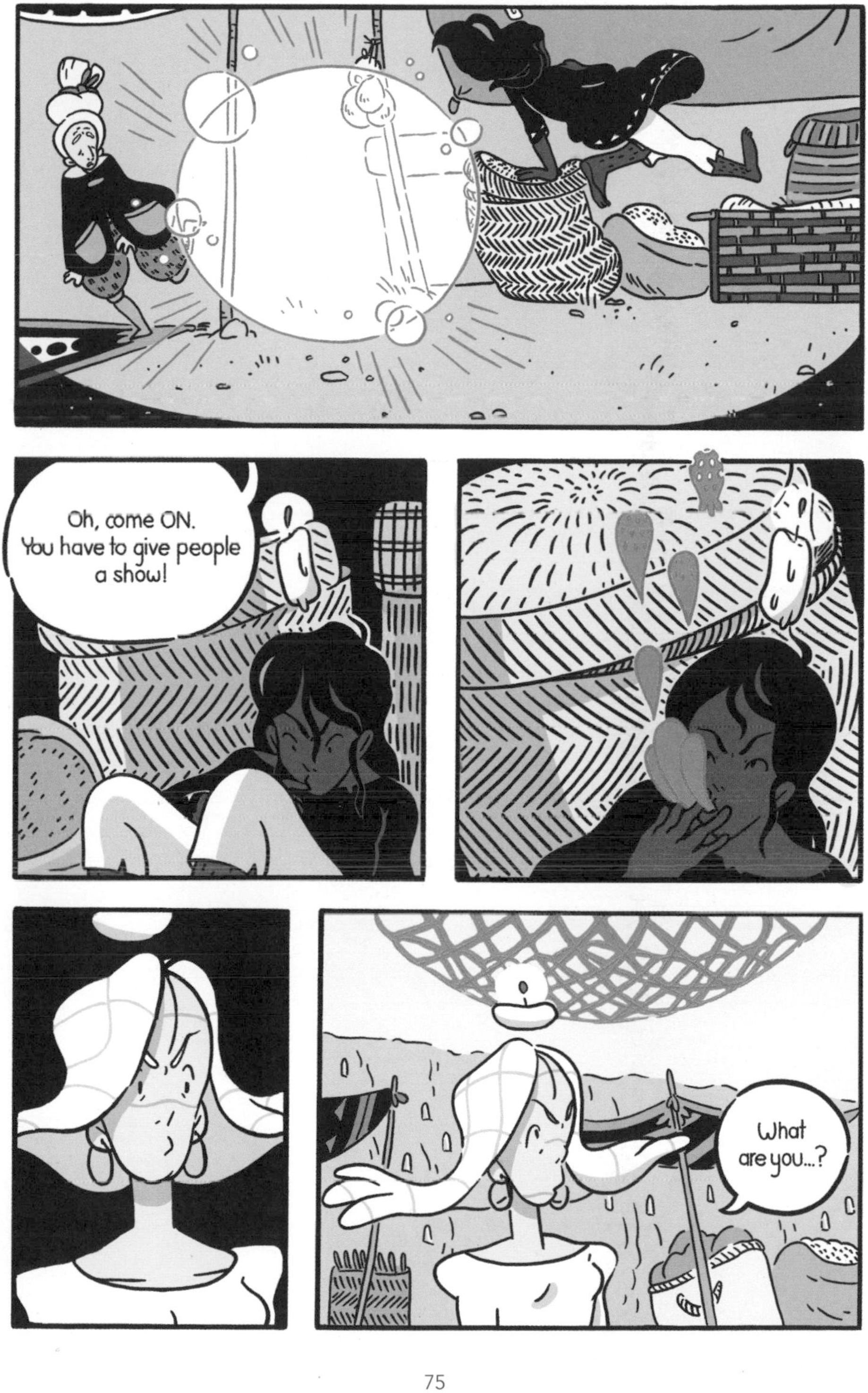
Oh, come ON.
You have to give people a show!
What are you...?

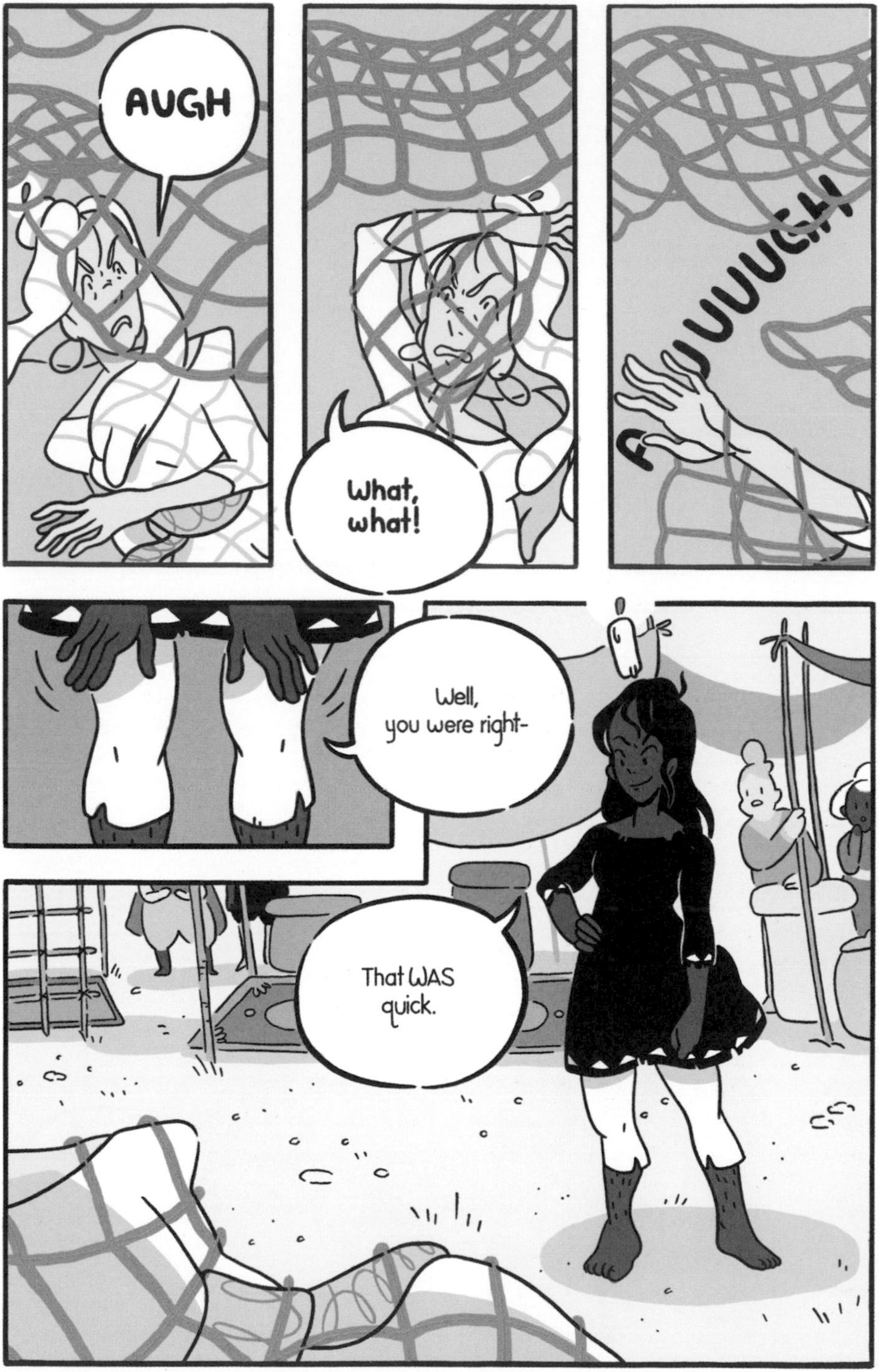
AUGH
What, what!
AUUUUGH
Well, you were right-
That WAS quick.

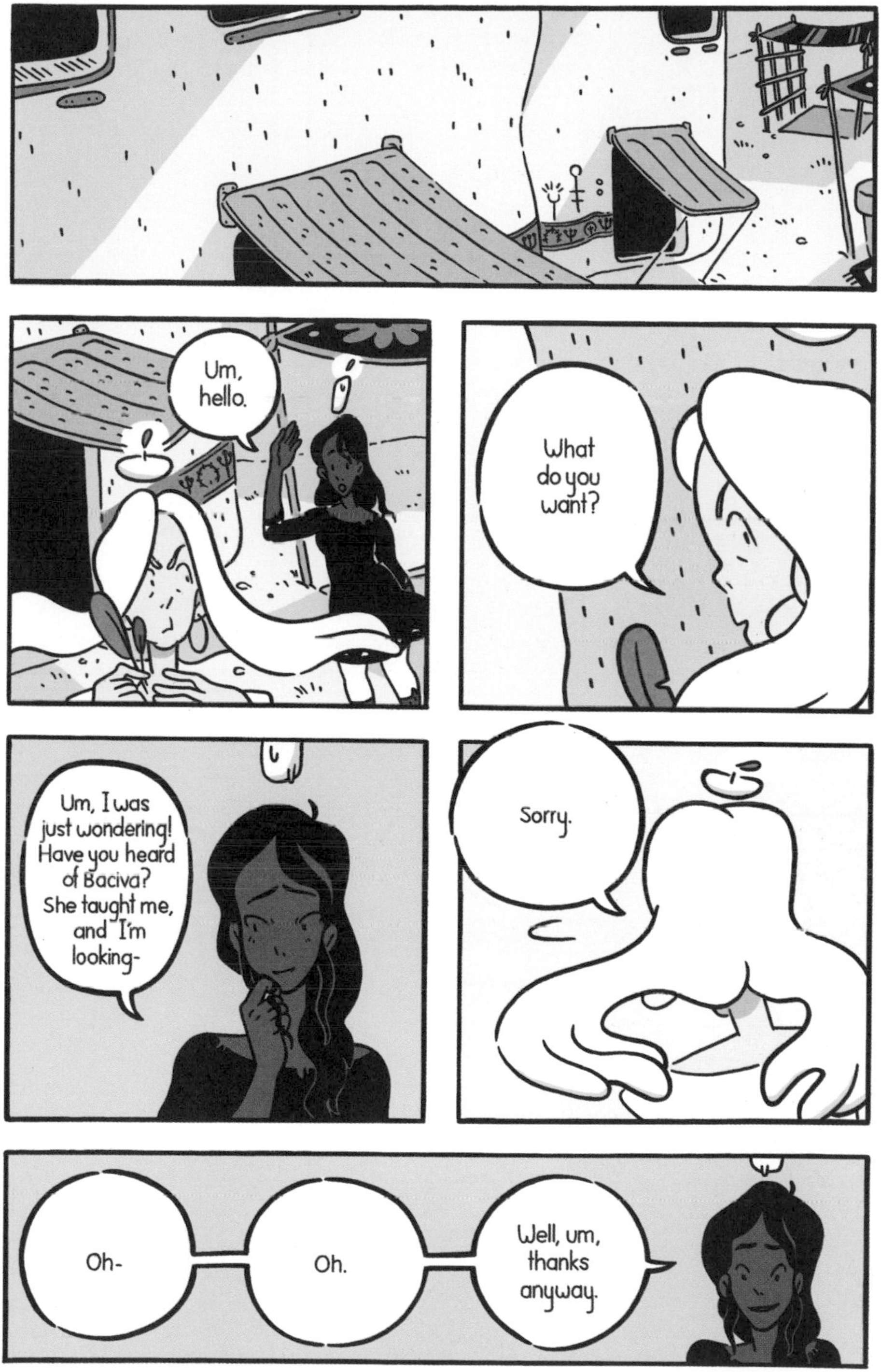
Um, hello.
What do you want?
Um, I was just wondering! Have you heard of Baciva? She taught me, and I'm looking-
Sorry.
Oh-
Oh.
Well, um, thanks anyway.

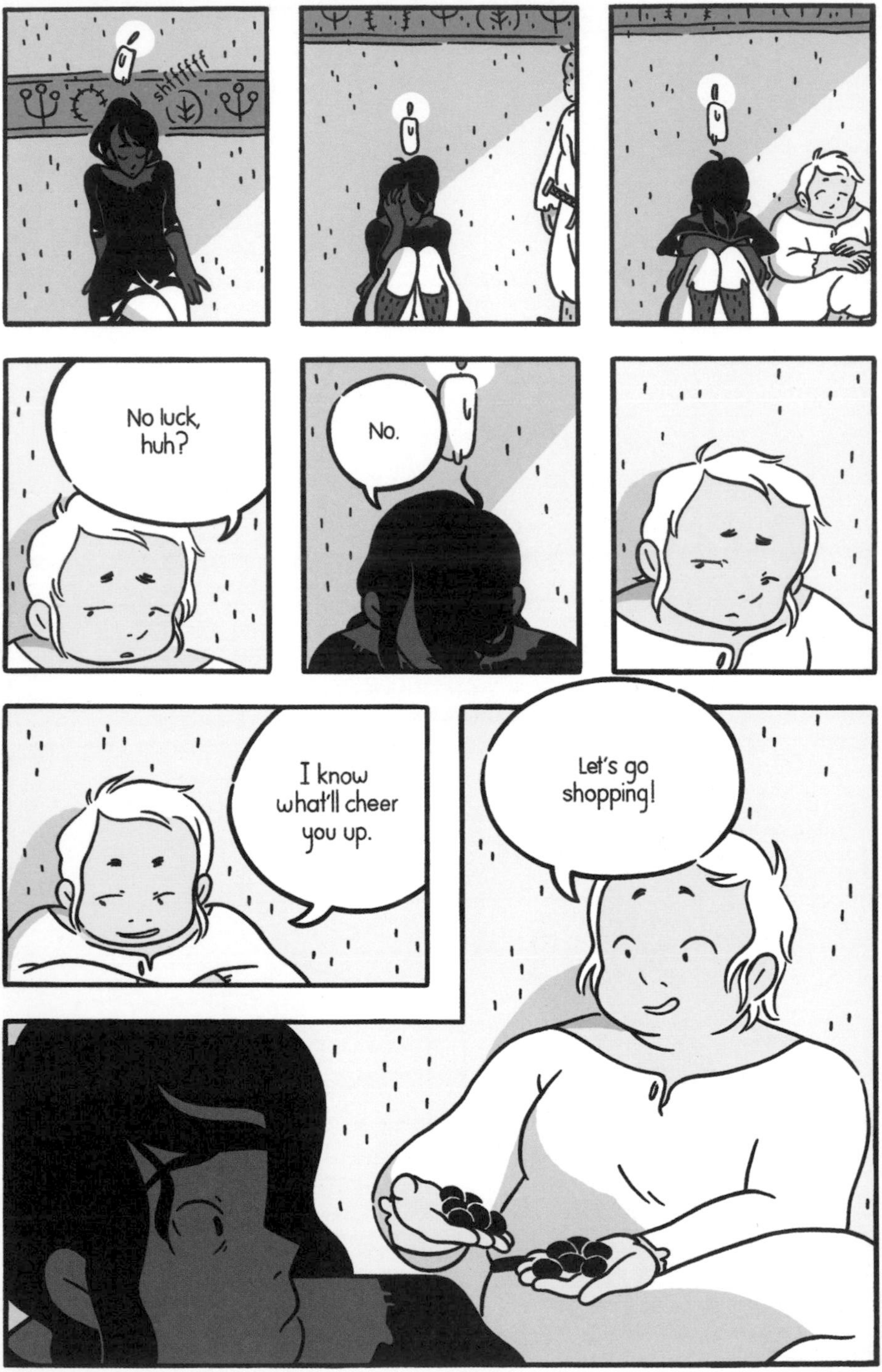

shffffff
No luck, huh?
No.
I know what'll cheer you up.
Let's go shopping!

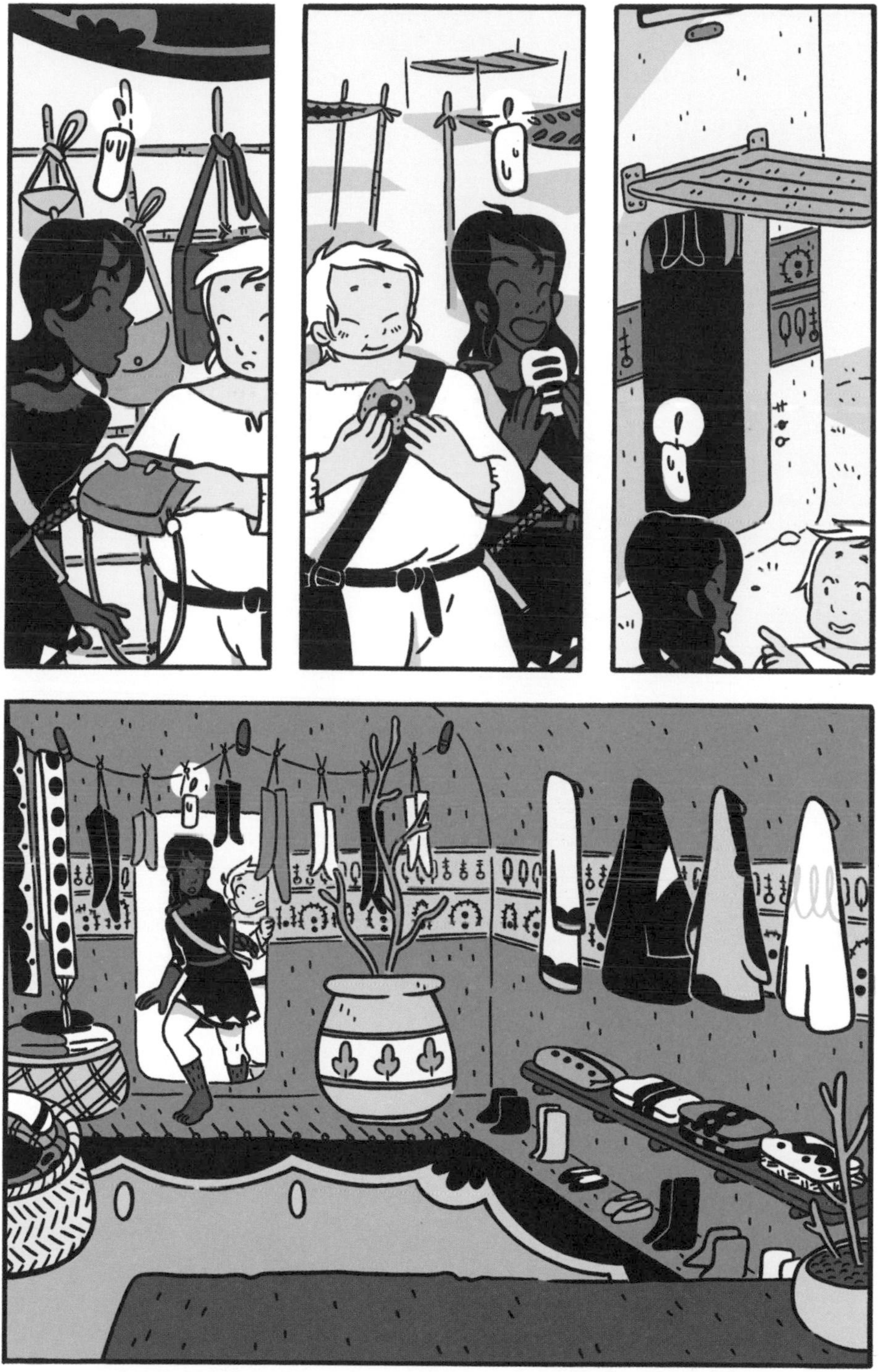

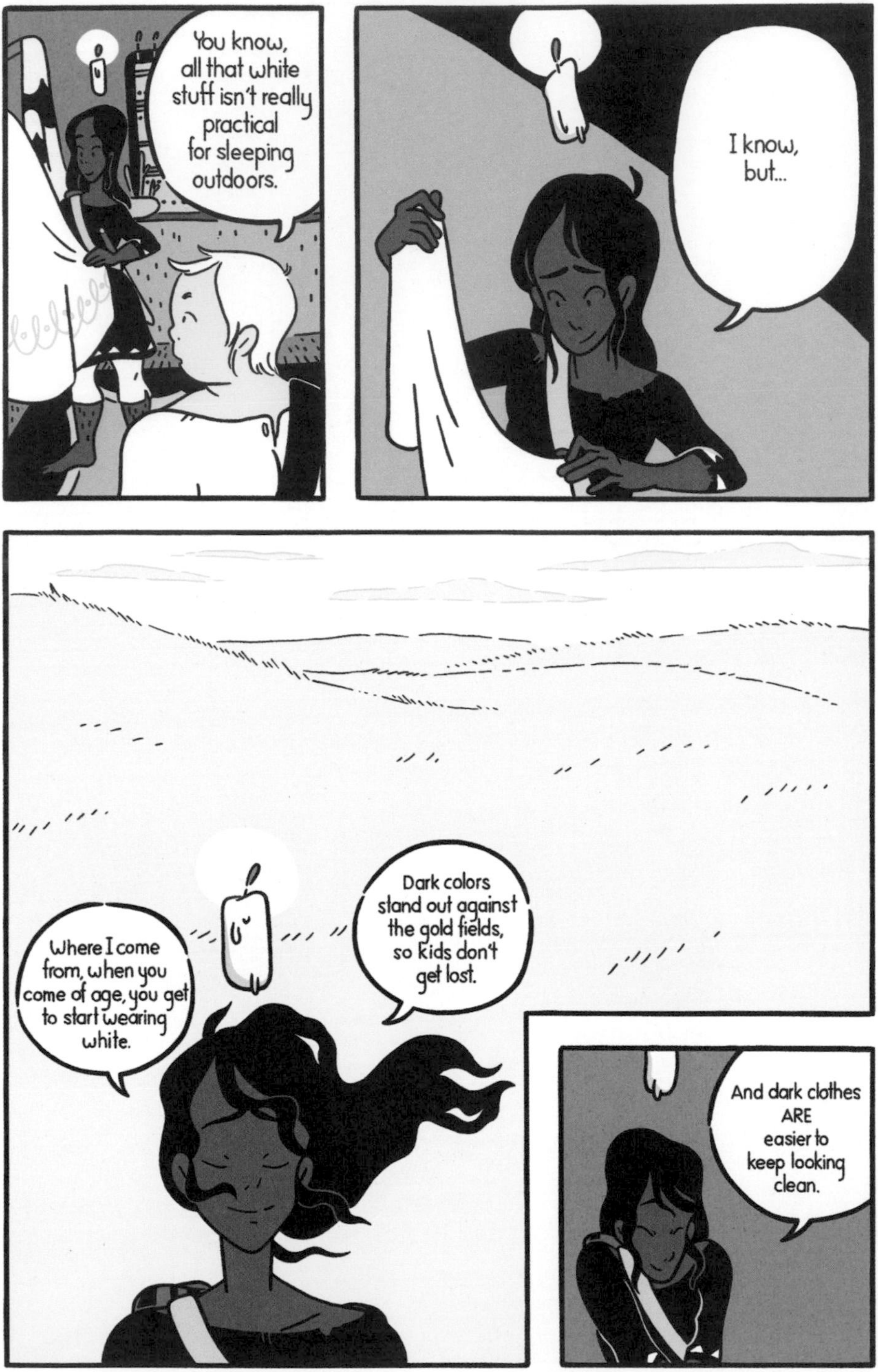
You know, all that white stuff isn't really practical for sleeping outdoors.
I know, but...
Where I come from, when you come of age, you get to start wearing white.
Dark colors stand out against the gold fields, so kids don't get lost.
And dark clothes ARE easier to keep looking clean.

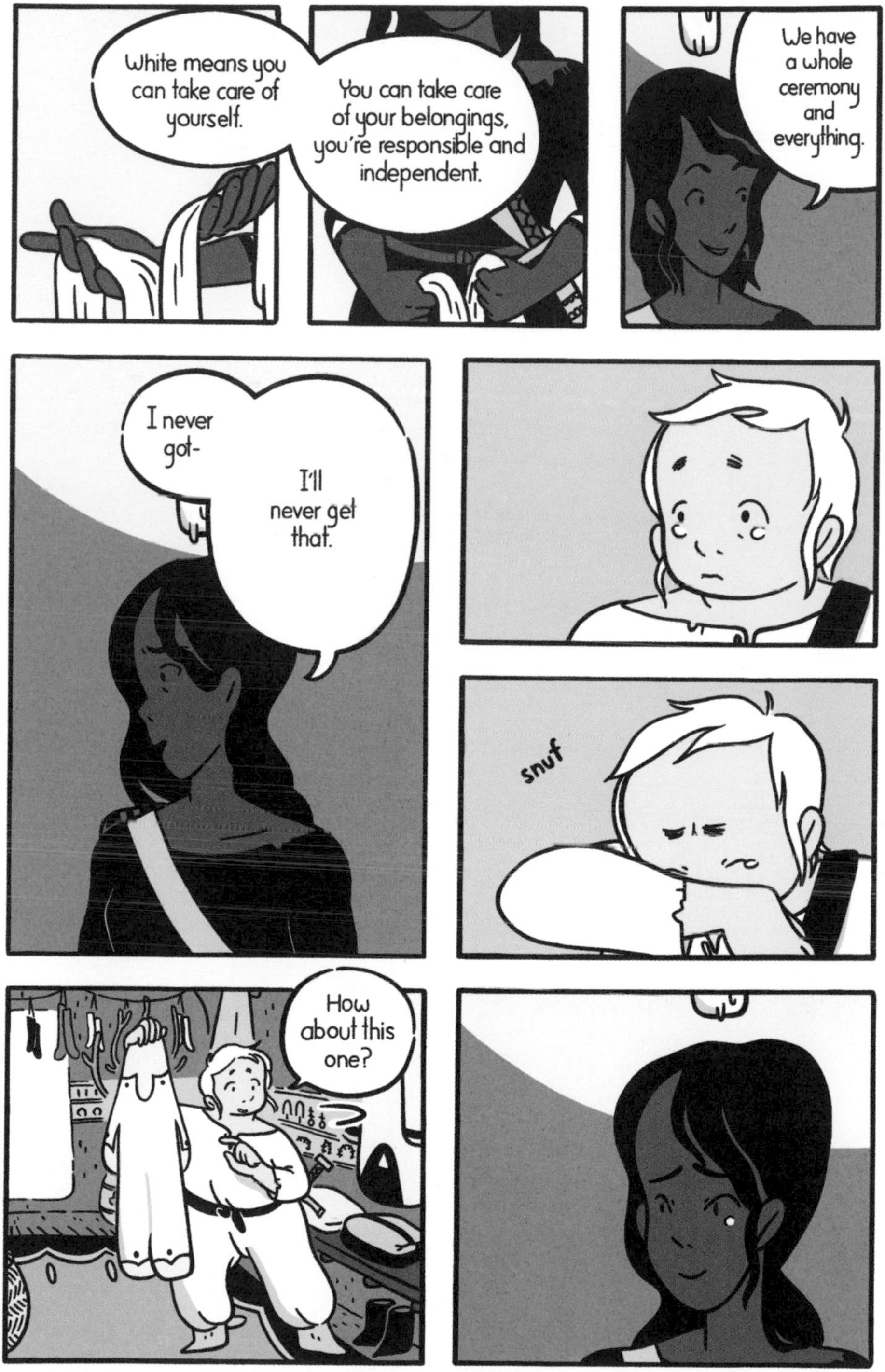
White means you can take care of yourself.
You can take care of your belongings, you're responsible and independent.
We have a whole ceremony and everything.
I never got-
I'll never get that.
snuf
How about this one?

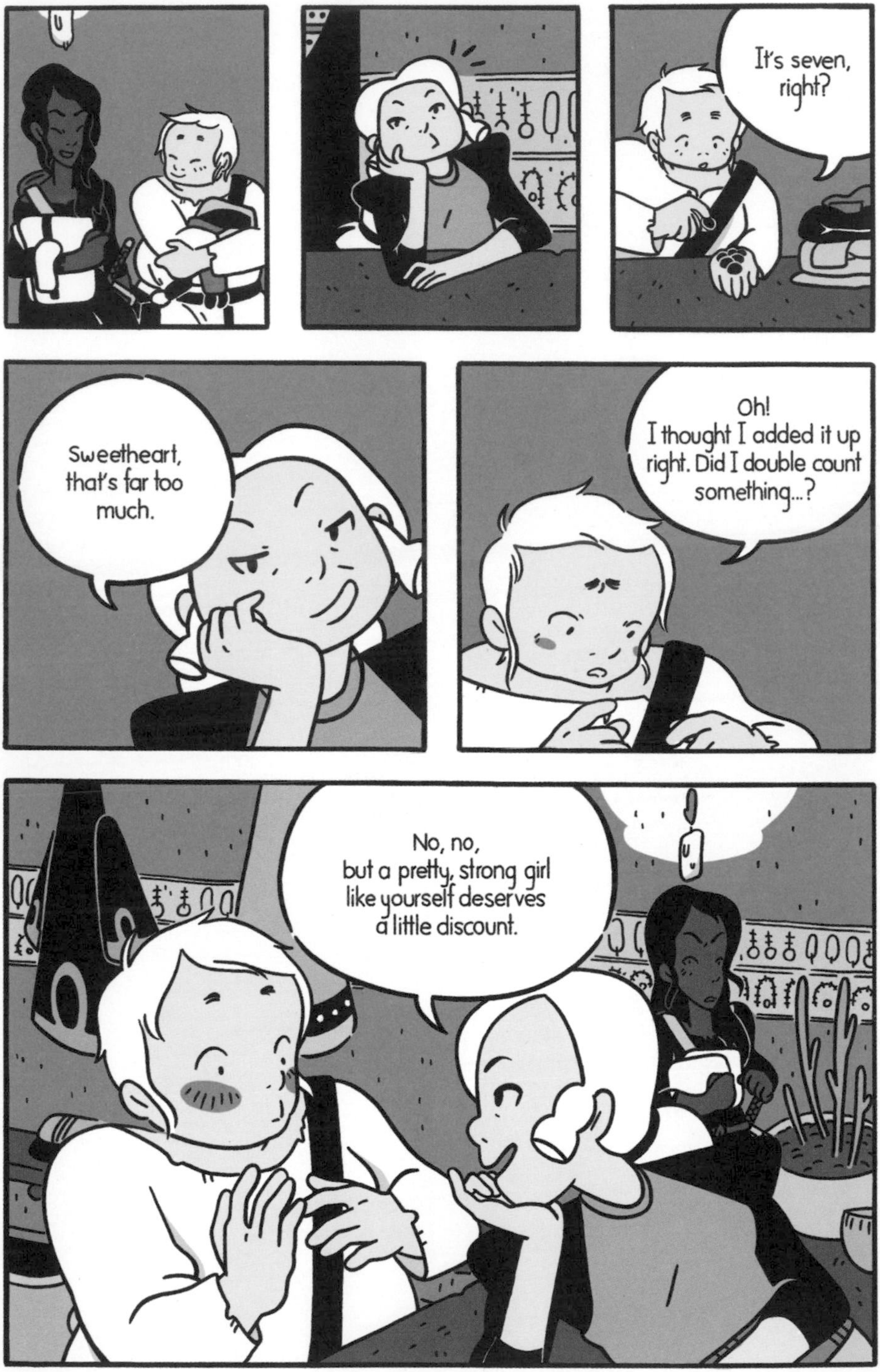
It's seven, right?
Sweetheart, that's far too much.
Oh! I thought I added it up right. Did I double count something...?
No, no, but a pretty, strong girl like yourself deserves a little discount.

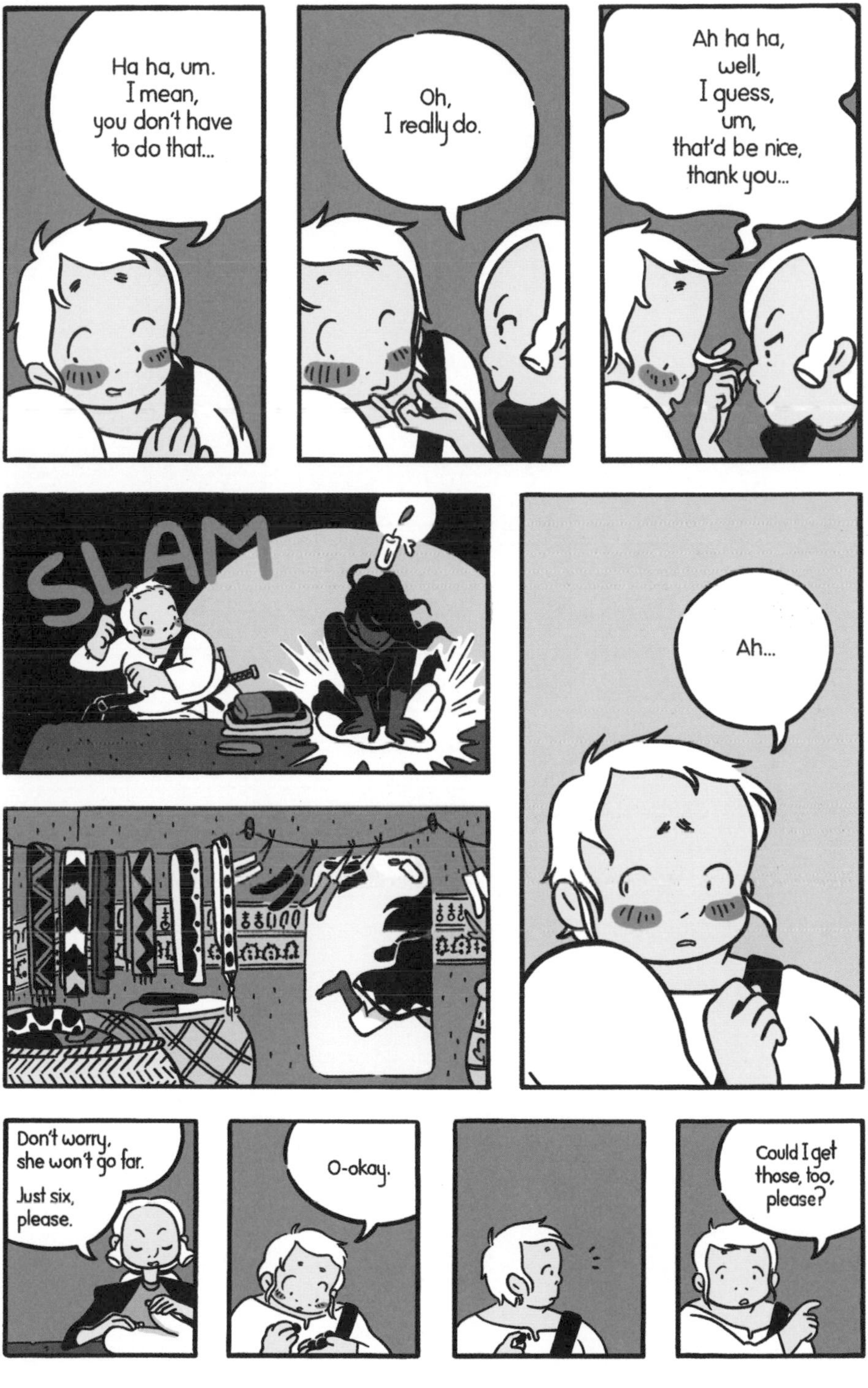
Ha ha, um. I mean, you don't have to do that...
Oh, I really do.
Ah ha ha, well, I guess, um, that'd be nice, thank you...
SLAM
Ah...
Don't worry, she won't go far.
Just six, please.
O-okay.
Could I get those, too, please?

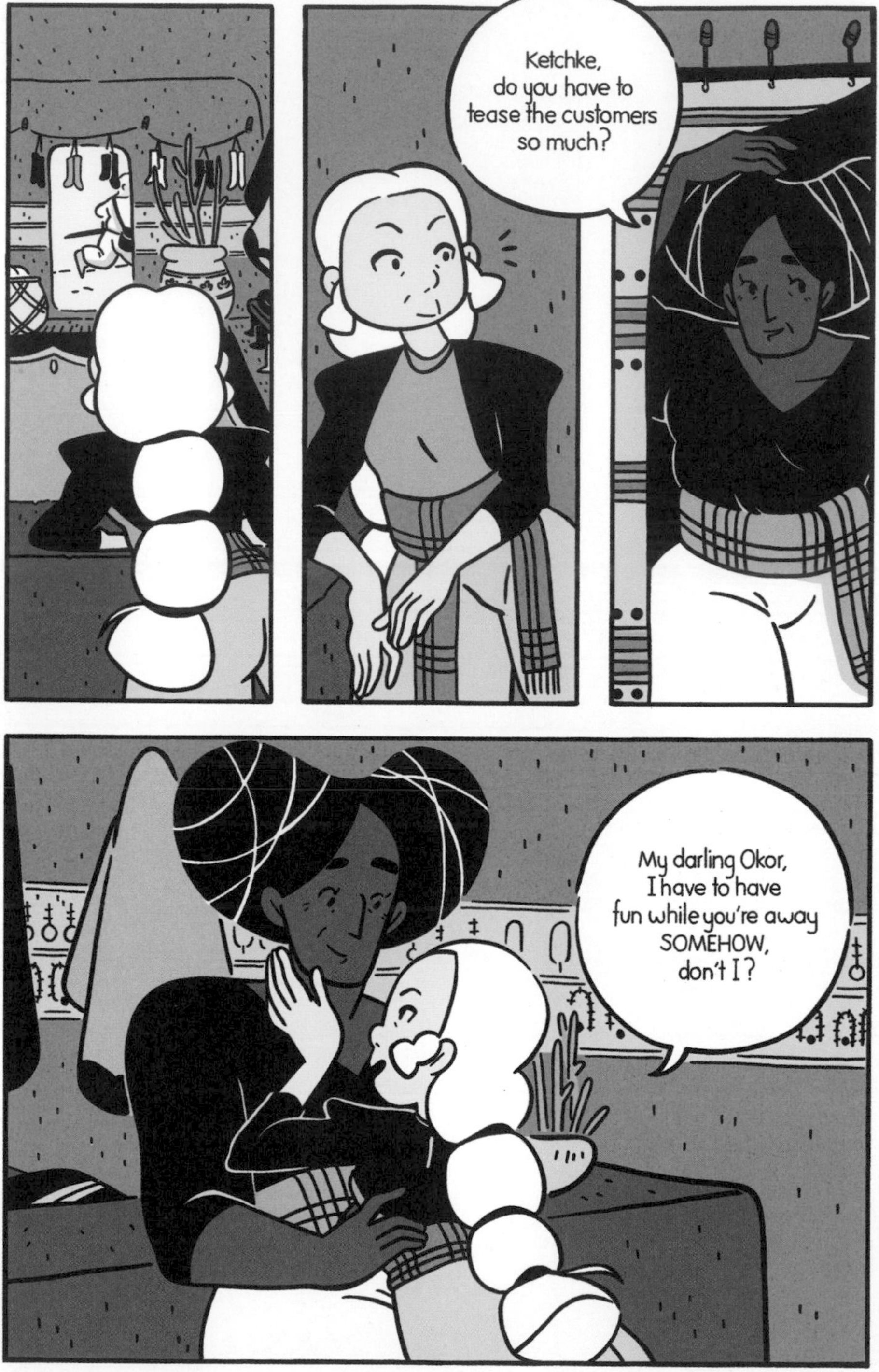
Ketchke, do you have to tease the customers so much?
My darling Okor, I have to have fun while you're away SOMEHOW, don't I?

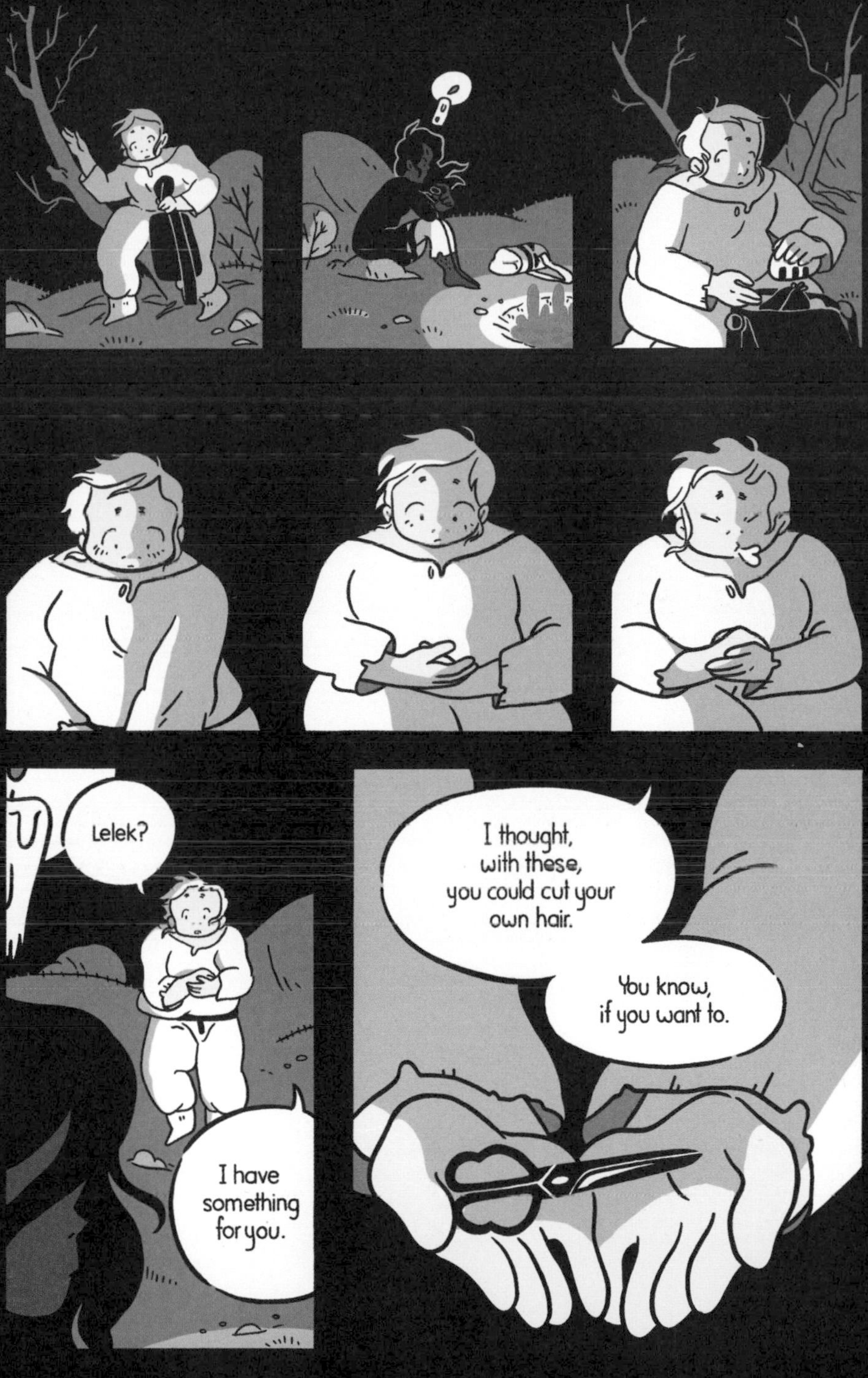
Lelek?
I have something for you.
I thought, with these, you could cut your own hair.
You know, if you want to.

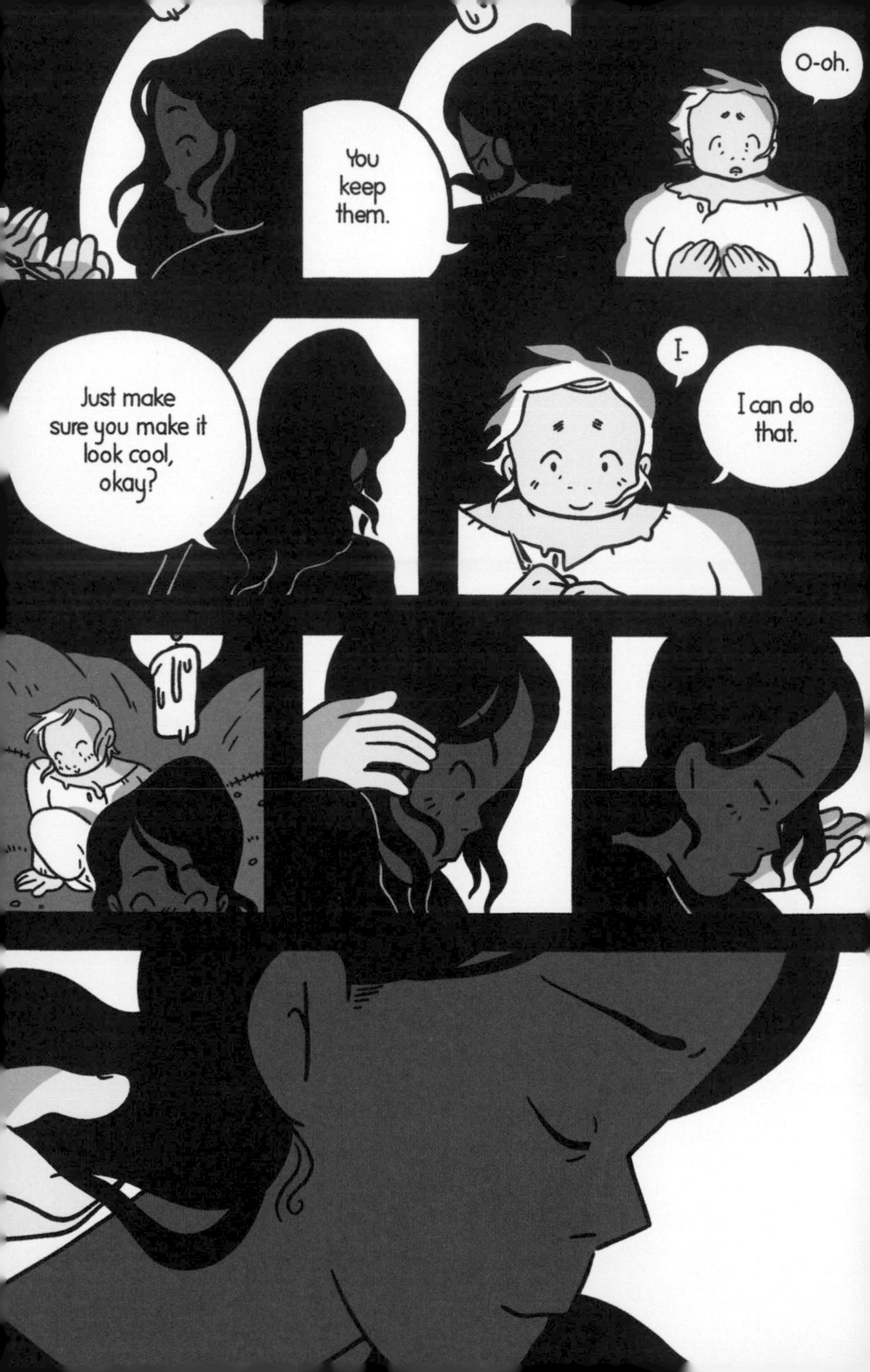
You keep them.
O-oh.
Just make sure you make it look cool, okay?
I-
I can do that.

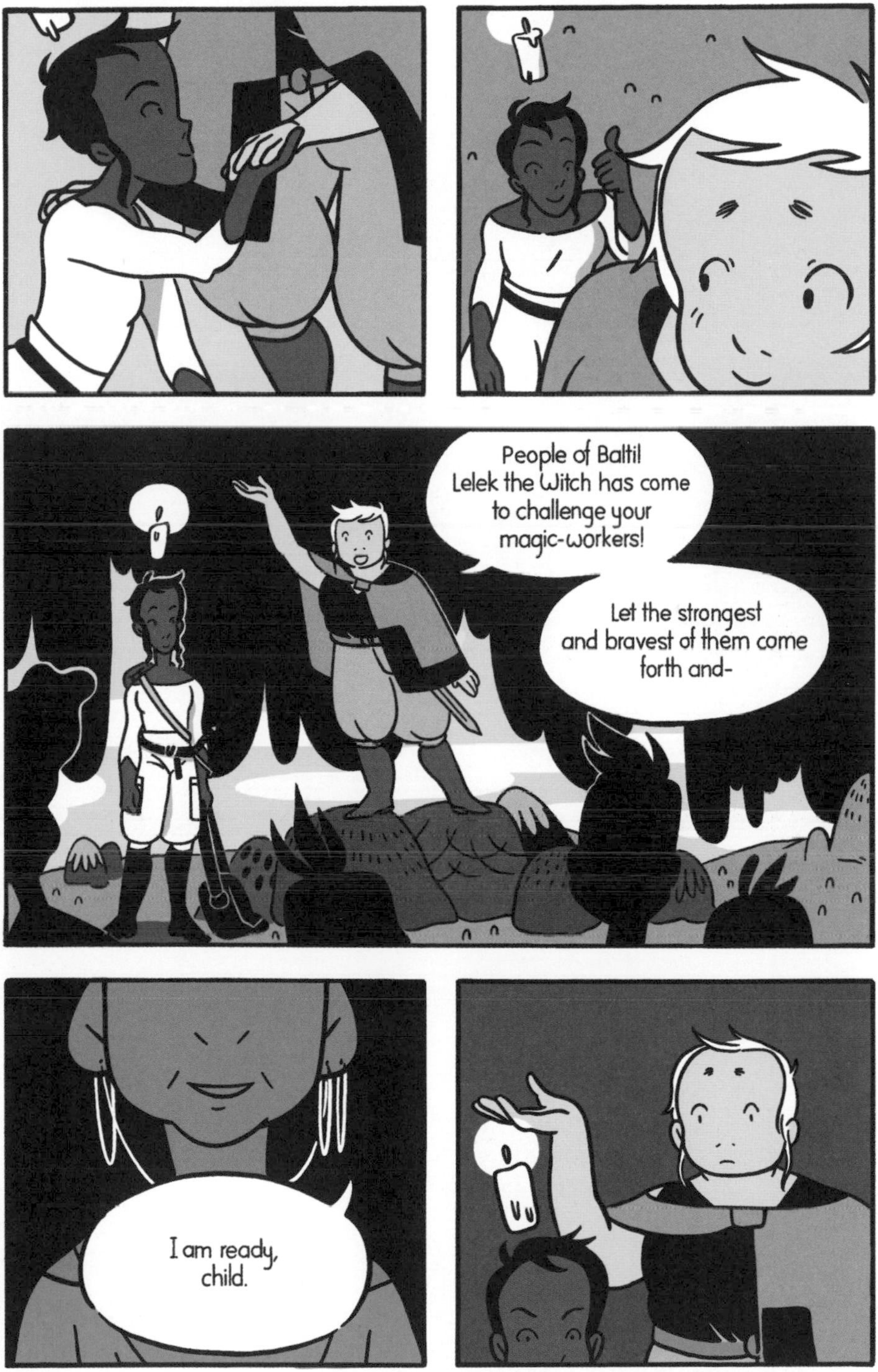
People of Balti! Lelek the Witch has come to challenge your magic-workers!
Let the strongest and bravest of them come forth and-
I am ready, child.

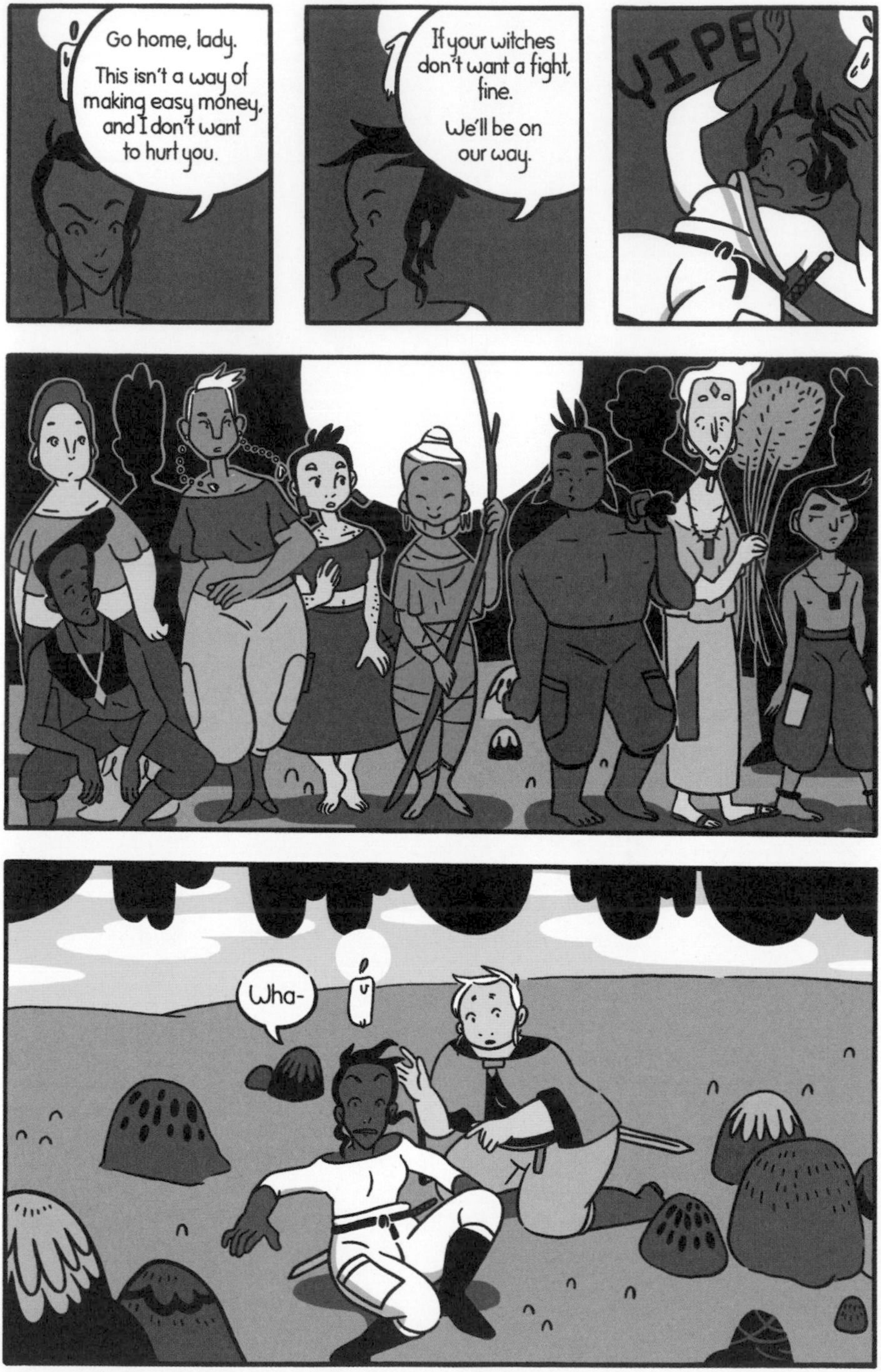
Go home, lady.
This isn't a way of making easy money, and I don't want to hurt you.
If your witches don't want a fight, fine.
We'll be on our way.
YIPE
Wha-

Part 4

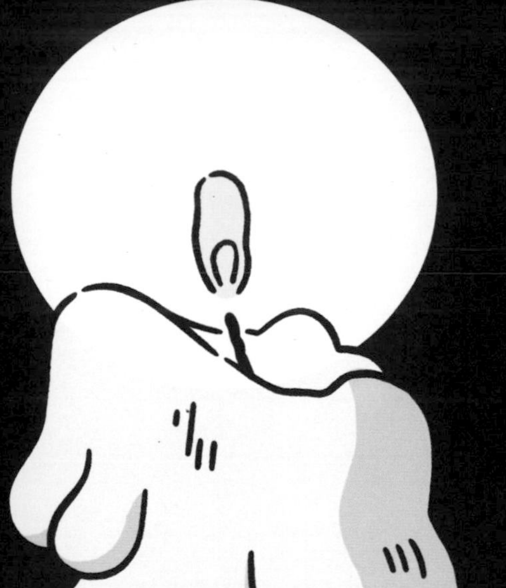

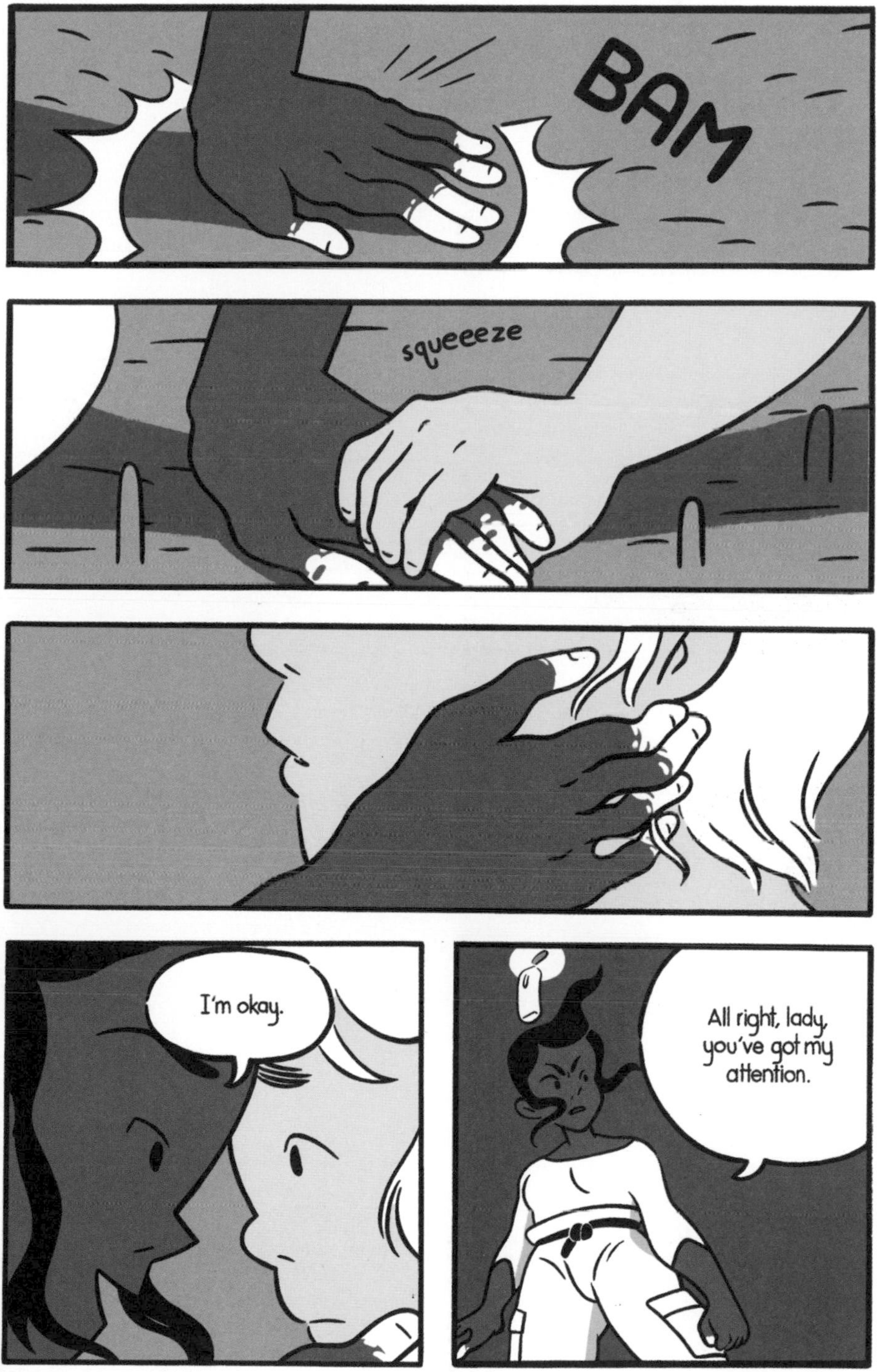
BAM
squeeeze
I'm okay.
All right, lady, you've got my attention.

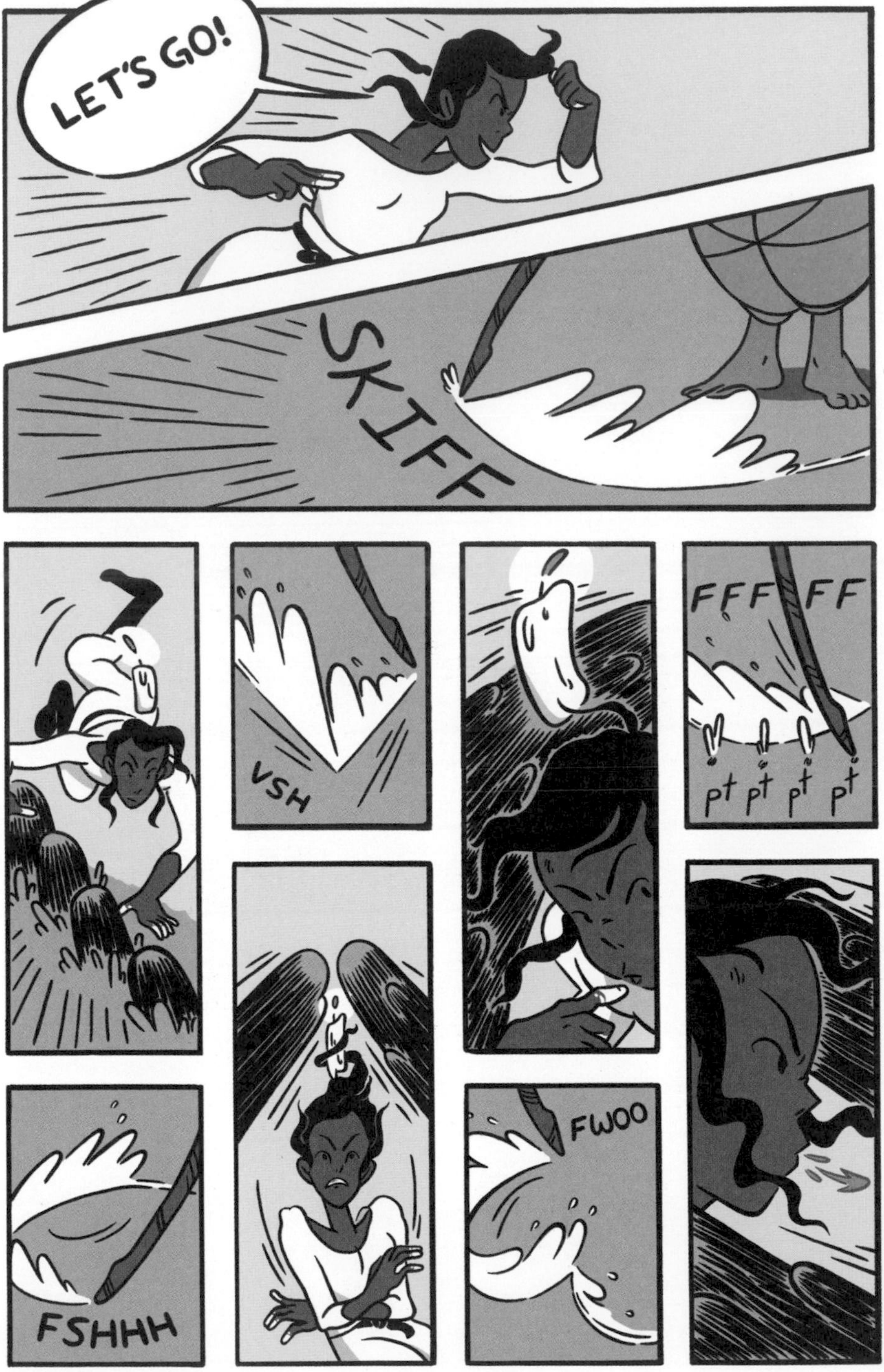
LET'S GO!
SKIFF
VSH
FFF FF
pt pt pt pt
FSHHH
FWOO

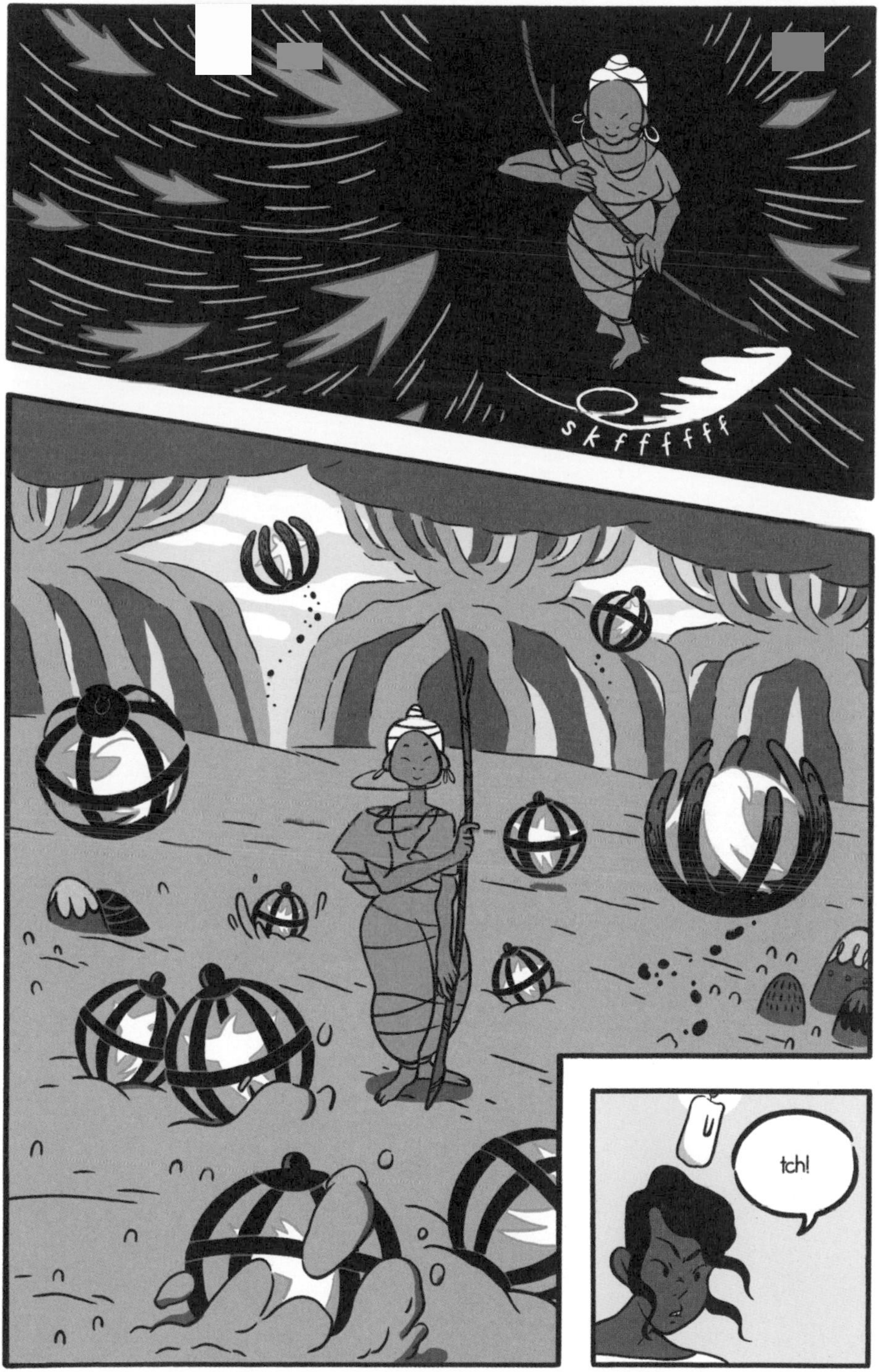
skffffff
tch!

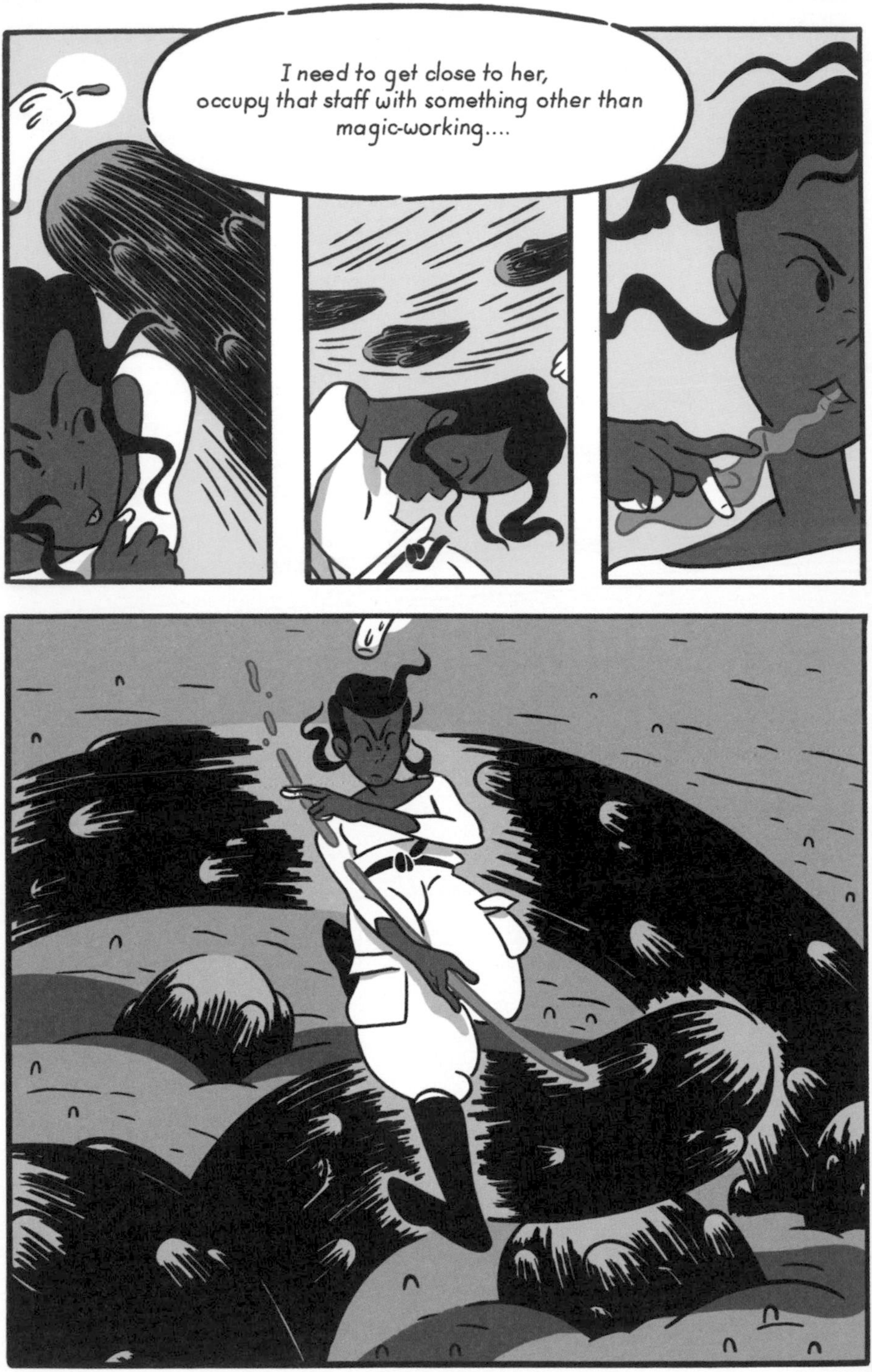
I need to get close to her, occupy that staff with something other than magic-working....

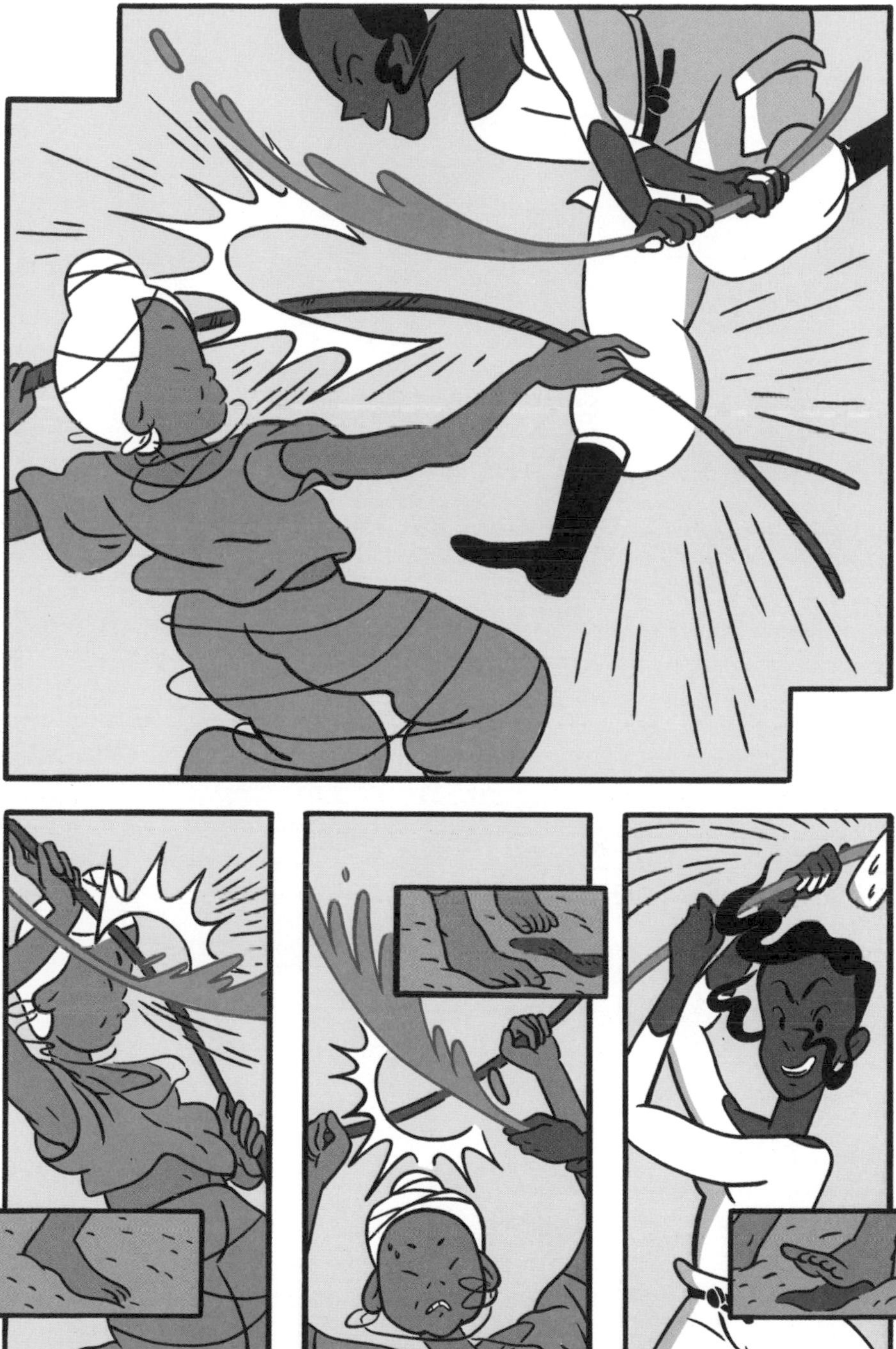

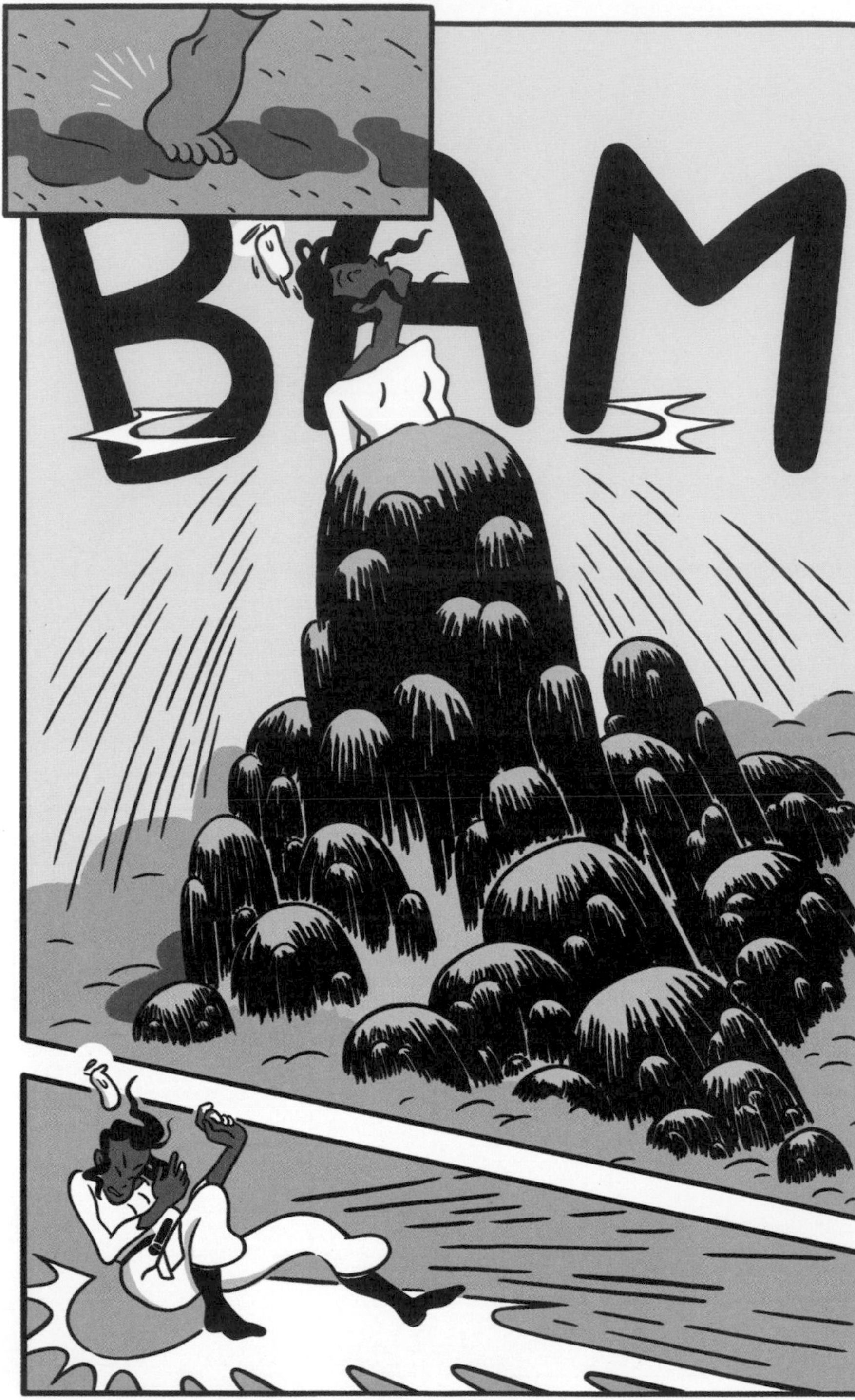
BAM

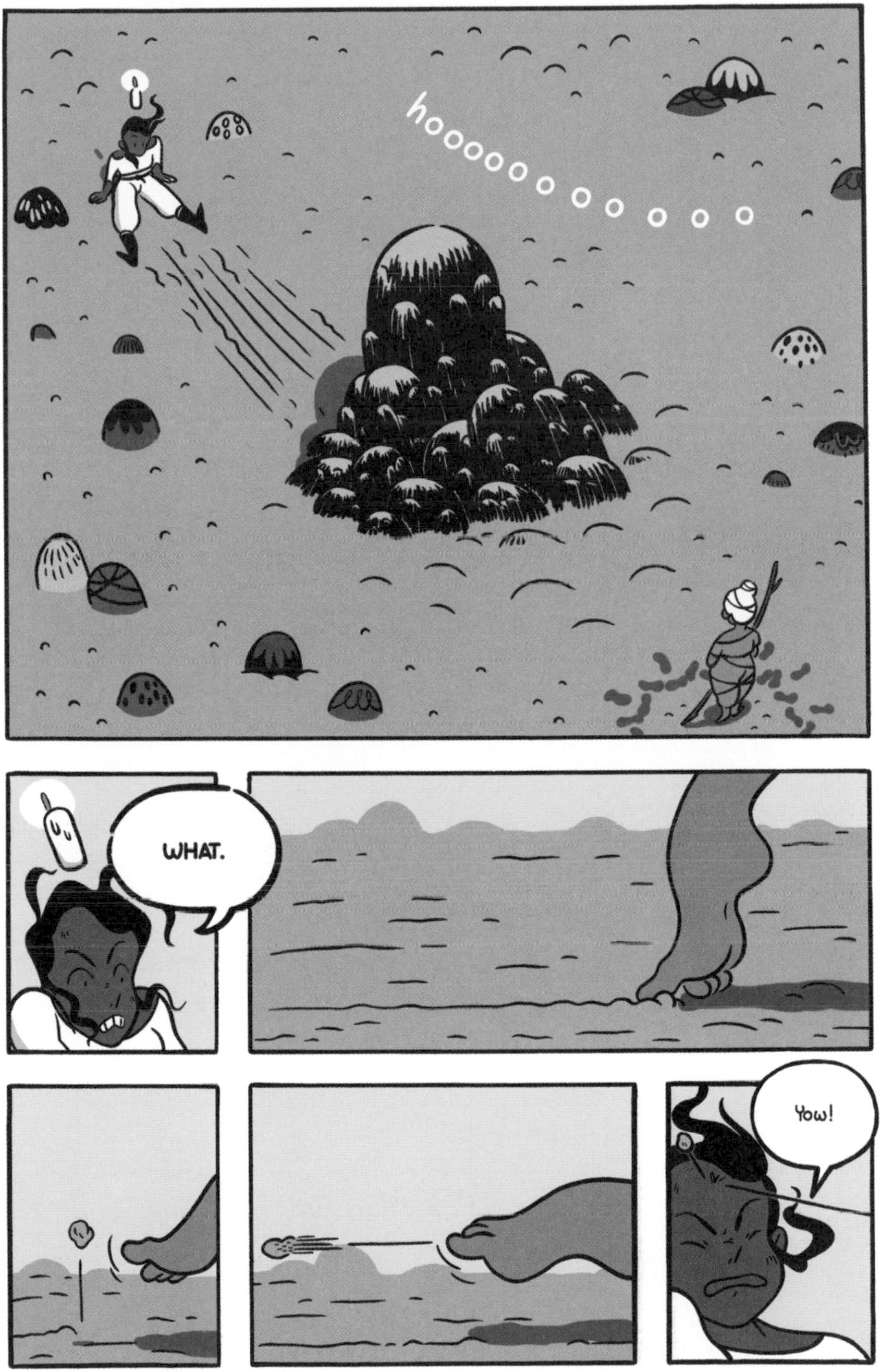
hooooooooooo
WHAT.
Yow!

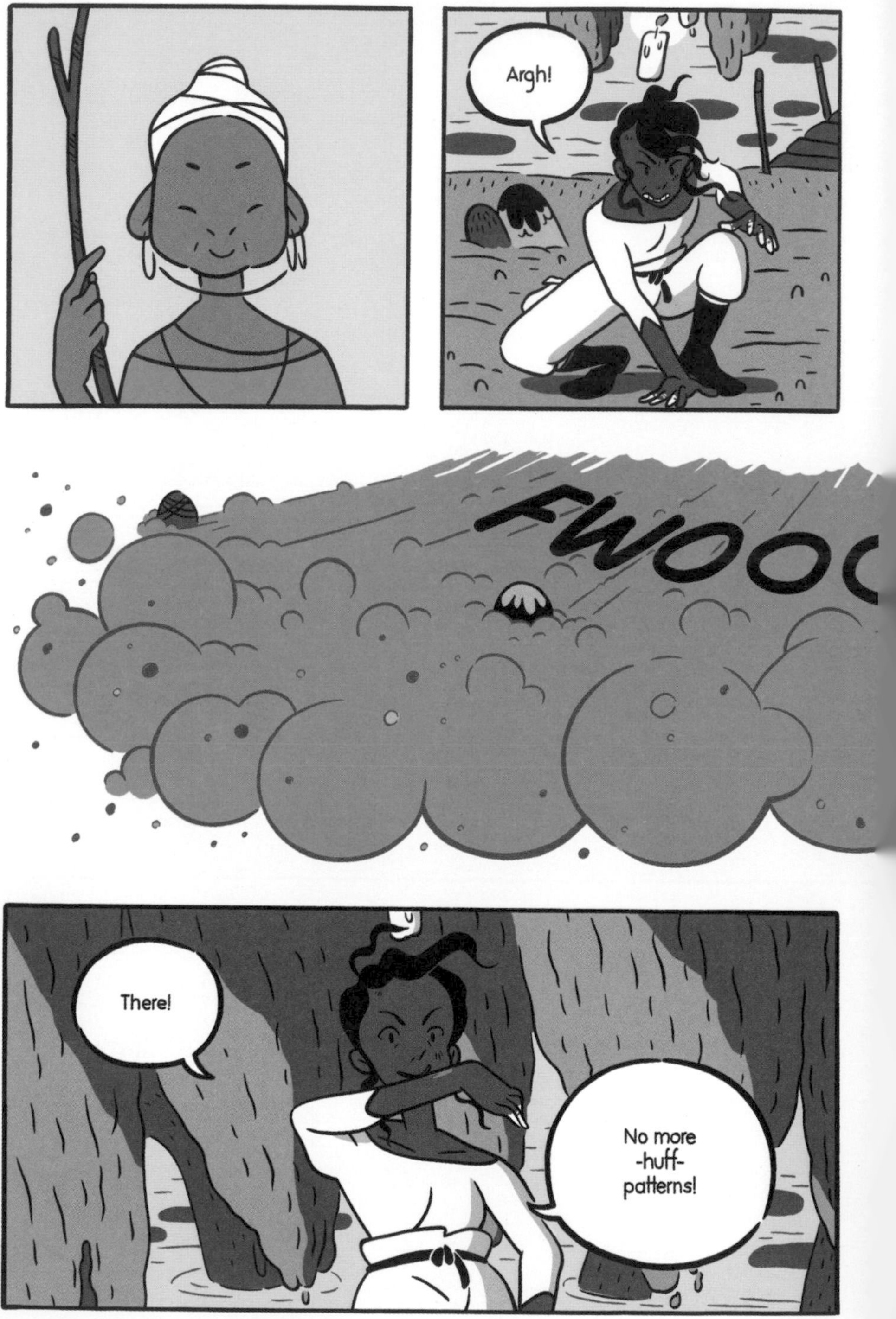
Argh!
FWOOO
There!
No more -huff- patterns!

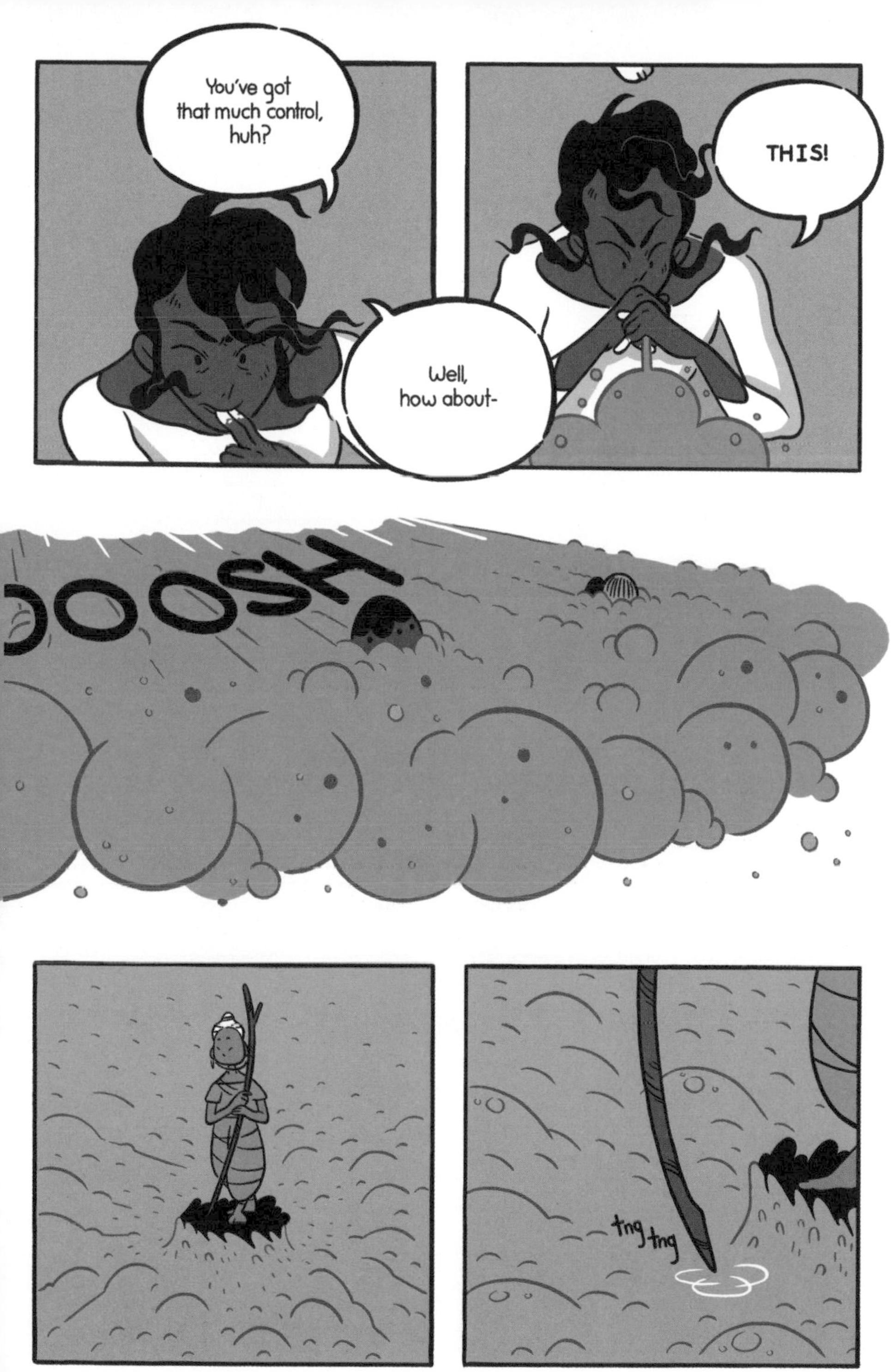
You've got that much control, huh?
THIS!
Well, how about-
OOSH
tng tng

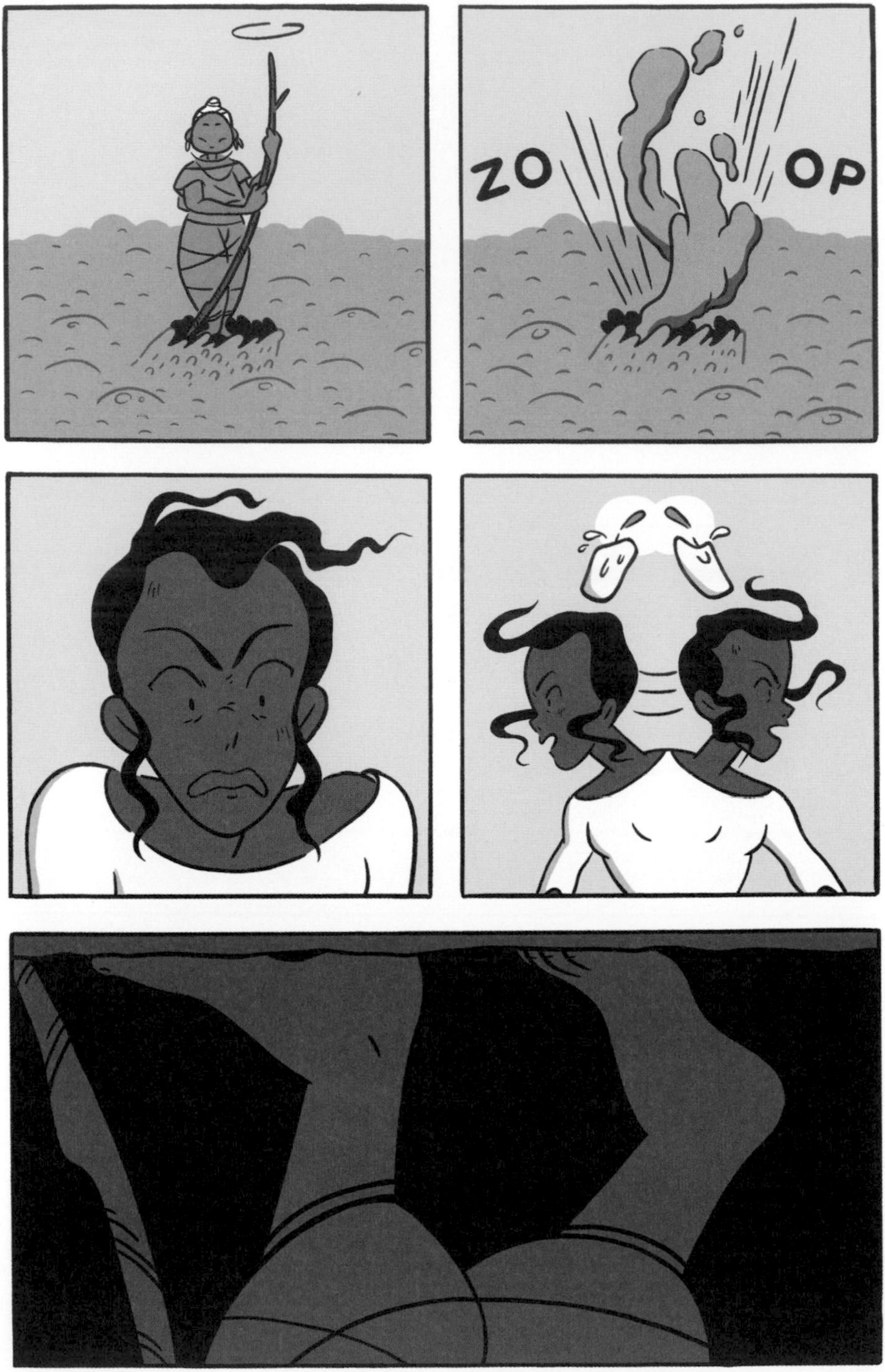
ZO
OP

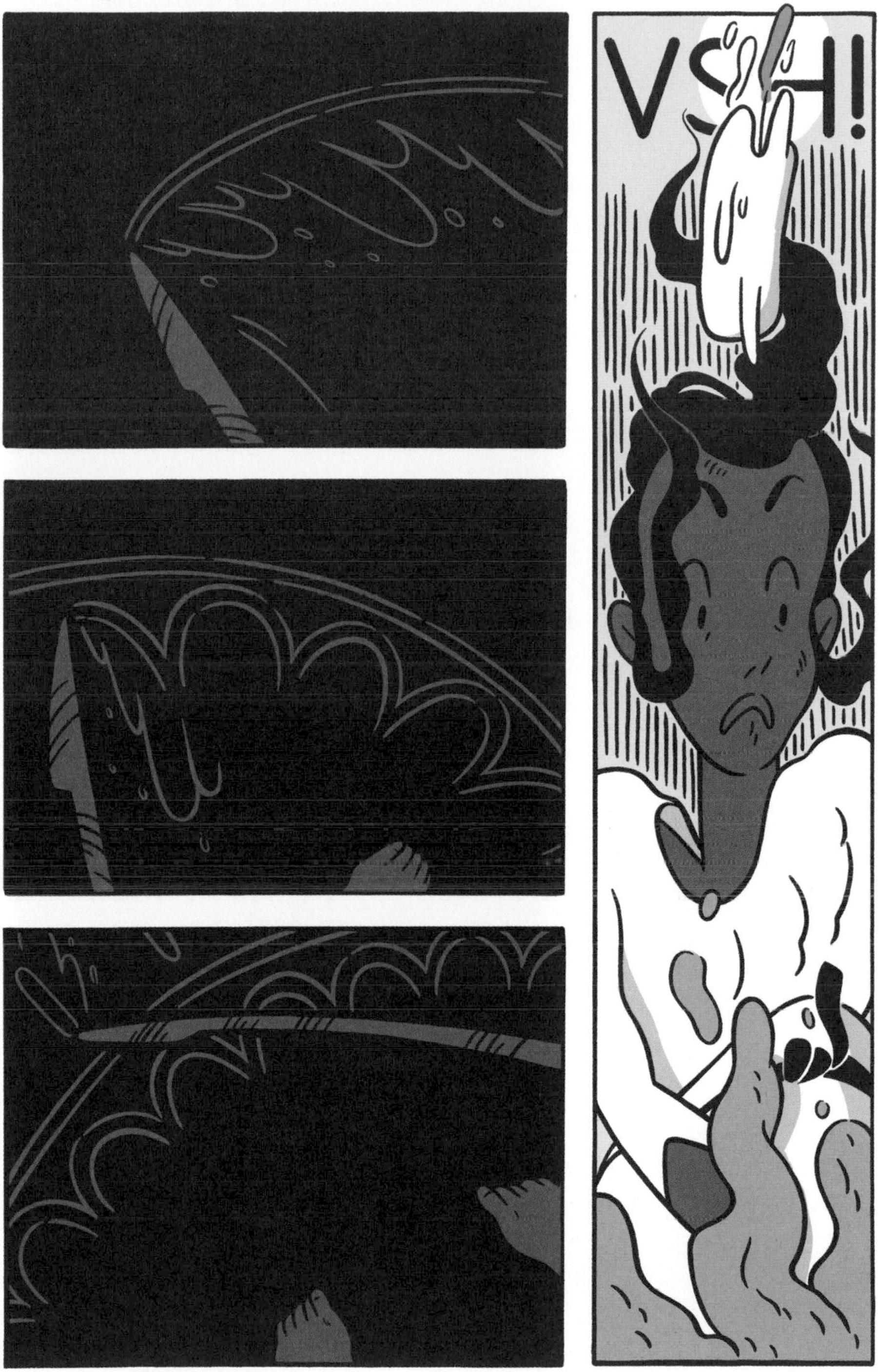
VSH!

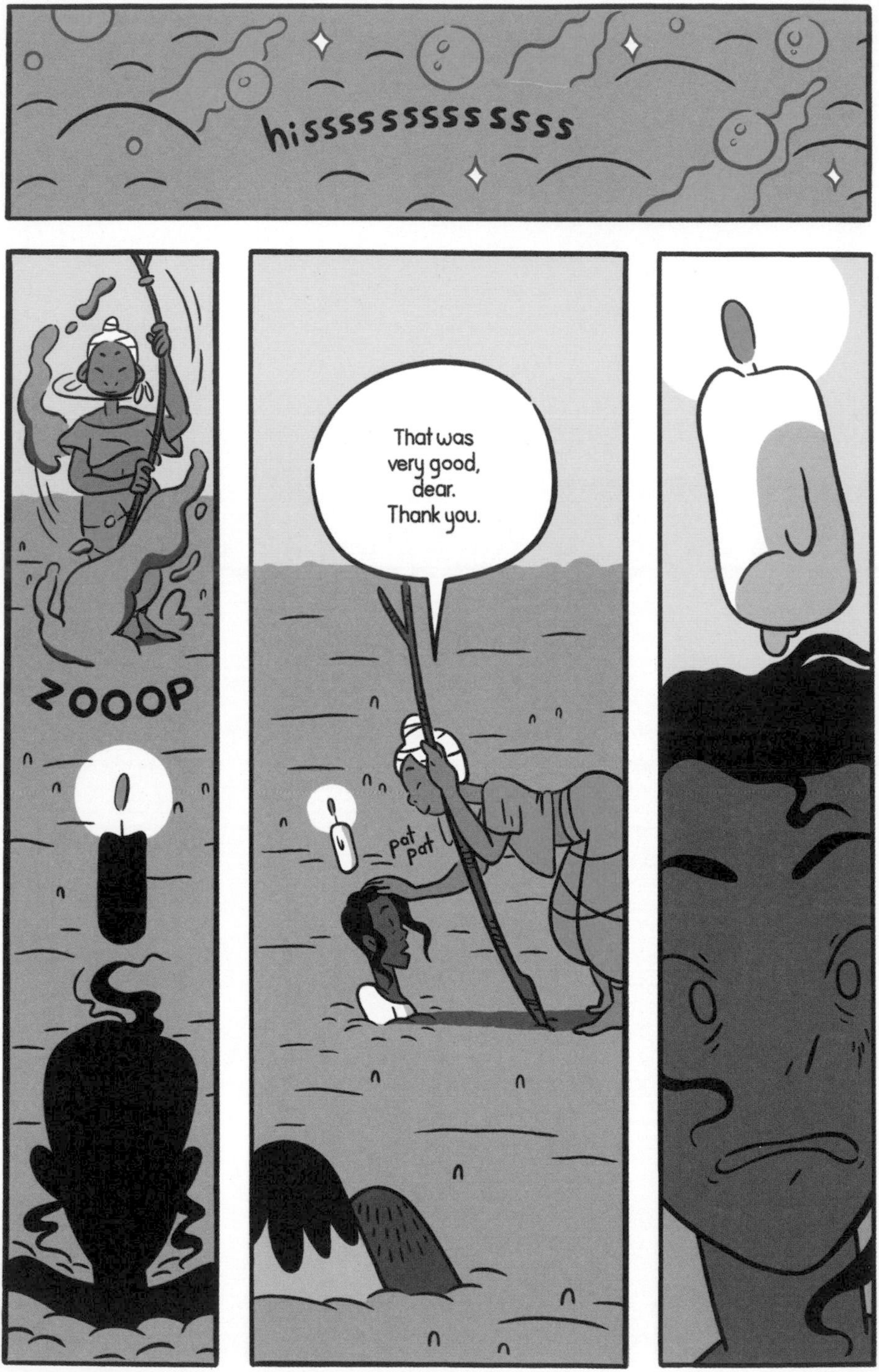
hissssssssssssss
ZOOOP
That was very good, dear. Thank you.
pat pat

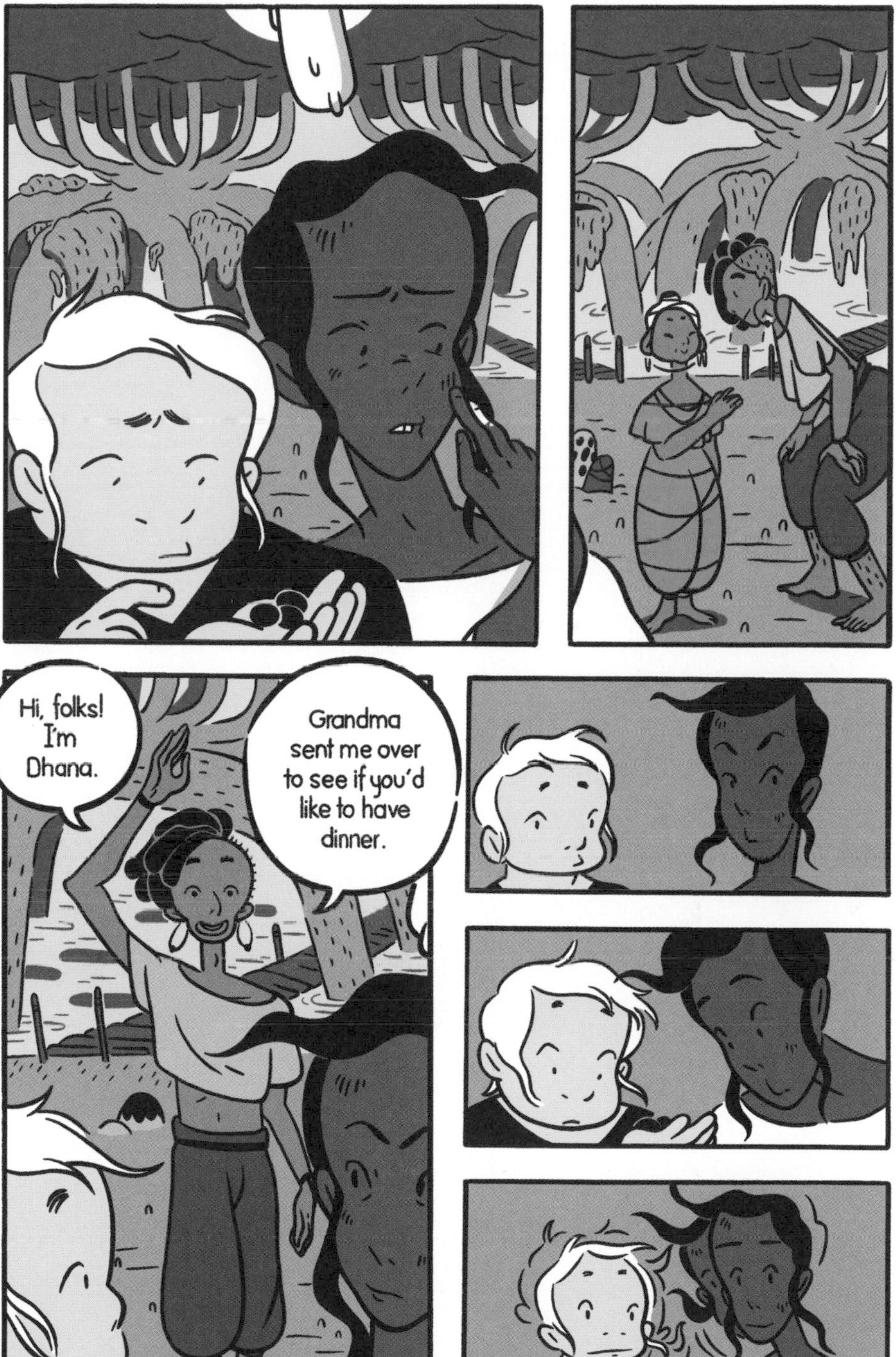
Hi, folks! I'm Dhana.
Grandma sent me over to see if you'd like to have dinner.

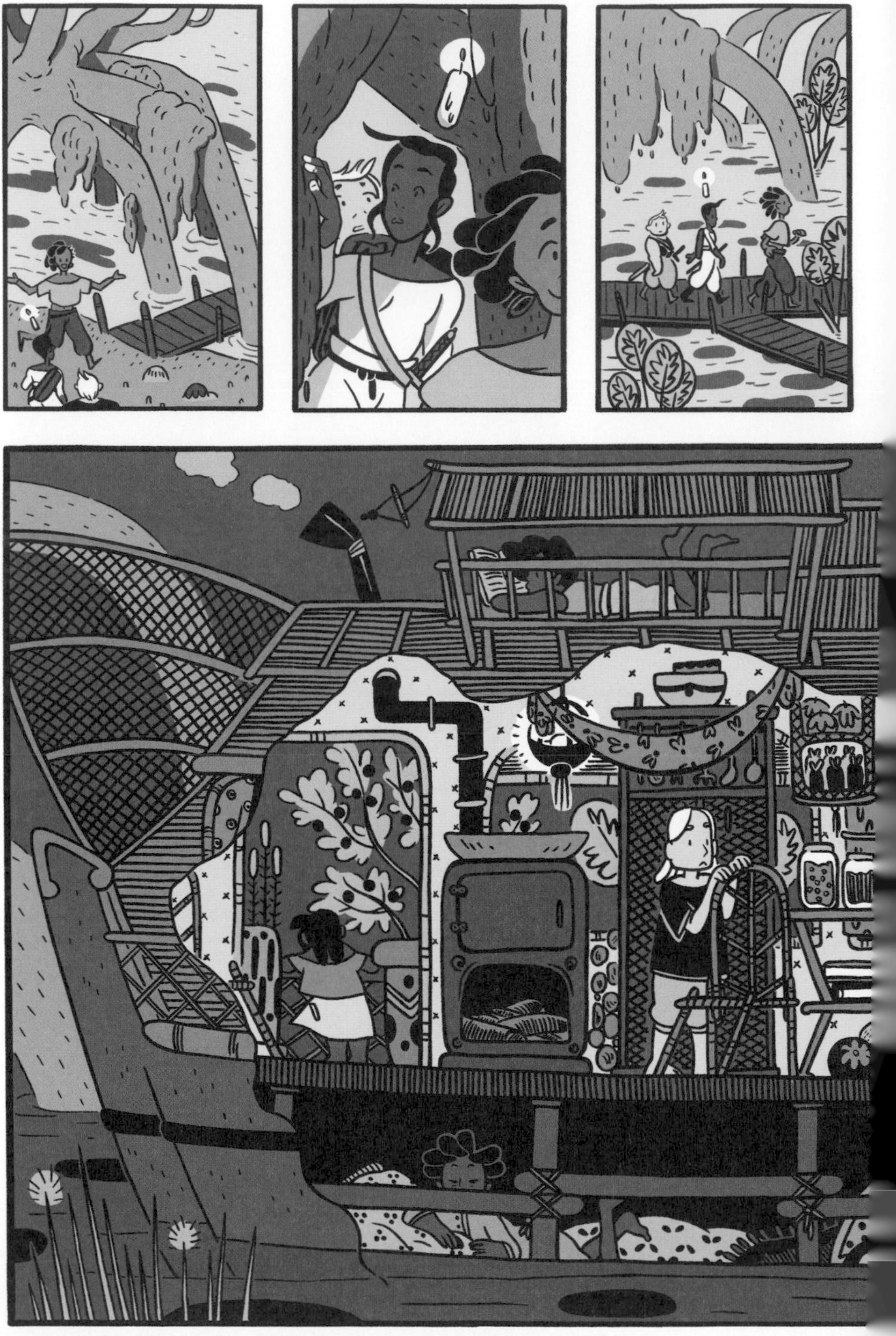

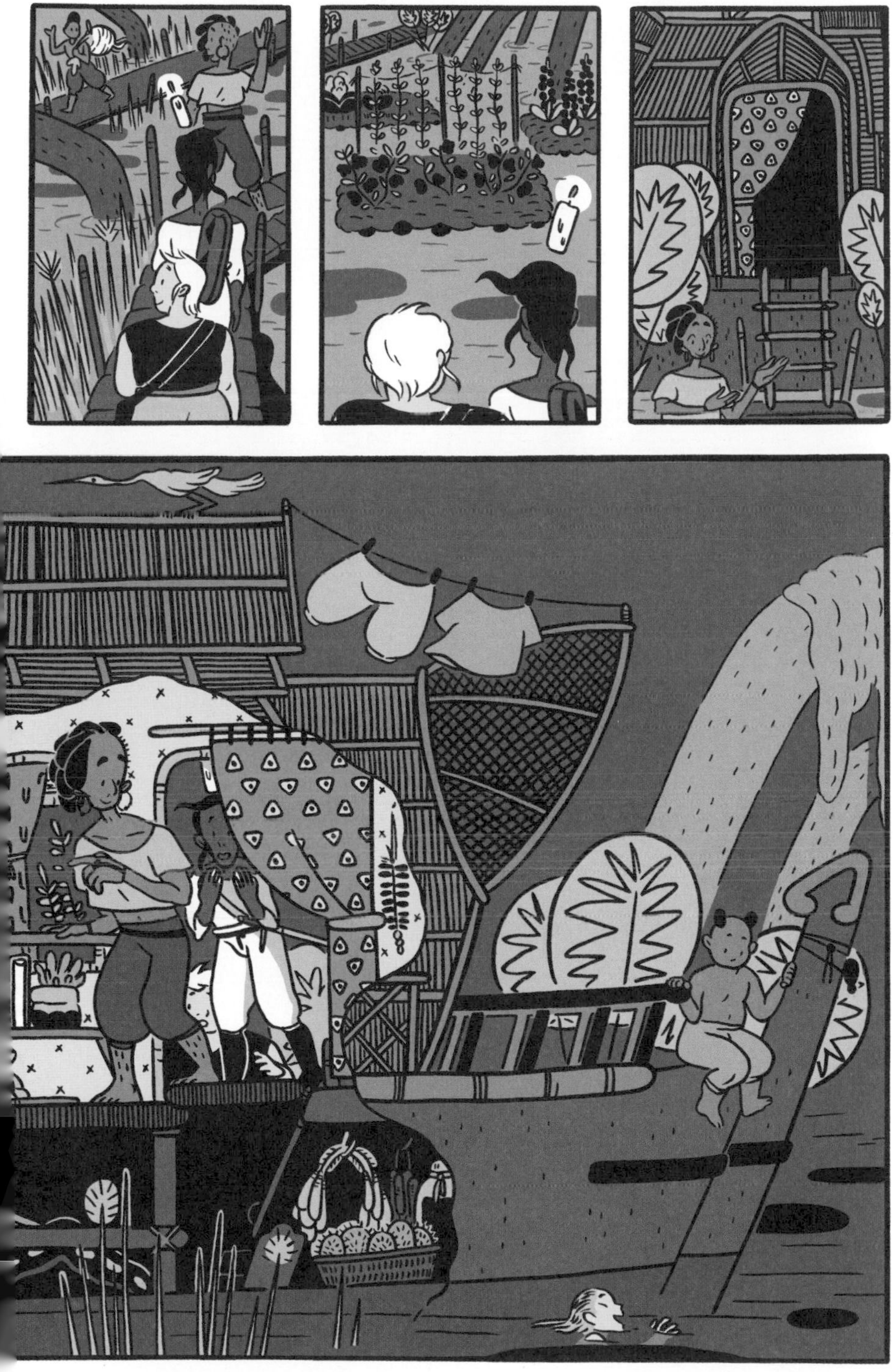

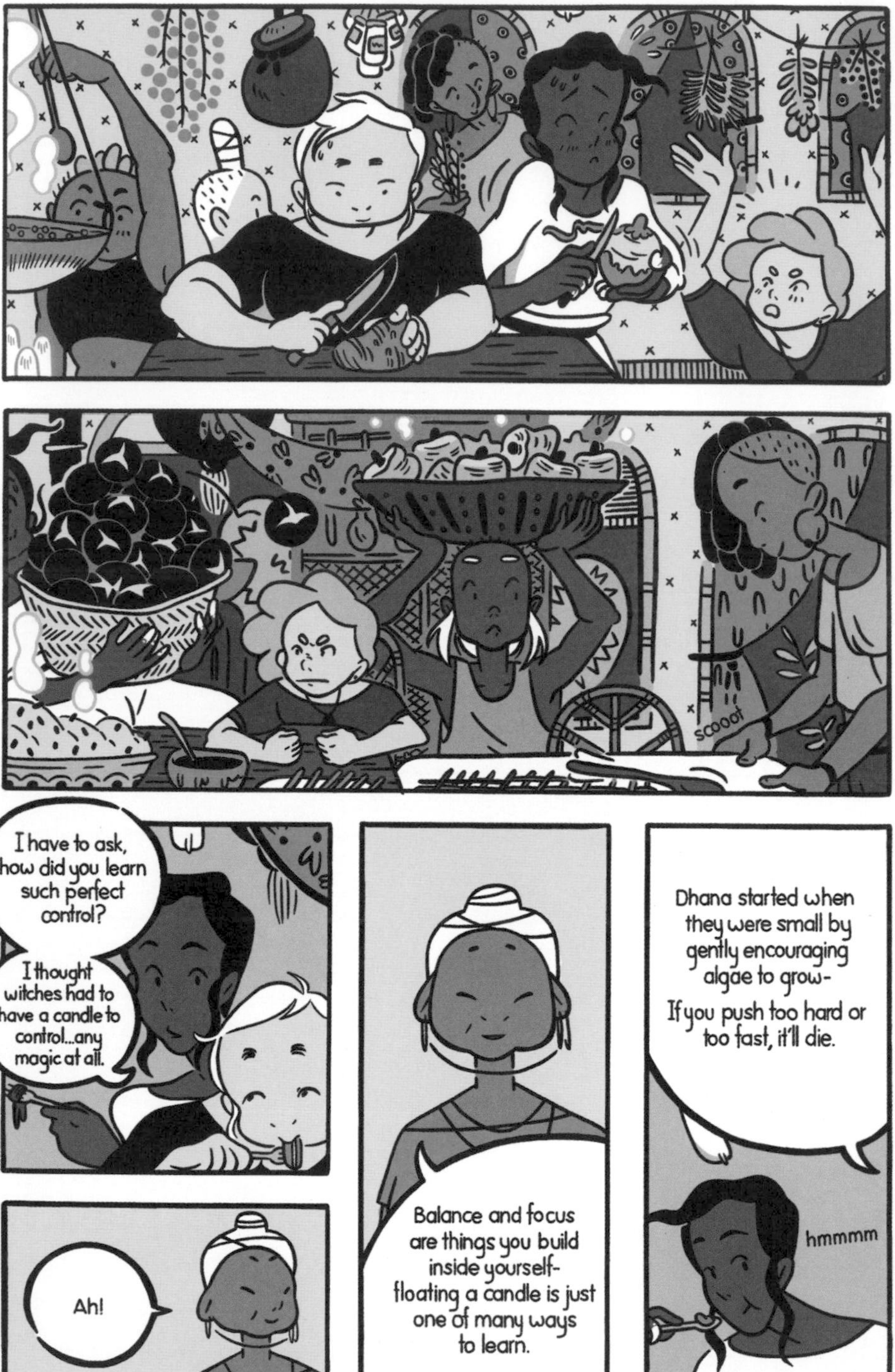
scooot
I have to ask, how did you learn such perfect control?
I thought witches had to have a candle to control...any magic at all.
Ah!
Balance and focus are things you build inside yourself- floating a candle is just one of many ways to learn.
Dhana started when they were small by gently encouraging algae to grow-
If you push too hard or too fast, it'll die.
hmmmm

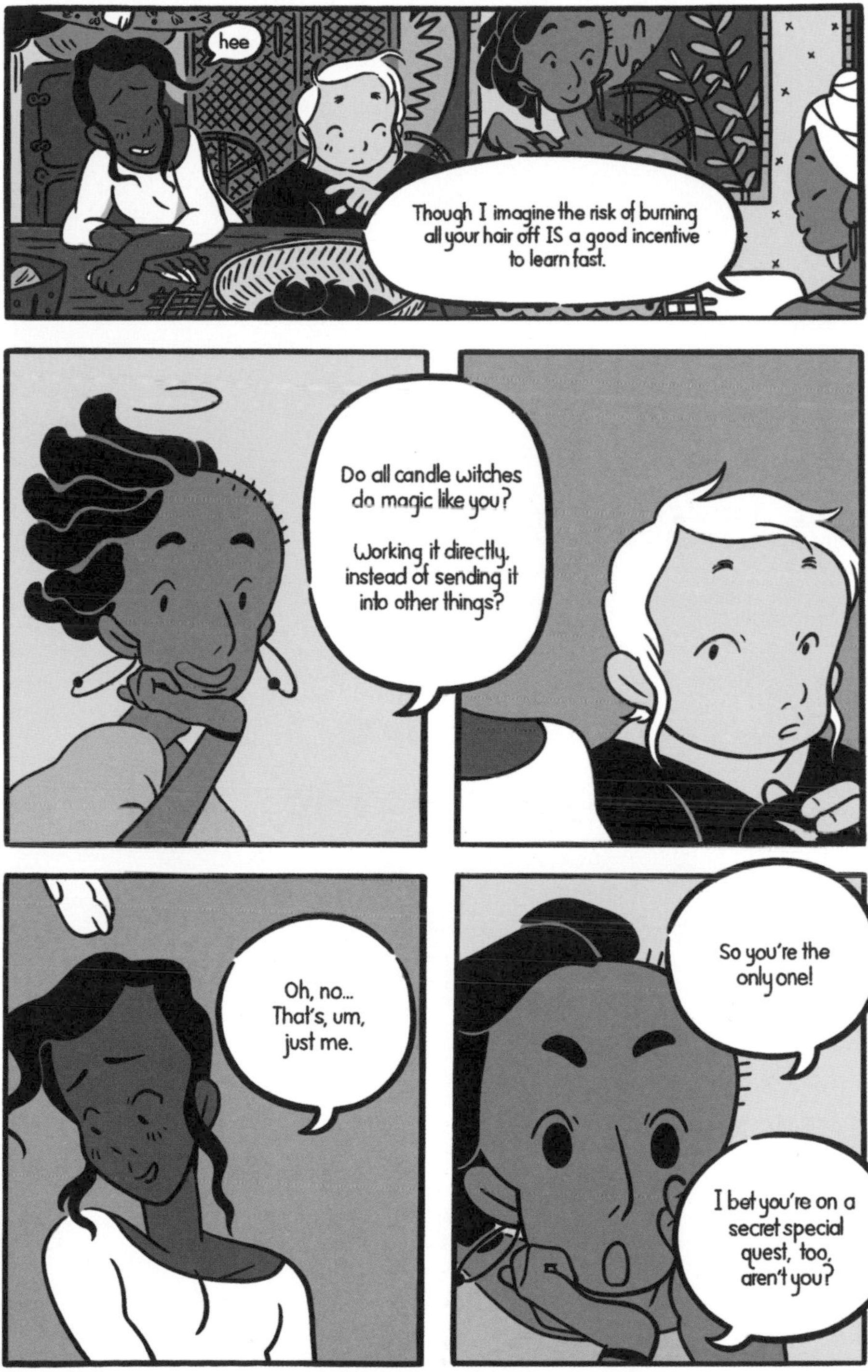
hee
Though I imagine the risk of burning all your hair off IS a good incentive to learn fast.
Do all candle witches do magic like you?
Working it directly, instead of sending it into other things?
Oh, no... That's, um, just me.
So you're the only one!
I bet you're on a secret special quest, too, aren't you?

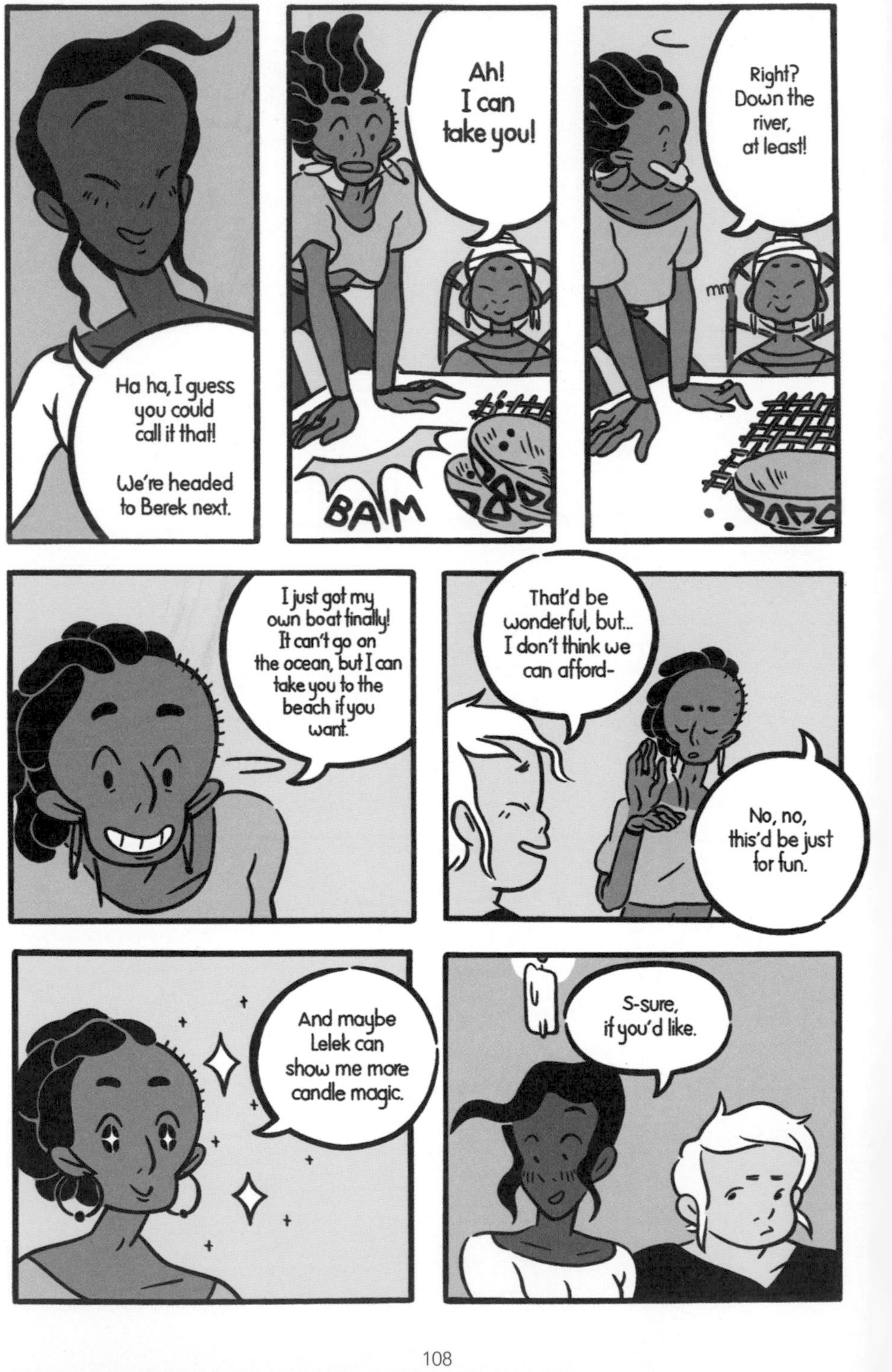
Ha ha, I guess you could call it that!
We're headed to Berek next.
Ah! I can take you!
BAM
Right? Down the river, at least!
mm
I just got my own boat finally! It can't go on the ocean, but I can take you to the beach if you want.
That'd be wonderful, but... I don't think we can afford-
No, no, this'd be just for fun.
And maybe Lelek can show me more candle magic.
S-sure, if you'd like.

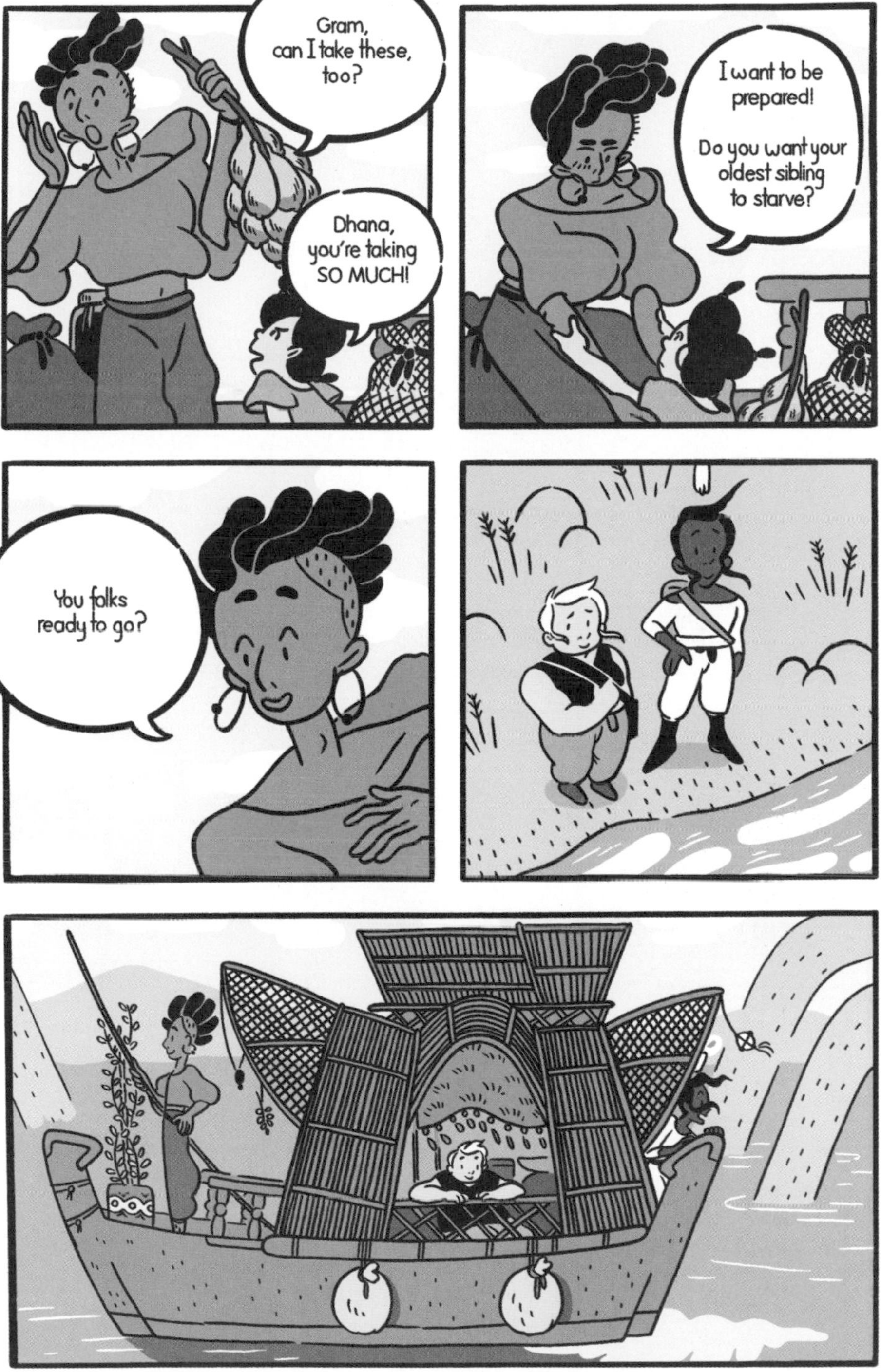

Gram, can I take these, too?
Dhana, you're taking SO MUCH!
I want to be prepared!
Do you want your oldest sibling to starve?
You folks ready to go?

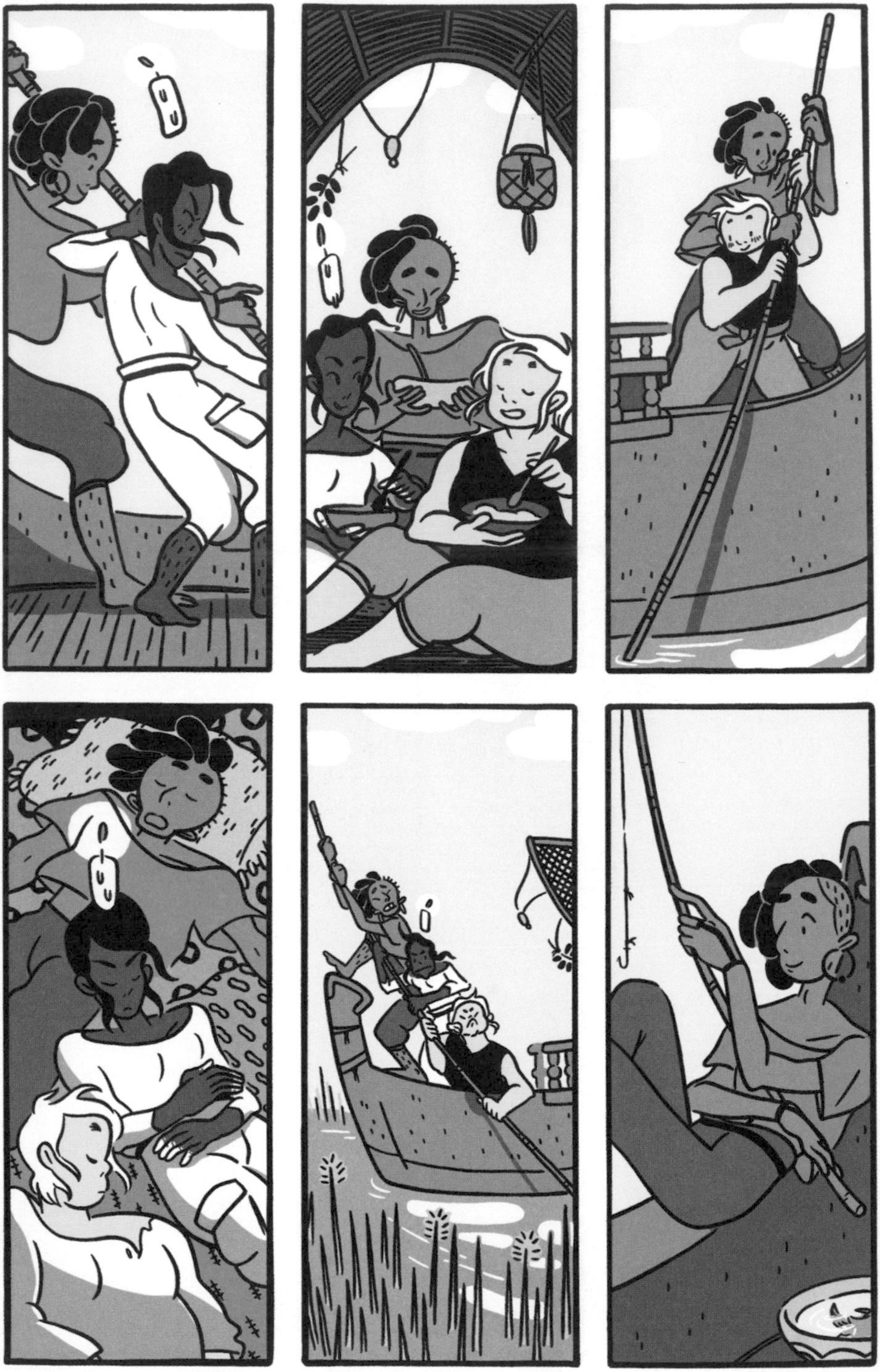

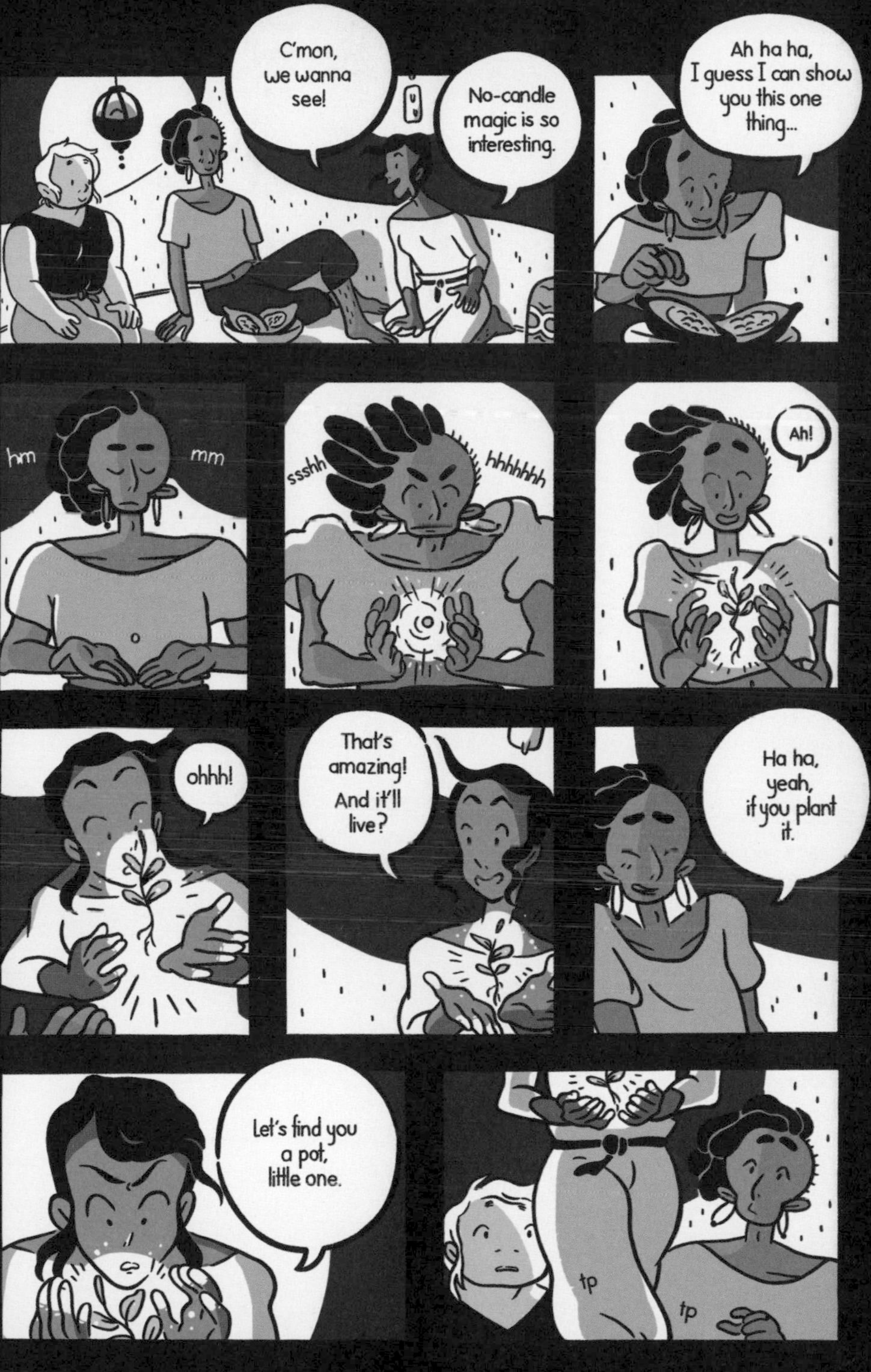
C'mon, we wanna see!
No-candle magic is so interesting.
Ah ha ha, I guess I can show you this one thing...
hm
mm
ssshh
hhhhhhh
Ah!
ohhh!
That's amazing! And it'll live?
Ha ha, yeah, if you plant it.
Let's find you a pot, little one.
tp
tp

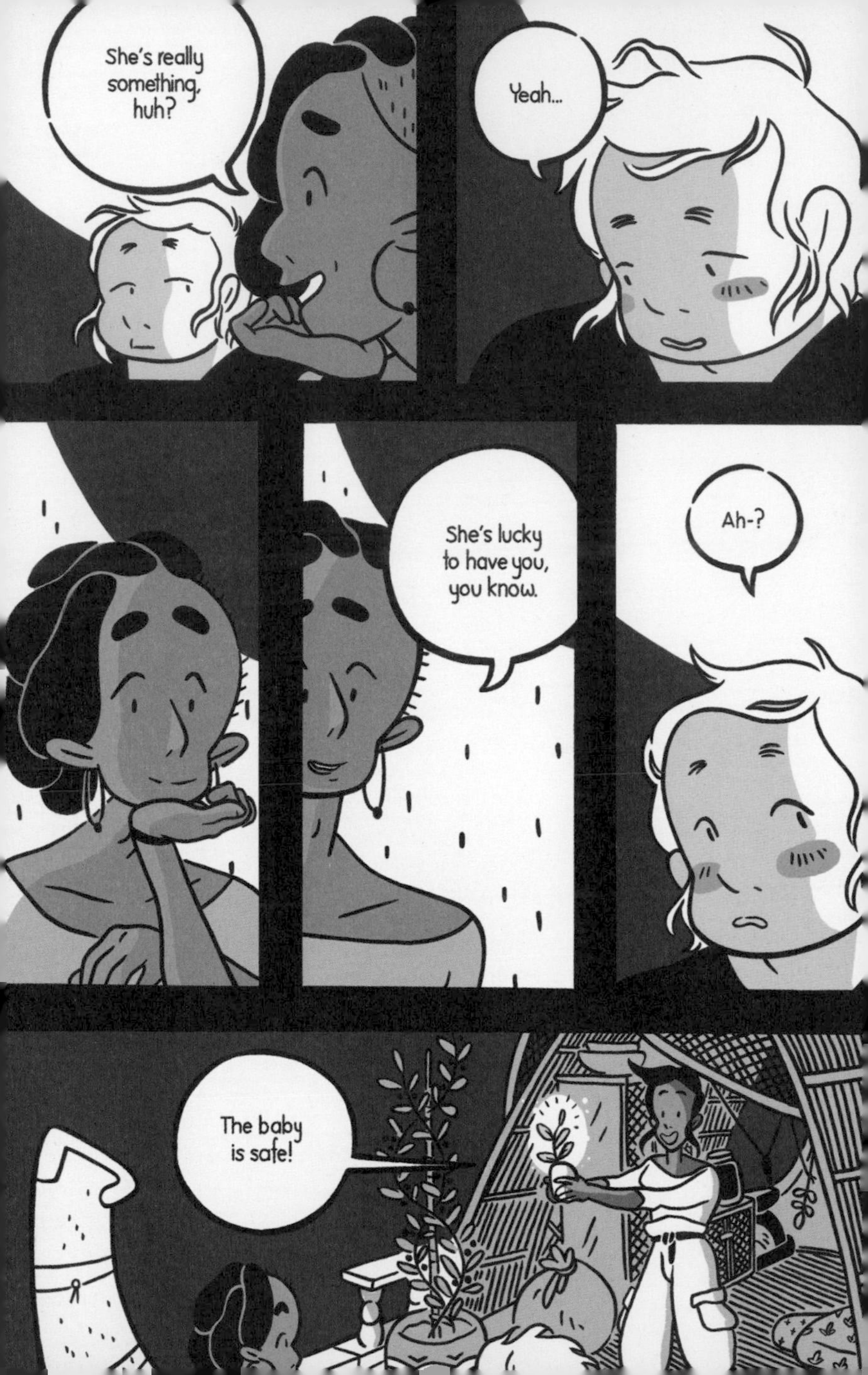
She's really something, huh?
Yeah...
She's lucky to have you, you know.
Ah-?
The baby is safe!

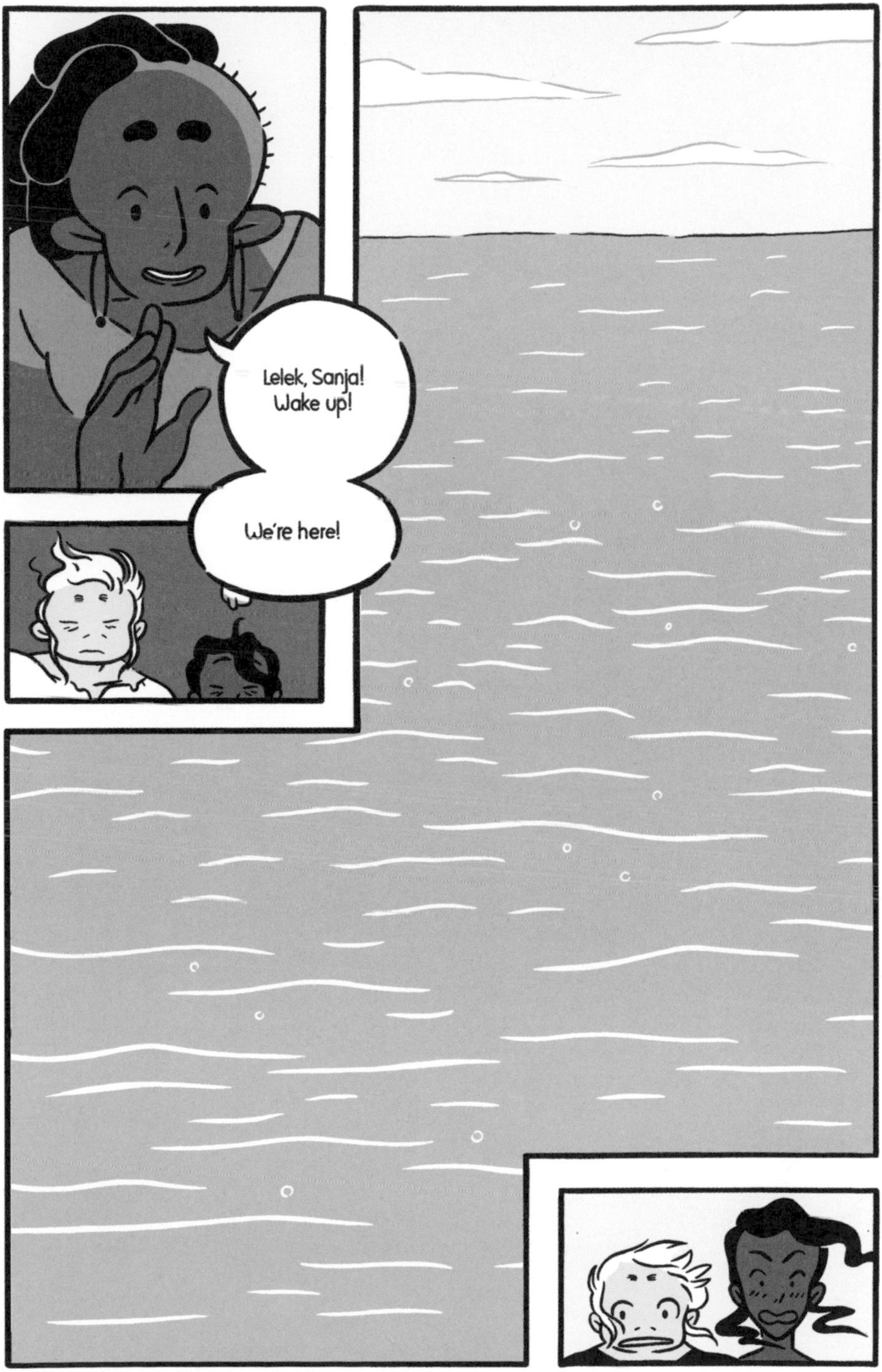
Lelek, Sanja! Wake up!
We're here!

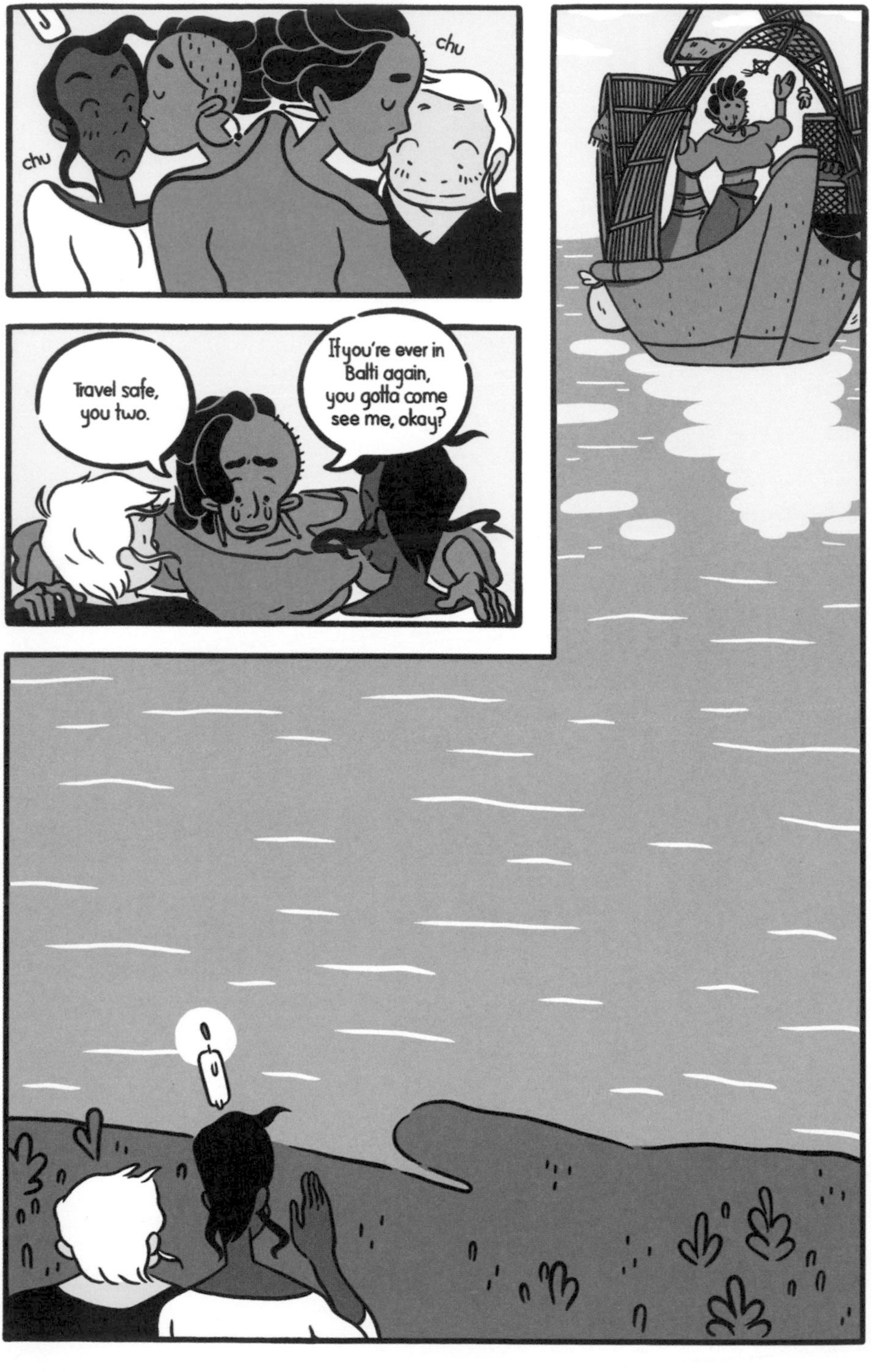
chu
chu
Travel safe, you two.
If you're ever in Balti again, you gotta come see me, okay?

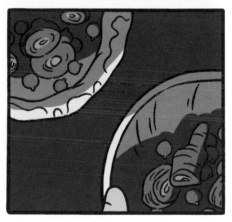

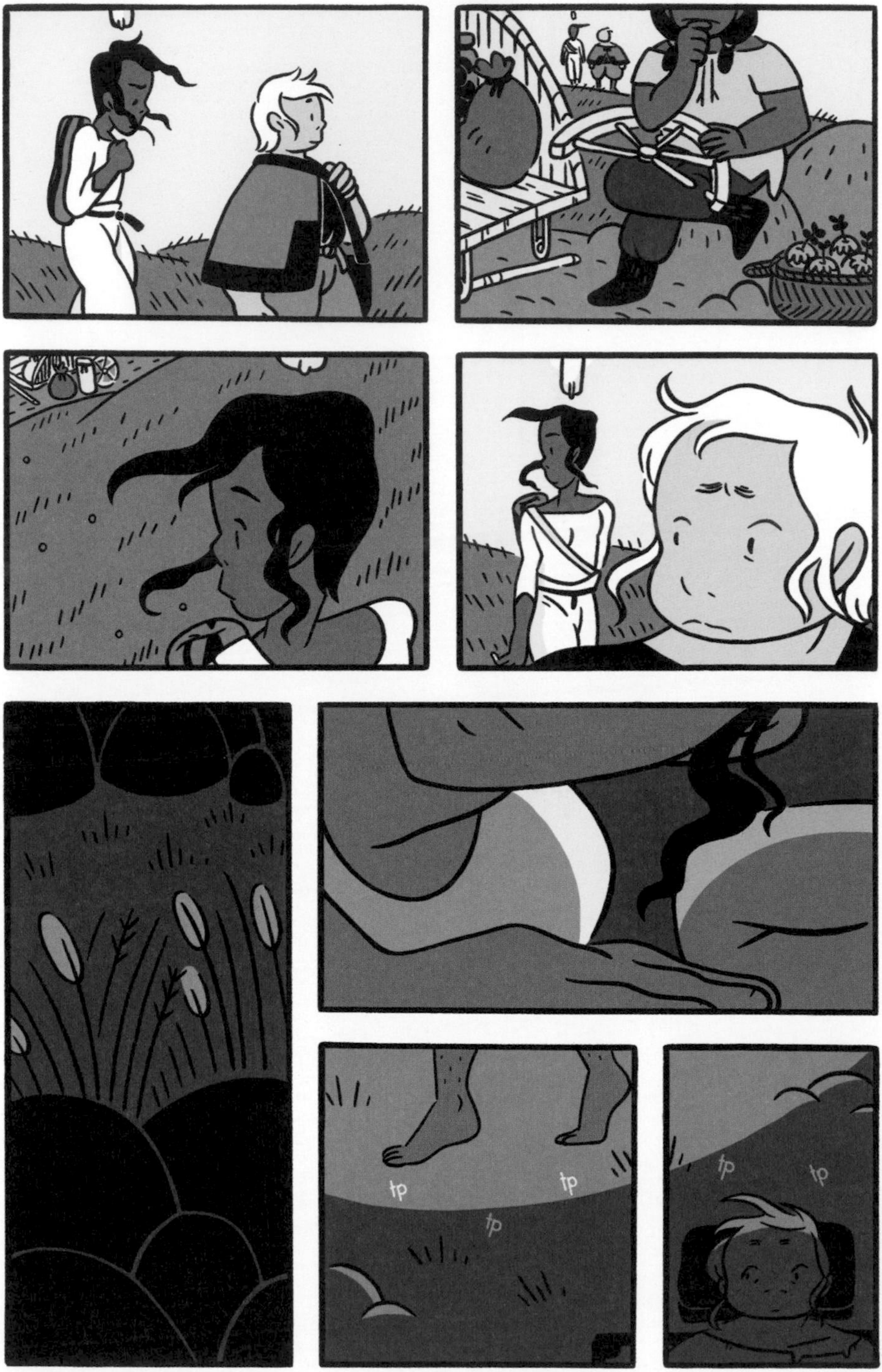
tp
tp
tp
tp
tp

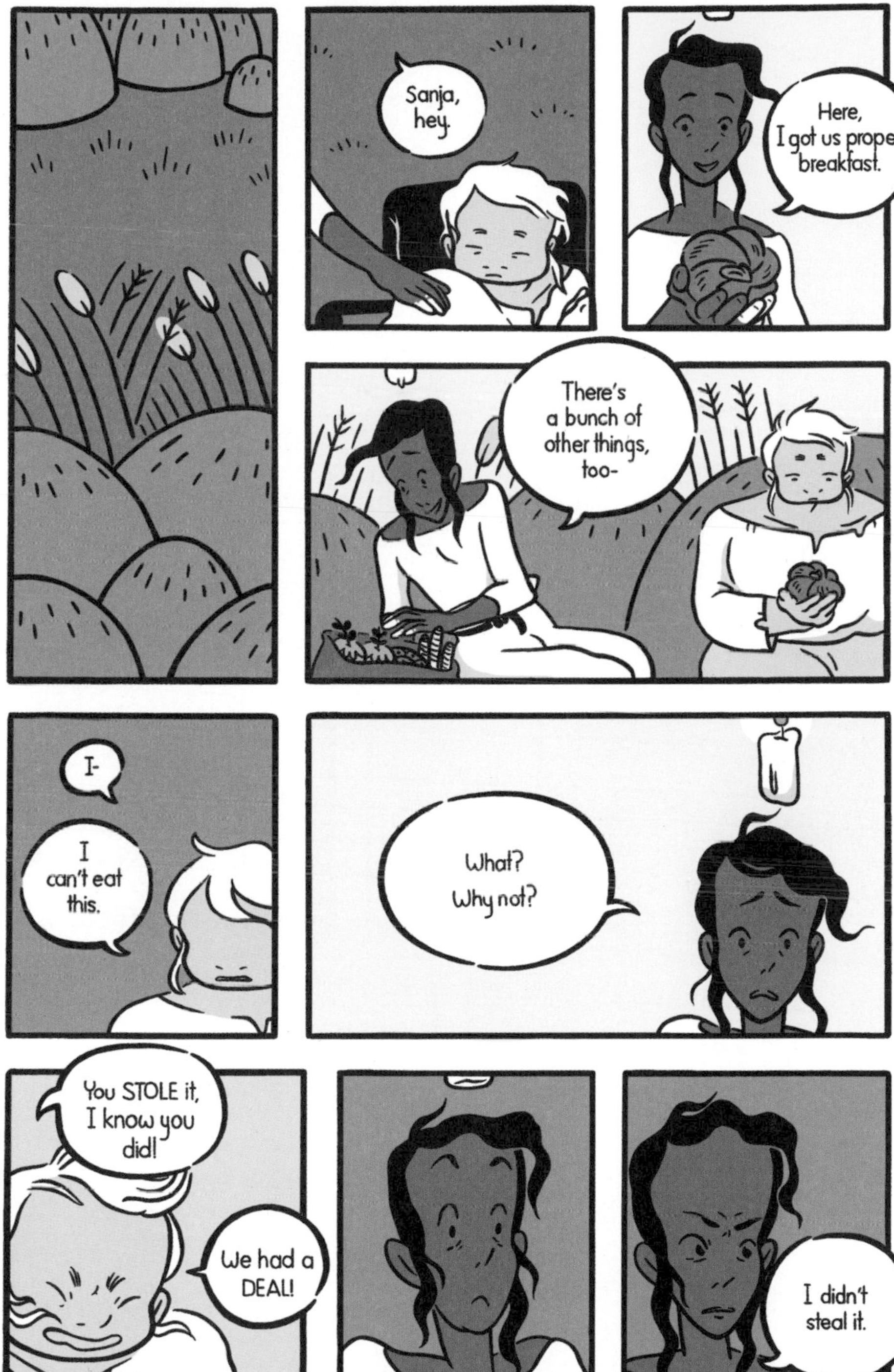
Sanja, hey.
Here, I got us proper breakfast.
There's a bunch of other things, too-
I-
I can't eat this.
What? Why not?
You STOLE it, I know you did!
We had a DEAL!
I didn't steal it.

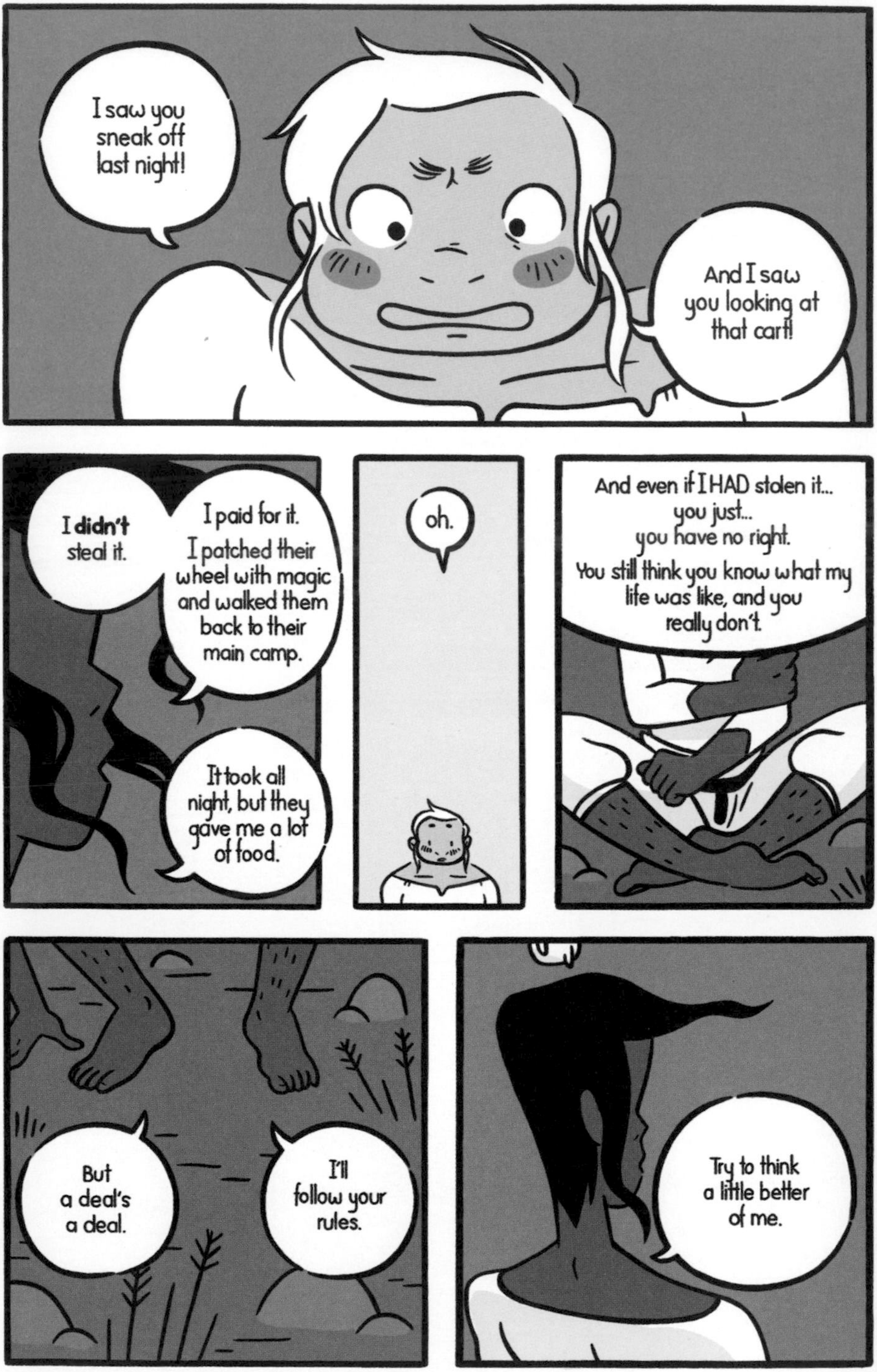
I saw you sneak off last night!
And I saw you looking at that cart!
I didn't steal it.
I paid for it. I patched their wheel with magic and walked them back to their main camp.
It took all night, but they gave me a lot of food.
oh.
And even if I HAD stolen it... you just... you have no right. You still think you know what my life was like, and you really don't.
But a deal's a deal.
I'll follow your rules.
Try to think a little better of me.

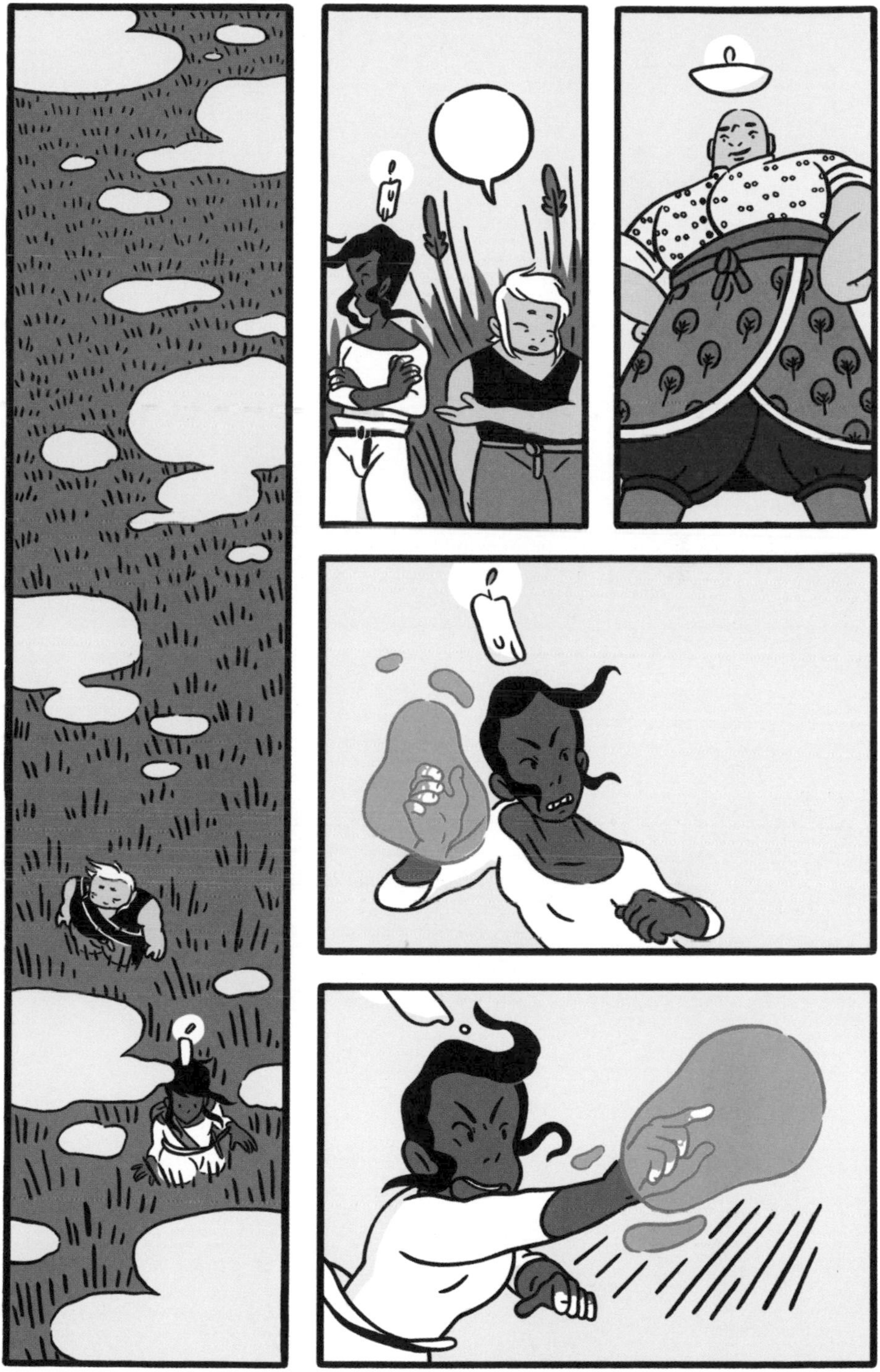

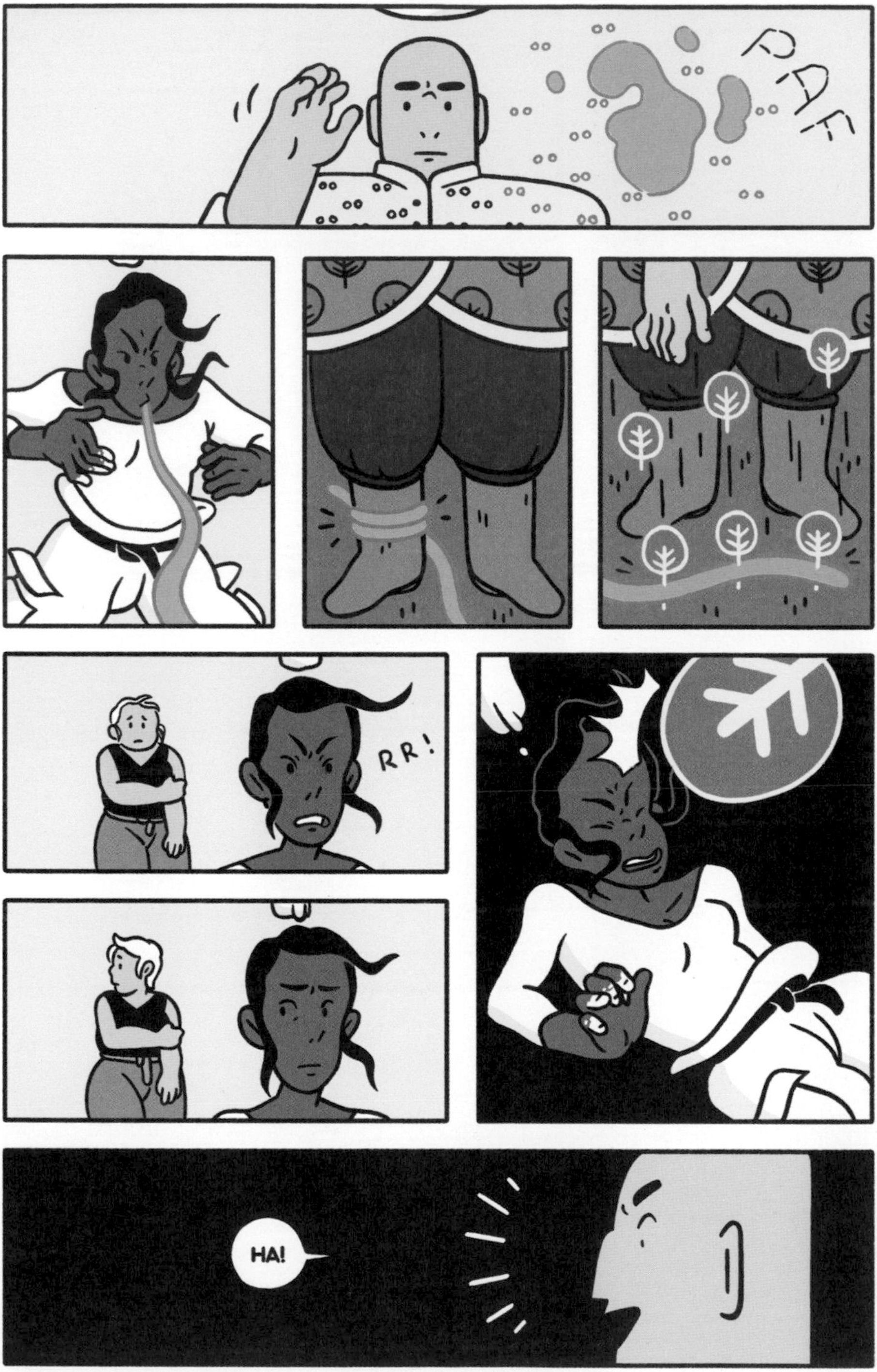
PAF
RR!
HA!

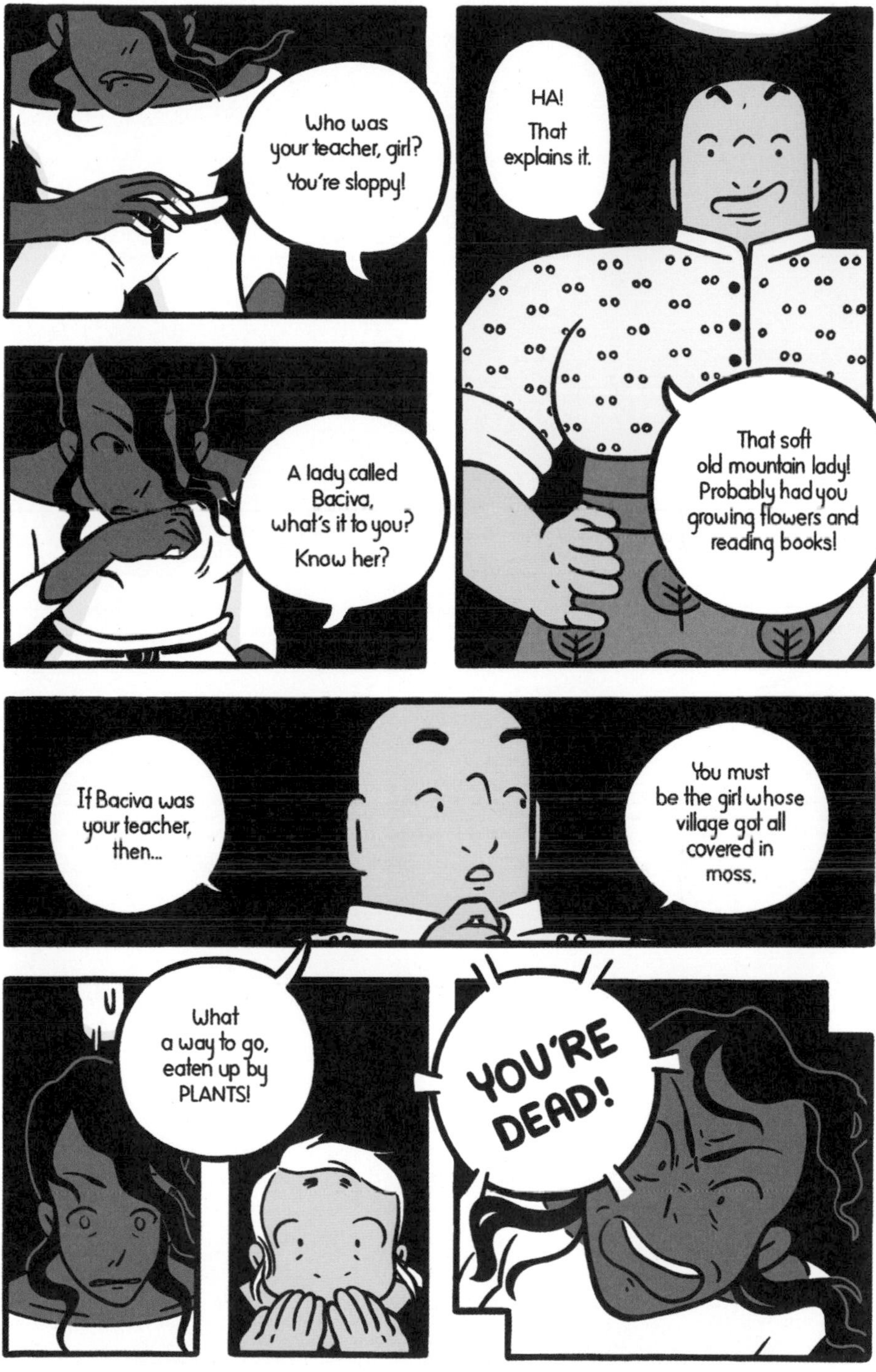
Who was your teacher, girl? You're sloppy!
HA! That explains it.
A lady called Baciva, what's it to you? Know her?
That soft old mountain lady! Probably had you growing flowers and reading books!
If Baciva was your teacher, then...
You must be the girl whose village got all covered in moss.
What a way to go, eaten up by PLANTS!
YOU'RE DEAD!

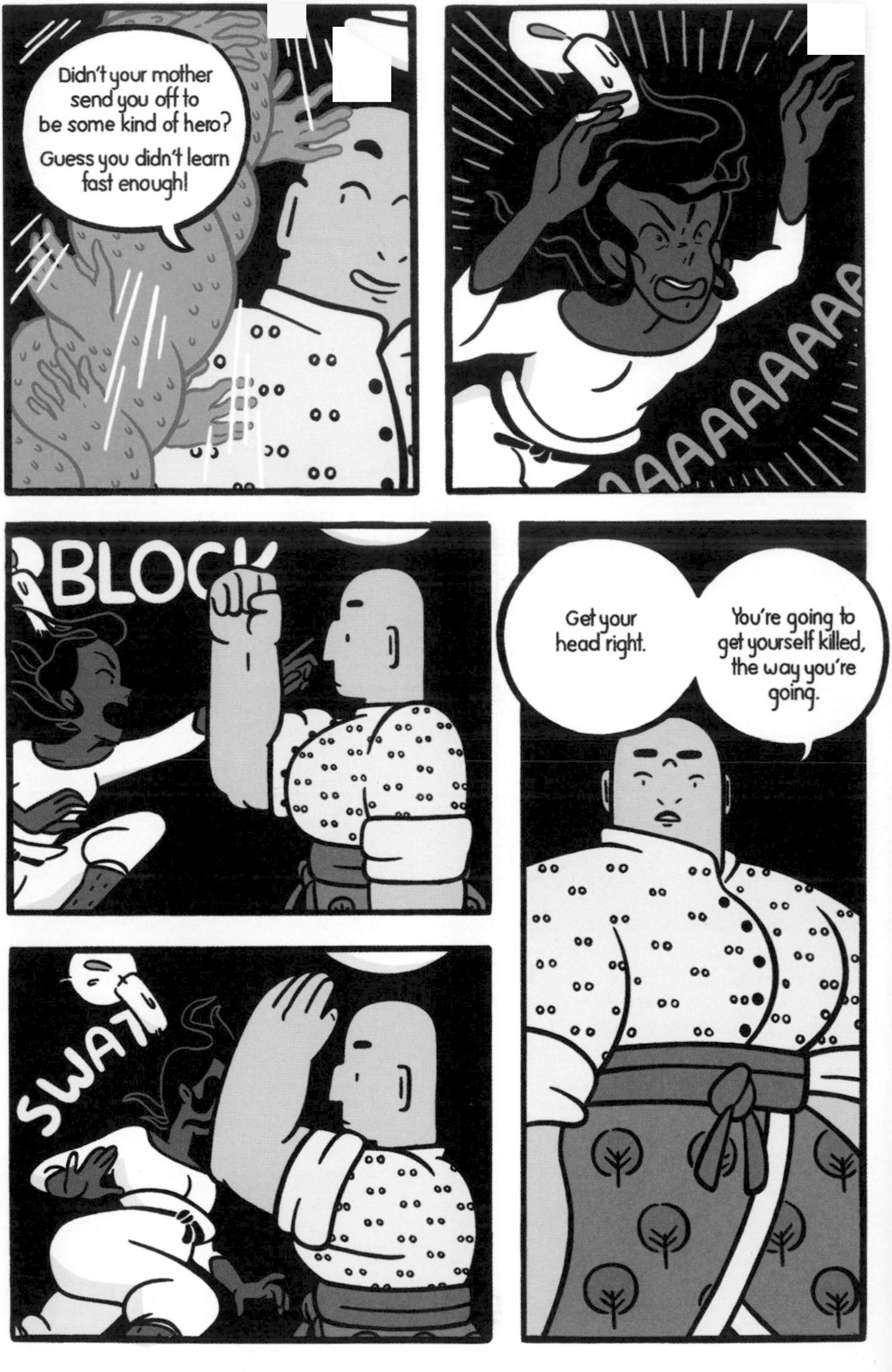
Didn't your mother send you off to be some kind of hero?
Guess you didn't learn fast enough!
AAAAAAAAA
BLOCK
SWAT
Get your head right.
You're going to get yourself killed, the way you're going.

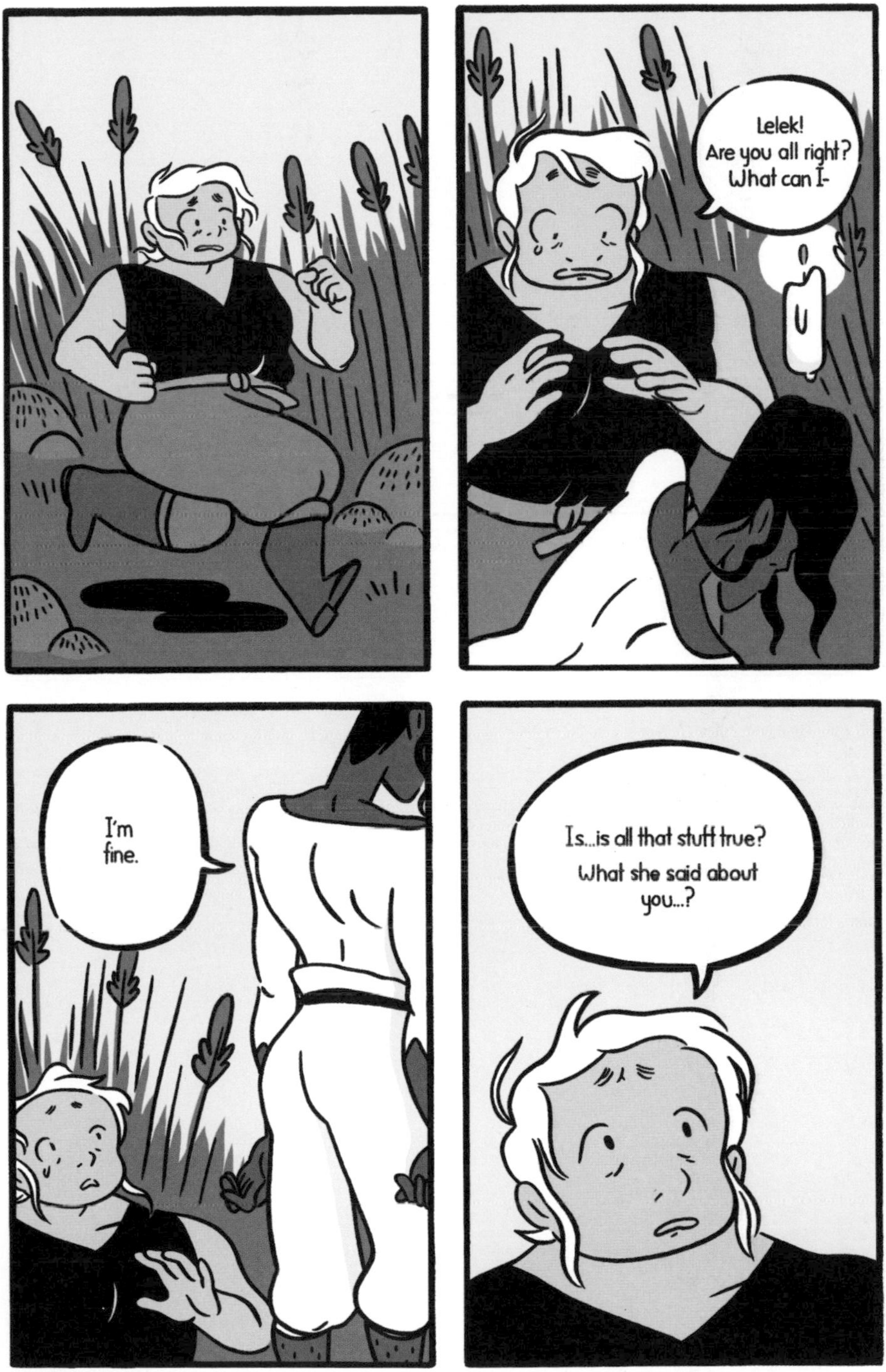
Lelek!
Are you all right? What can I-
I'm fine.
Is...is all that stuff true? What she said about you...?

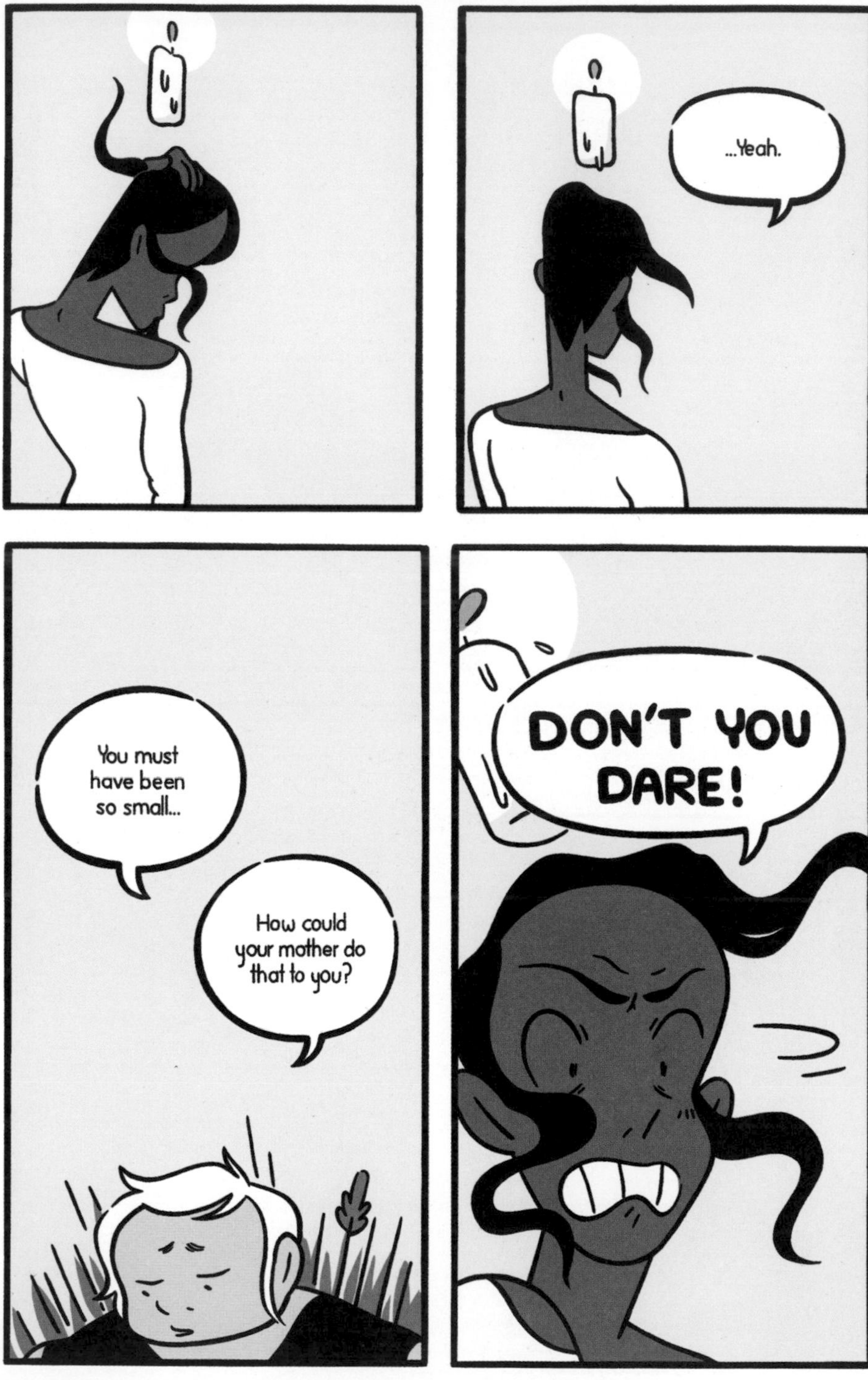
...Yeah.
You must have been so small...
How could your mother do that to you?
DON'T YOU DARE!

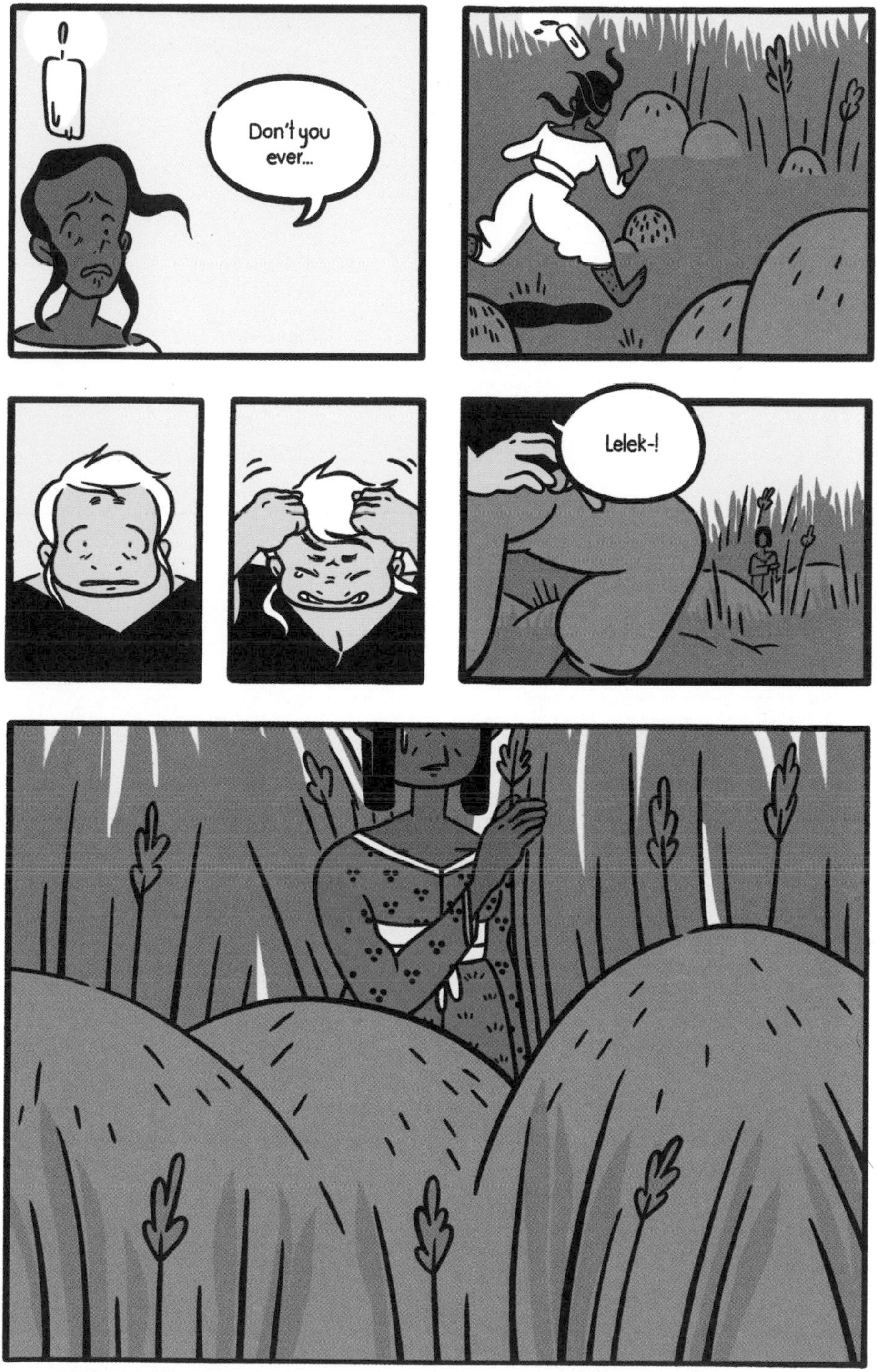

Don't you ever...
Lelek-!

Part 5

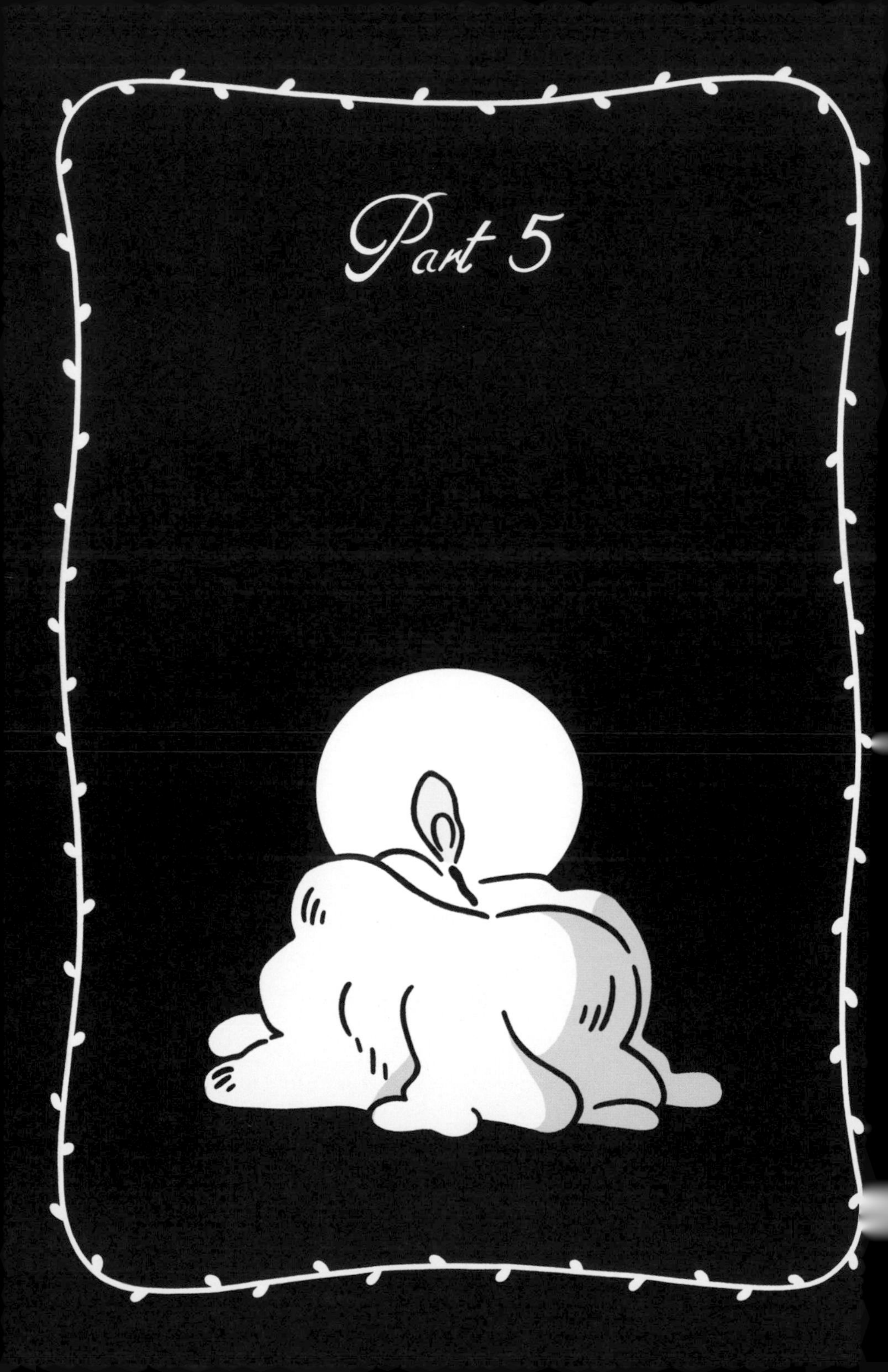

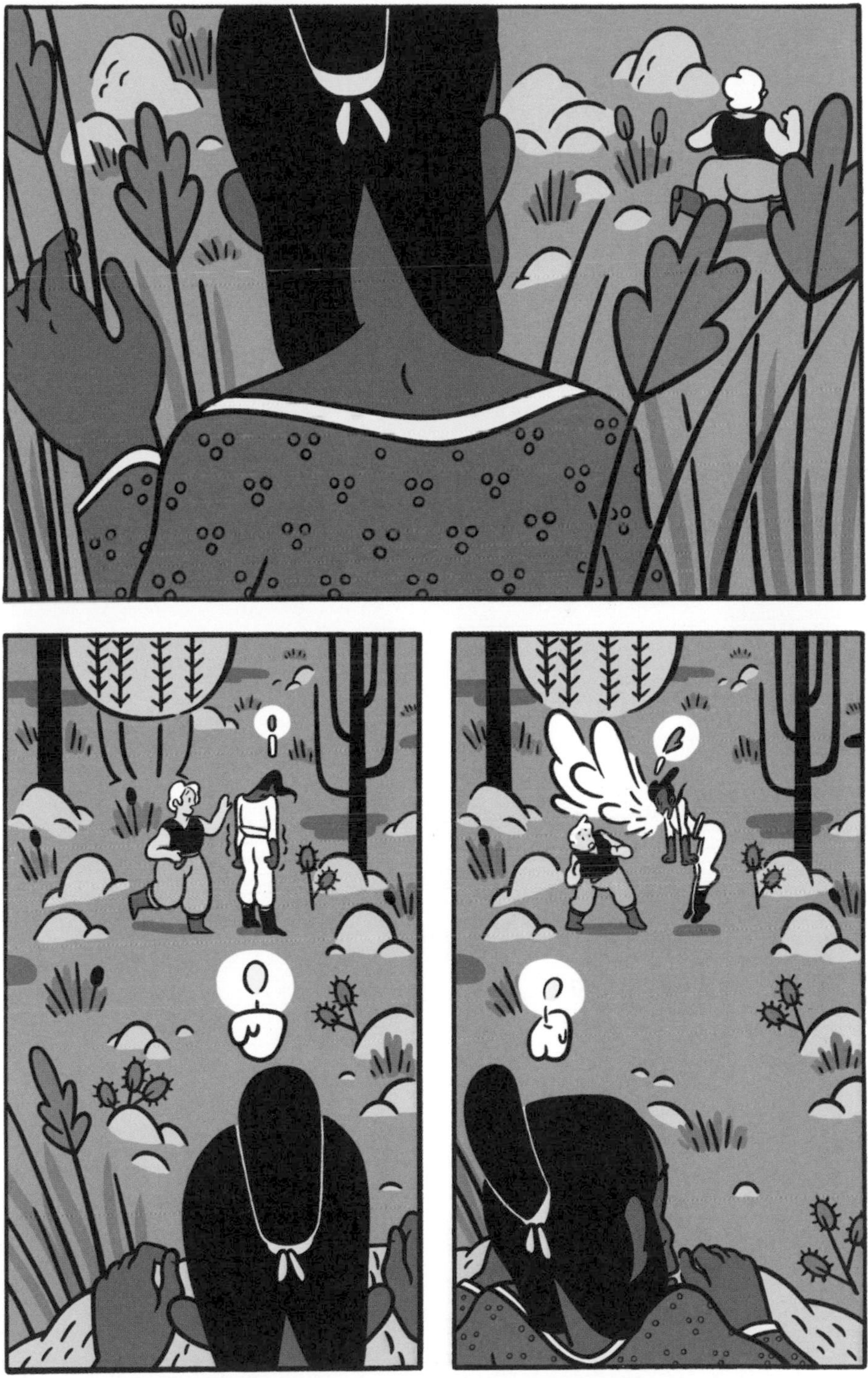

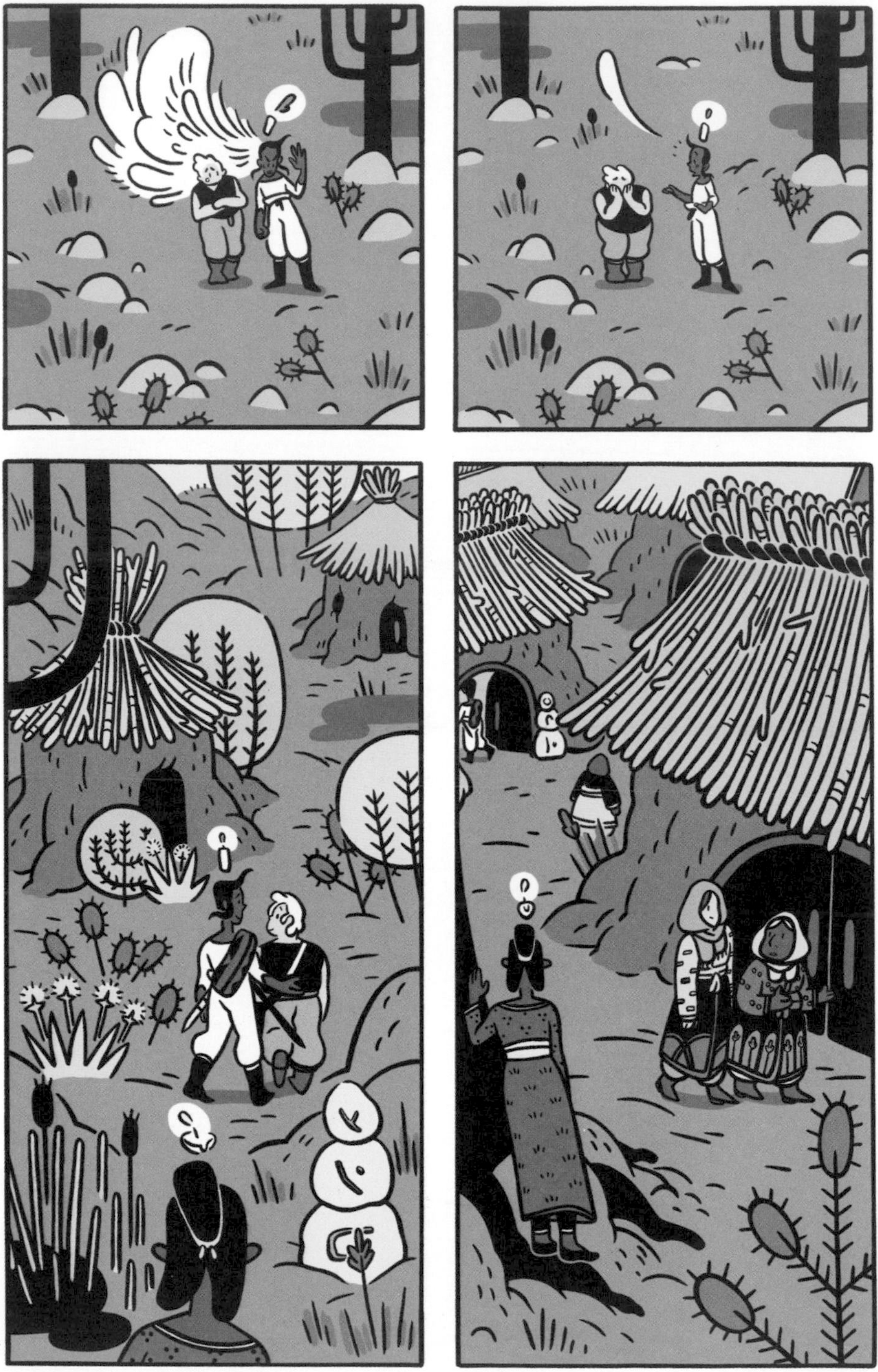

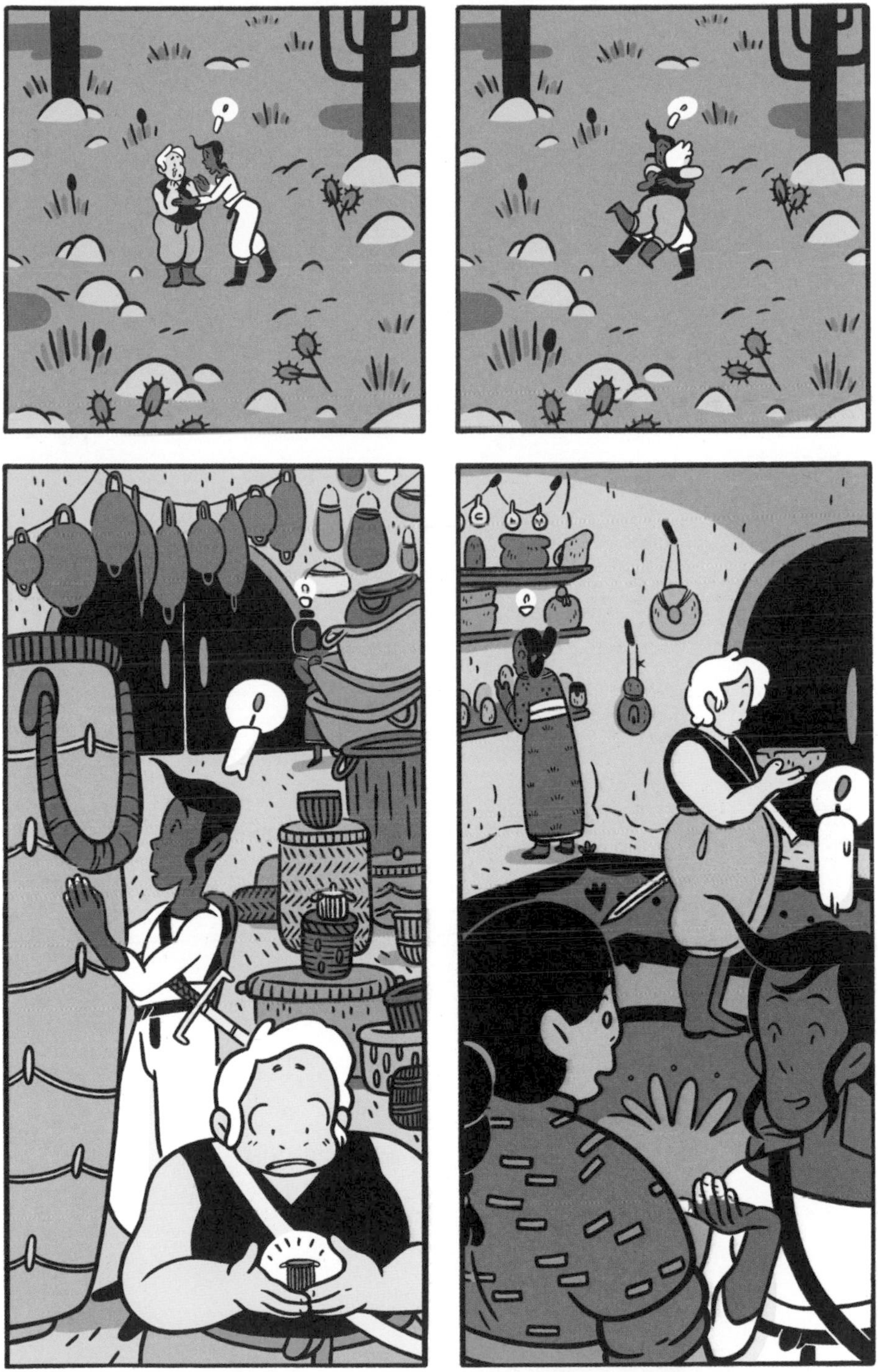

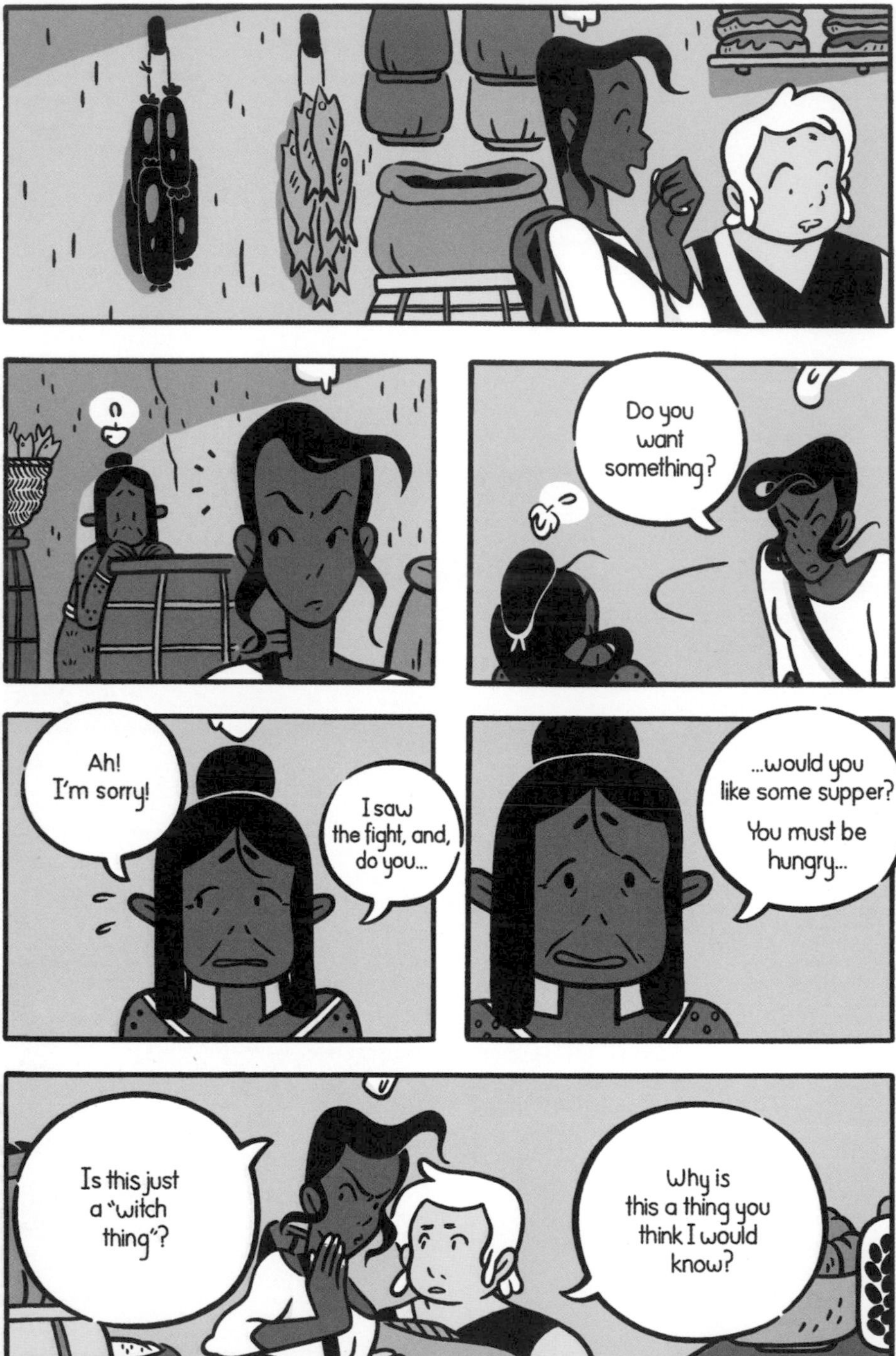
Do you want something?
Ah! I'm sorry!
I saw the fight, and, do you...
...would you like some supper?
You must be hungry...
Is this just a "witch thing"?
Why is this a thing you think I would know?

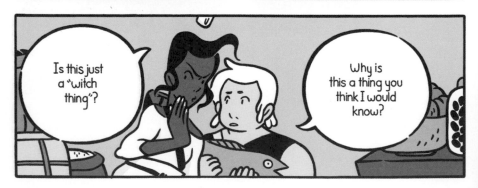

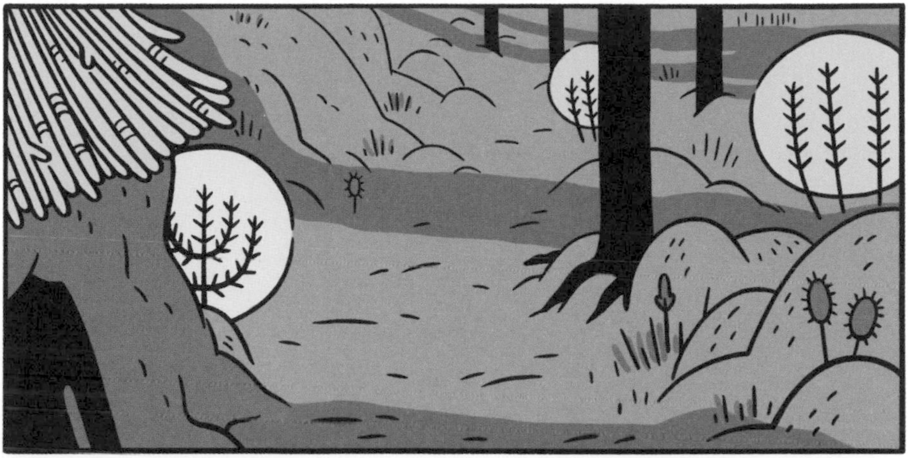

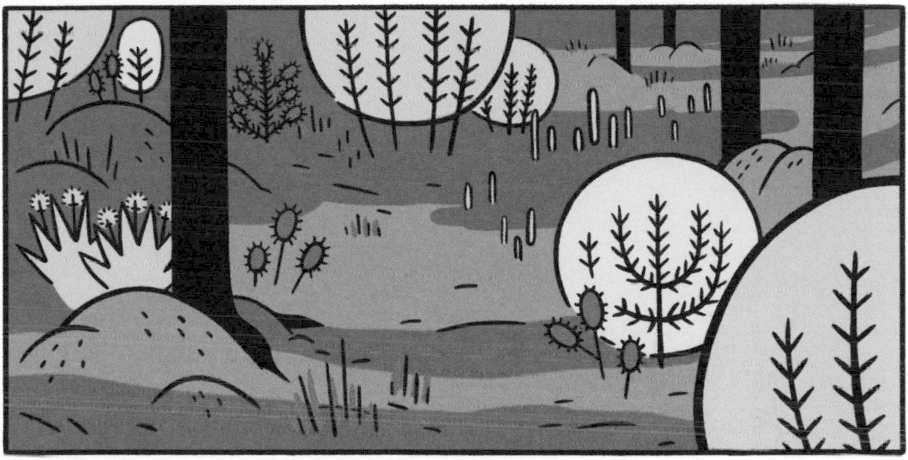

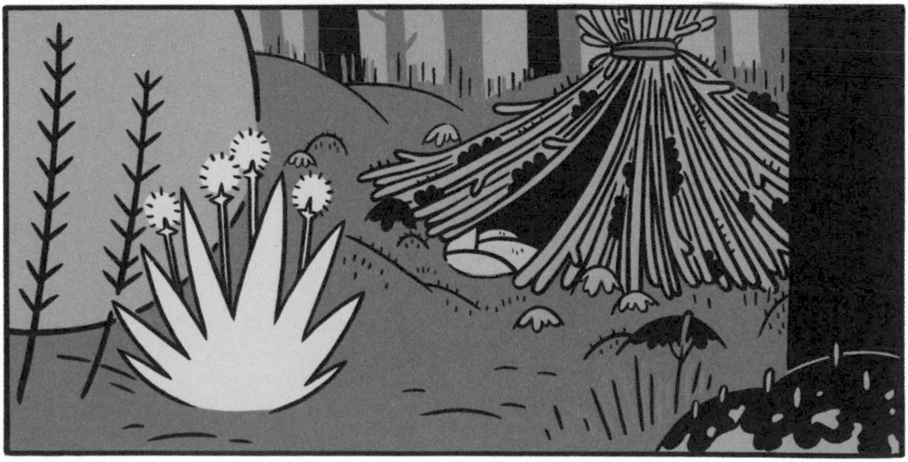

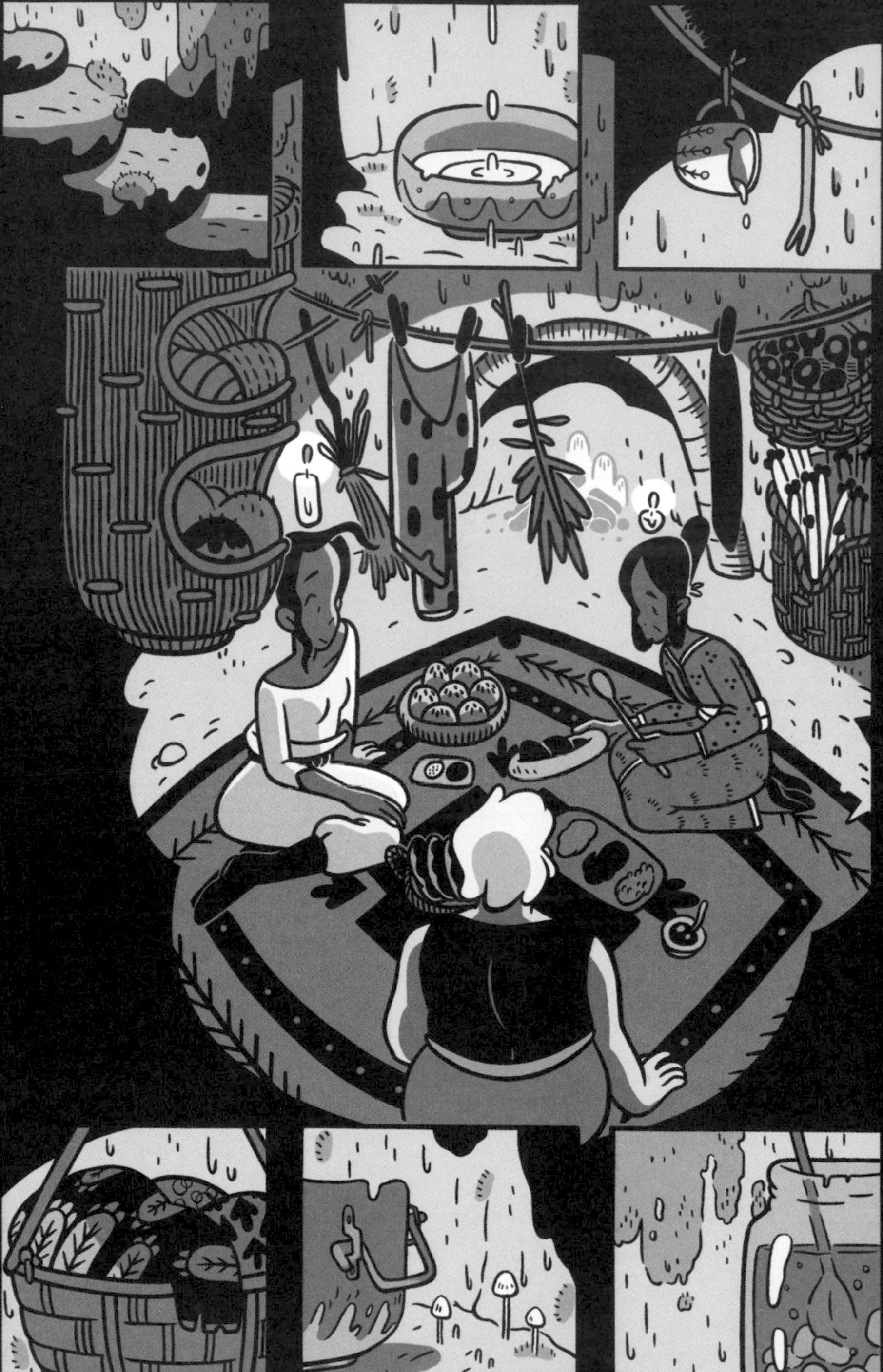

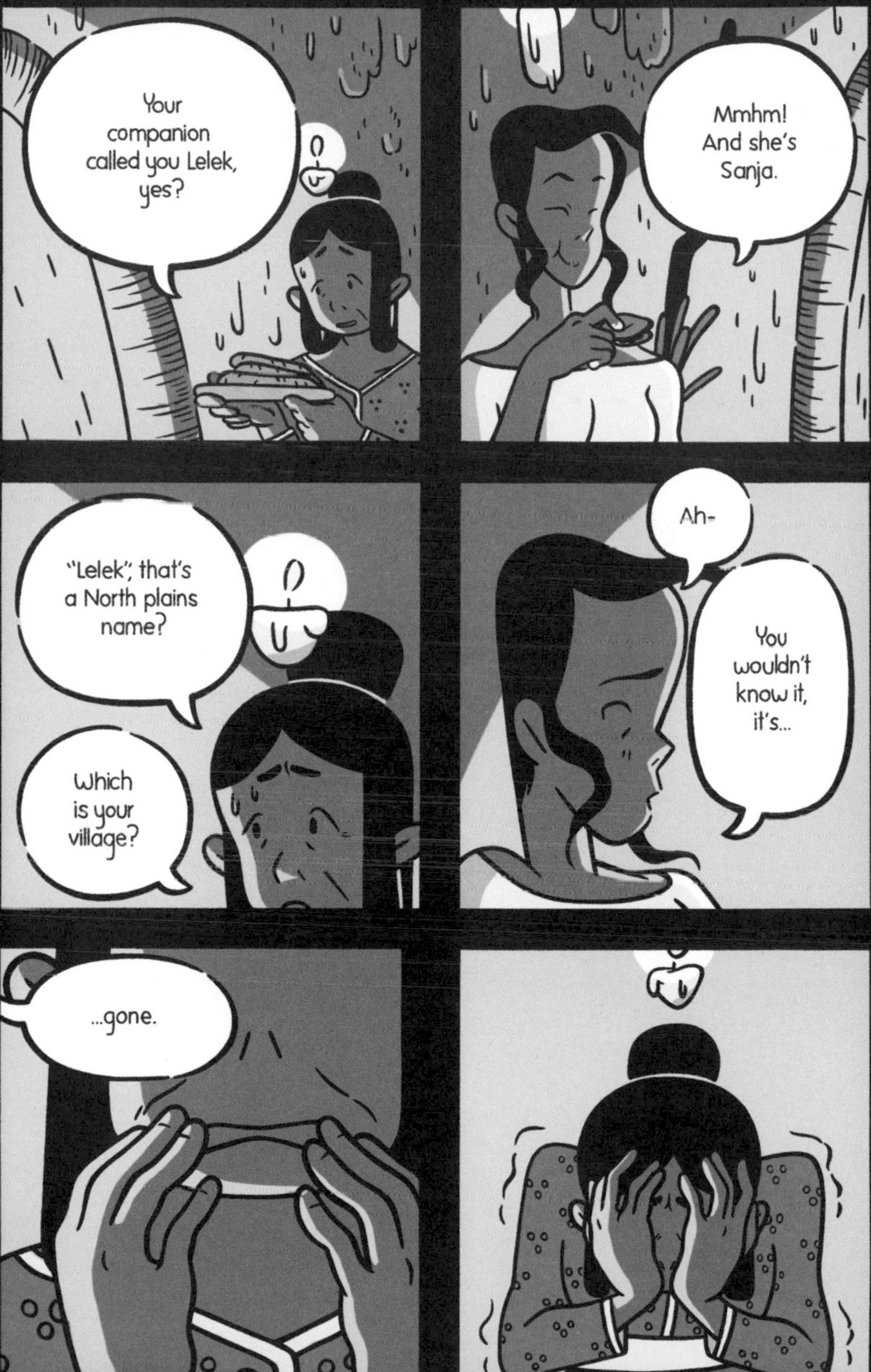

Your companion called you Lelek, yes?
Mmhm! And she's Sanja.
"Lelek", that's a North plains name?
Which is your village?
Ah-
You wouldn't know it, it's...
...gone.

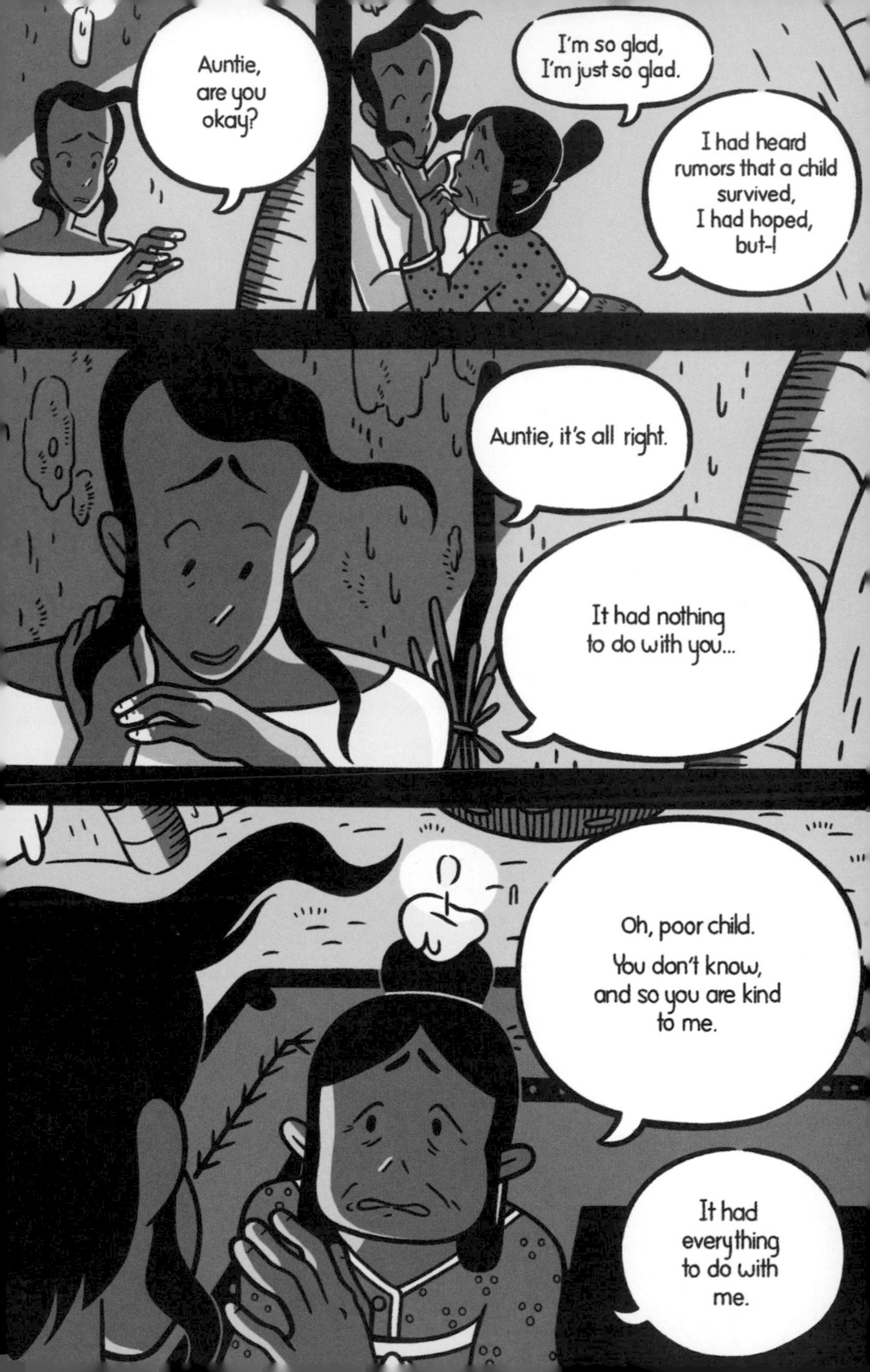

Auntie, are you okay?
I'm so glad, I'm just so glad.
I had heard rumors that a child survived, I had hoped, but-!
Auntie, it's all right.
It had nothing to do with you...
Oh, poor child.
You don't know, and so you are kind to me.
It had everything to do with me.

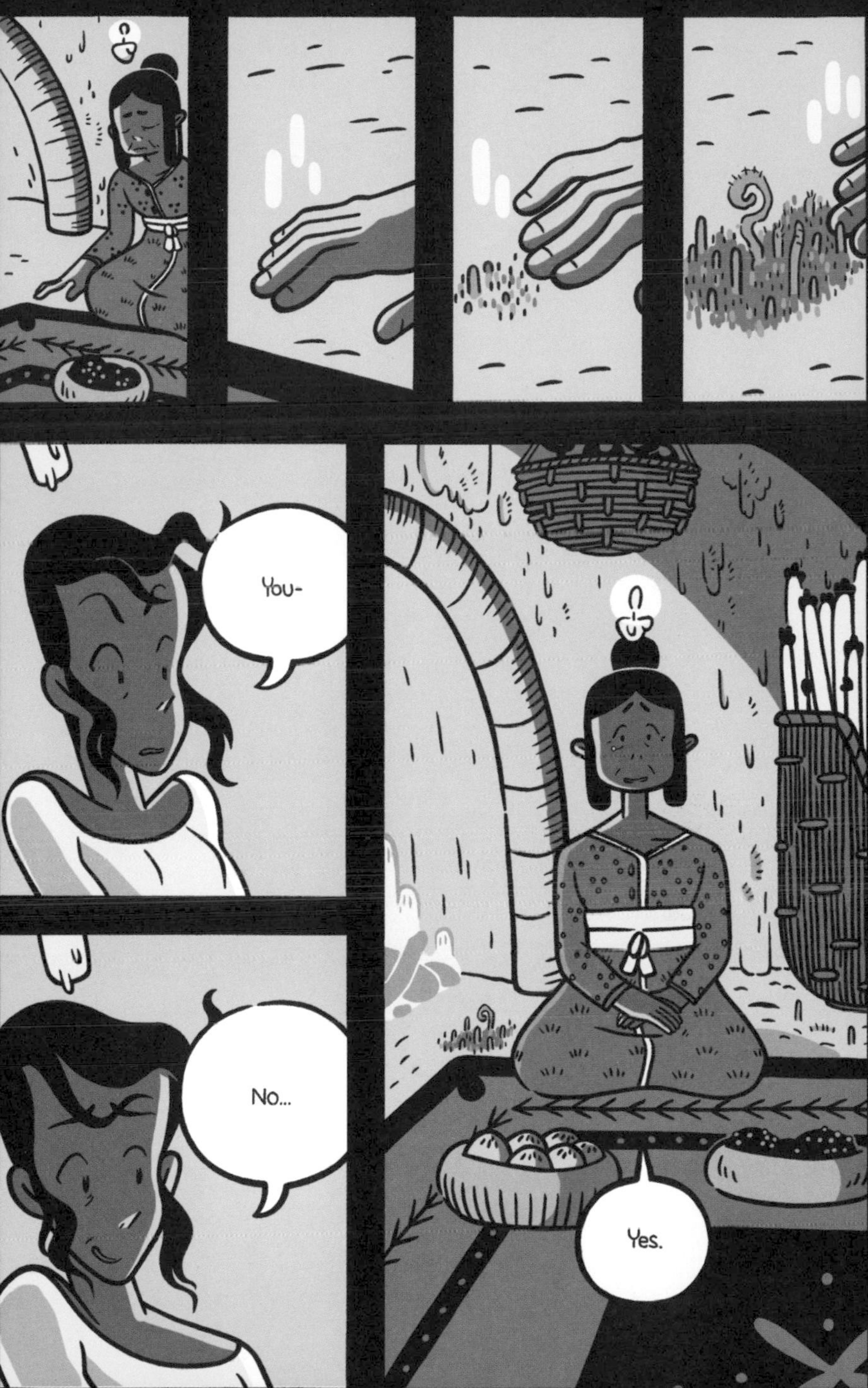
You-
No...
Yes.

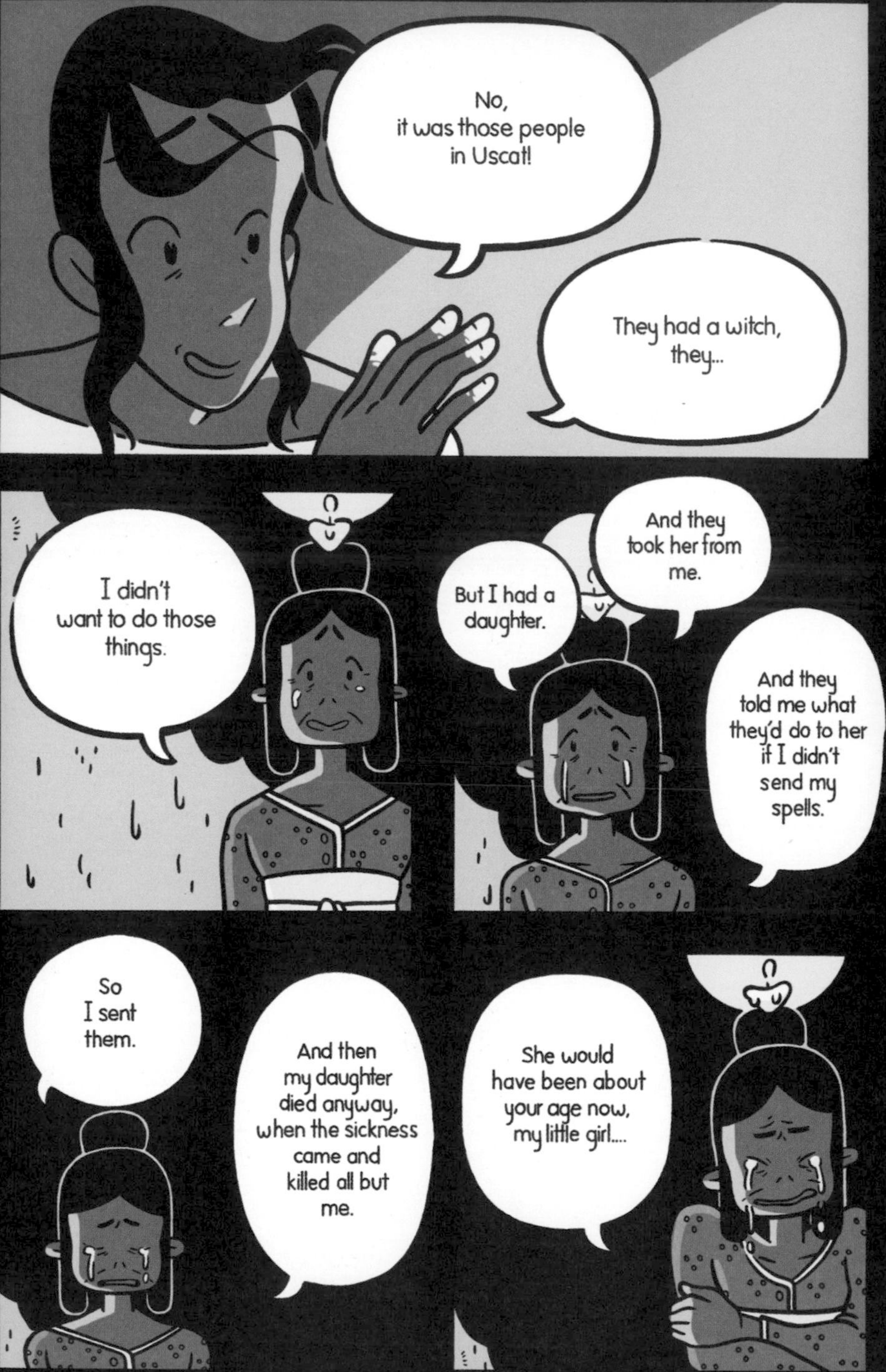
No, it was those people in Uscat!
They had a witch, they...
I didn't want to do those things.
But I had a daughter.
And they took her from me.
And they told me what they'd do to her if I didn't send my spells.
So I sent them.
And then my daughter died anyway, when the sickness came and killed all but me.
She would have been about your age now, my little girl....

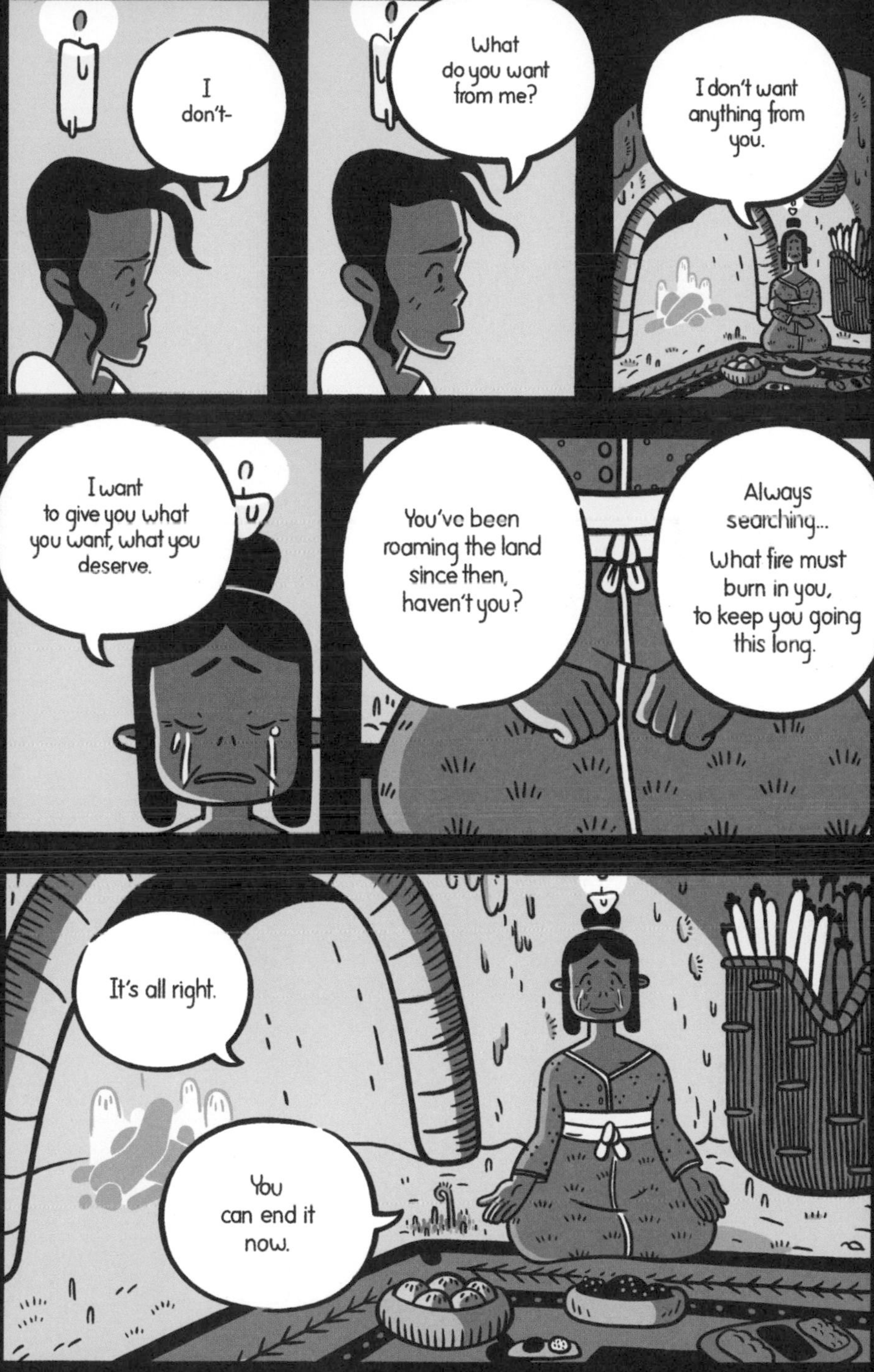
I don't-
What do you want from me?
I don't want anything from you.
I want to give you what you want, what you deserve.
You've been roaming the land since then, haven't you?
Always searching...
What fire must burn in you, to keep you going this long.
It's all right.
You can end it now.

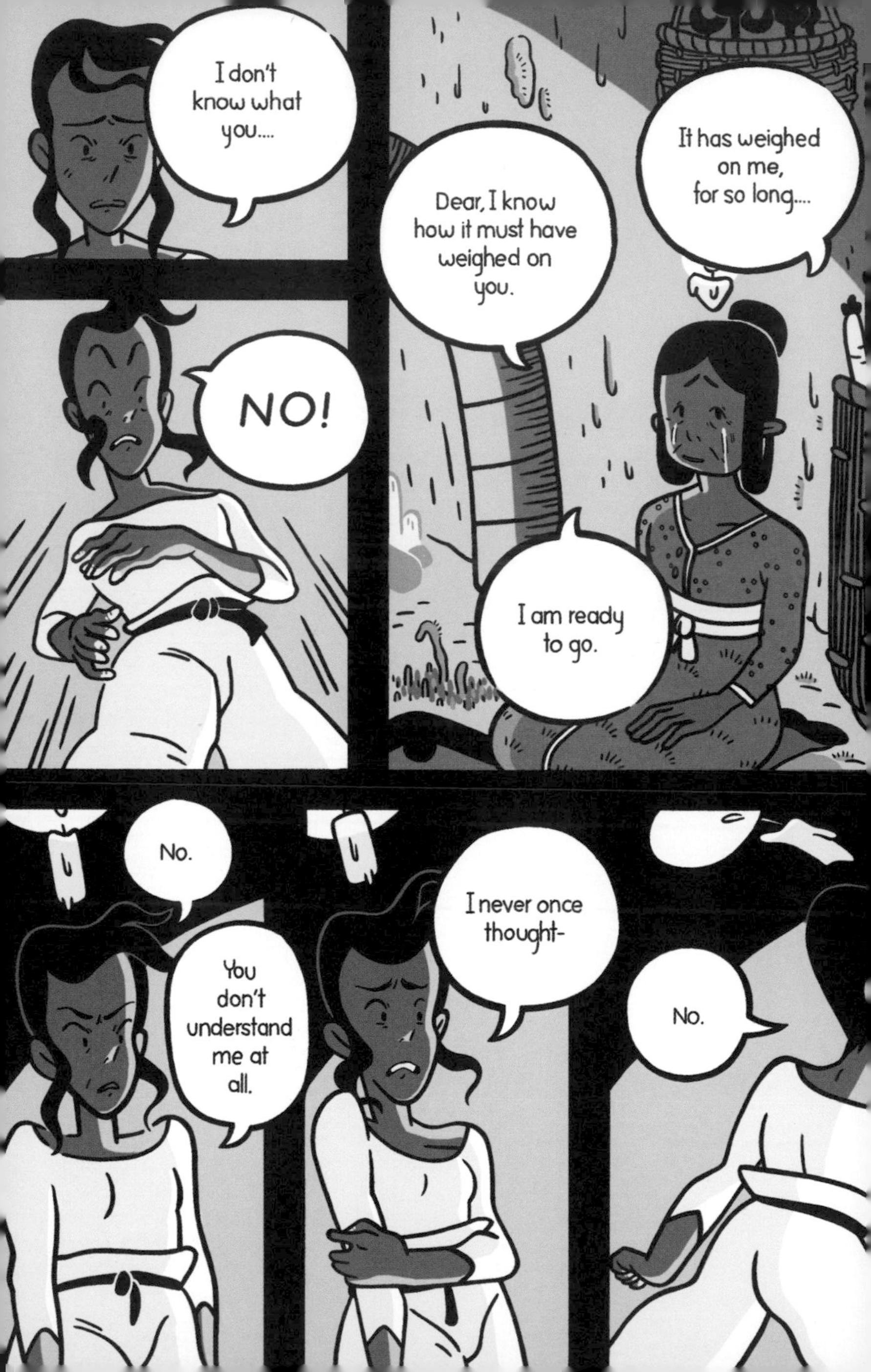

I don't know what you....
NO!
Dear, I know how it must have weighed on you.
It has weighed on me, for so long....
I am ready to go.
No.
You don't understand me at all.
I never once thought-
No.

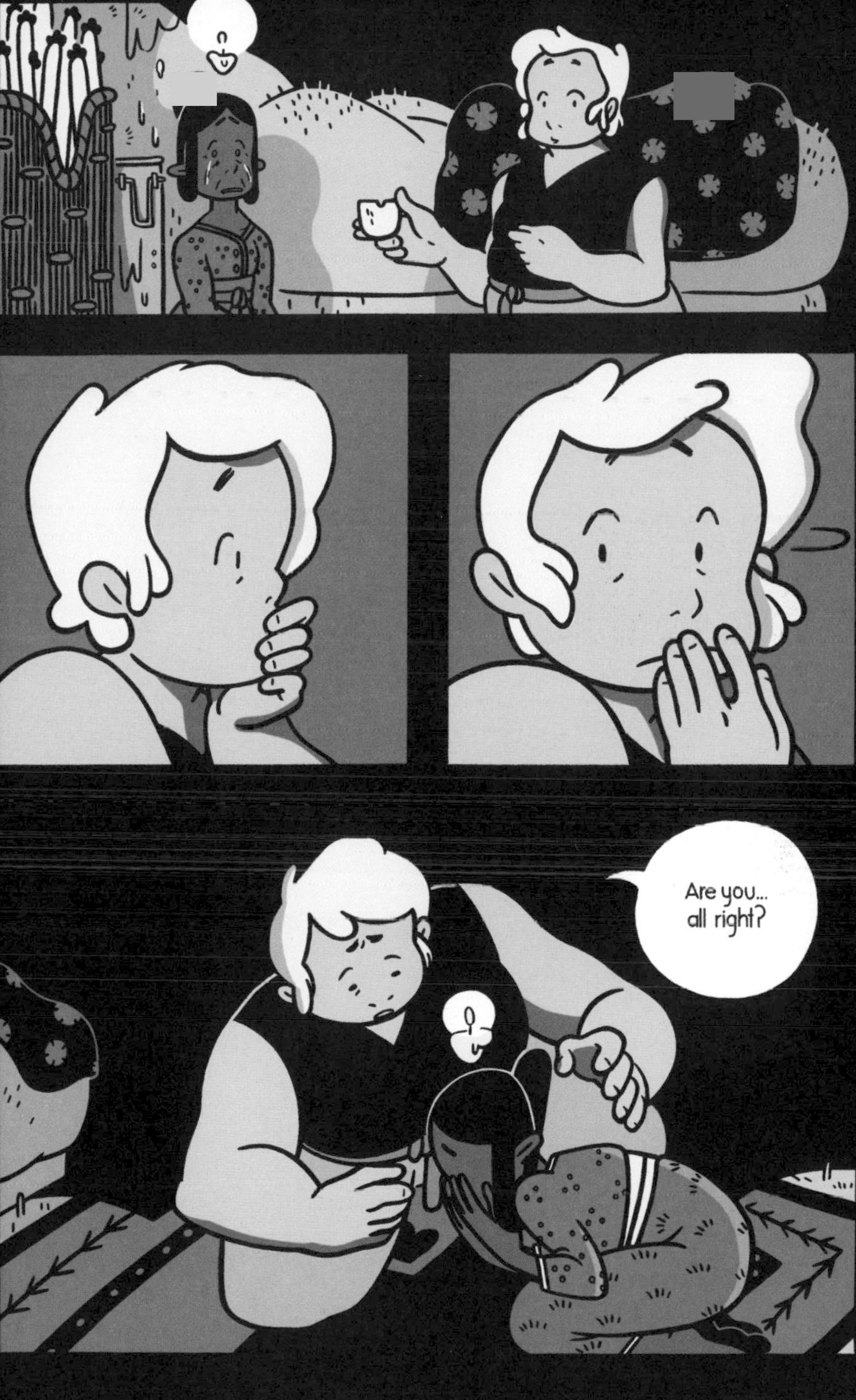
Are you...
all right?

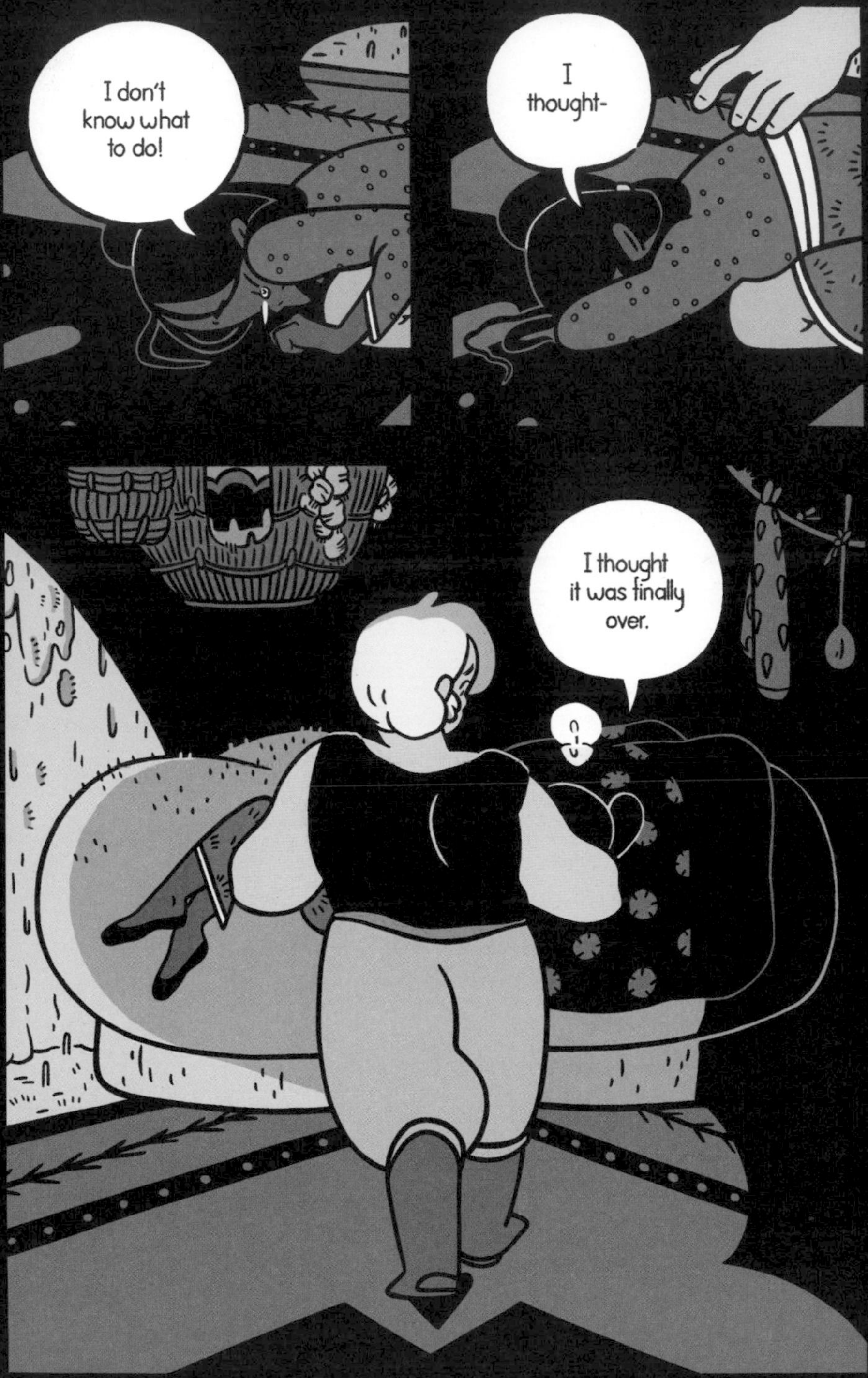
I don't know what to do!
I thought-
I thought it was finally over.

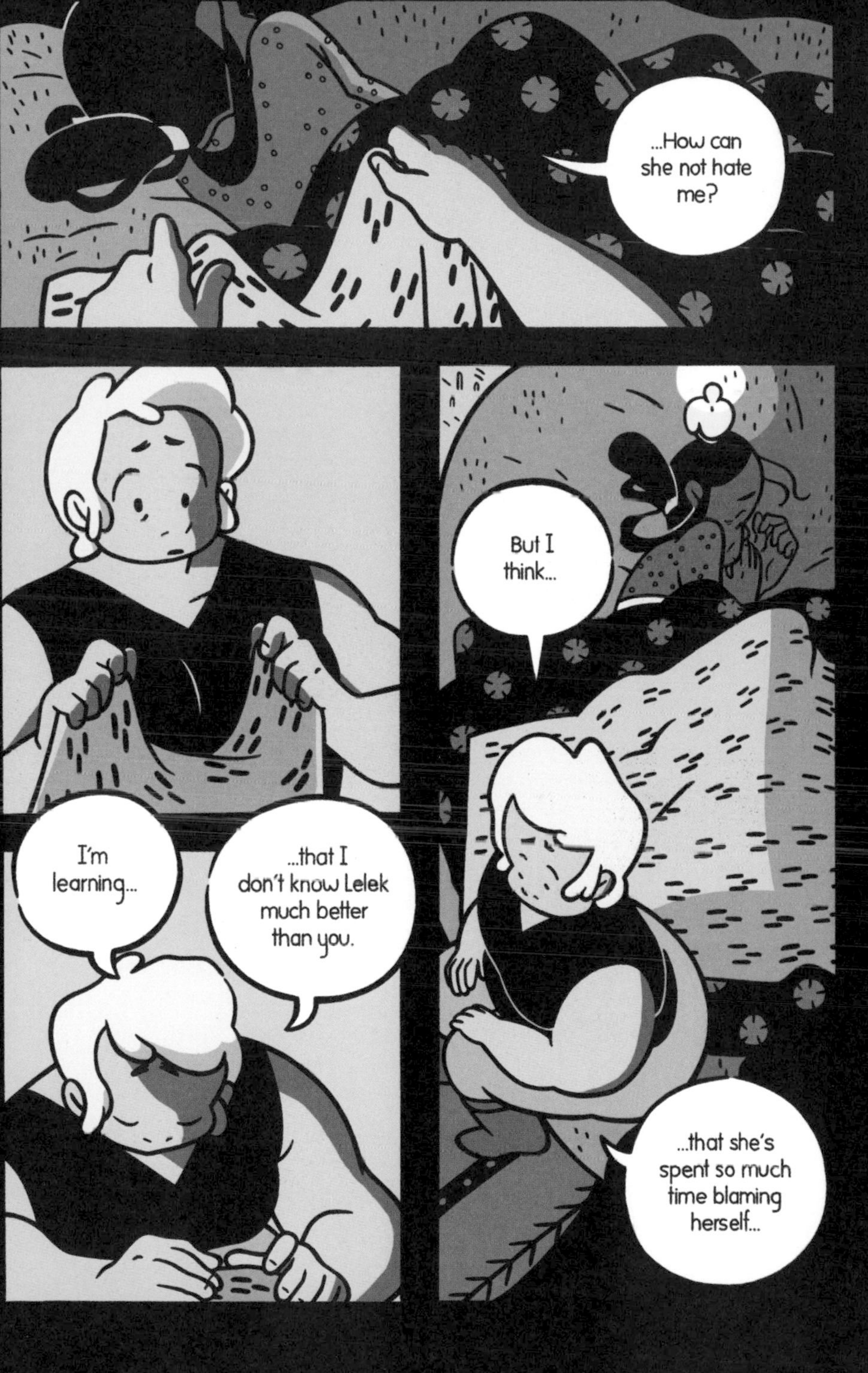
...How can she not hate me?
But I think...
I'm learning...
...that I don't know Lelek much better than you.
...that she's spent so much time blaming herself...

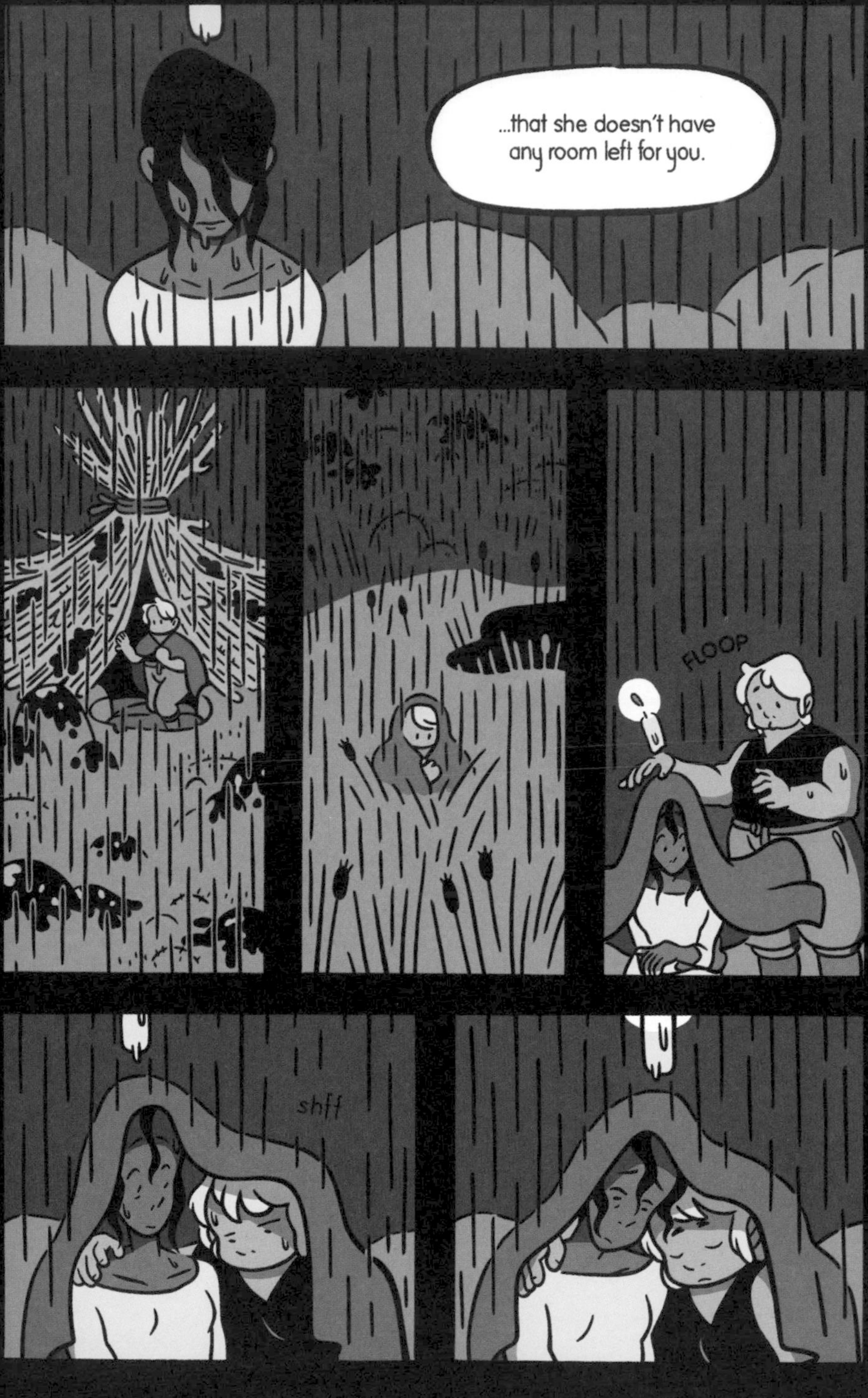
...that she doesn't have
any room left for you.
FLOOP
shft

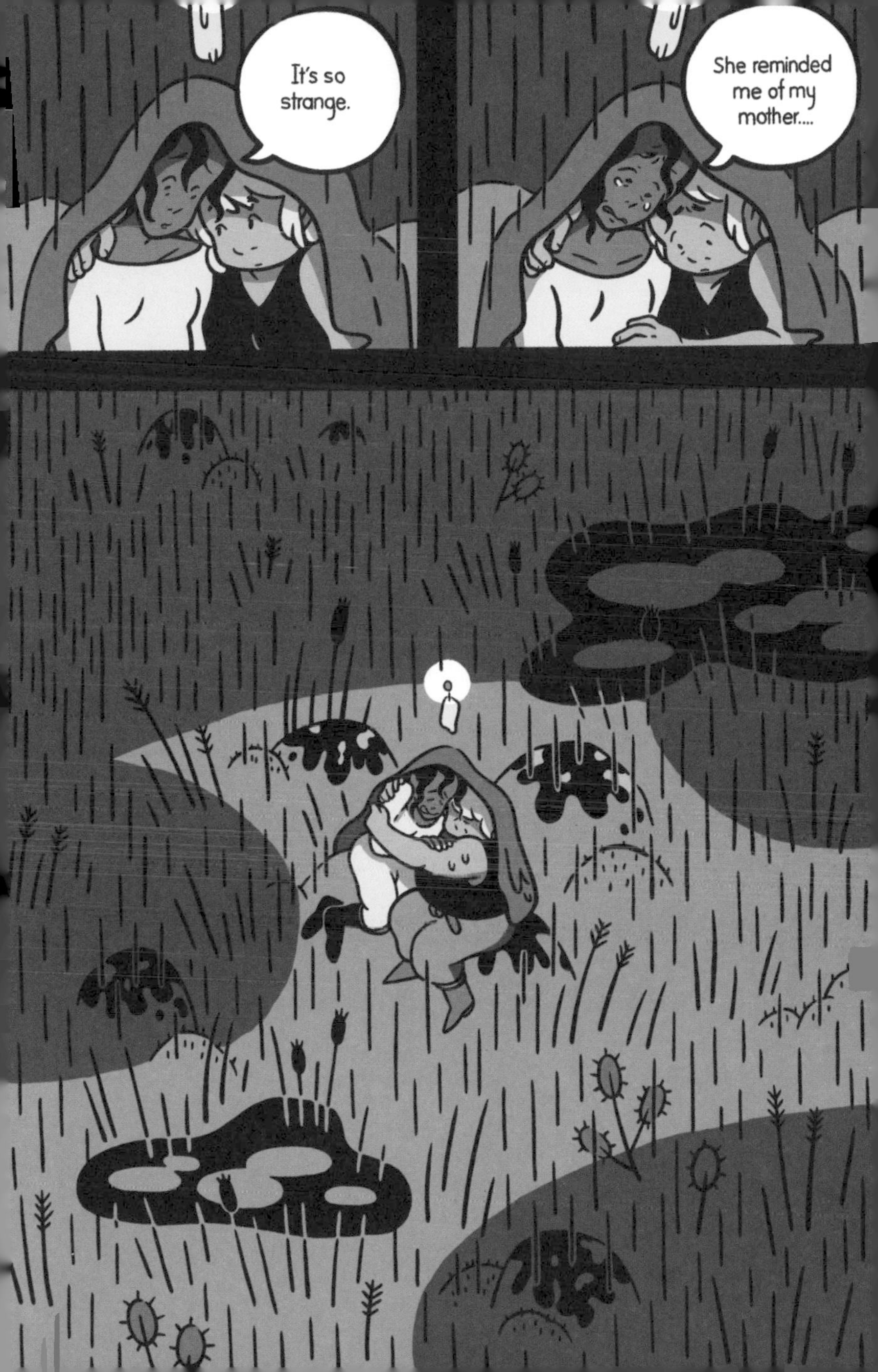

It's so strange.
She reminded me of my mother....

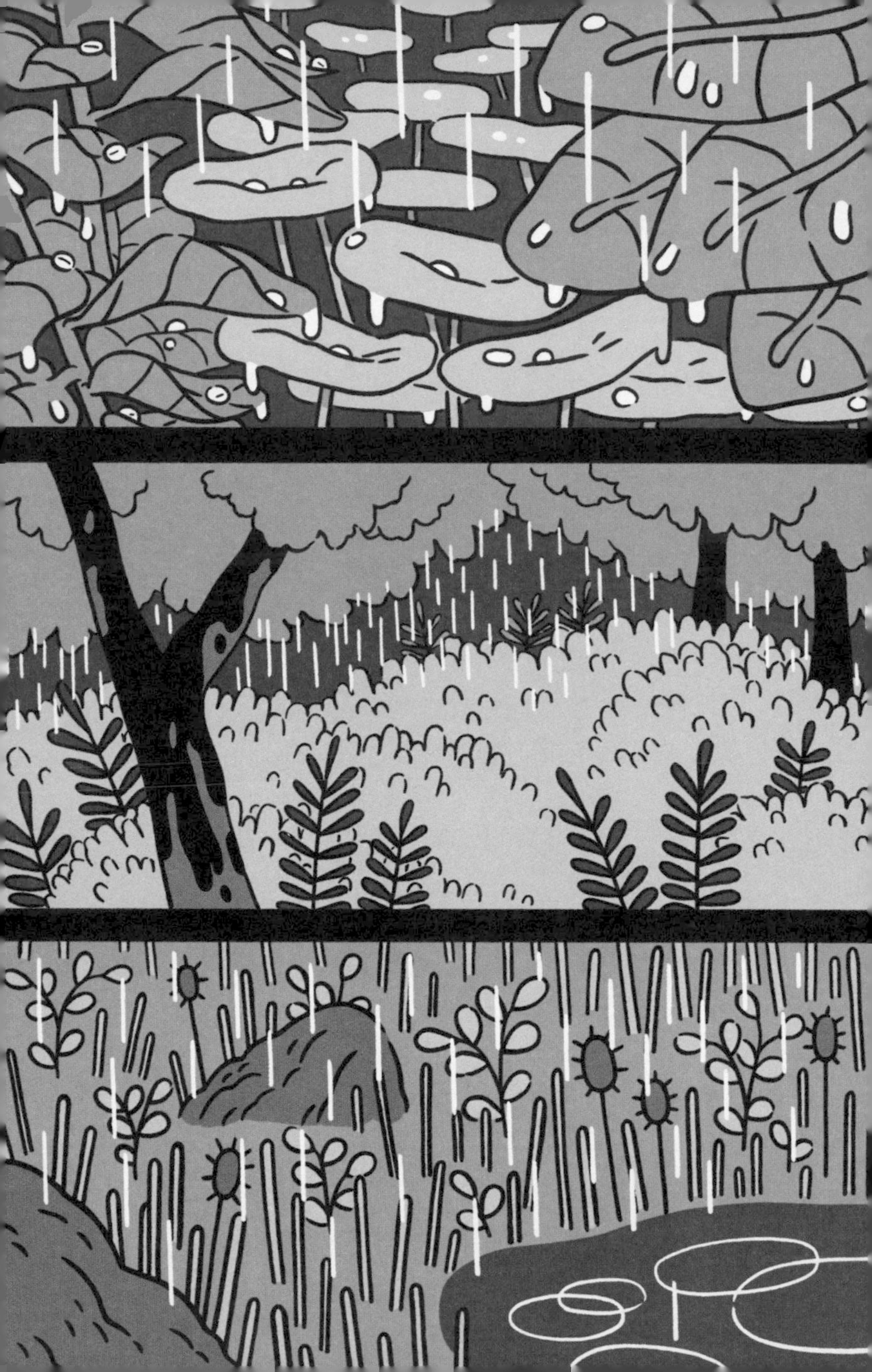

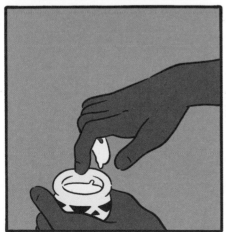

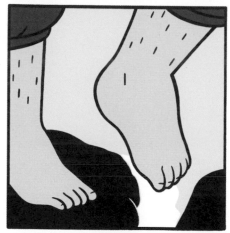

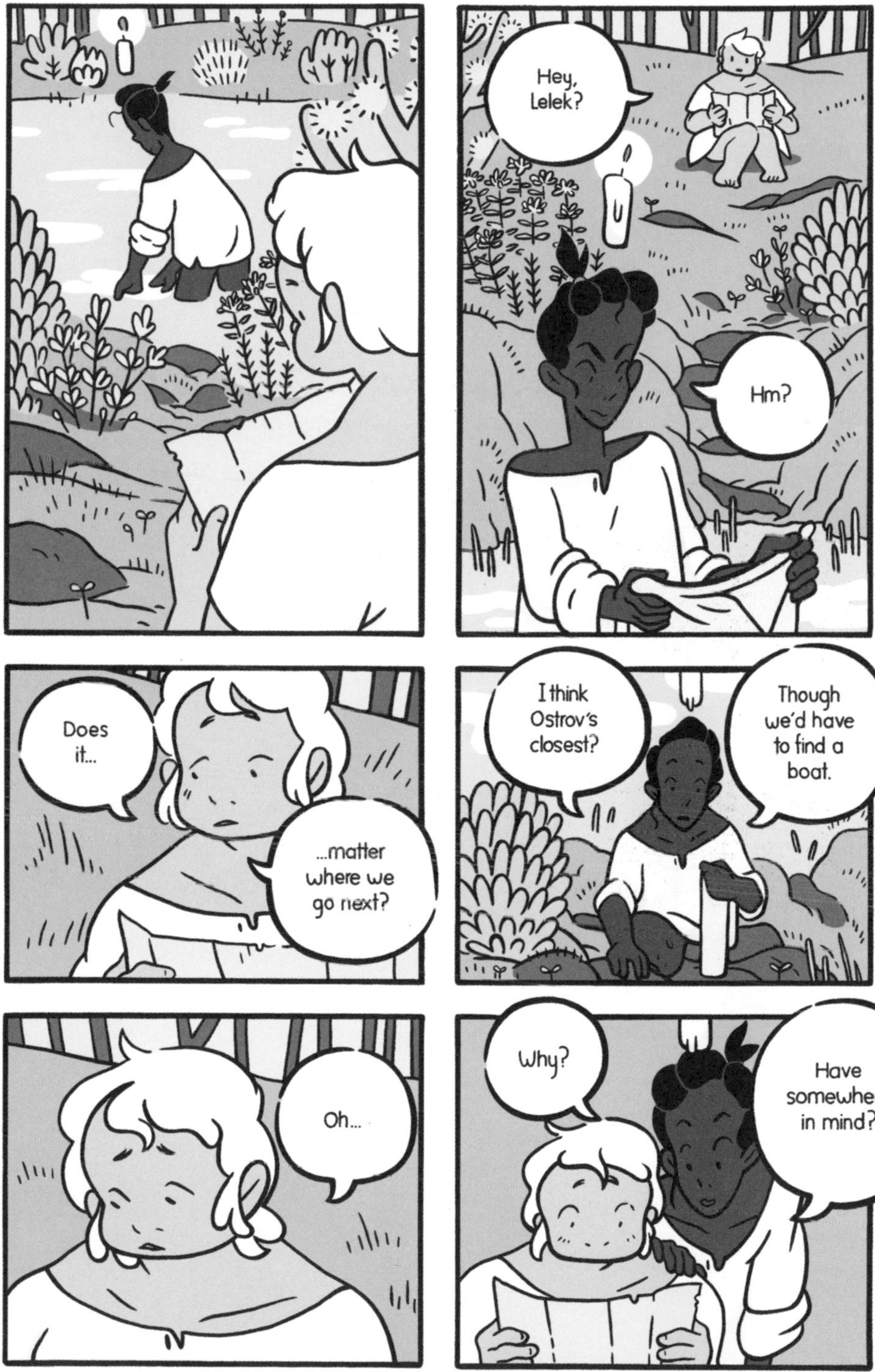
Hey, Lelek?
Hm?
Does it...
...matter where we go next?
I think Ostrov's closest?
Though we'd have to find a boat.
Oh...
Why?
Have somewhere in mind?

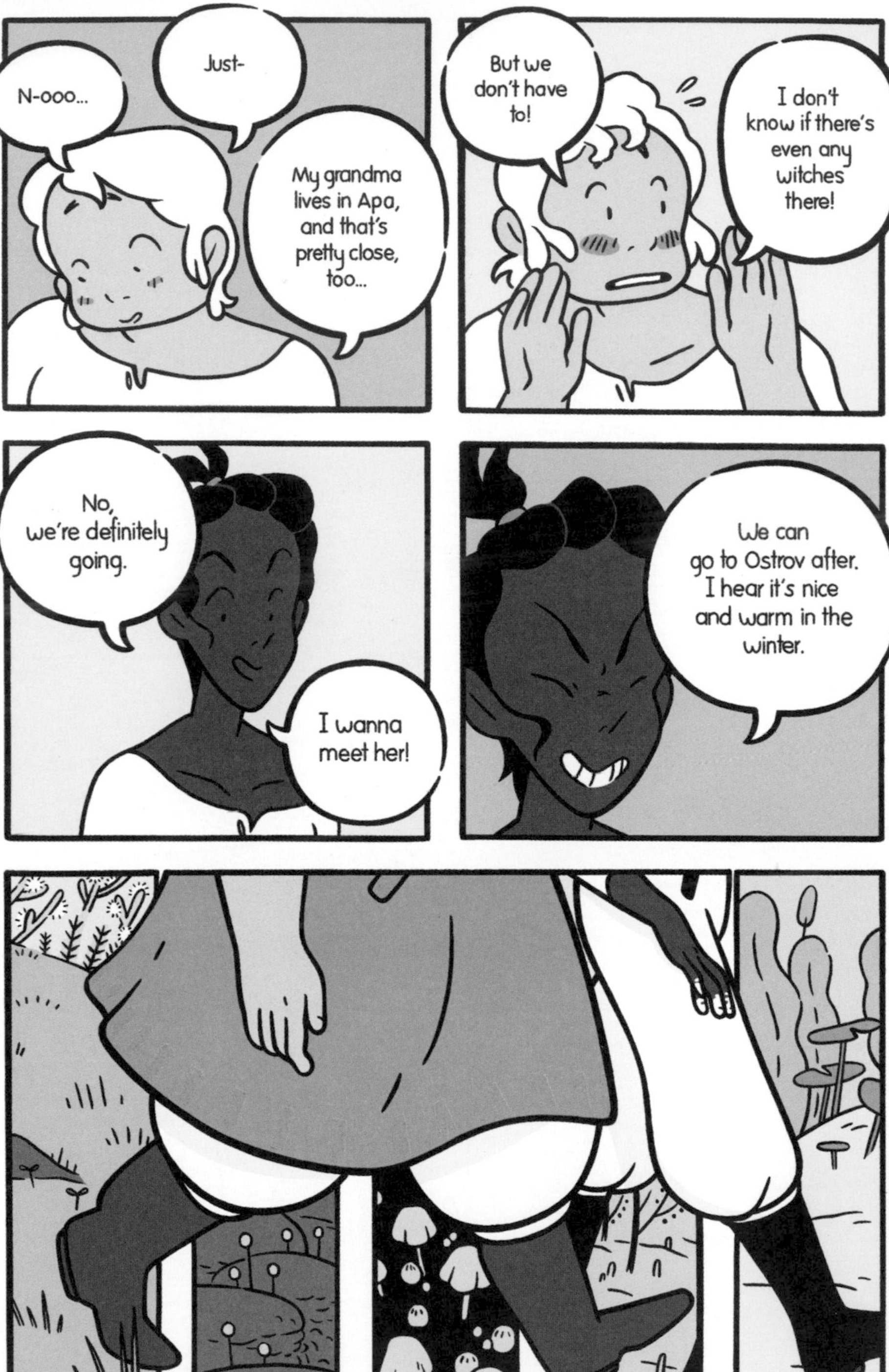
N-ooo...
Just-
My grandma lives in Apa, and that's pretty close, too...
But we don't have to!
I don't know if there's even any witches there!
No, we're definitely going.
I wanna meet her!
We can go to Ostrov after. I hear it's nice and warm in the winter.

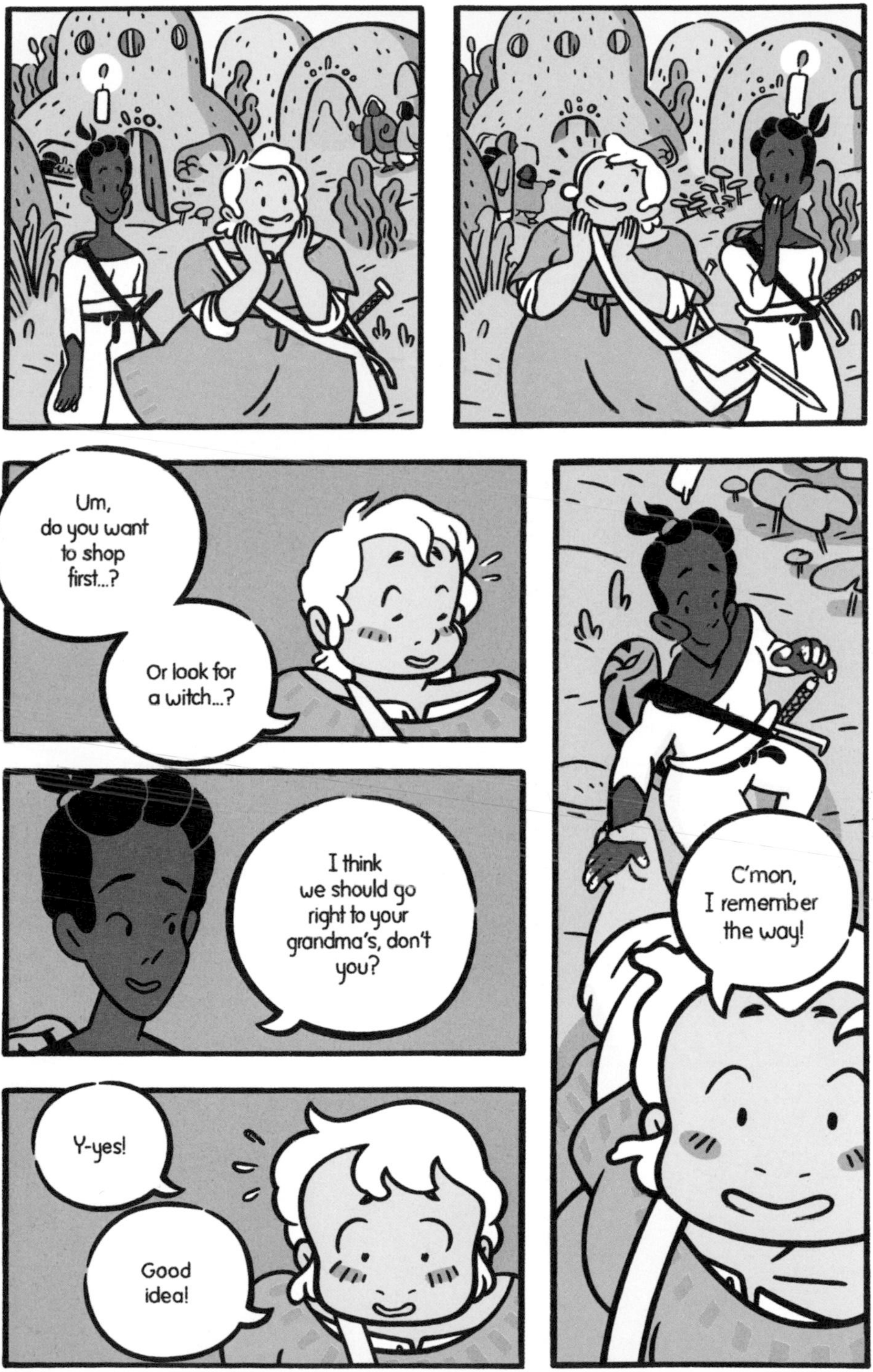
Um,
do you want
to shop
first...?
Or look for
a witch...?
I think
we should go
right to your
grandma's, don't
you?
Y-yes!
Good
idea!
C'mon,
I remember
the way!

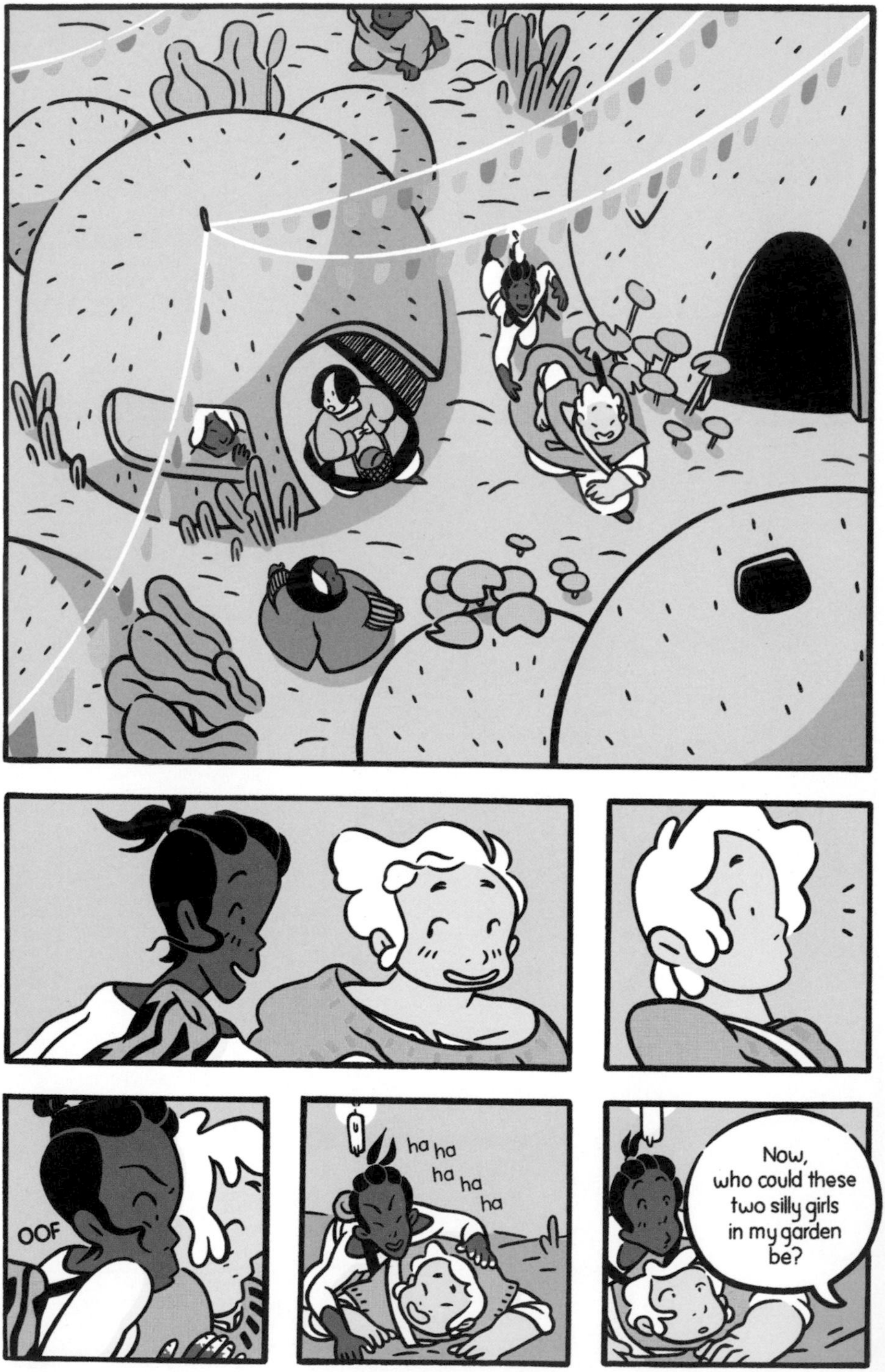
OOF
ha ha ha ha ha
Now, who could these two silly girls in my garden be?

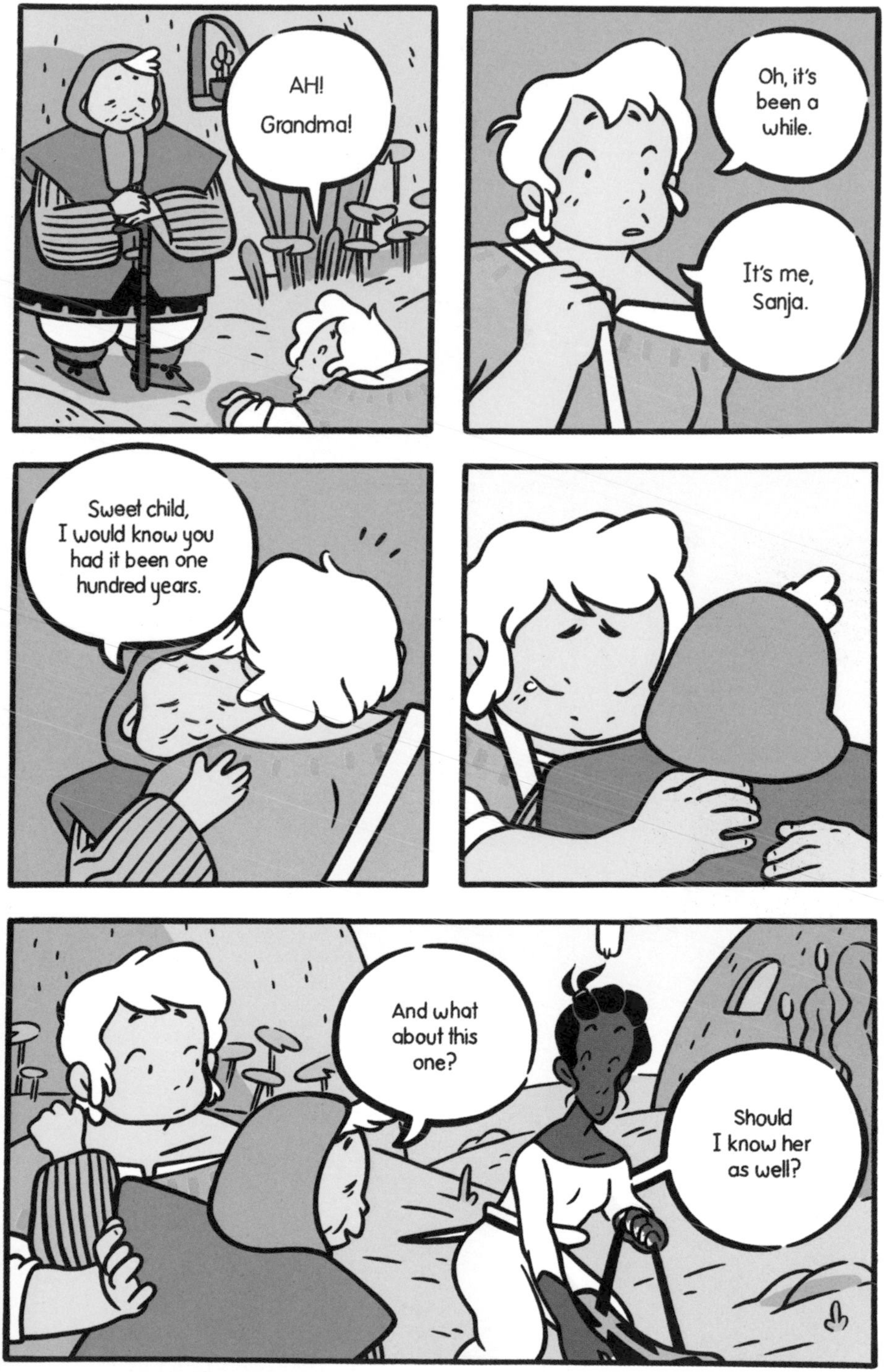
AH!
Grandma!
Oh, it's been a while.
It's me, Sanja.
Sweet child, I would know you had it been one hundred years.
And what about this one?
Should I know her as well?

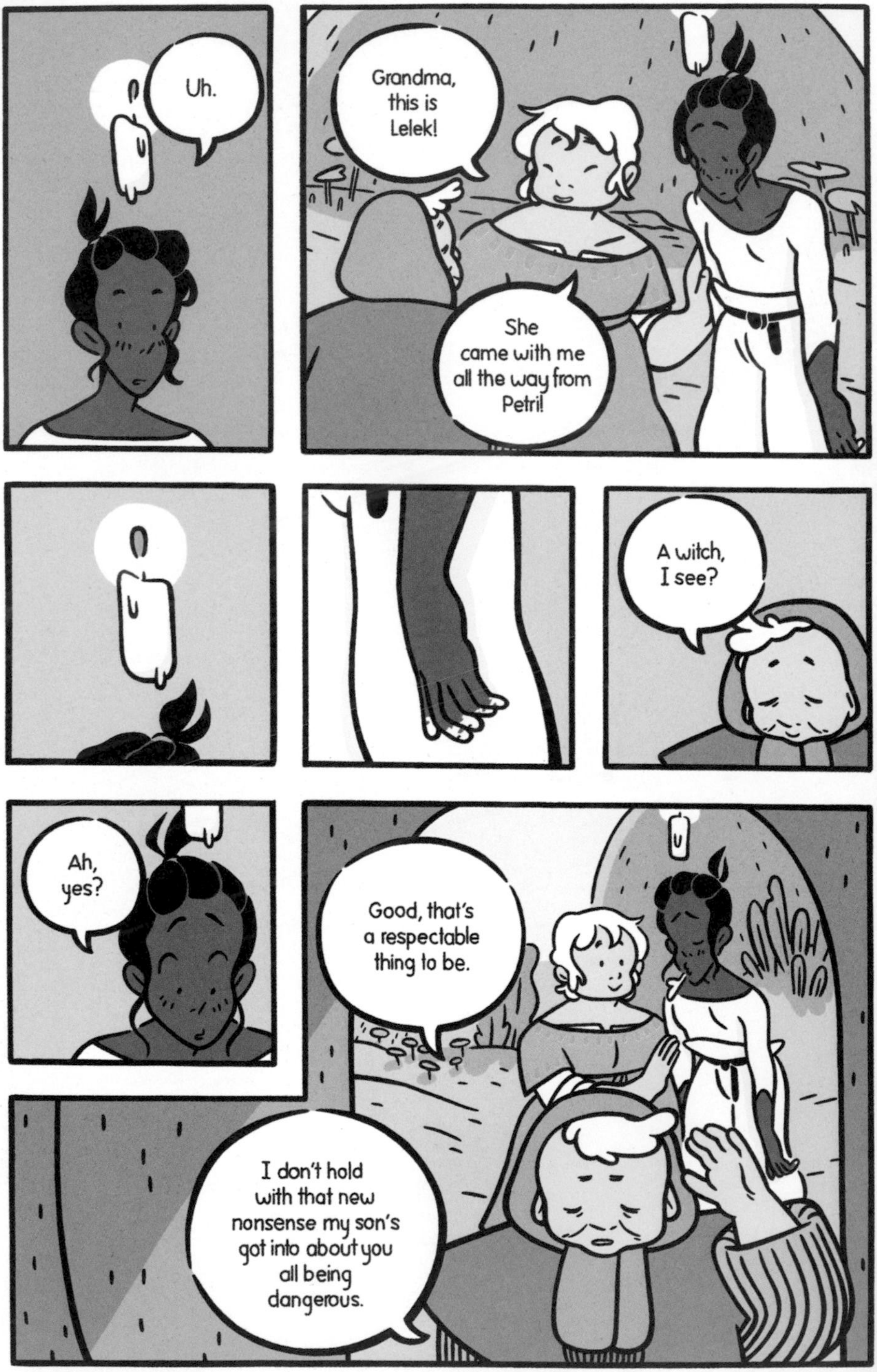
Uh.
Grandma, this is Lelek!
She came with me all the way from Petri!
A witch, I see?
Ah, yes?
Good, that's a respectable thing to be.
I don't hold with that new nonsense my son's got into about you all being dangerous.

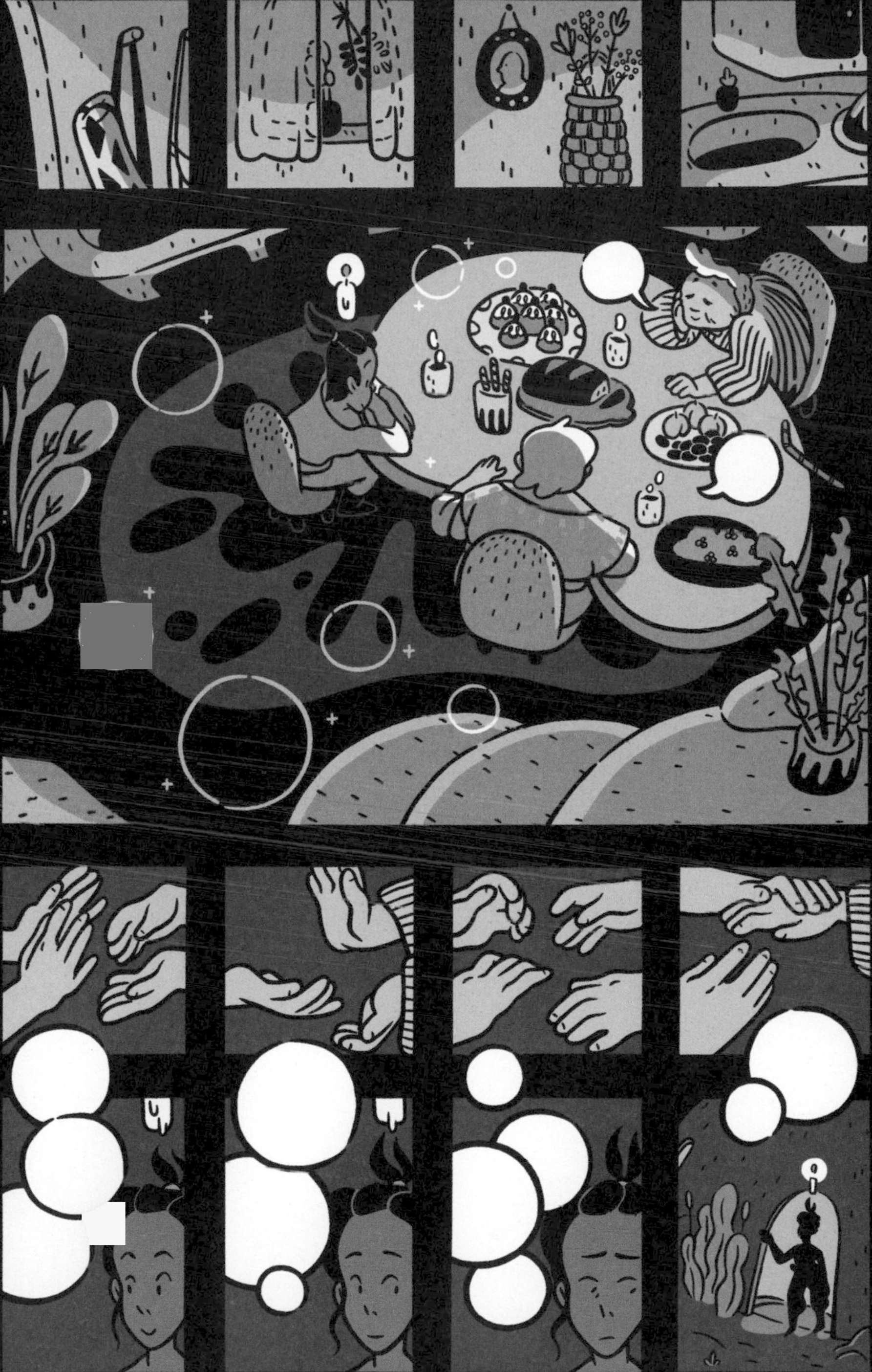

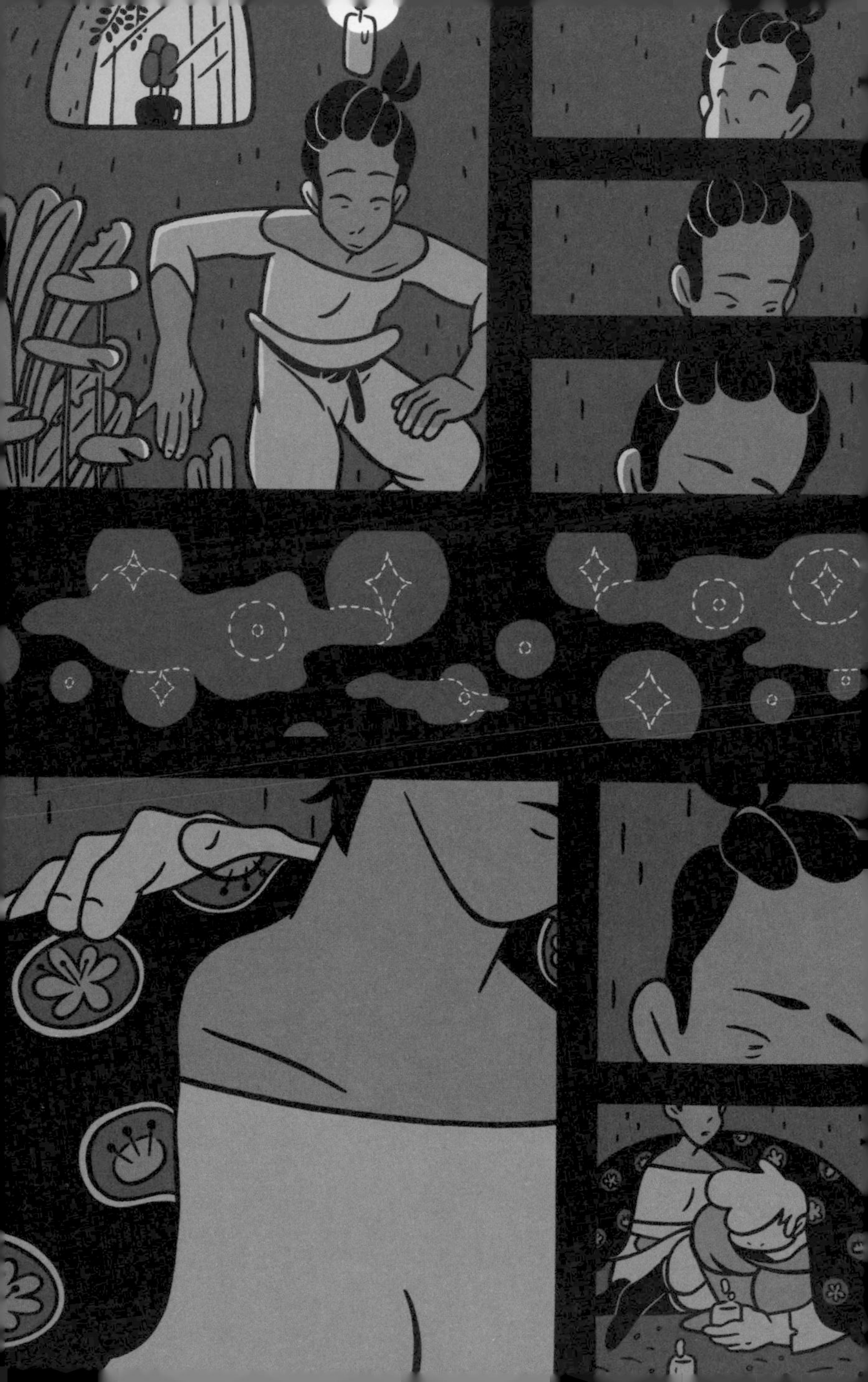

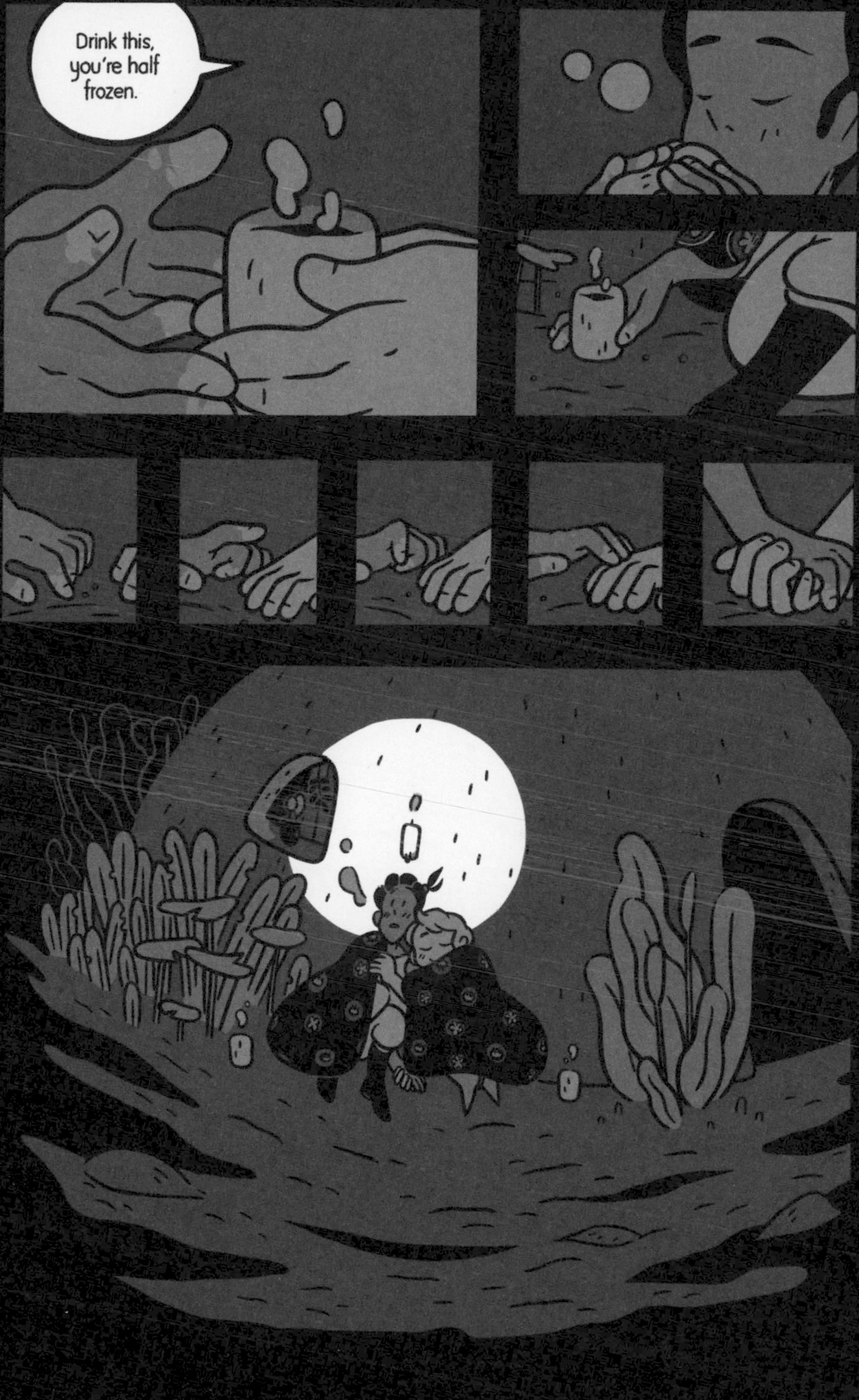
Drink this, you're half frozen.

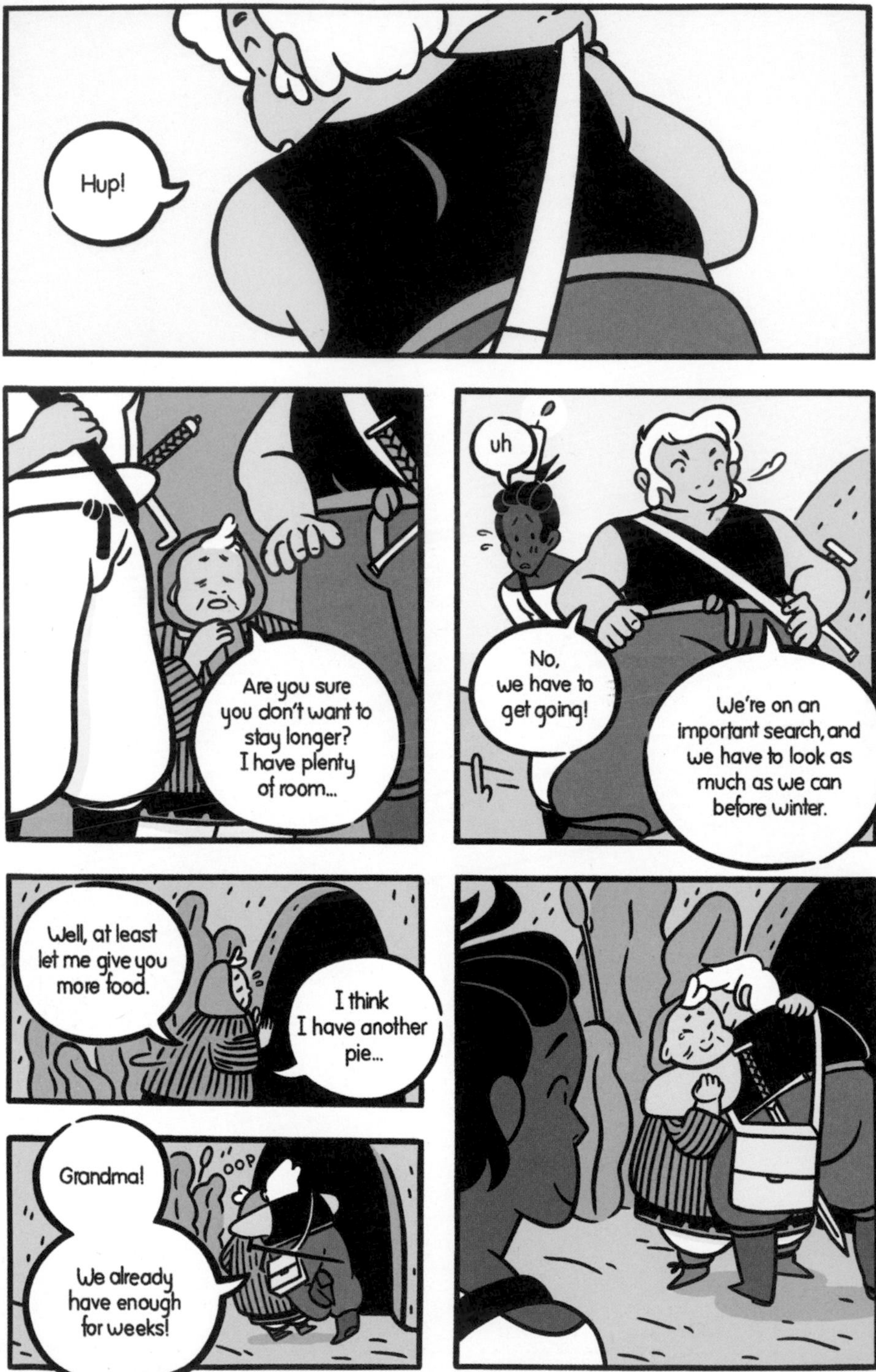
Hup!
Are you sure you don't want to stay longer? I have plenty of room...
uh
No, we have to get going!
We're on an important search, and we have to look as much as we can before winter.
Well, at least let me give you more food.
I think I have another pie...
Grandma!
OOP
We already have enough for weeks!

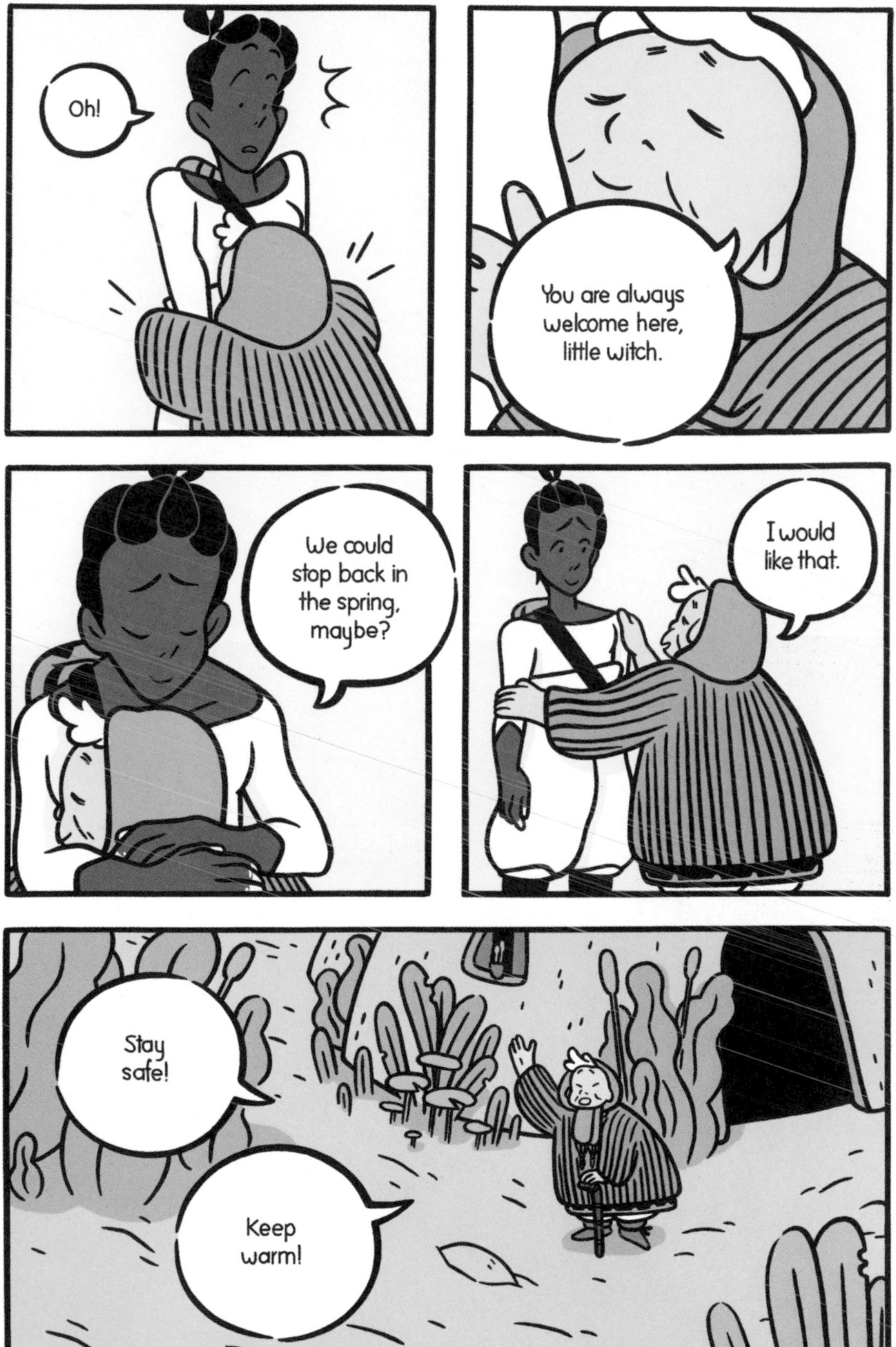
Oh!
You are always welcome here, little witch.
We could stop back in the spring, maybe?
I would like that.
Stay safe!
Keep warm!

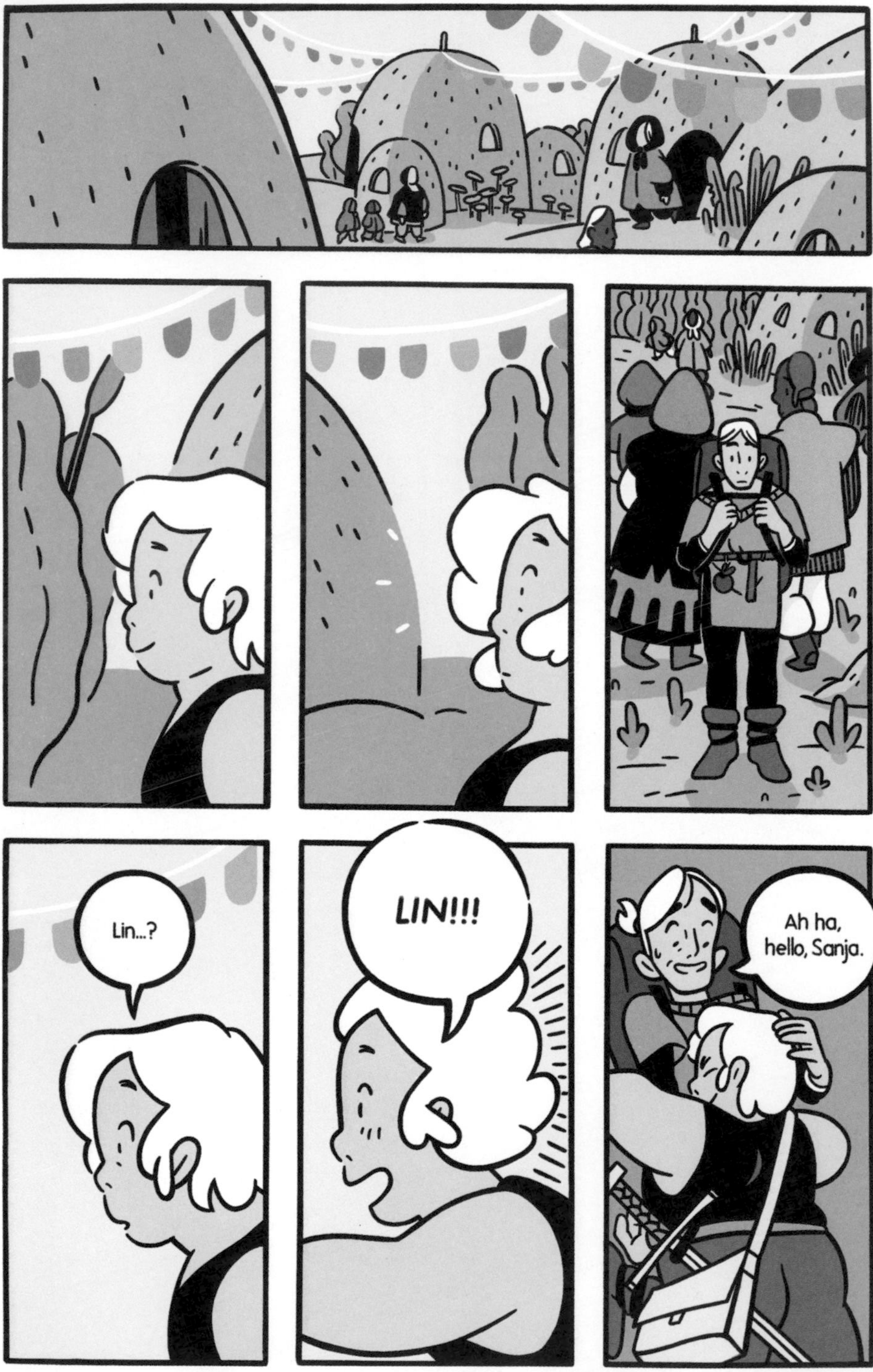
Lin...?
LIN!!!
Ah ha, hello, Sanja.

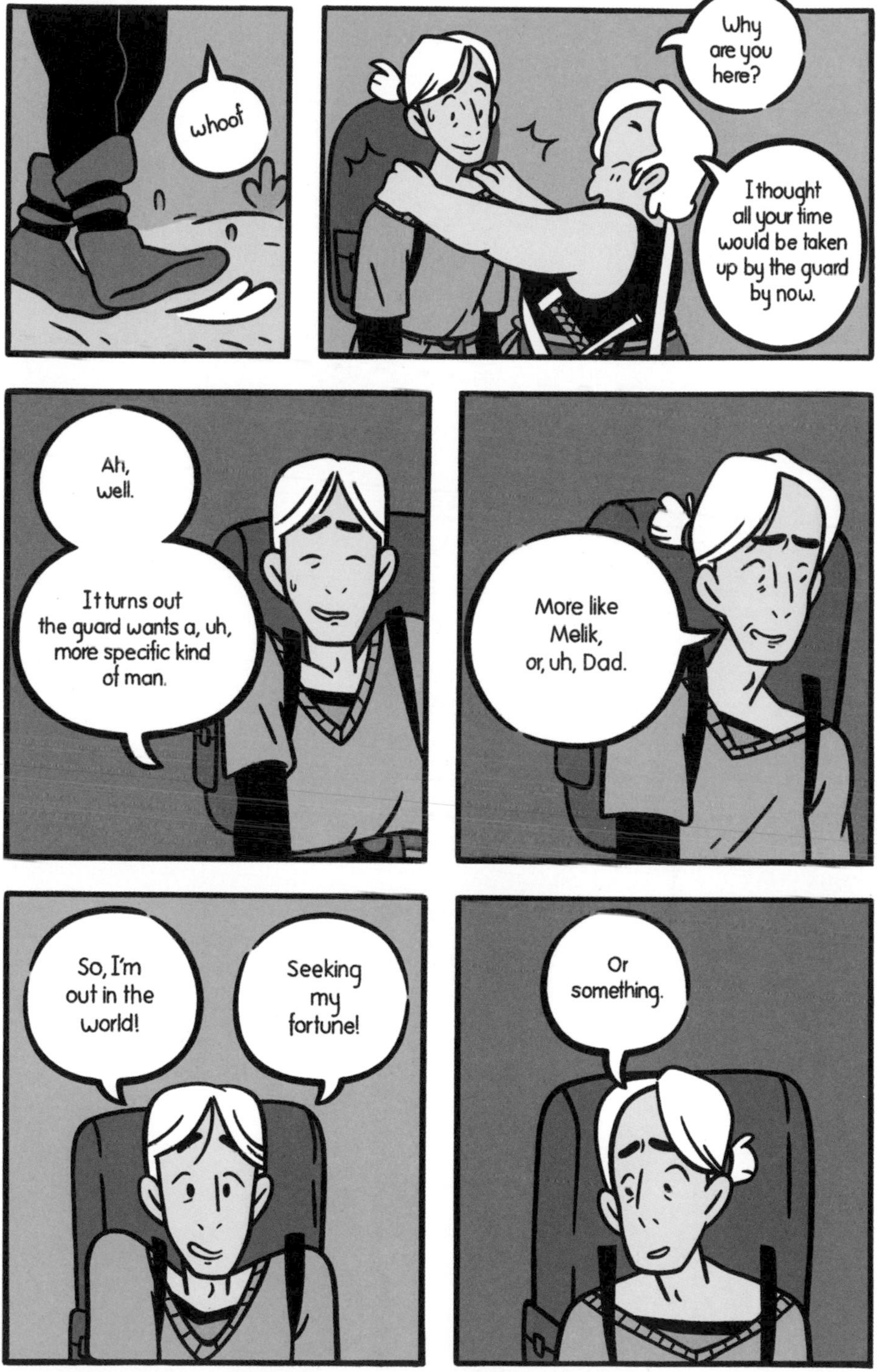
whoof
Why are you here?
I thought all your time would be taken up by the guard by now.
Ah, well.
It turns out the guard wants a, uh, more specific kind of man.
More like Melik, or, uh, Dad.
So, I'm out in the world!
Seeking my fortune!
Or something.

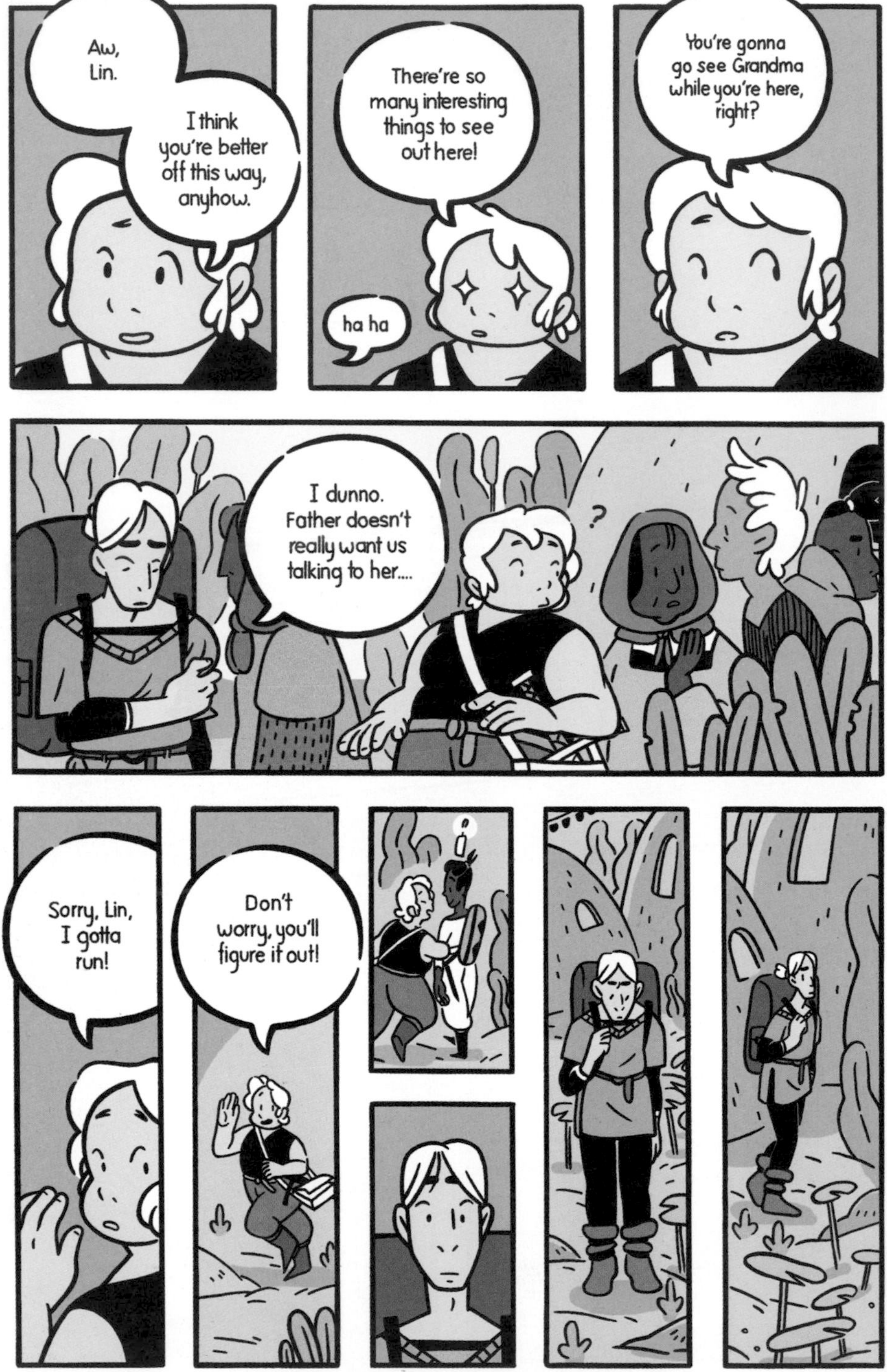

Aw, Lin.
I think you're better off this way, anyhow.
There're so many interesting things to see out here!
ha ha
You're gonna go see Grandma while you're here, right?
I dunno. Father doesn't really want us talking to her....
?
Sorry, Lin, I gotta run!
Don't worry, you'll figure it out!

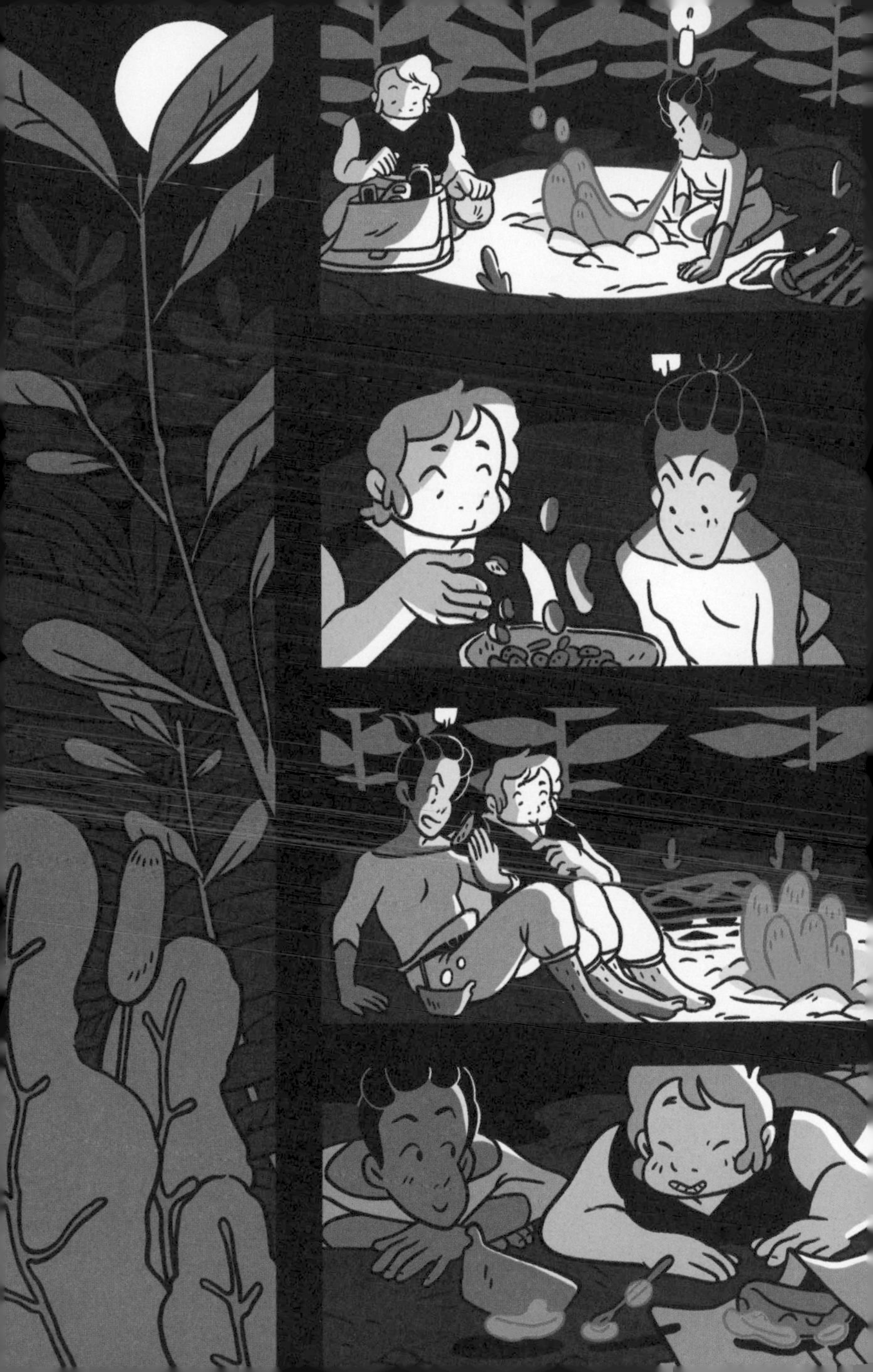

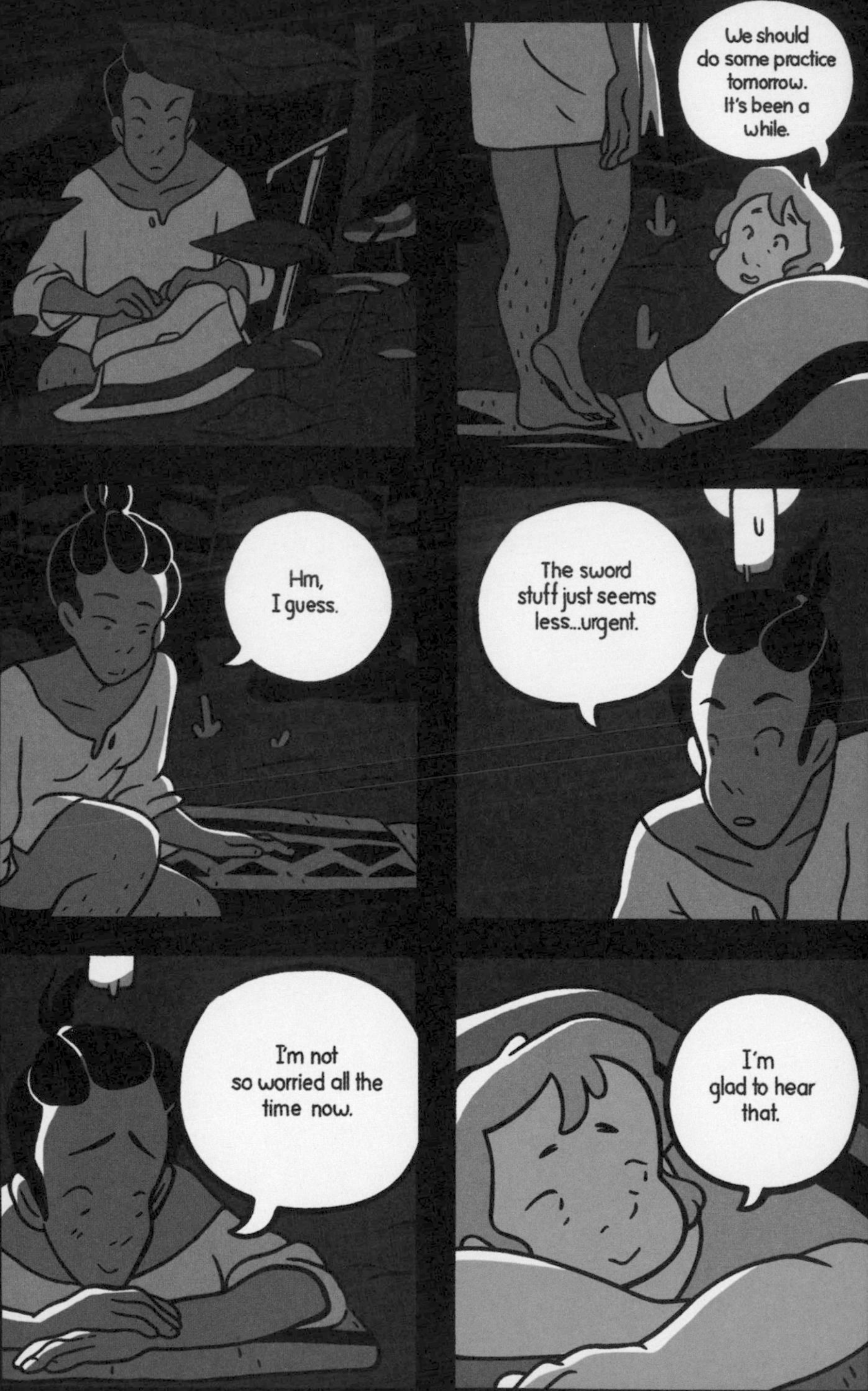
We should do some practice tomorrow. It's been a while.
Hm, I guess.
The sword stuff just seems less...urgent.
I'm not so worried all the time now.
I'm glad to hear that.

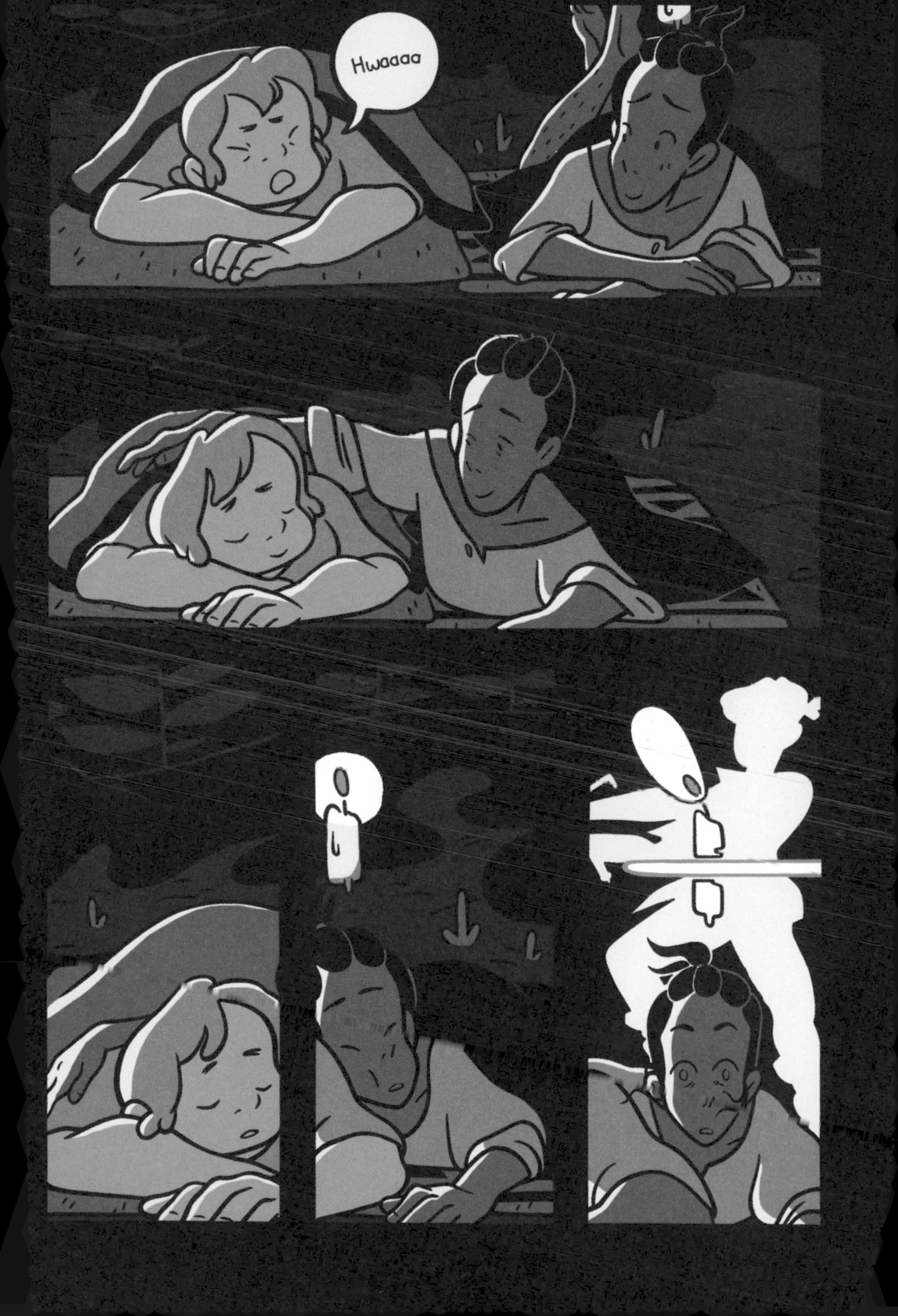
Hwaaaa

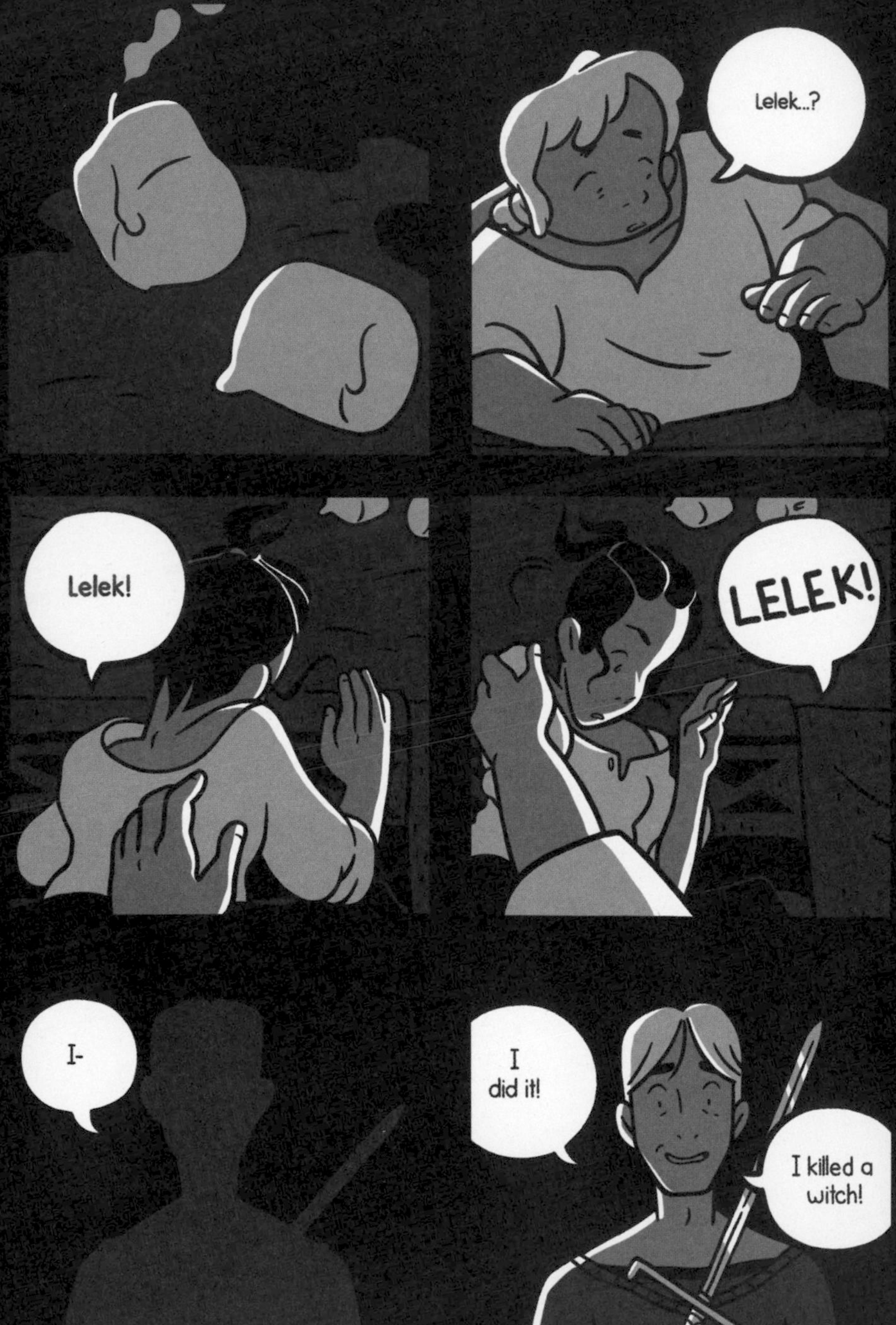
Lelek...?
Lelek!
LELEK!
I-
I did it!
I killed a witch!

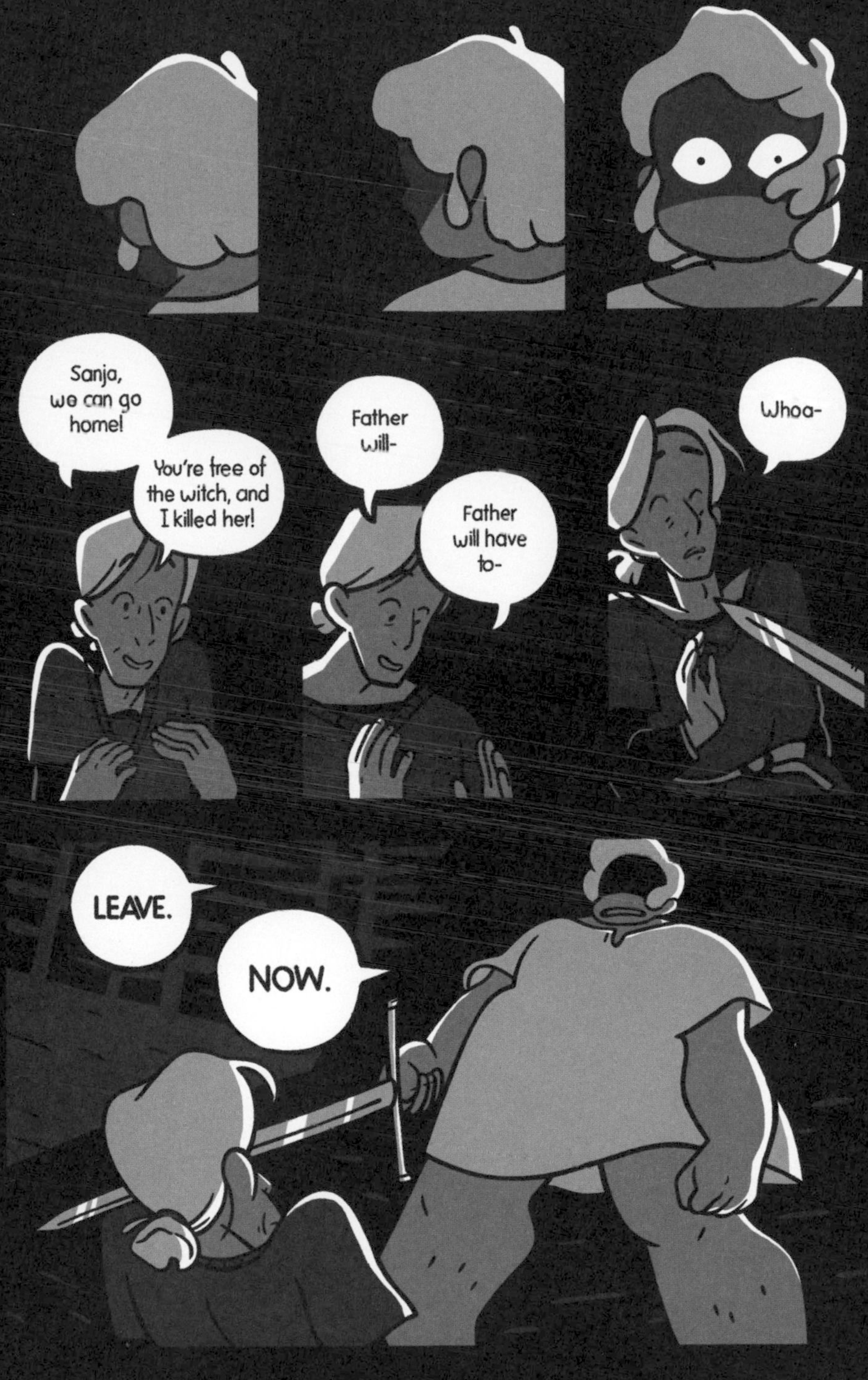
Sanja, we can go home!
You're free of the witch, and I killed her!
Father will-
Father will have to-
Whoa-
LEAVE.
NOW.

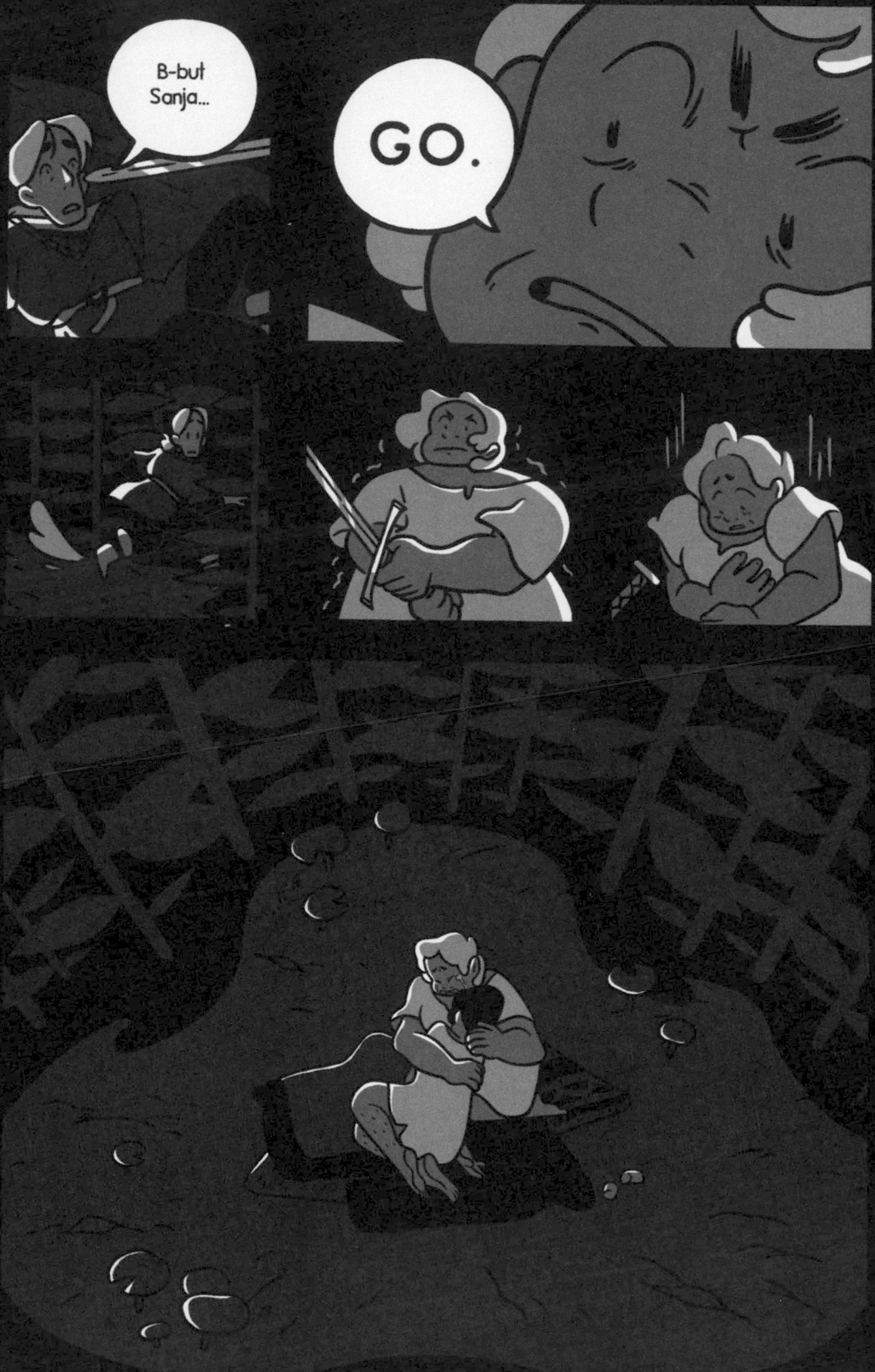
B-but Sanja...
GO.

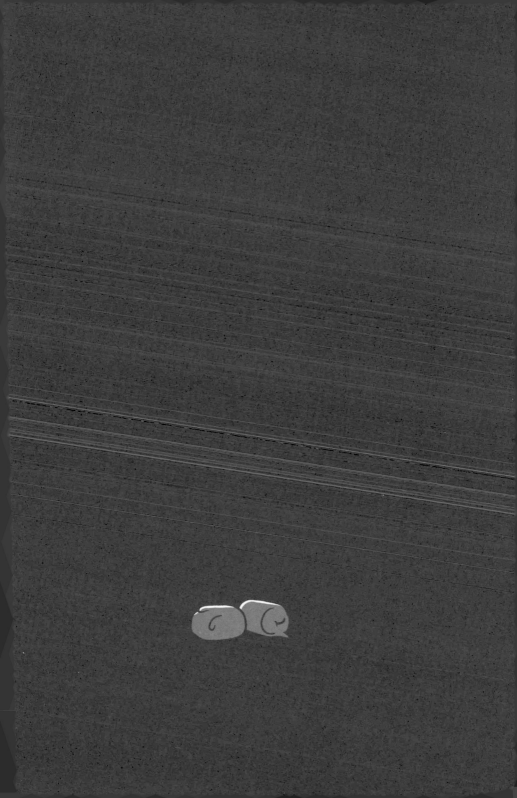

Part 6

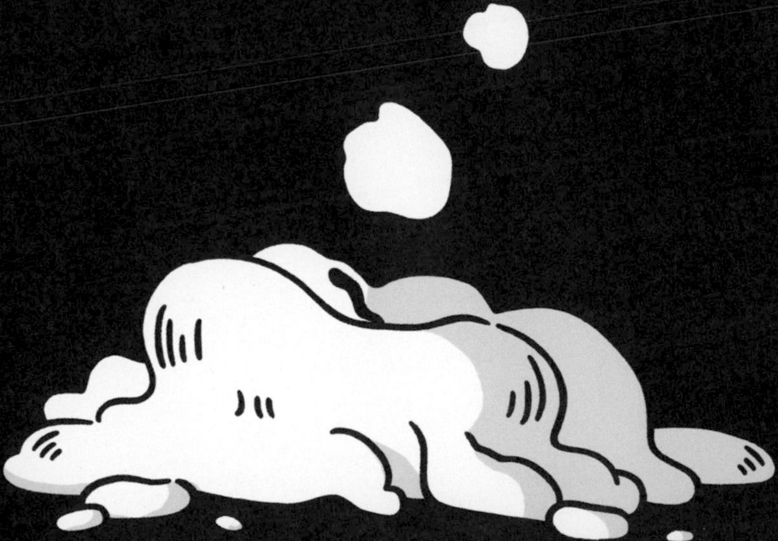

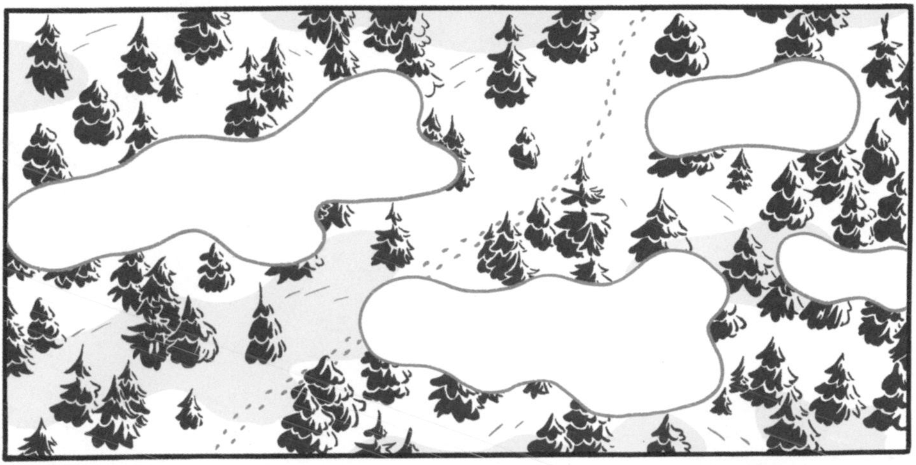

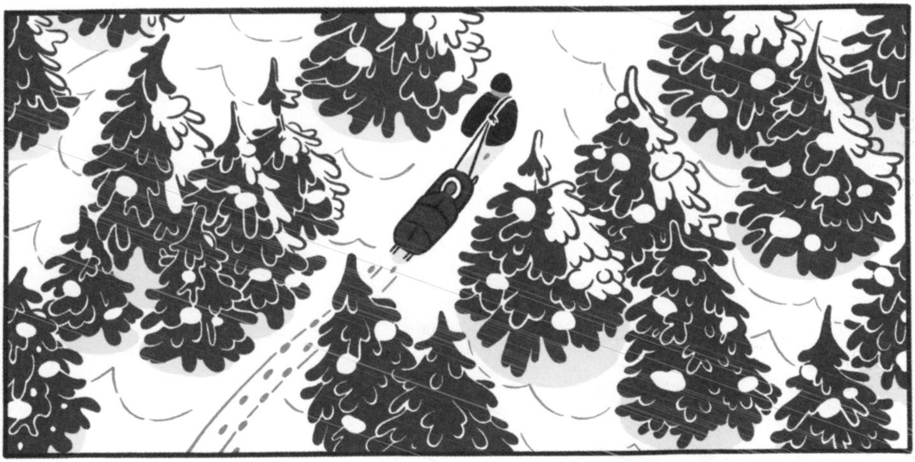

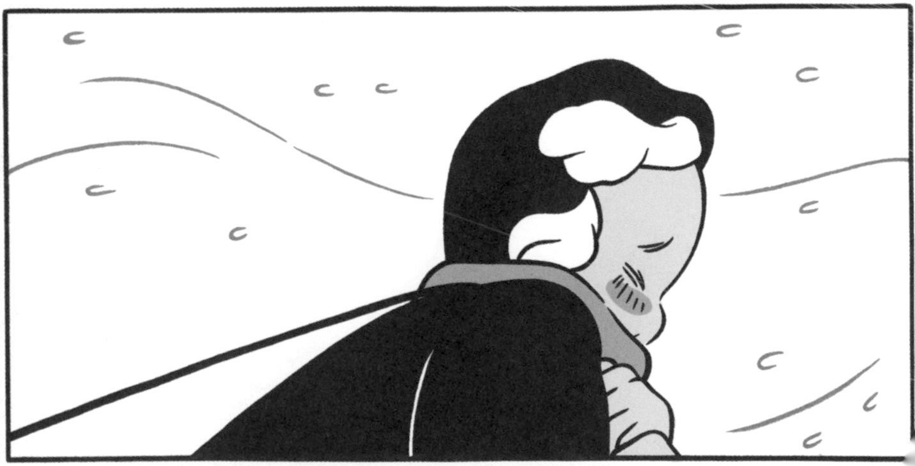

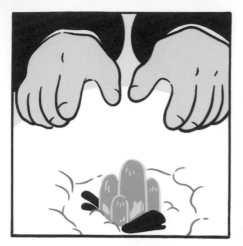

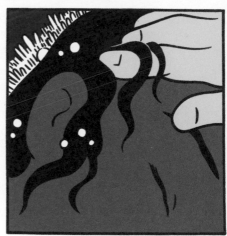

I don't know what I'm doing, Lelek.

I don't know where I'm going.

I'm just hoping this mark on the map is Baciva.

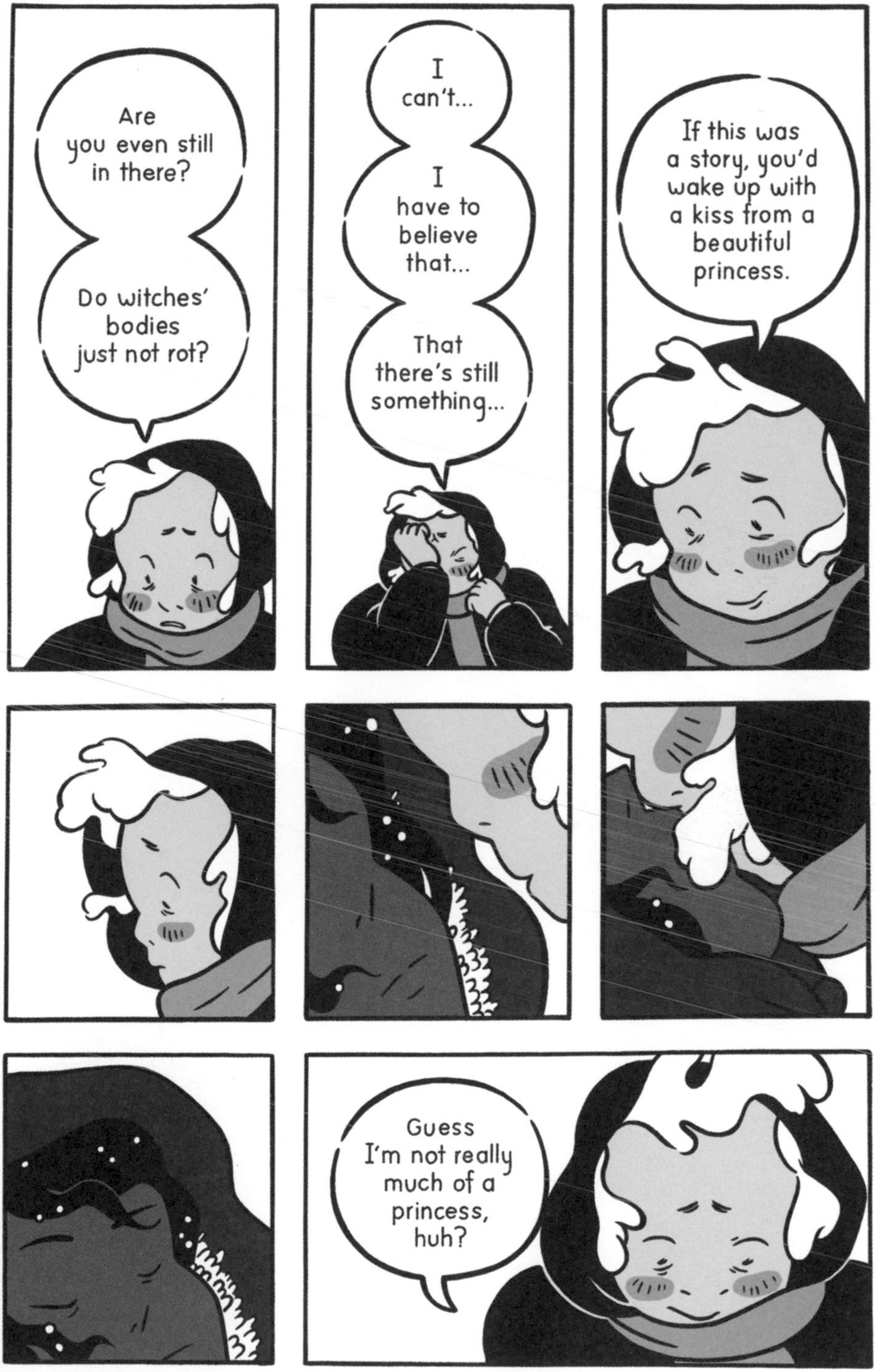
Are you even still in there?
Do witches' bodies just not rot?
I can't...
I have to believe that...
That there's still something...
If this was a story, you'd wake up with a kiss from a beautiful princess.
Guess I'm not really much of a princess, huh?

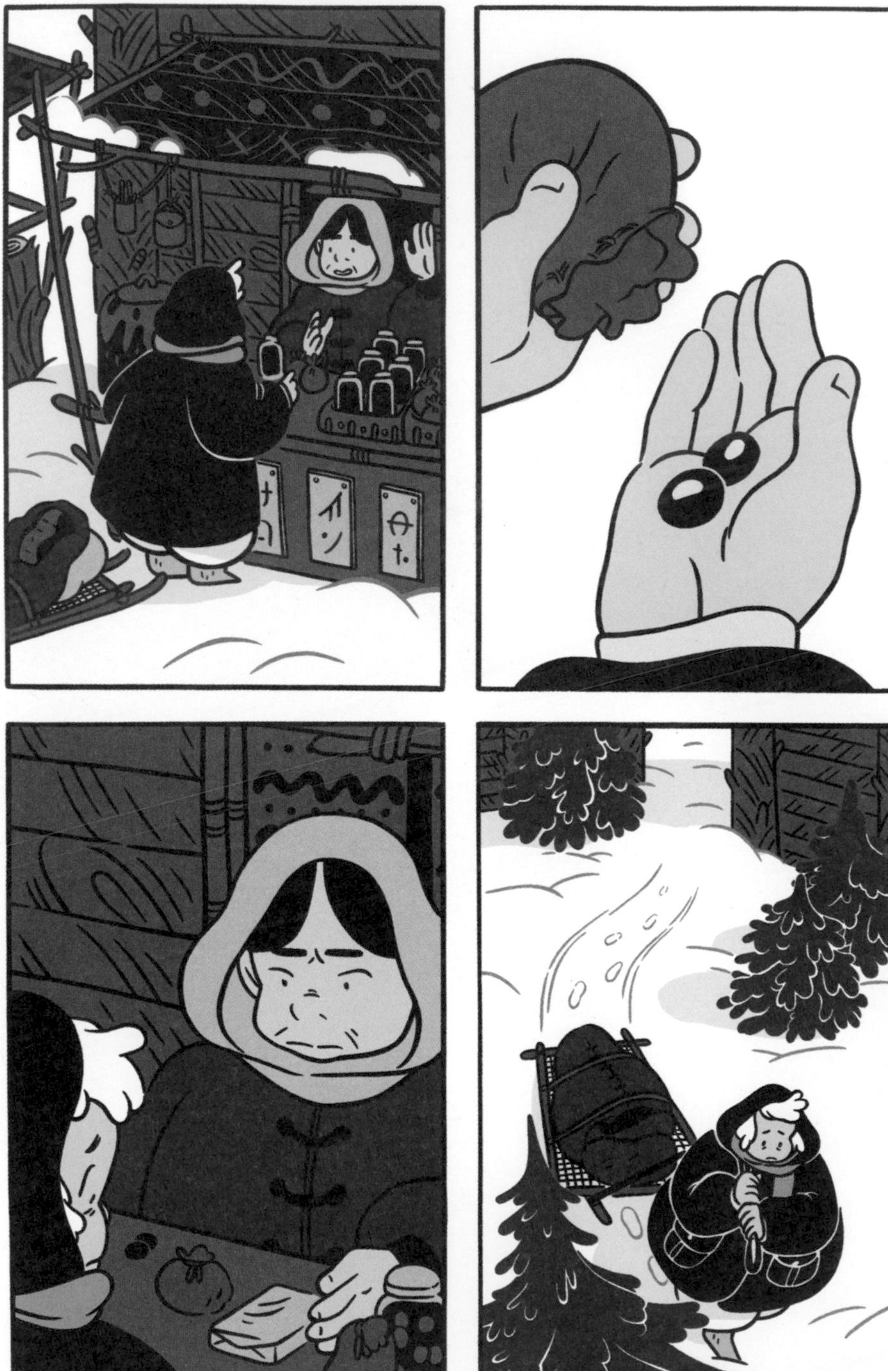

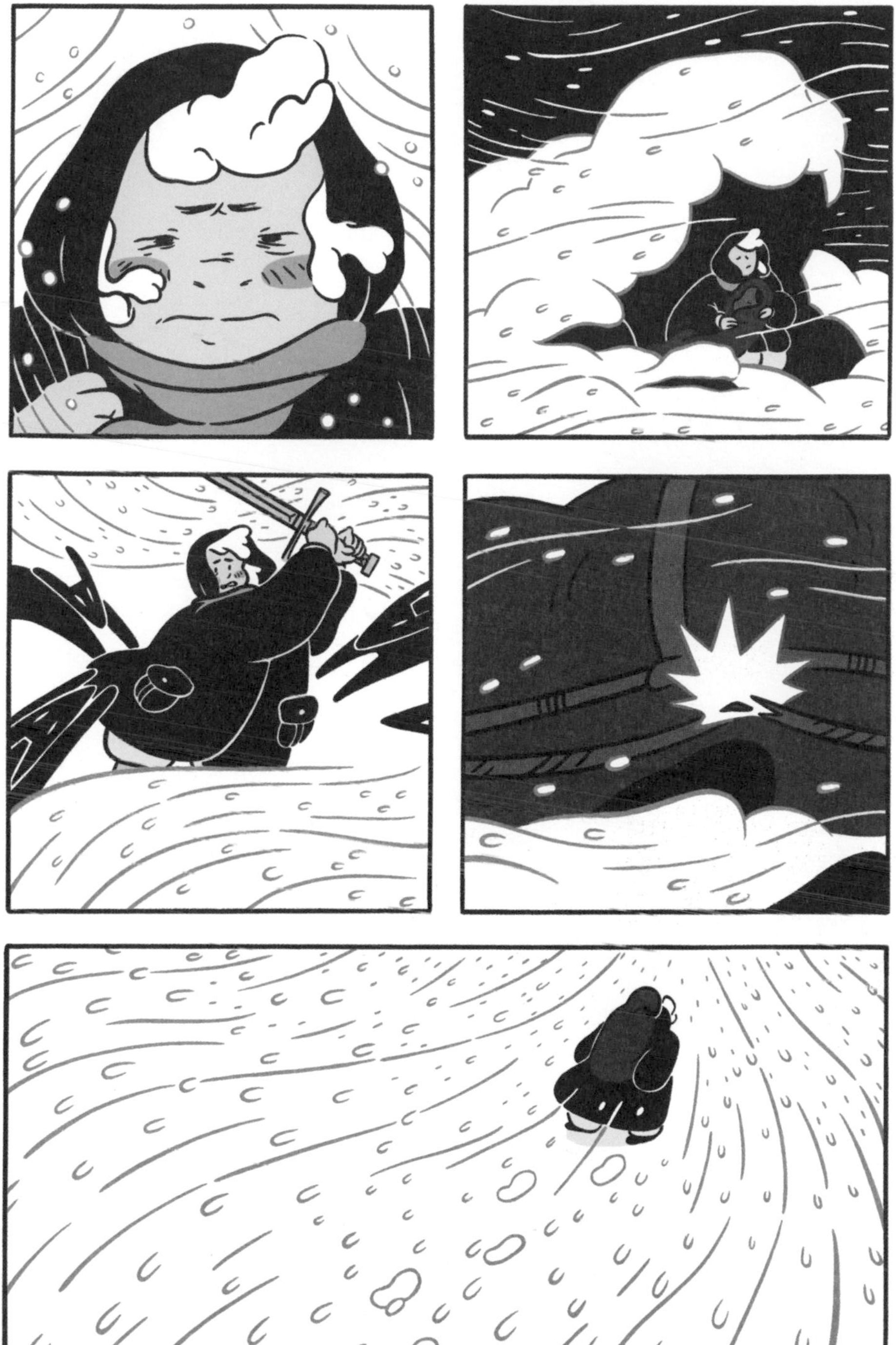

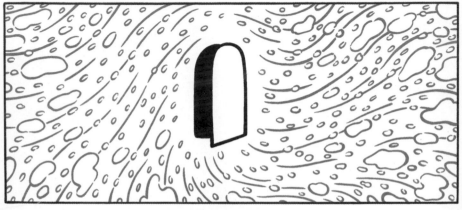

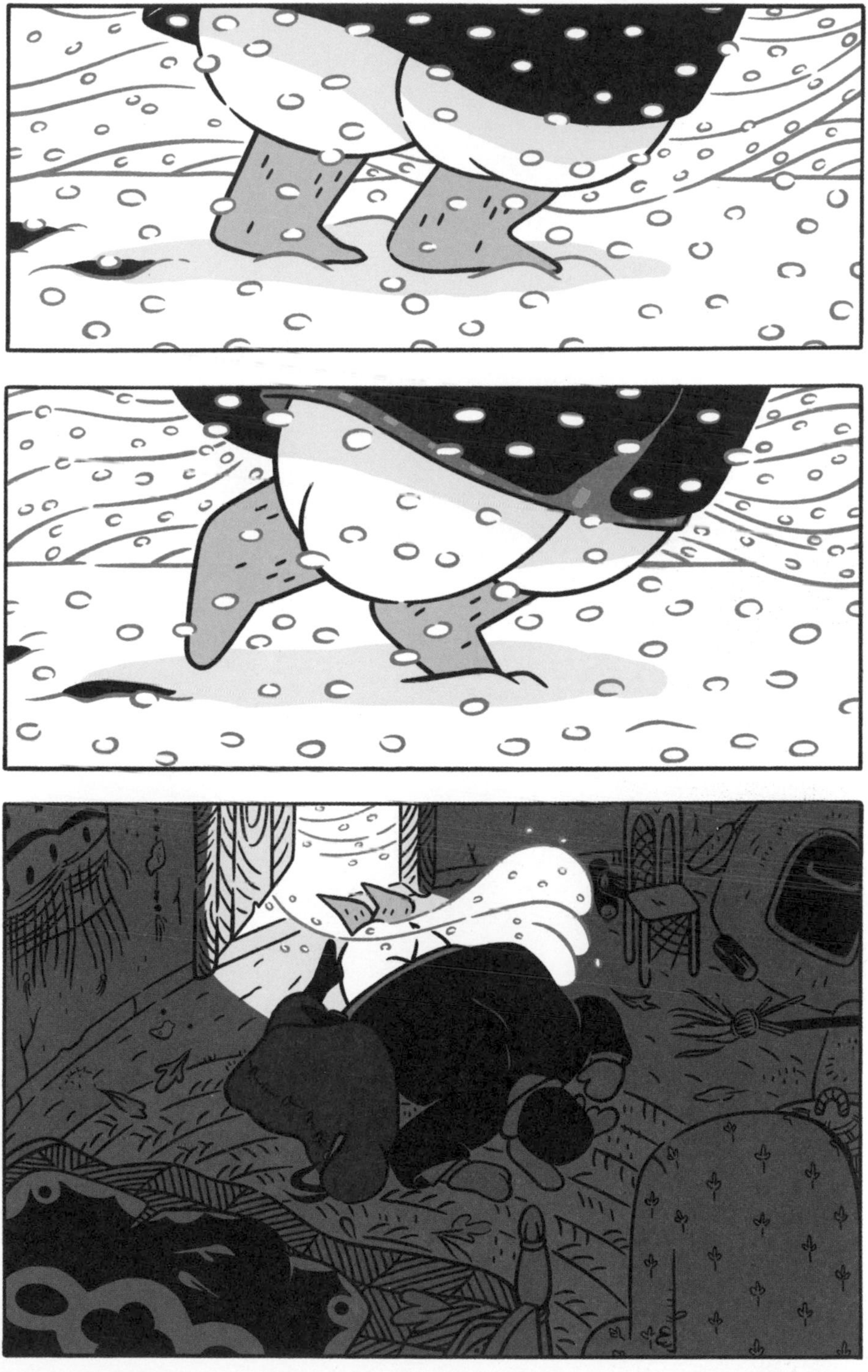

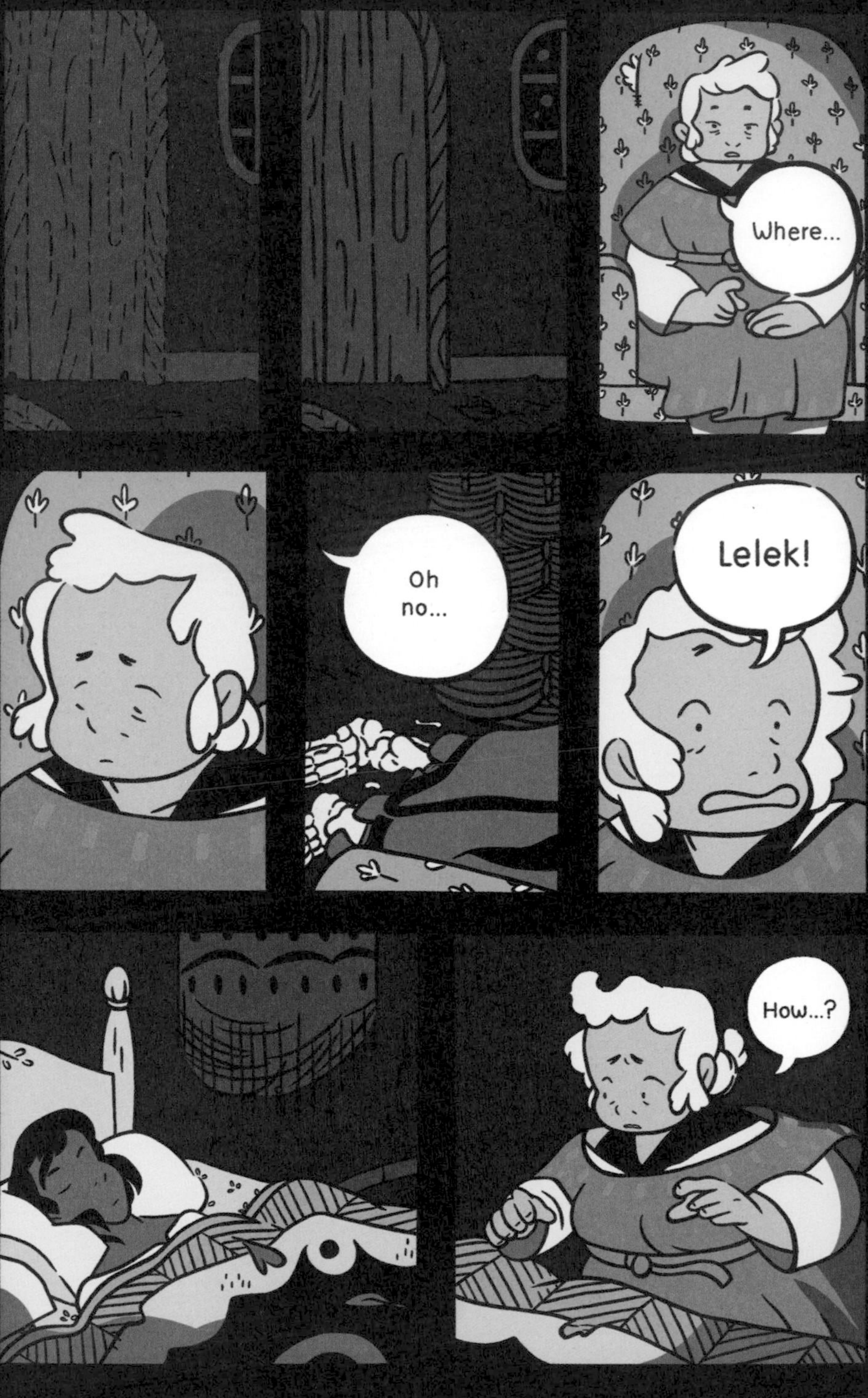
Where...
Oh
no...
Lelek!
How...?

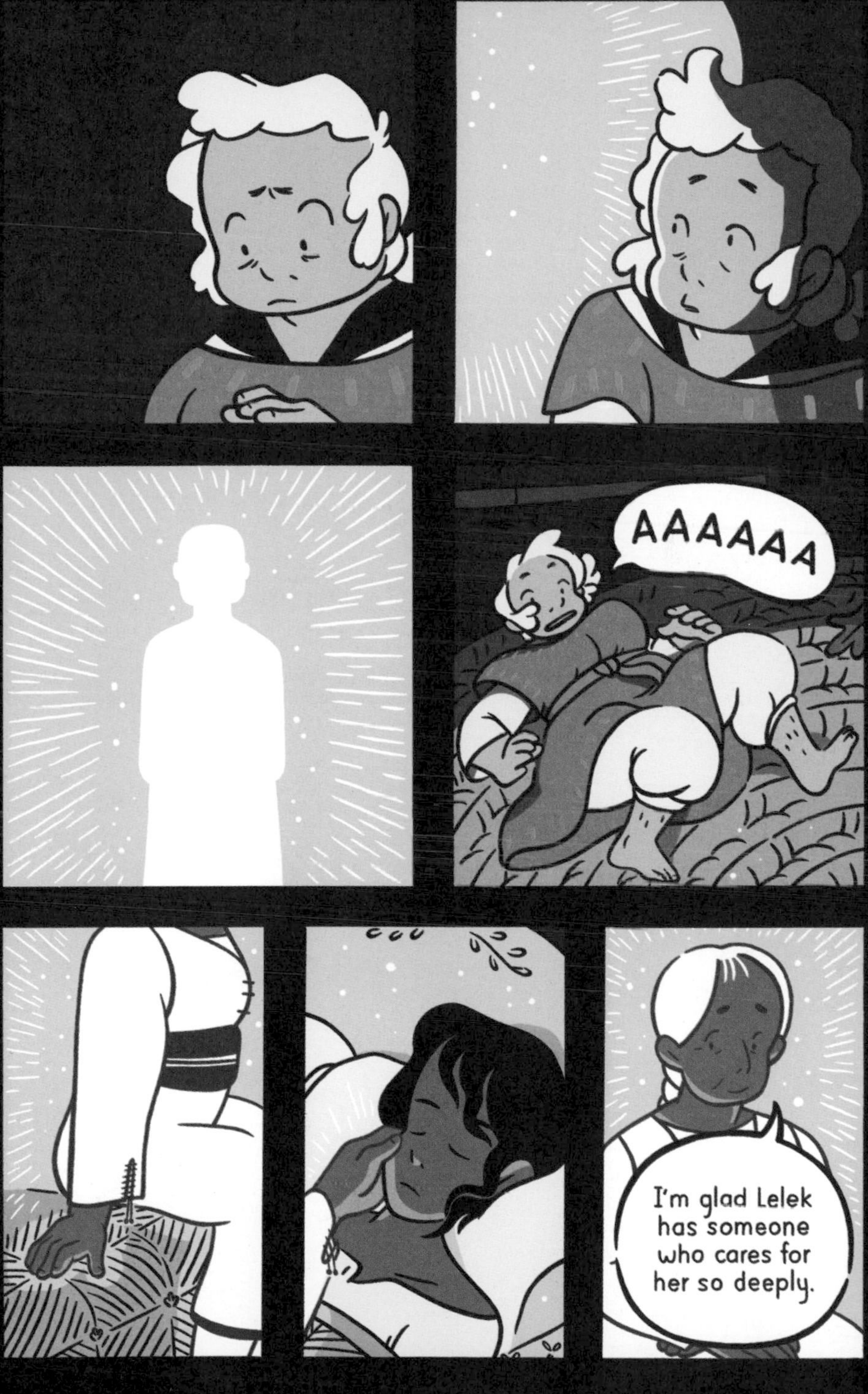
AAAAAA
I'm glad Lelek has someone who cares for her so deeply.

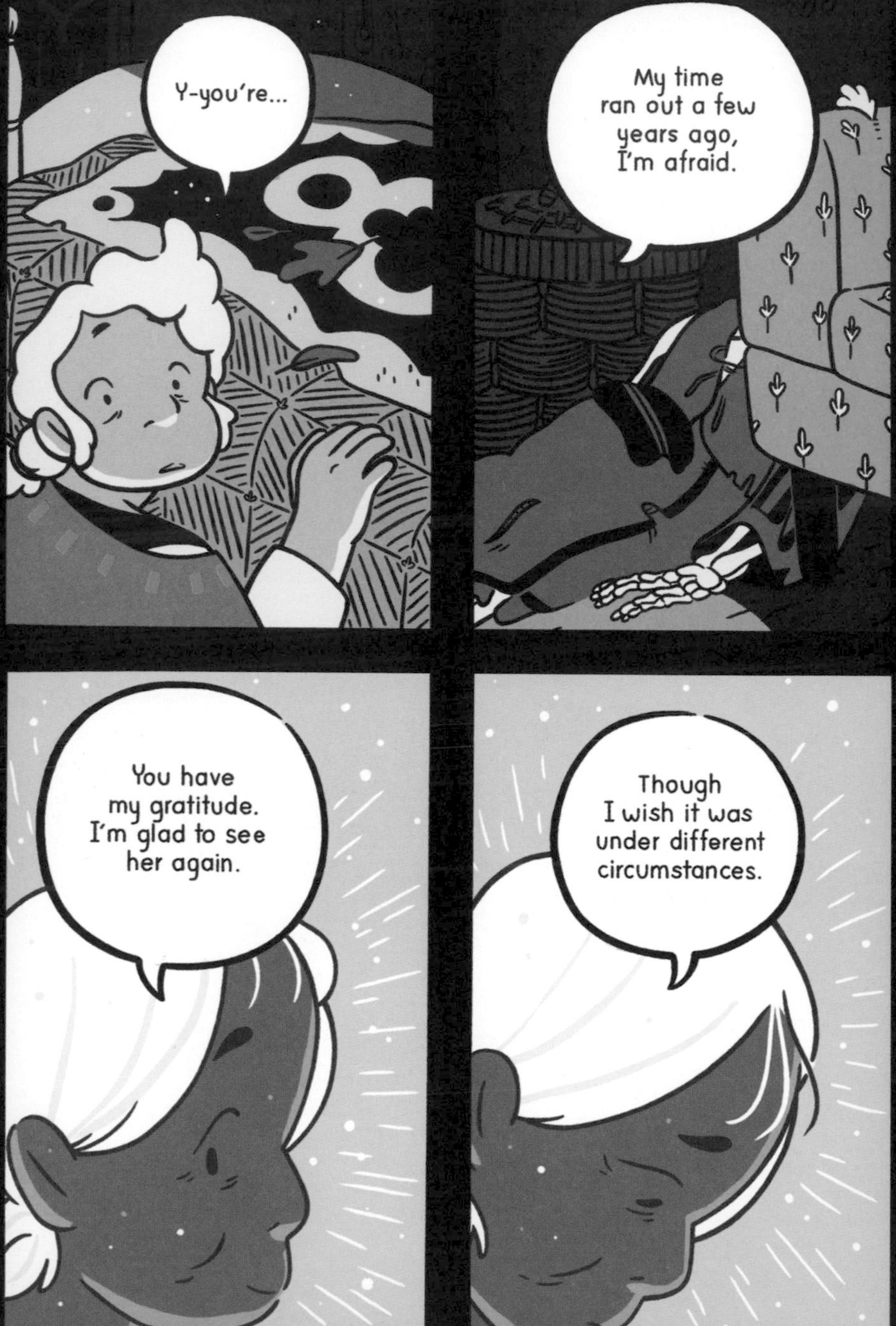
Y-you're...
My time ran out a few years ago, I'm afraid.
You have my gratitude. I'm glad to see her again.
Though I wish it was under different circumstances.

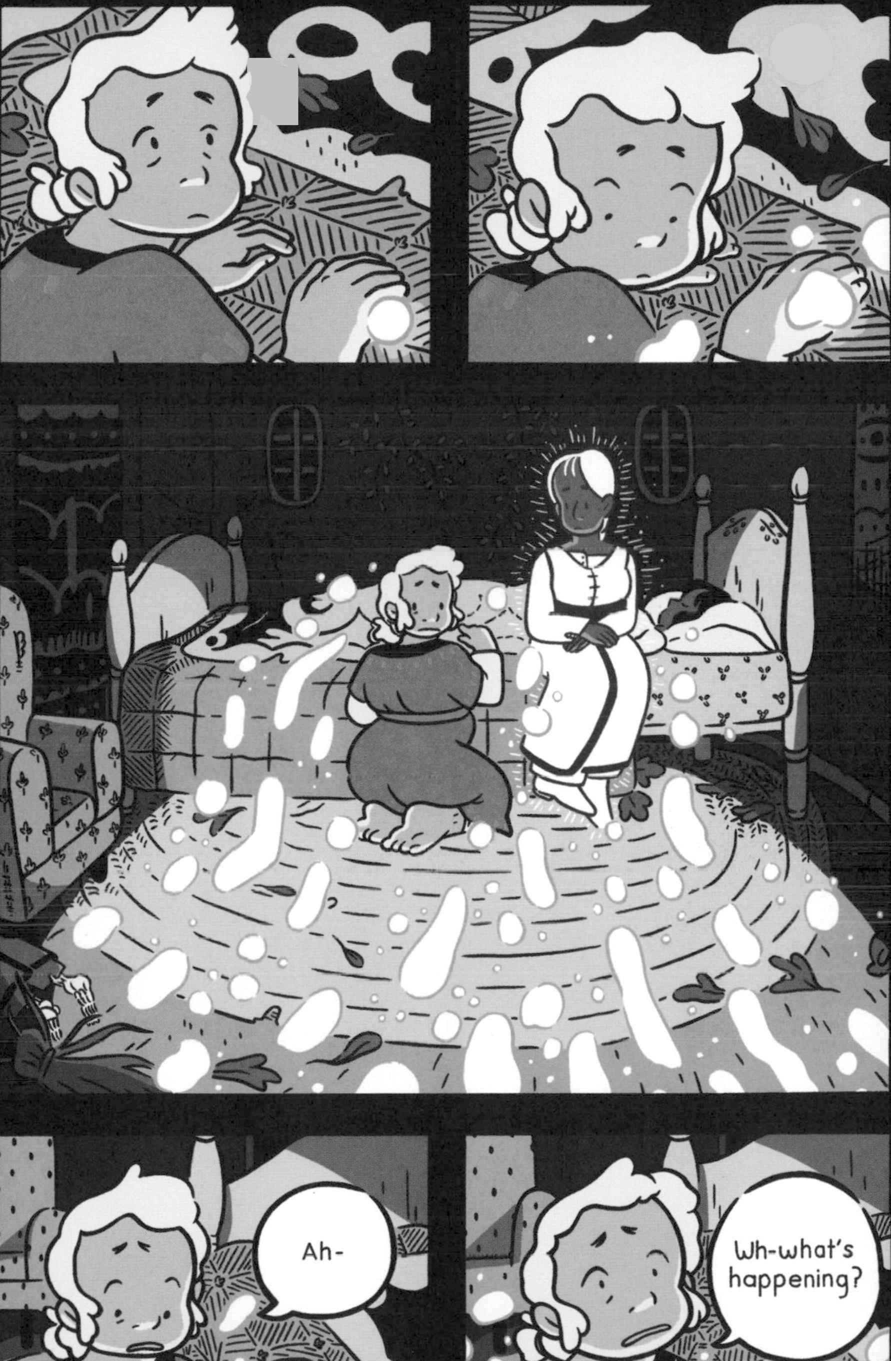
Ah-
Wh-what's happening?

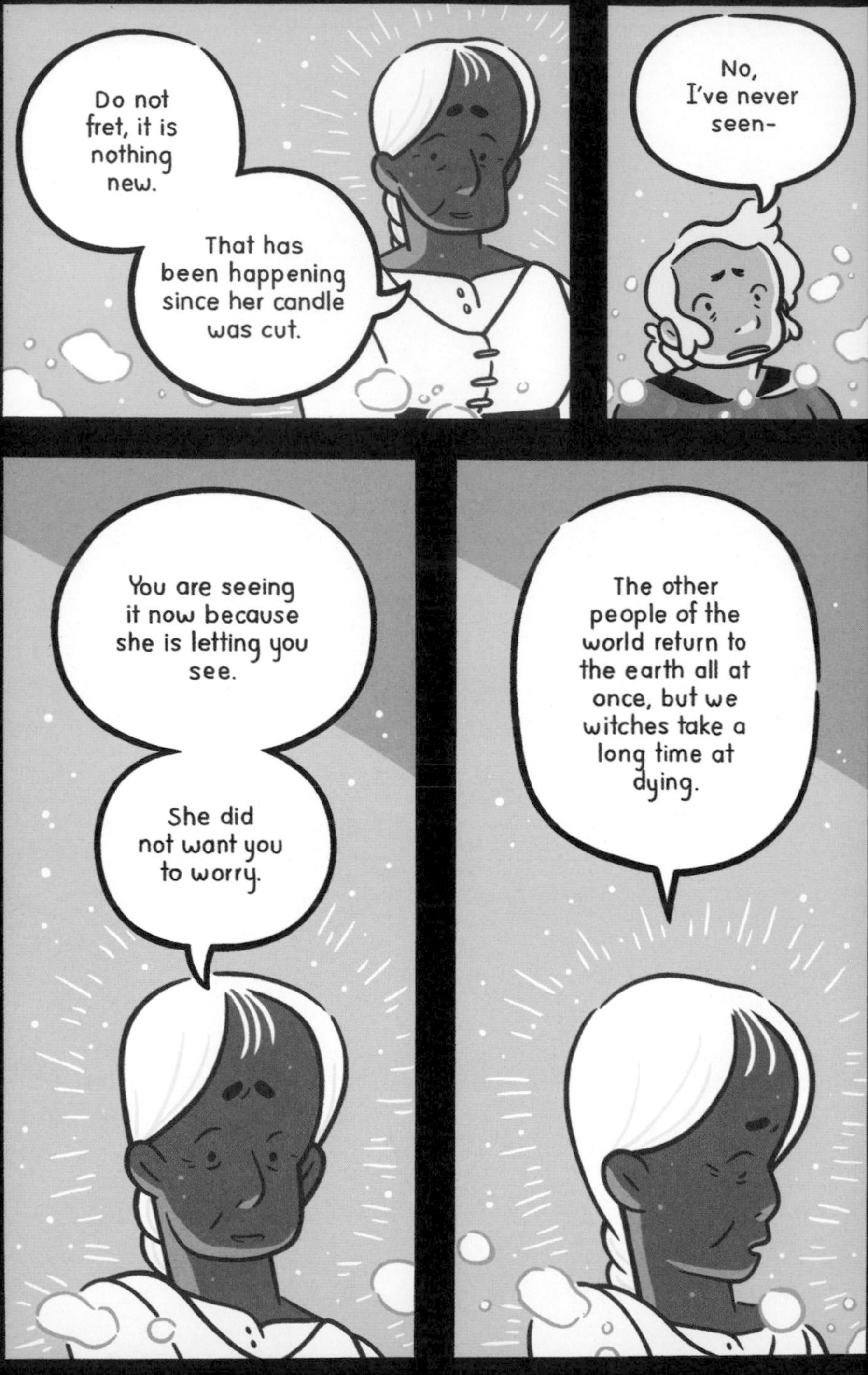
Do not fret, it is nothing new.
That has been happening since her candle was cut.
No, I've never seen-
You are seeing it now because she is letting you see.
She did not want you to worry.
The other people of the world return to the earth all at once, but we witches take a long time at dying.

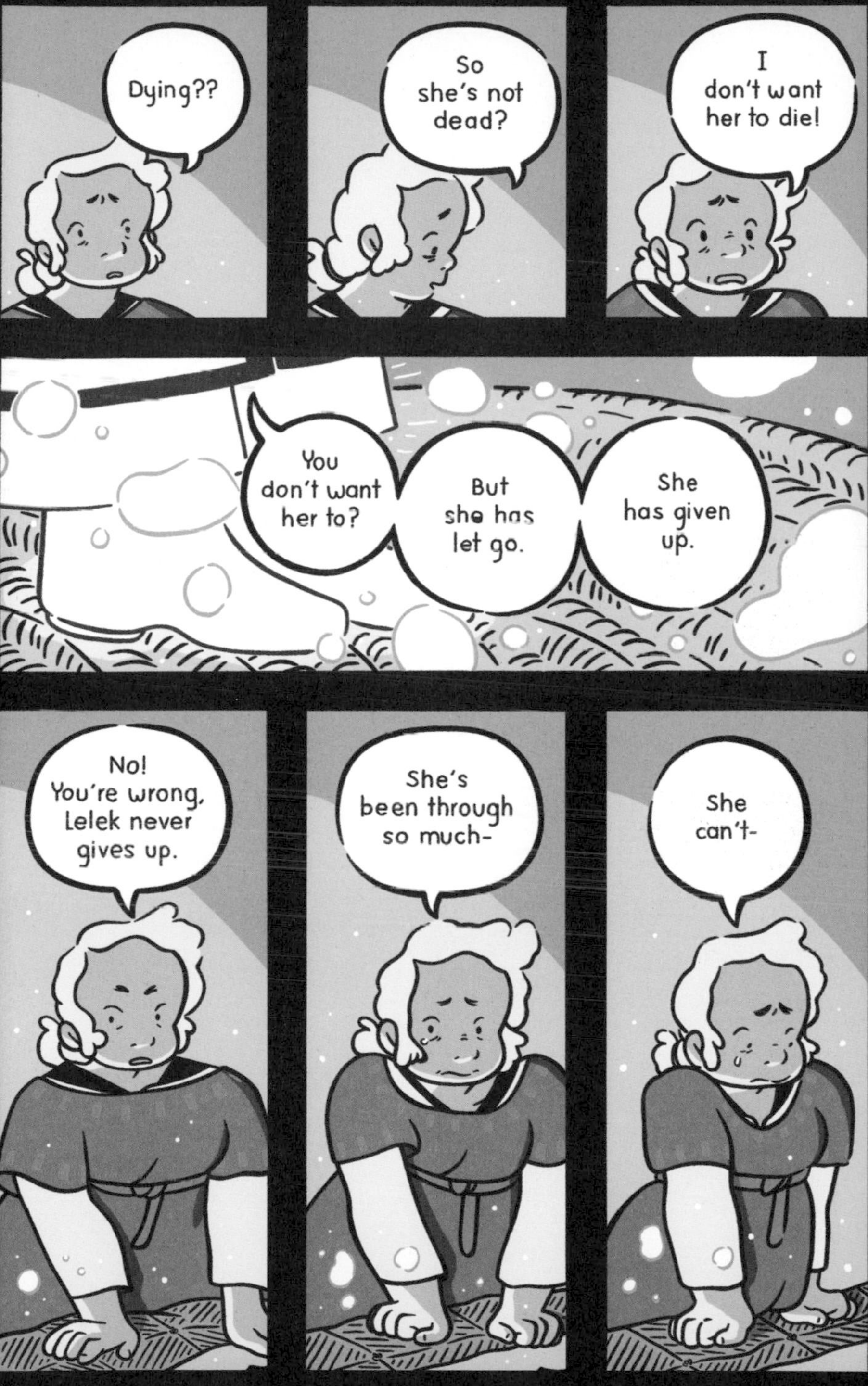
Dying??
So she's not dead?
I don't want her to die!
You don't want her to?
But she has let go.
She has given up.
No! You're wrong, Lelek never gives up.
She's been through so much-
She can't-

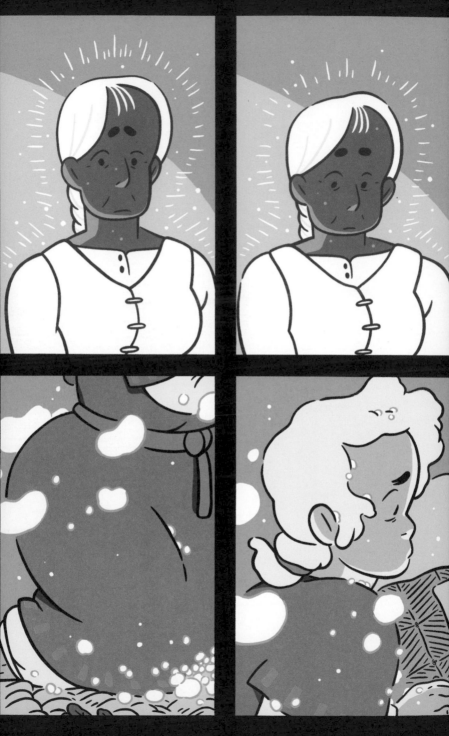

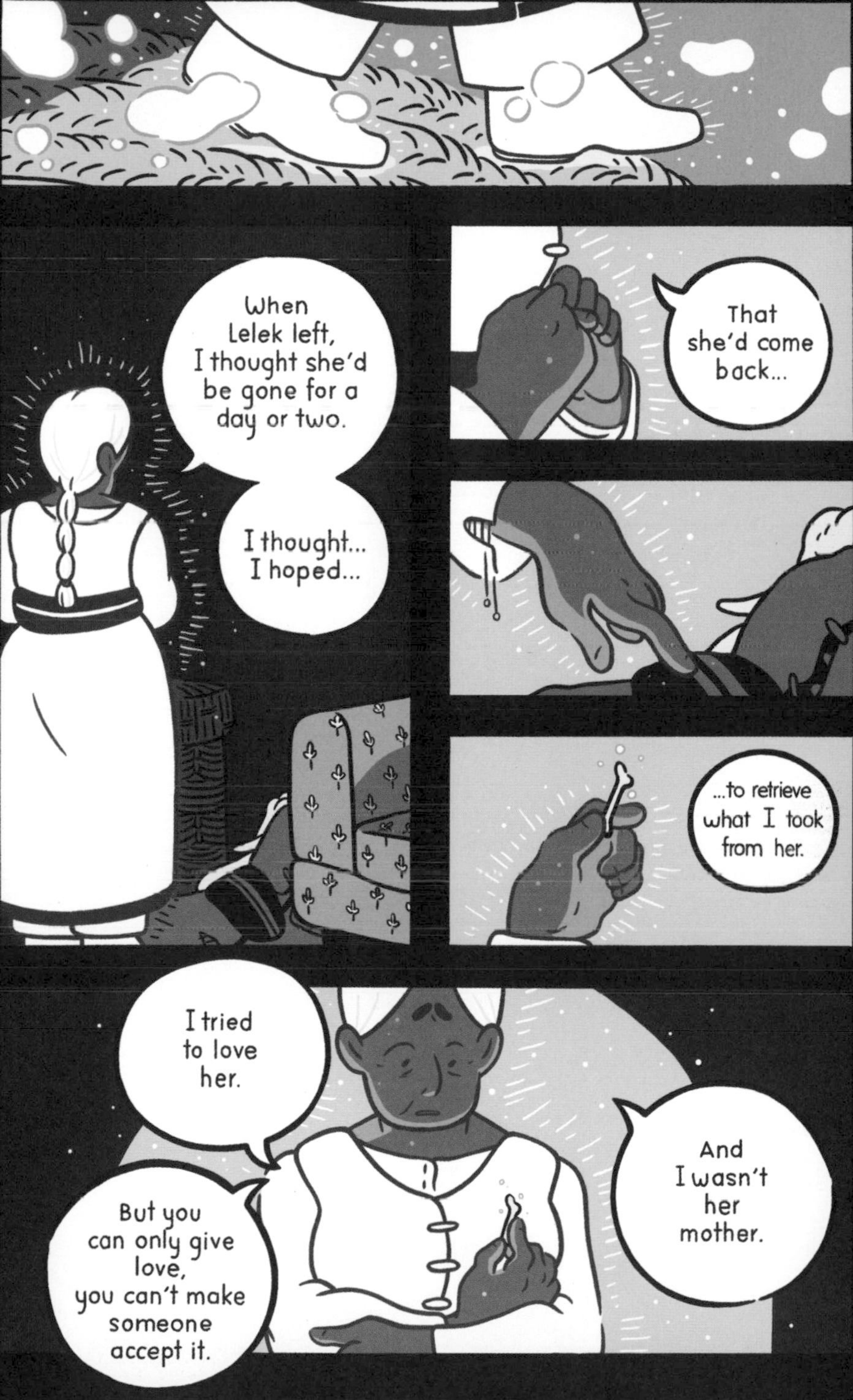
When Lelek left, I thought she'd be gone for a day or two.
I thought... I hoped...
That she'd come back...
...to retrieve what I took from her.
I tried to love her.
But you can only give love, you can't make someone accept it.
And I wasn't her mother.

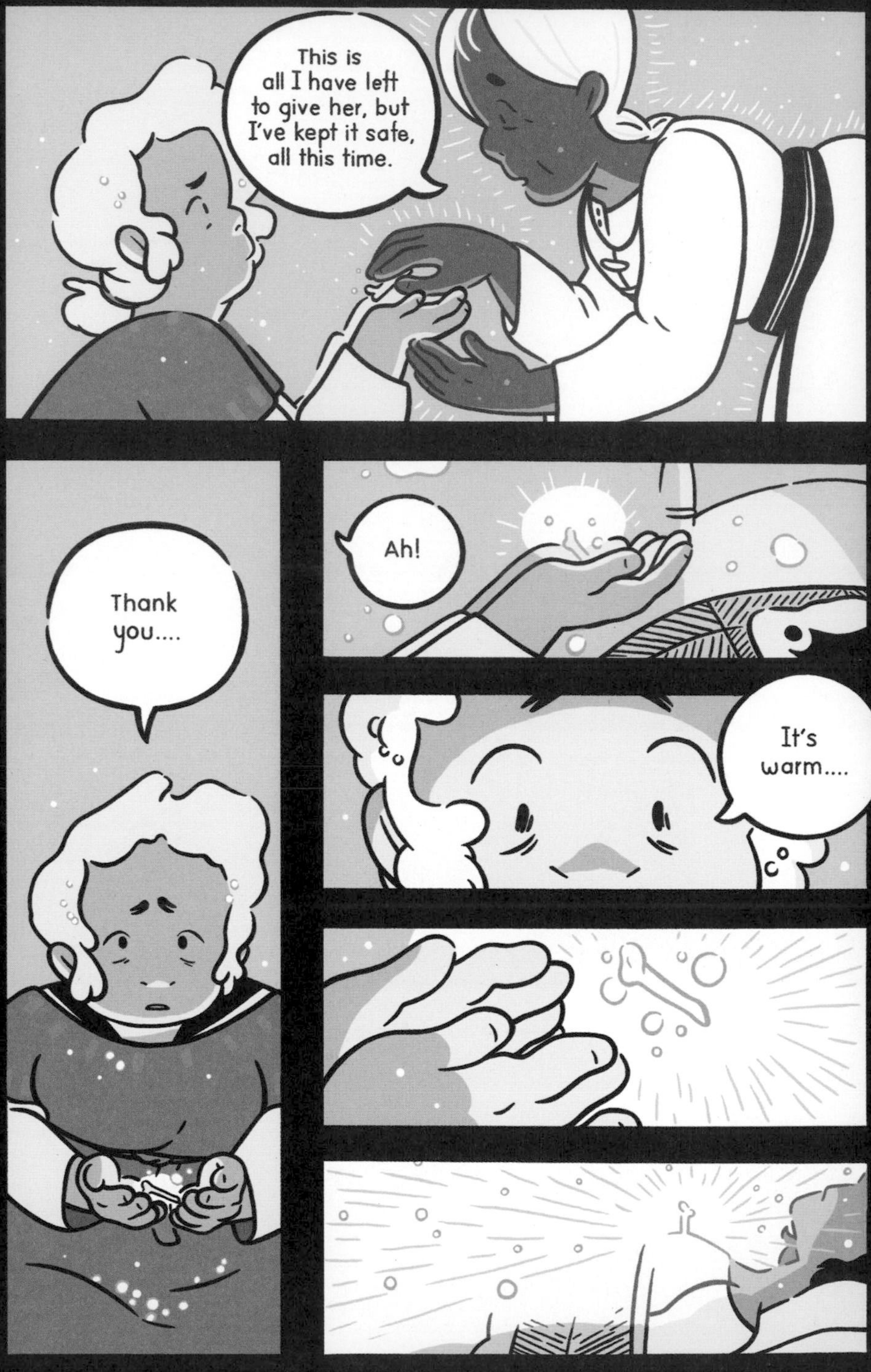
This is all I have left to give her, but I've kept it safe, all this time.
Thank you....
Ah!
It's warm....

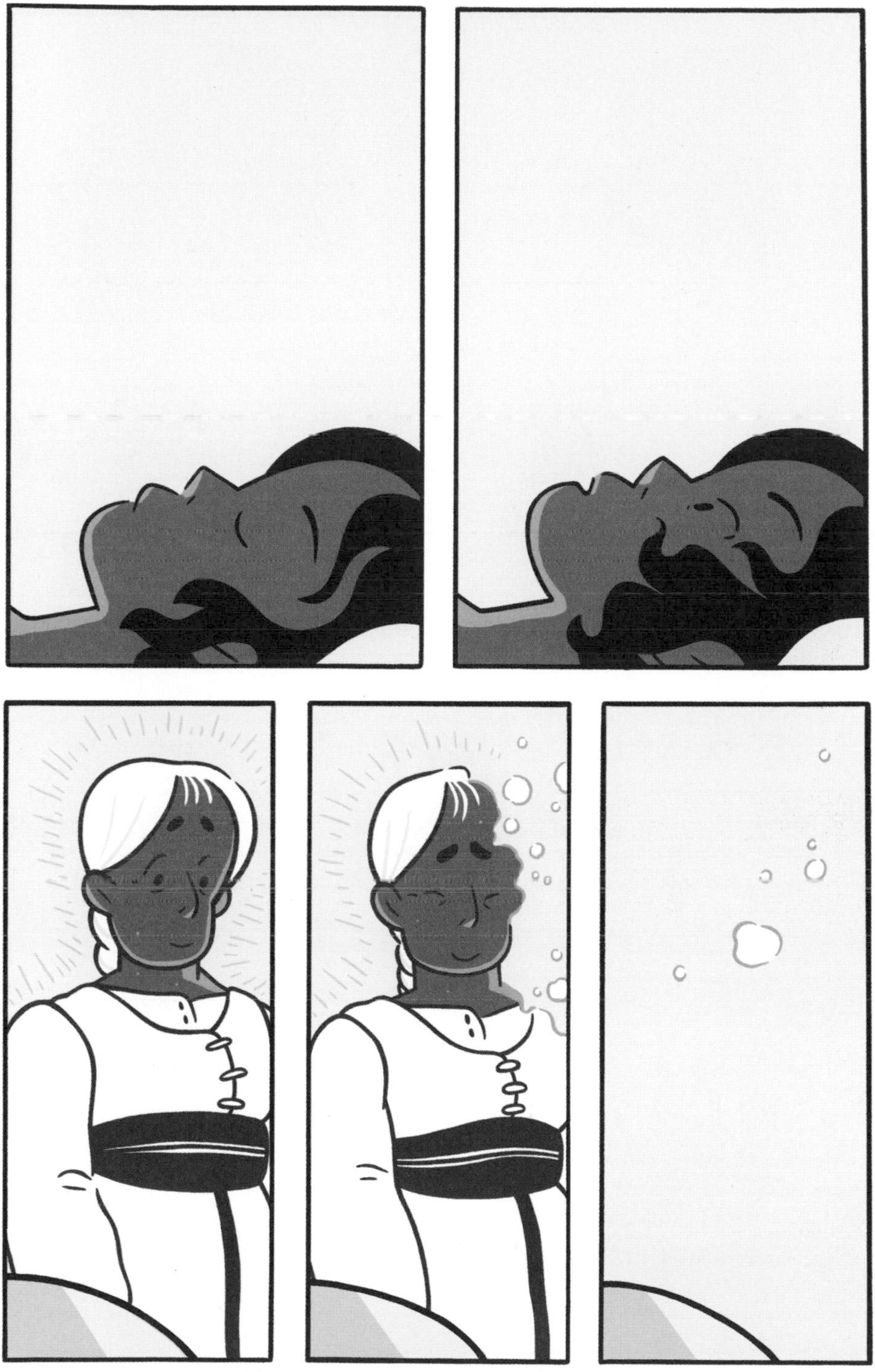

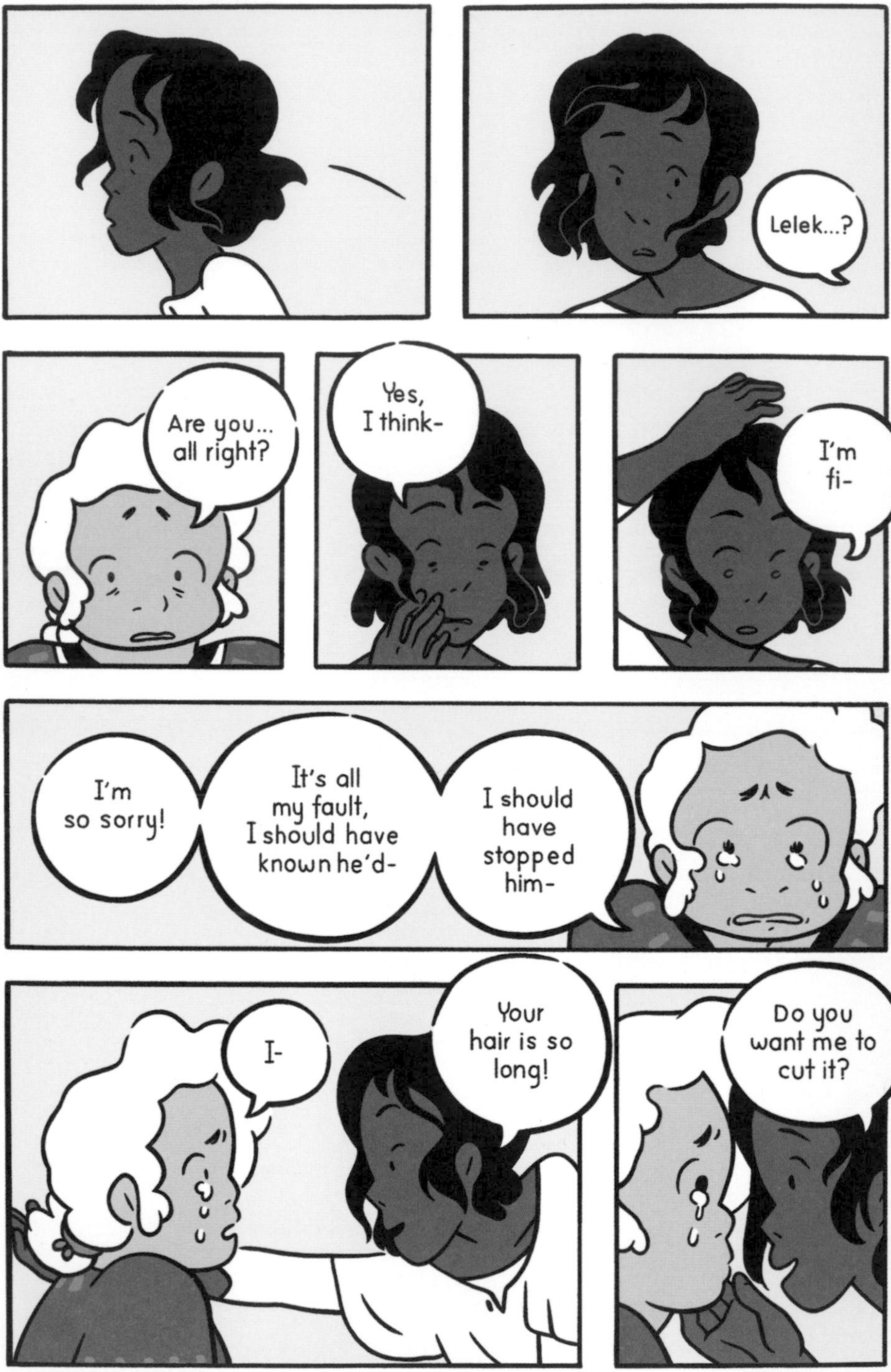
Lelek...?
Are you... all right?
Yes, I think-
I'm fi-
I'm so sorry!
It's all my fault, I should have known he'd-
I should have stopped him-
I-
Your hair is so long!
Do you want me to cut it?

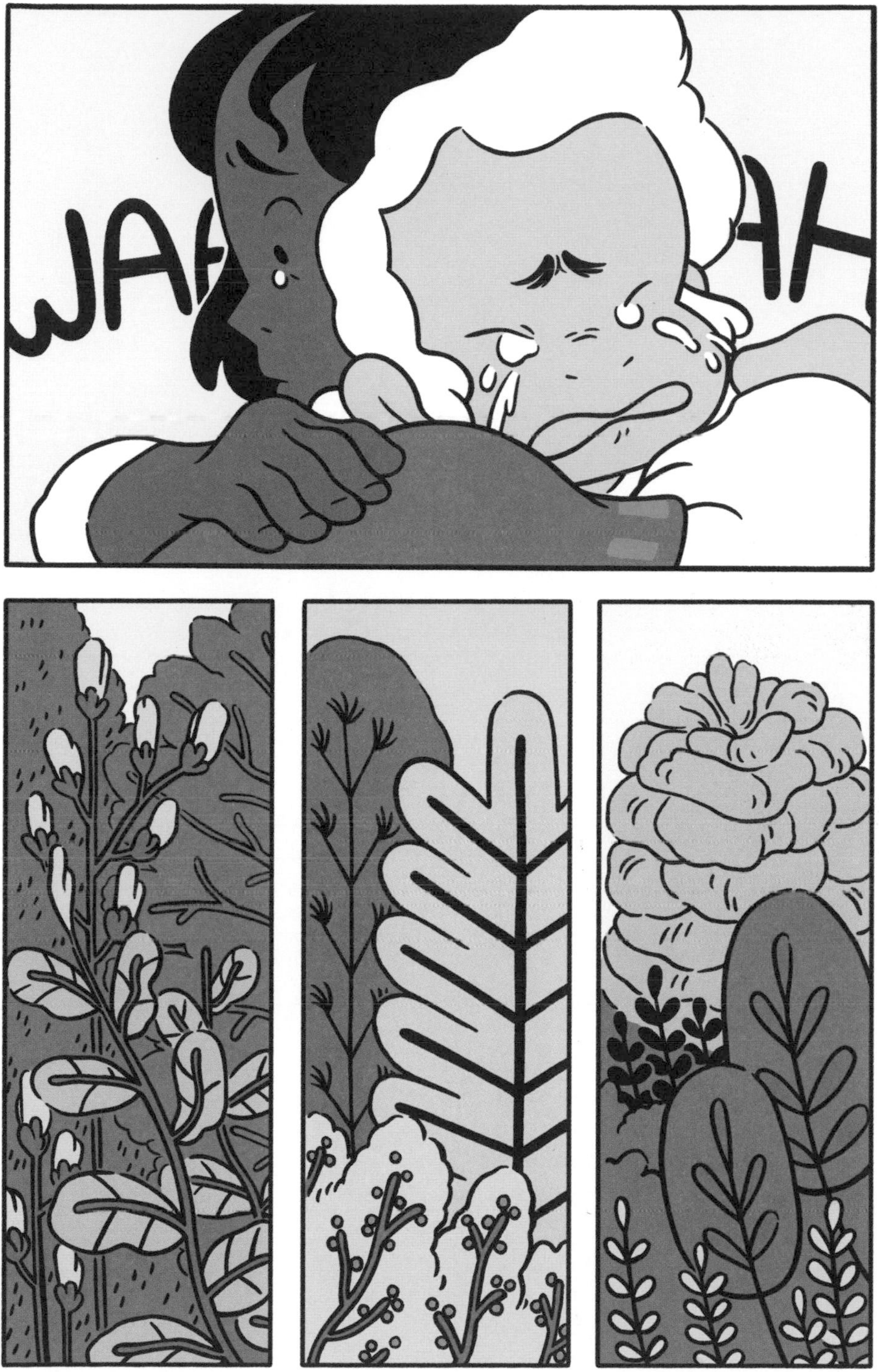
WA
AH

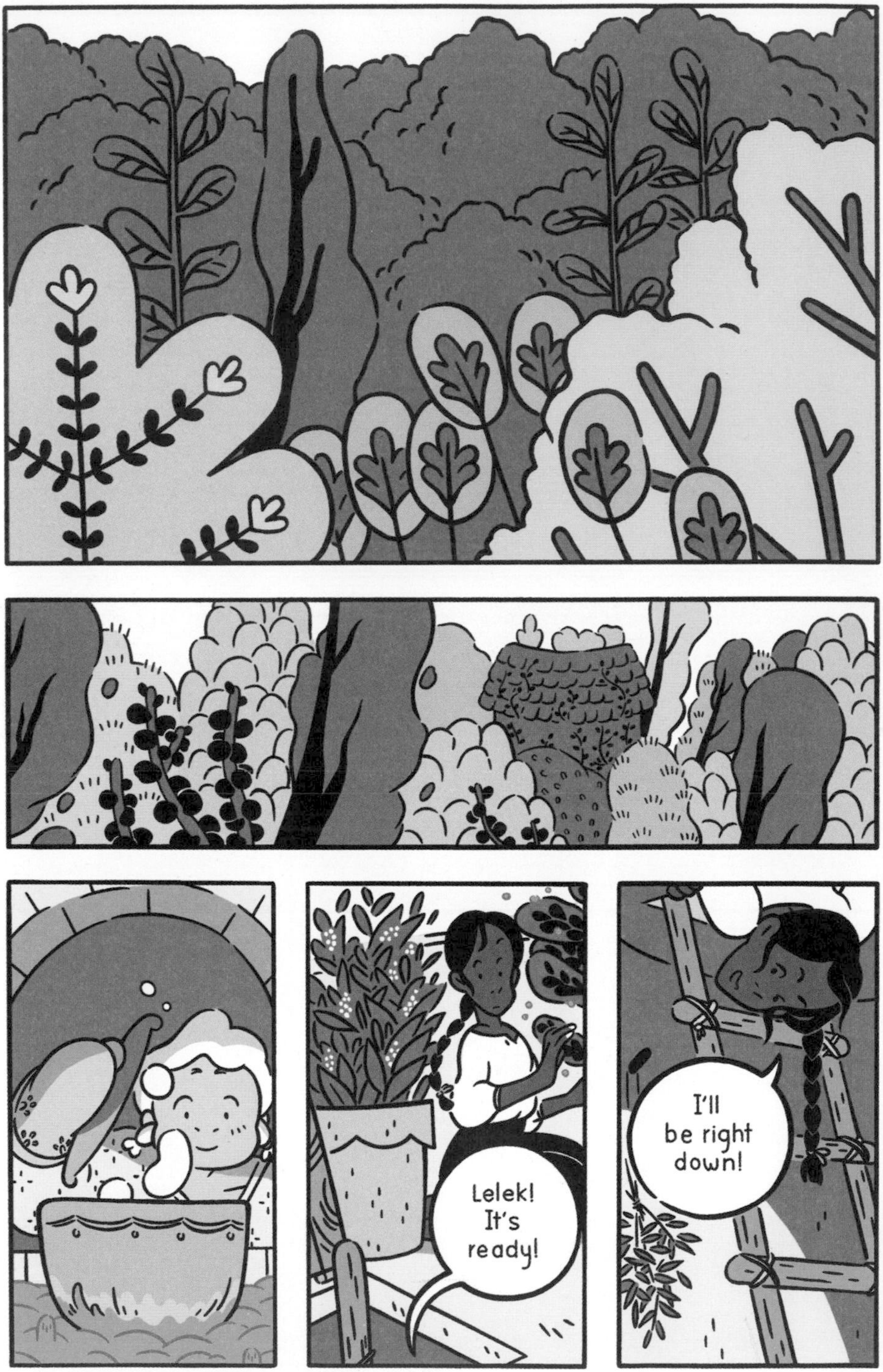
Lelek! It's ready!
I'll be right down!

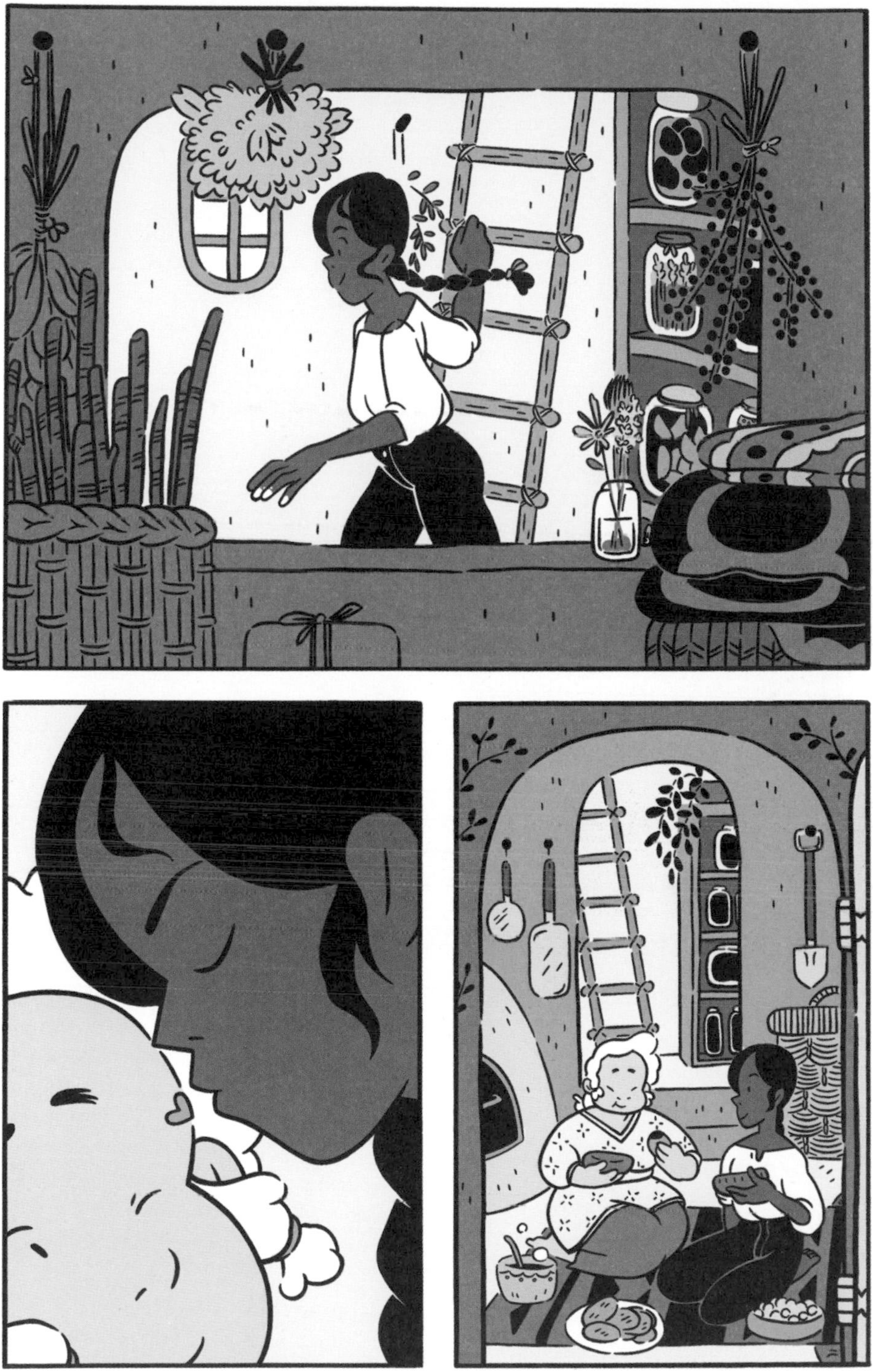

Epilogue

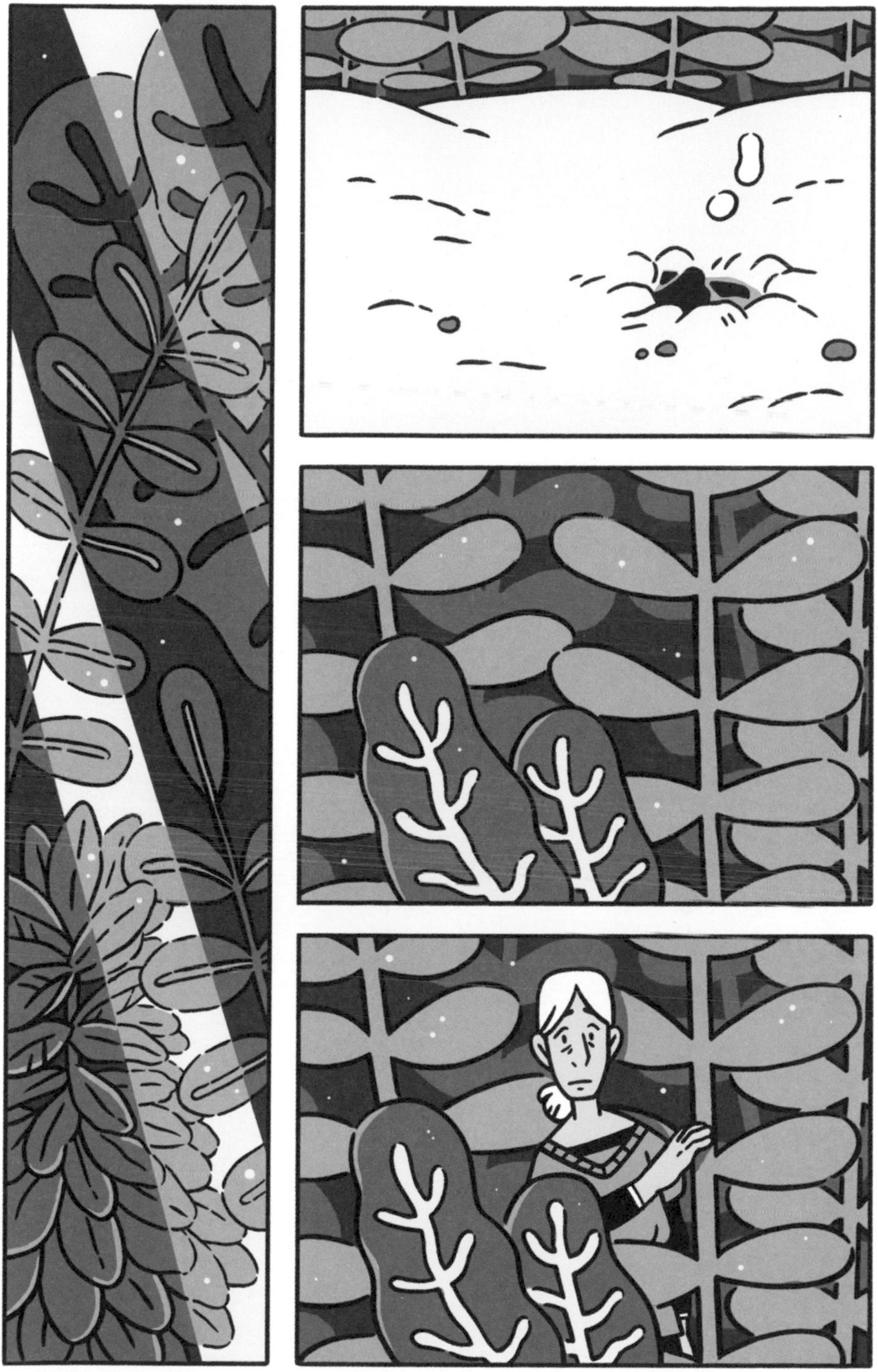

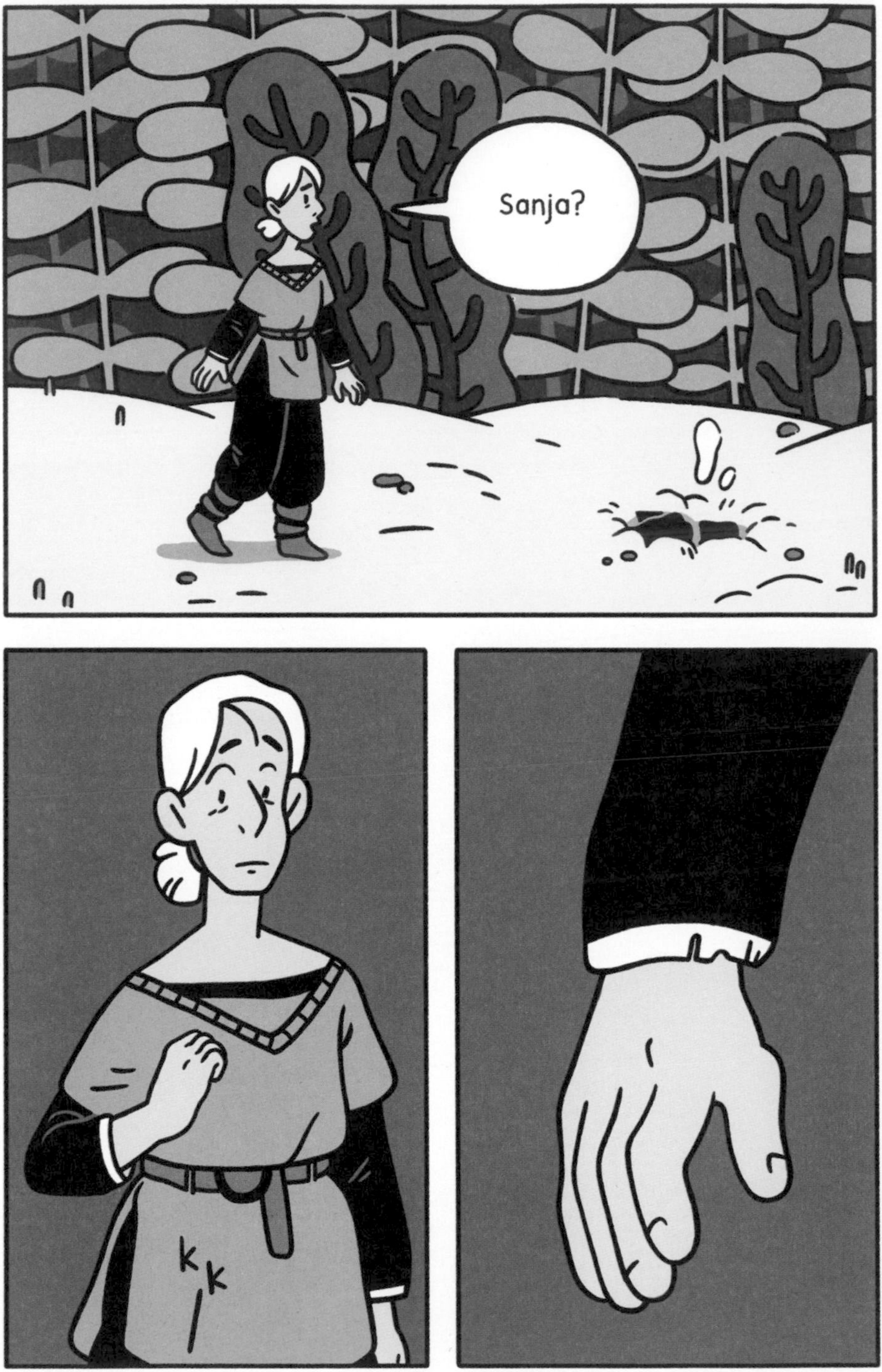
Sanja?
KK

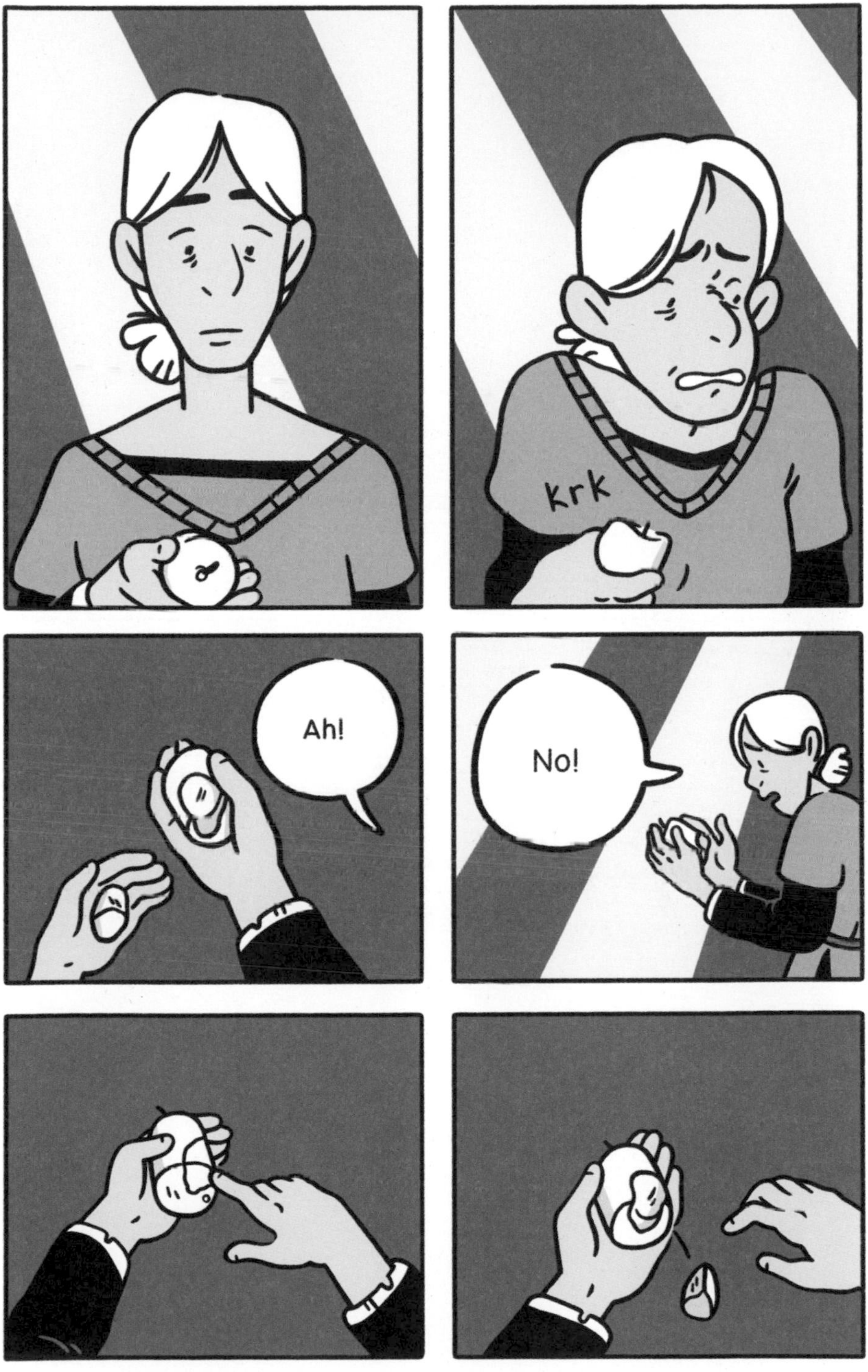
krk
Ah!
No!

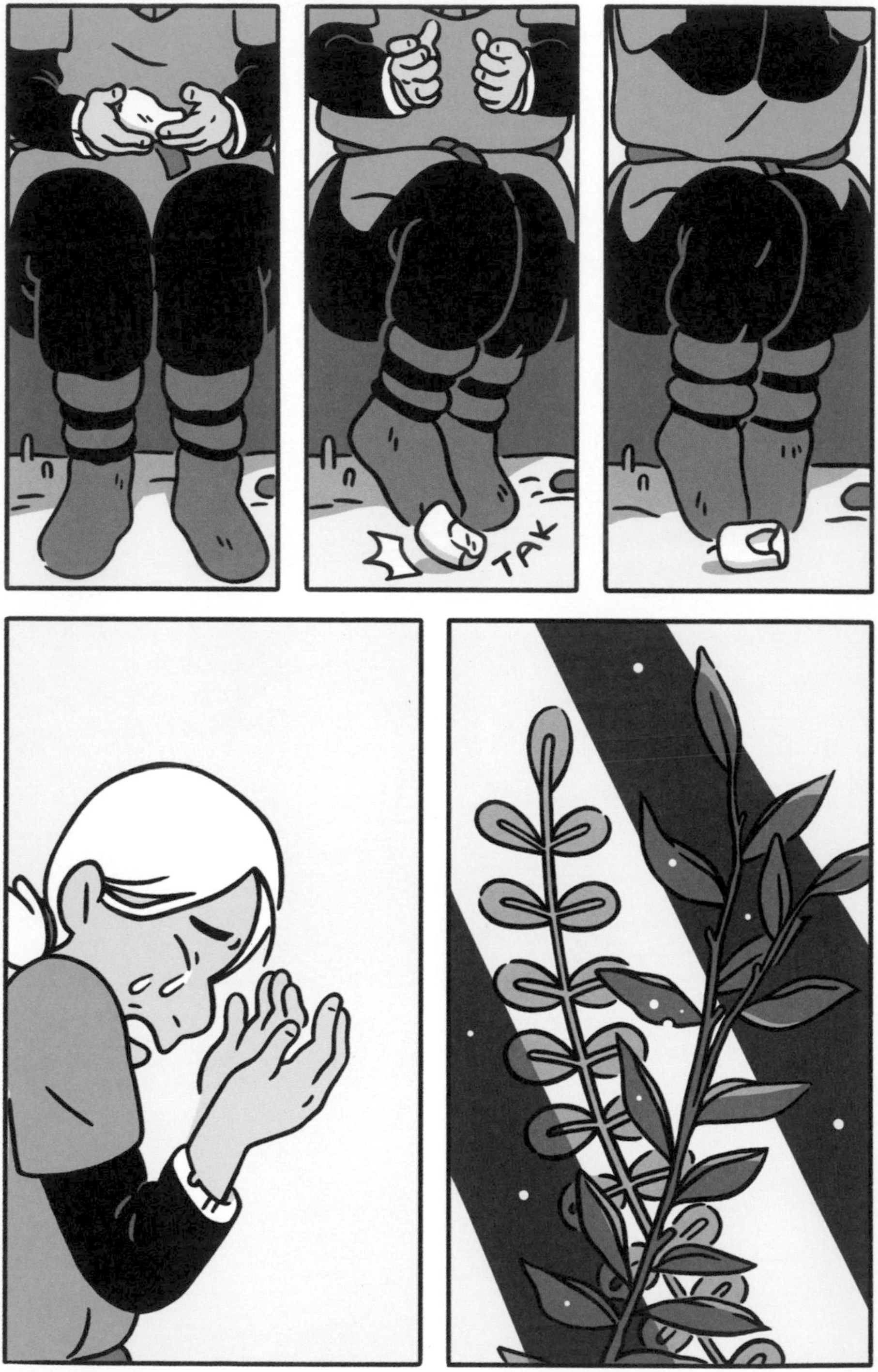
TAK

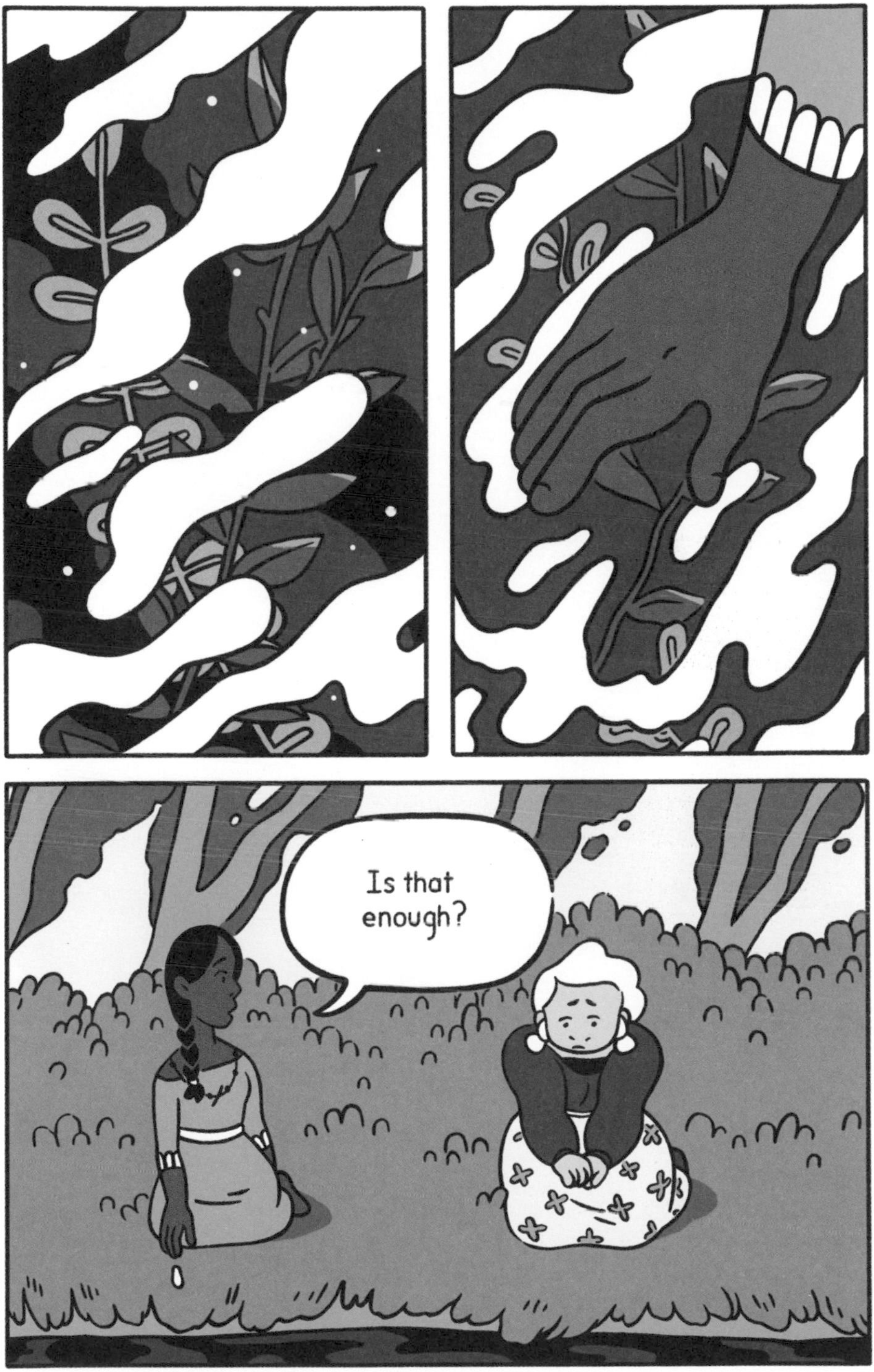
Is that enough?

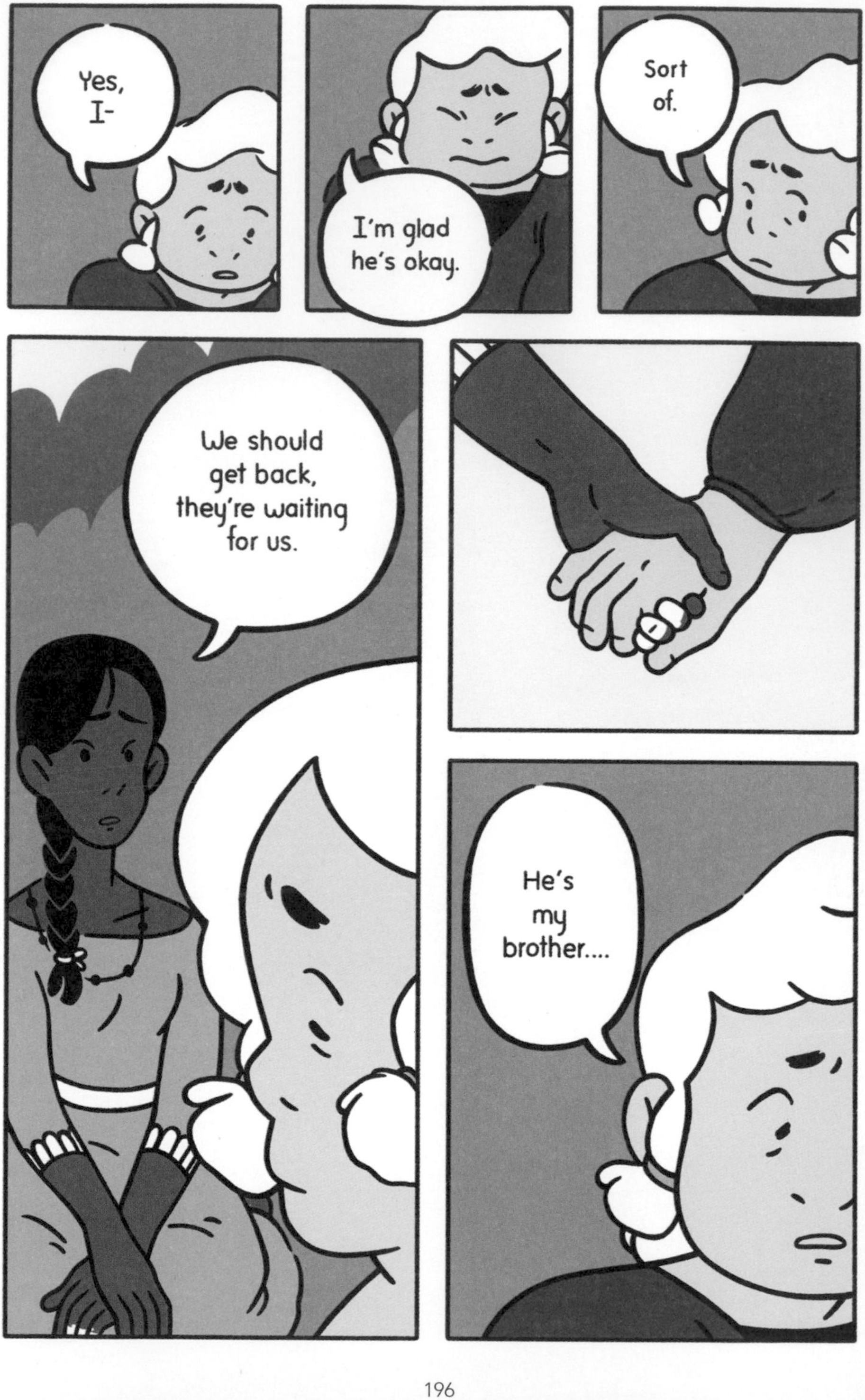
Yes, I-
I'm glad he's okay.
Sort of.
We should get back, they're waiting for us.
He's my brother....

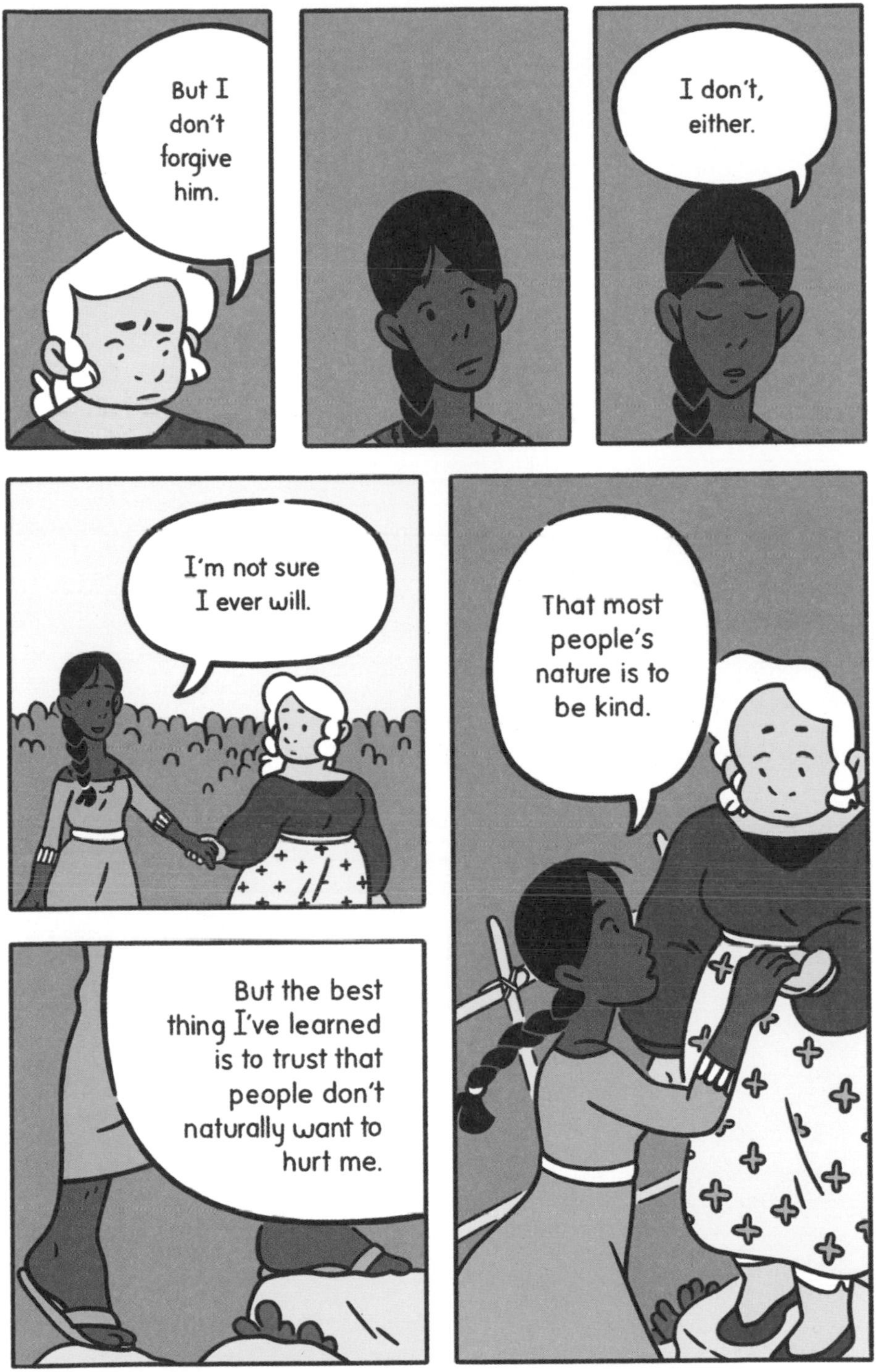
But I don't forgive him.
I don't, either.
I'm not sure I ever will.
But the best thing I've learned is to trust that people don't naturally want to hurt me.
That most people's nature is to be kind.

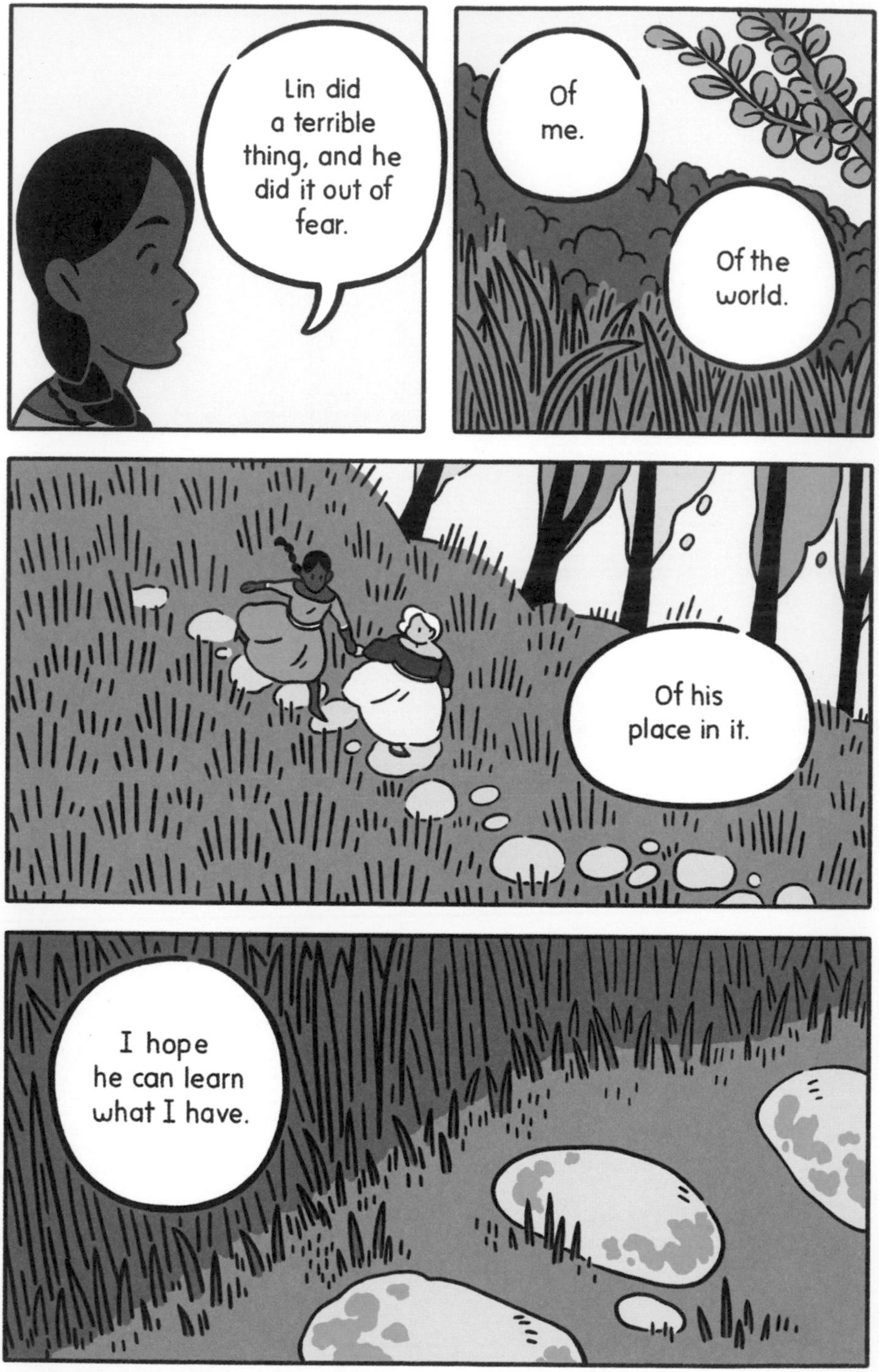
Lin did a terrible thing, and he did it out of fear.
Of me.
Of the world.
Of his place in it.
I hope he can learn what I have.

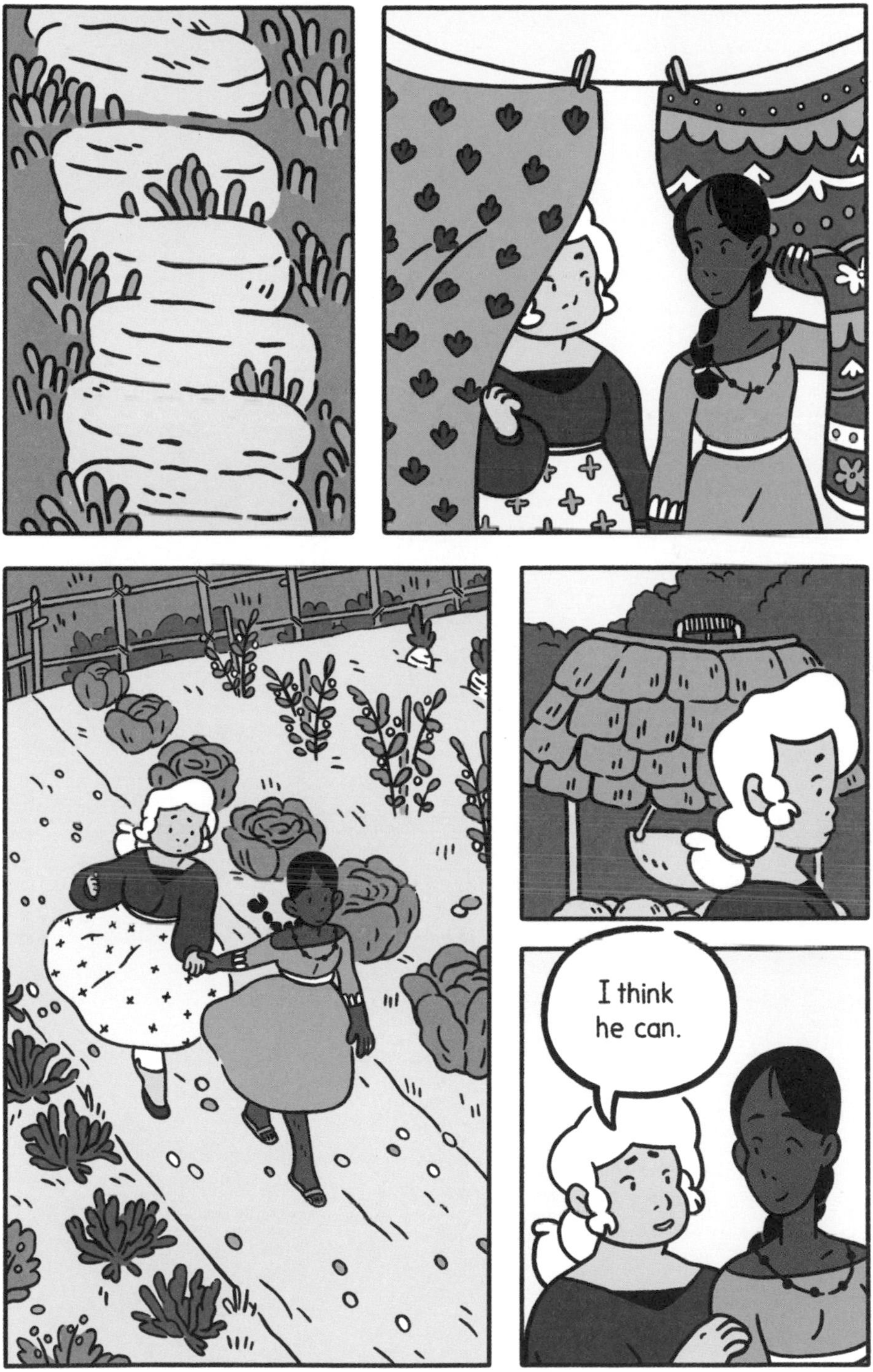
I think he can.

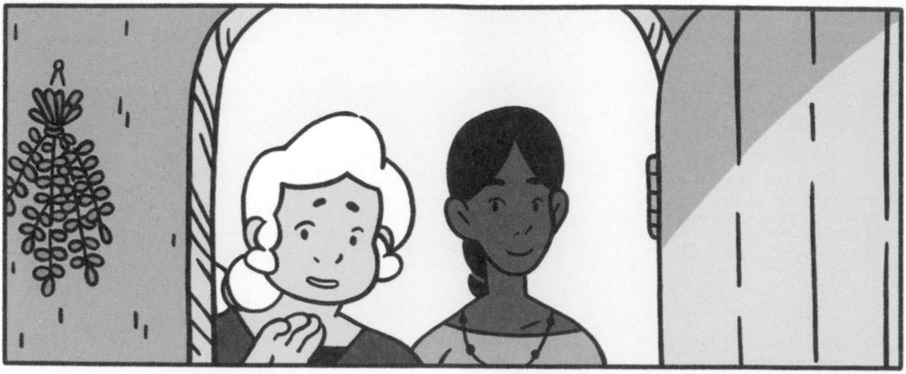

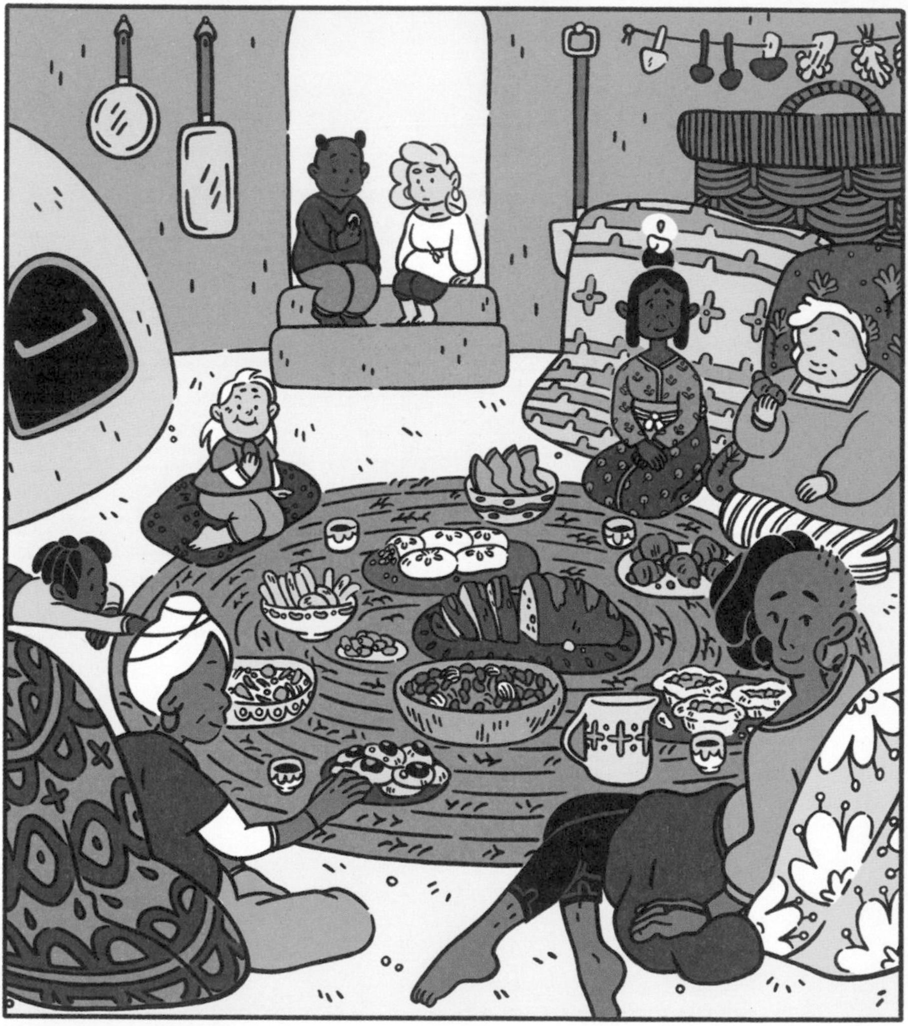

A note from the author:

From the start, *Witchlight* was an experiment in making exactly what I wanted to, and not worrying about what anyone thought it should be. I am incredibly grateful that so many people have embraced it.

A full half of *Witchlight* was made while listening to the podcast *Friends at the Table*, and I'm not sure how it could have gotten done otherwise. Their work has taught me so much about the joy and vulnerability at the core of all good storytelling. I am at heart a solitary and secretive creature, but their show makes me marvel at what can come out of true collaboration and trust.

Thank you to my parents for taking me to parks and museums and libraries, for teaching me how light works and the names of trees. Most of all, thank you for showing me how to tell stories for fun and taking the fear out of writing.

Thank you to Claire, for the good times. I hope we'll have more.

Above all others, thank you to Kevin Czap. When I first met them, I thought, "Who's this nerd?", one of many examples of my rude first impressions of the people who end up most dear to me. They were the first stranger to read my comics and say not just kind things, but insightful and true things about them. I am powered almost constantly by a brash and indestructible determination, but where that resolve stumbles, I keep going because I know Kevin believes I will.

RH GRAPHIC

THE DEBUT LIST

BUG BOYS
LAURA KNETZGER

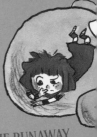

BUG BOYS
By Laura Knetzger

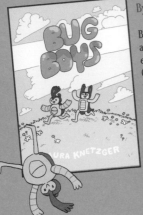

Bugs, friends, the world around us—this book has everything!
Come explore Bug Boys for the fun, thoughtful adventure about growing up and being yourself.

Chapter Book

THE RUNAWAY PRINCESS
Johan Troïanowski

THE RUNAWAY PRINCESS
By Johan Troïanowski

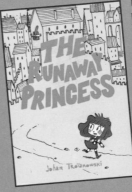

The castle is quiet.
And dull.
And boring.
Escape on a quest for excitement with our runaway princess, Robin!

Middle-Grade

Aster and the ACCIDENTAL MAGIC
THOM PICO
KARENSAC

ASTER AND THE ACCIDENTAL MAGIC
By Thom Pico & Karensac

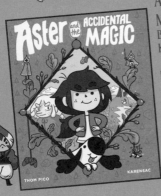

Nothing fun ever happens in the middle of the country . . . except maybe . . . magic?
That's just the beginning of absolutely everything going wrong for Aster.

Middle-Grade

Witchlight
Jessi Zabarsky

WITCHLIGHT
By Jessi Zabarsky

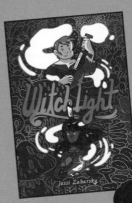

Lelek doesn't have any friends or family in the world. And then she meets Sanja. Swords, magic, falling in love . . . these characters come together in a journey to heal the wounds of the past.

Young Adult

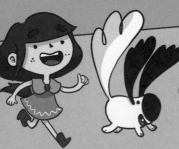

FIND US ONLINE AT @RHKIDSGRAPHIC AND RHKIDSGRAPHIC.COM